THE FEATHERED EDGE: TALES OF MAGIC, LOVE, AND DARING

Edited by Deborah J. Ross

Sky Warrior Book Publishing, LLC.

ISBN-13: 978-0-61559-993-9
ISBN-10: 0-615599-93-1

Published by Sky Warrior Book Publishing
PO Box 99
Clinton, MT 59825
www.skywarriorbooks.com

This is a work of fiction. All characters and events portrayed in this book are fictitious, and any resemblance to real people is purely coincidental.

Editor: Deborah J. Ross.
Cover art by Mitch Bentley.
Publisher: M. H. Bonham.

Printed in the United States of America

0   9 8 7 6 5 4 3 2 1

Copyrights

CONTENTS

INTRODUCTION by Deborah J. Ross 7

FEATHERWEIGHT by Kari Sperring 11

THE ART OF MASKS by Sherwood Smith 27

CULVERELLE by Sean McMullen 51

FORTUNE'S STEPCHILD by Sheila Finch 77

THE WOMAN WHO FELL IN LOVE WITH THE
HORNED KING by Judith Tarr 93

A WREATH OF LUCK by Madeleine E. Robins 115

EMBERS by Shannon Page & Jay Lake 133

QUESTION A STONE by Tanith Lee 147

A SWAIN OF KNEADED MOONLIGHT by Dave
Smeds 171

FIRE AND ICE AND BURNING ROSE by
Rosemary Hawley Jarman 201

THE GARDEN OF SWORDS by K. D. Wentworth
217

BLUE VELVET by Diana L. Paxson 245

OUTLANDER by Samantha Henderson 269

INTRODUCTION

by Deborah J. Ross

Come with me on a voyage of discovery to the "feathered edge," a realm where magic and adventure coalesce into wonder, where rapier wit is as prized as rapier steel. Where is it to be found? In the deadly silence of an owl's flight or the fall of a single feather? In the clash of steel or the unfolding of one heart to another? In a ghostly dance through a garden of swords? In the touch of a lover spun from living moonlight? On the border between the lands of mortal men and those of Faerie?

Joseph Campbell wrote eloquently about "the hero's journey," in which a character leaves the familiar, embarks upon adventure, and returns transformed. Fantasy at its finest is also a journey, one that can take us to places both inside and outside ourselves. It summons us to venture beyond the safe and familiar.

There are many sorts of journeys—voyages from one geographical location to another, leaving-home and returning-home, travel in time or imagination or into our darkest nightmares. We emerge with insights and resources previously unguessed.

If a tale of adventure is a journey, how does it end? In a meeting, as Shakespeare wrote—of lover and beloved, of soul and self, of friends and mirrors, of partners in a dance.

I welcome you to a banquet of journeys with surprising beginnings and even more startling destinations. Some have exotic settings, from the borders of Faerie to an Algerian brothel, from Renaissance Venice to the deck of a pirate ship, from newly-discovered America to lands beyond all known maps. Others begin more quietly as the alchemy of lyric imagination leads us on, gently but inexorably.

Ancient maritime charts used to label unknown waters, "Here There Be Dragons." Dragons and gods and ghosts and pirates and swordswomen and much more.

Bon voyage!

Deborah J. Ross

Boulder Creek, CA

Kari Sperring grew up dreaming of joining the musketeers and saving France, only to discover that the company had been disbanded in 1776. Disappointed, she became a historian instead, and as Kari Maund has written and published five books and many articles on Celtic and Viking history, and co-authored (with Phil Nanson) a book on the real people behind her favourite novel, *The Three Musketeers*. She's also worked as a barmaid, a tax officer, a personal assistant, and a university lecturer. She started writing fantasy in her teens, inspired by J. R. R. Tolkien, Alexandre Dumas and Thomas Malory. Her first novel, *Living with Ghosts* (DAW, 2009), evolved from her love of France and its history, ghosts, mysteries, Celtic culture, sharks, and sword-fights; her forthcoming novel, *The Grass King's Concubine*, has even found a creative role for book-keeping.

She lives in Cambridge, England, with her partner Phil (who helps design the sword-fights) and three very determined cats, who guarantee that everything she writes will have been thoroughly sat upon. Her website is http://www.karisperring. com/ and she also writes a regular blog on LiveJournal.

FEATHERWEIGHT

by Kari Sperring

After the alchemical queen died, she turned into feathers. In life, she had been whipcord and lemons, yet in death she came apart in peace. Her peace—her pieces—floated out into the city she had guarded so long, carried by wind and chance to roost in trees and sink in drains, to burn in grates and drift away on the currents of the river, caught in the signs of shops and the hats of merchants, blown every which way to do what they would or could or wished. Here, a long pinion brushed the lips of a newborn child, so that all her days she stuttered and blushed in company yet, once alone, possessed a laugh that warmed the souls of those who chanced to hear it. There, a fluff of down leavened the sour hands of the Sog Street baker, and ever after his loaves rose lighter and higher than any others in the city. A single tail feather fell in through the broken window in the attic of the Markgraf's Theatre and landed on the papers of its harried play-maker as he struggled to write just one last play that might bring him favour, and his words turned from dross to gold from that night.

Two came spiralling down onto the steep roof of the Old Gate Inn. The smaller, a soft breast feather, disappeared into a chimney. The larger was washed by the light spring rains into the gutter, and thence down to the cobbled yard below, to mingle with clean straw and road dust. It squeezed out through the iron lattice into the ditch outside and came to rest at the foot of the crumbling Artofan family memorial. And there it lay, as spring turned to summer, and summer to autumn, and the leaves grew brown and fell, and dust washed away, and the feather itself shrank to a single strong shank, unnoticed by anyone.

By anyone living, that was. Carts and hacks rumbled past, men and women strode or minced or ambled, all without knowing that the last of the queen lay at their feet. On a chill day at the very start of winter, the ghost of Tharinn Arliss stumbled to the foot of the memorial and put his unsubstantial hand on the feather. The sharp tine pricked his absent skin, so that he pulled his hand away with a curse, then looked down in surprise that anything might touch him. It had been so long. Even in life, he had felt remote from most of the things and people around him. Most things and most people apart from Ingret Fell, the inn-master's daughter. Ingret Fell—now Ingret Vane—with the smile that included him and the laugh that made him almost real.

He was—had been—a skinny, inept young man, all big feet and clumsy elbows, always oversetting stools and spilling tankards, so that old Mr Fell shook his fist and ordered him out of the taproom. He would hang around the inn's yard, hoping for a glimpse of Ingret through a window or open door, dreaming of impressing her with a poem or a song, and she would see him out there, sometimes, and smile or wave, so that he went back to his lodgings warmed and happy.

What killed him in the end was his habit of venturing out in all seasons and all weathers in the hopes of winning her smile. The city was full of young people like him, half-starved and ill-housed, coughing their slow way into the grave. But most of them had not crept out before dawn every morning to squander their coppers on a handful of last night's red and orange and yellow flowers from the lobby of the Opera House. He had run with them full tilt through the early bustle, to be sure of leaving them on the inn steps before Ingret opened the door to sweep out last night's dust. Rain pounded its way through his thin coat, ran down his neck, seeped in through the holes in his shoes, dripped from his ragged fringe.

Perhaps the rain in his eyes was why he did not see the rag cart coming round the corner. Perhaps it was the cold air and the reek of cold dust making him cough and duck his head. Or perhaps it was just one of those flat jokes that the lesser gods were said to play. He did not know: he had no way of knowing. He remembered only the suddenness of it, the jolt and the thud. Then he was lying at the foot of the monument, and the carter was shouting and the dray-horse stamping, and there were boots and clogs everywhere too close to him, and all he could think of was his flowers turning red, petal by slow petal, spoiled beyond repair.

Had Ingret cried for him? He did not know. The flowers were spoiled and his hopes alongside them, and here he was, hovering still at the fringes of her ambit, craning his insubstantial neck to watch her at her work. In death, it seemed, he grew closer than he ever had been to her and all the others who lived and worked in Old Gate Street. He saw them far more clearly, now that life no longer filmed his eyes. On the corner, the short-tempered barber still cursed the weather and the queen and his customers, yet night after night, he rubbed the twisted limbs of his wife and read to her from yellowed library books. The retired guardsman who rented the long attic over the cobbler's shop gave fencing lessons to no-one at night, his shadow striking and parrying, lunging and dodging all alone in the greasy rush light. Each morning, the wife of the chandler's clerk waved her husband goodbye from her clean-scrubbed doorstep, but each afternoon she kissed other men in the privacy of her chamber. They all gathered, at this time or that, around the monument, the women in the mornings, perhaps on their way back from the markets, the children after chores or schools let out, the men in the evenings on their way home, each group telling each other— telling him—the news of their day. He watched and listened and learned them, and grew more and more awake. And most of all, he watched Ingret, hour by hour.

As that first winter turned into spring, her father married her off to Ruric Vane, the butcher's strapping second son. *A good match for an inn-wife*, said the gossips, gathered by his monument to watch the bridal party. *A good match for both, an heiress for the boy, and a guaranteed meat supply for the girl and her inn.*

Ruric Vane drank too much and yelled too much and never once brought Ingret flowers. From the shelter of the monument, Tharinn watched her as she swept floors and baked pies, nursed her children and haggled with traders, while her father grew older and her husband grew drunker and the seasons went on changing. *Well, she's a hard worker,* said the gossips. *She'll do right by the business, though her husband's less use than a paper fan in a blizzard.*

Five years passed, and old Mr Fell died and his ashes were sent to the flame. The barber's wife died, and he grew taciturn and sour. Ruric yelled more and Ingret's crooked smile grew rare, though Tharinn still longed for it. Ten years more, and Ruric's breadth turned to fat and grey hairs wove themselves into Ingret's brown hair. The clerk caught his wife one afternoon and drove her lover from the house with curses and thrown shoes. At fifteen years, Ingret's son went out every morning to learn his letters at the temple, while her pretty daughter waited tables and smiled at the soldiers who drank at the inn, and Ruric scolded. Seventeen years, and the girl ran away with a wool merchant's journeyman. Ingret wept and Ruric turned purple in the face and choked and staggered and died.

Ruric's ghost, if ghost he had, must be haunting his daughter, for Tharinn saw no trace of him ever again. He did not mind that at all, for Ruric, of late, had made Ingret cry at night in her kitchen as she put away her dishes, unseen by anyone save Tharinn and the inn cat. He would drift close to her then, and wish for hands of flesh to wipe away her tears, and breath to speak words of comfort to her. But she did not see him, though the cat fluffed out its tail and spat at him, and her son complained that the kitchen was always cold. Tharinn had discovered by then that he could go half a street or more from the monument, so long as the light was dim and there were not too many people. He sat in the hallway while Ingret slept, and sang soft unheard songs to sweeten her dreams. He could never have done that while Ruric lived. Ruric snored and disrupted everything. The son—his name was Horic—moaned of draughts under his door and noise from the streets, but day by day the pain eased out of Ingret's face.

That was the year after the old queen died, eighteen years since the cart and the wedding. *Ingret Vane's still a fine-looking woman,* said the gossips. *Young enough, too, to get herself another man to help with that inn and that boy of hers.*

It seemed to Tharinn that Ingret was perfectly happy as she was, though the inn was busy and Horic often troublesome. But no one had listened to him when he was alive. There was even less reason for them to do so now, if any of them even remembered him.

As that year moved on, old Guthran, the candle-merchant, took to arriving early and leaving late each market day, and the widowed deputy of the Drapers' Guild brought gifts of thread or ends of rolls of cloth. Ingret was still pretty. More to the point, she had money and property and the only male in her household was fourteen years old. *Ripe for the picking,* said the gossips, wisely, *and she'll fall, sooner or later. Better it's into the marriage bed than any other kind.* Other women took to looking at her askance, or gripped their husbands' hands tightly should she chance to pass by. *The boy needs a father,* the gossips said. *The priest should tell her.*

Listening to them, Tharinn's throat stung with retorts he could not utter. When Guthran tried to linger at closing time, Tharinn hovered close by, so that the old man's hands turned blue. He walked through the plates that Horic brought out to the draper, so that his meals were cold. Such men, with their counting-house hearts, were not for Ingret. She merited a man who saw her, not her goods and chattels. But though the draper found himself another widow, and Old Guthran moved away to live with his daughter, suitors kept coming to the inn, following Ingret with covetous eyes.

On a damp day in late autumn, Tharinn put his hand on the feather. He stared at it for long moments as its texture imprinted on what passed for his skin. Brittle and waxy, solid and slick, his fingers closed over it. It fitted neatly under them, resting against the callous on his right forefinger where his pen used to rest. He tucked it into the pocket of his shirt and it stayed, held up by the nothingness there, his to hold, the sole thing, besides himself, that he might call his own.

The very same day, a cavalry sergeant blew in, his scarlet coat and blue eyes driving out the greys and browns of the season. He doffed his cap to the shop-wives as he passed, and they dimpled and smiled at his back. He was in town for the winter, he told the chestnut vendor. His whole regiment had been summoned while the high-ups decided what war they would pursue next summer. He had rooms in a lodging house four streets over, but he'd been told by a trooper of the excellence of the beer to be had at the Old Gate Inn.

"And here I am," he finished, with a quick bright grin. "Here for a good pint and good company."

Tharinn watched him anxiously as he went into the inn. There were three other inns between here and the barracks, all with perfectly respectable beer. Four streets was quite close enough for Ingret's circumstances to be known and discussed. And soldiers were known to be always in want of money.

Tharinn drifted in his wake to the inn door and found, as all too often, he might go no further. The taproom was busy, crowded with apprentices and craftsmen, market sellers and clerks, all washing away the strains of the day's labour. The sergeant strode inside, to be swallowed in the throng. Tharinn hovered, shadowy limbs taut with anxiety and alarm as Ingret served drinks and meals and nodded and smiled at her customers, the sergeant amongst them. If he troubled her, if she remarked him, Tharinn could not tell.

Her face was tired when at last she swept out the taproom and barred the door. It was like that so many nights, though since Ruric's death she no longer wept.

Tharinn stopped where he always did, just outside her room. Under his shirt, the feather prickled. He reached in to touch it and his fingers tingled. He drew it out. In the dark hallway, it glowed with a faint amber light. He cupped it against him as he sang to her of love and comfort and rest, and it seemed to him that the glow grew brighter. His words floated out on it, gathering warmth and strength, seeped through the wood of her door to wrap her as she slept and keep out the autumn chill.

Night thickened, carried with it the snap of frost to pattern windows and rime cobbles. Slipping through the inn door just as dawn came, Tharinn hesitated. In his hand, the feather twitched. He squatted and there on the frosty step he began to draw. With each stroke of the feather, a petal took shape out of the frost, until there on the stone lay a single fresh bloom, white and bright as new snow, the first he had given her since the day before he died. The first anyone had given her since her wedding day, so far as he remembered.

He reached out a finger and extended it carefully. The petals were soft and fragrant under his touch. Carefully, he lifted the blossom by its stem and placed it where Ingret would be sure to see it.

Then he tucked himself into the shadiest corner of the inn-yard, the precious feather once more inside his shirt. The heat of it spread through him, so that he did not tremble when the first thin rays of autumn sun crossed the yard. It had changed everything. It had given him back communication and touch.

From the dirty lane behind the cobbler's shop, a cock crowed, and Ingret opened the inn door. Her long hair was still in its night-time braid, hanging over her shoulder; her eyes were sleepy. But as her gaze fell on the flower, her smile—her old, lost, crooked smile—spread across her face. She knelt to pick it up and all the worry was for an instant gone from her.

In his corner, Tharinn hugged the feather to him. She looked out into the yard for a long moment, still smiling, then she turned back into the inn. "Horic! See what someone brought me."

"What?" The boy's voice was grumpy. "Just a flower. What use is that?"

"This close to midwinter? This took thought and trouble."

The boy's reply was inaudible. Tharinn took the feather from his shirt and smiled at it.

oOo

Frost settled the next night, and the next, and on the two mornings that followed, Tharinn left his white gifts on Ingret's doorstep. With the feather close to him, he found it easier to bear the press of people, the weight of light, and he spent more and more of his time watching the taproom from the stair that led from it.

The sergeant was there on that second night, too, and the third, with his cheerful jacket and his cheerful smile. He was always polite, never trying to touch Ingret's hand when she served him, nor using words to her that were vulgar or familiar, speaking kindly to the boy and listening without rancour or disdain to the fulminations of his neighbours at the bar. Tharinn hoped that his regiment would soon march him away.

But the sergeant kept coming. Tharinn hovered next to him at the bar, and the sergeant smiled and praised the cool air. He walked through the man's dinner, and the sergeant only observed that Ingret's cooking was as fine when cold as when hot.

The sergeant would not be shifted or discommoded in any way. On the morning of the third day, he had the brass nerve to walk down Old Gate Street as Ingret returned from her daily trip to the market. As Tharinn watched and glowered, the man bowed and took the laden basket from her, escorting her the last few yards to the inn and carrying her shopping inside for her. Tharinn's hand clenched about his feather.

Ingret walked the sergeant to the door, thanking him, and, as he touched his hat to her, she smiled her old crooked smile. And then—*oh, then!*—she laughed.

The sound of it filled Tharinn with despair and alarm and delight all in one. He could barely recall the last time he had known Ingret to laugh. Not since her daughter ran away. Perhaps not since her marriage to Ruric.

He looked again at the sergeant, and cold settled about his heart. A dead man could love, but he could not hold or comfort. And Ingret was lonely.

Tharinn shut his eyes on his own pain and followed the sergeant home. If Ingret liked this man, if she wanted him, then first he must be proved worthy of her and then, if worthy, he must somehow be taught to treat her well.

The sergeant whistled as he walked, bowing to women and touching his cap to men, and several of the shop-keepers called out friendly greeting to him. Tharinn bristled, shook himself. It had to speak well of the man, surely, if he was treated thus after so few days in the neighbourhood. He stopped at a corner bakery to buy fresh pastries, and gave the few coppers' change to the baker's boy with another grin. This was a kind man, a generous man, then, a man to whom people warmed.

Tharinn hated him.

The sergeant jangled the bell at his lodging house door and waited, his hands behind his back. The landlady frowned when she saw him, and Tharinn's heart warmed a little. But before she could speak, the sergeant bowed and presented her with the box of pastries. "For all your kindness, Mistress."

The woman's face softened. "Well..."

"I hear that you've a shutter loose. I thought perhaps I could take a look at it for you: I've sometimes a knack for fixing things of that kind. And," the sergeant shook his head, "it might go some way to make up for me being so late with my rent. You know how it goes with the army paymaster. It'd be a weight off my mind if I could do something for you."

The frown vanished entirely as the landlady stepped back to let the sergeant in. "That'd be a help, certainly. Come this way, Sergeant."

Tharinn took the shortest route back to his monument, extinguishing fires and spooking pets as he passed. Then he sat down on the steps, head in his hands, and began to brood.

The feather had come to him for a reason. It had helped him give Ingret some small pleasure in her life. But it could not give him the life he needed to wed her. In which case....

Round and round the thoughts went, bitter and happy, hopeful and sad. Ingret deserved love in her life, a love that could do more than sing lullabies and draw flowers. The sergeant had made Ingret laugh.

By dusk, he had made his decision. The sergeant should

marry Ingret. Tharinn and his feather would somehow arrange that. He found a corner of wrapping paper, blown against the monument, and began to write upon it with the feather. Then he tucked both into his shirt and went to slide his letter under the door of the sergeant's lodging house.

That evening, the sergeant arrived at the inn with a bunch of yellow and orange flowers for Ingret. She blushed as she took them, eyes downcast. "Thank you."

"I thought they might please you," the sergeant said.

"They're lovely." Ingret touched one bloom with a finger. "Someone used to bring me flowers like these. It's been years since I saw them." For a moment, her eyes rested on the corner where Tharinn crouched. Then she smiled back at the sergeant. "I'll put them in water, then get your ale. On the house."

That night, Tharinn sang her songs of love and marriage, and made himself hope they would fill up her dreams. In the morning, he found a leaf torn from a schoolchild's copybook and wrote the sergeant another letter. And so a week passed and another, and Ingret's chamber filled up with flowers and she sang to herself as she swept floors and made bread. The sergeant came every night, and sat at the bar and smiled at her and made her laugh. Tharinn watched and clutched the feather and told himself he was glad that ghosts do not weep.

oOo

The boy Horic changed everything. He was meant to help his mother and her maid in the inn at nights, but as often as not he shirked or skimped his duties when it came to serving and cleaning. But he was keen as steel over matters of money, his father's son to the core. The sergeant had taken to lingering, helping Ingret clear tables and carry trays to the kitchen. A sign, Tharinn told himself, of the man's kindness. But on this particular evening, as the sergeant made to rise, Horic sat down beside him and handed him a piece of paper. The sergeant smiled. "Another billet?"

"A bill, more like." The boy had his father's eyes, cold and pale. "It's been three weeks since you paid us. And word is your regiment's off the day after tomorrow."

"Then I'll pay you tomorrow." The sergeant folded the bill and made to put it in a pocket. "Now, let me help your mother, seeing you don't care to."

"Tonight, if you please," Horic said. "I spoke to your landlady, too. She says you flitted on her this morning. Said you thought you'd get away with payment in pastries. I won't have you flitting on us."

"Seems to me," said the sergeant, "that you've the vice of listening to gossip."

In his corner, Tharinn froze. Three weeks or more had passed since he last spent any time heeding the gossips at the monument, preoccupied as he was with Ingret. Had he missed something? He stepped forward, hand on the feather.

The sergeant rose. "And if there's anything owed, it's by you. I've spent enough on flowers for your mother." He looked again at the bill, crumpling it into a ball. "So I'll be collecting *my* dues, if you please." He flung the paper into the fire.

"Why, you..." Horic swung a fist at the sergeant's face. The man caught it in a hand and held on to it.

Ingret came back in from the kitchen. Under Tharinn's hand, the feather began to tingle. She stopped, empty tray in hand, and said, "What's this?"

"Your boy has some odd ideas," the sergeant said, still smiling, still holding on to Horic.

"Really?" For a moment, it seemed to Tharinn that Ingret looked straight at him. He trembled. Then she said, "He may have. But I'll thank you to let go of him."

"With pleasure," the sergeant said and released Horic. The boy staggered back, rubbing his hand. "It's you I'd rather have hold of, anyway. You owe me, mistress. You've had your boy pandering you to me for weeks."

"I don't think so," Ingret said, bringing the tray up in front of her. The sergeant laughed, harsh and cold, and made a grab for her.

Tharinn stepped between him and Ingret. The feather was burning hot now, too heavy for his shirt to hold. He drew it out.

A glow emanated from it, bright as firelight, spreading up his arm, across his chest, out over all of him.

The boy gasped. The sergeant stared. From behind Tharinn, Ingret said, "At last."

"Stage tricks," the sergeant said. "I don't scare so easily." But his face was wary, and his hand went to the knife at his belt.

"Please leave," Ingret said.

The sergeant hesitated, eyes on the feather. Then Horic said, "Pay up first," and made a snatch at the man's purse.

The sergeant drew his knife and twisted. Horic cried out, dropping to his knees.

Tharinn's hand tightened on the feather and he lunged for the sergeant. He had never had a day's formal training in fighting in his life. But in death, he had watched the guardsman duel shadows for night after night.

The feather stretched, lengthened. Its tip shone sharp in the firelight. The sergeant gasped as a long slash opened in the sleeve of his jacket. Blood began to trickle down his arm. Tharinn pulled back and thrust again, this time at the man's chest.

The sergeant stepped backwards hastily. "The old queen's magic... They said she died...."

Tharinn followed him, cutting another red runnel, this time in the left thigh. The sergeant brought up his knife, but the feather twisted round it to draw a bleeding line across his cheek. Tharinn brought the tip down to rest at the base of the sergeant's throat. The latter swallowed, staring at Ingret. Then he flung his purse at her feet and ran for the door.

Tharinn made to follow. Ingret said, "Don't," and he stopped, turned. She was still looking towards him, looking *at* him. The feather shrank back to its normal size.

From the floor, Horic said, "What happened?"

Ingret put the tray down on the nearest table. Still looking at Tharinn, she said, "You stay right there." Then she knelt beside her son. "This inn's protected. I told you that, remember, when you were little?"

"It's a story." Horic did not sound convinced.

"It's my guardian," Ingret said firmly, and for an instant

her eyes met Tharinn's and she smiled——really smiled—at him. Then she busied herself inspecting her son's cut hand. "Let's get that washed and bandaged, and then you can go to bed."

Escorting Horic to the kitchen, she looked back and her face repeated the injunction for Tharinn to wait for her. He crossed to the hearth and began to draw in the cooling ashes. Flowers, red and orange and yellow.

"Well," she said, a few minutes later when she returned alone. "Here you are, then. At last." Her face softened as she saw the flowers he had placed on the bar. But she said only, "It'll take more than those to sort this."

"You can see me."

"Yes. And hear you, too, and spot your meddling. Who else ever left me flowers on the doorstep?"

Tharinn looked down.

She went on, "I sent no notes to that man, and neither did my son. But I knew you were plotting. You sang such ridiculous songs to me."

Ghosts do not blush. Tharinn shuffled his feet and gripped the feather.

Ingret continued, "What were you thinking?"

"He made you laugh," Tharinn said to the floor. "And people said you were lonely."

"People!" She shook her head. "People have told me what to do quite enough in my life. I'm done with it."

"I'm sorry. I wanted..." Tharinn looked up. "I wanted you to be happy. I can't do it myself. I...I died."

"Bringing me flowers." Her voice was soft. "I missed them, you know. I missed you. I used to hope and hope you'd speak, to me, to my father, but you just stared and brought flowers. And then..."

He had no words. He stared at her, longing for the tears that death denied him.

She said, "And then when we finally have another chance, you try and palm me off on a...a

"I'm sorry," Tharinn said again.

"So you should be."

There was a silence. He fidgeted, looked over his shoulder at the door.

Ingret said, "Don't you dare, Tharinn Arliss. I don't need a new husband, or any of those fools who've been courting me, I just need you, and I'm not letting you go this time."

He said, "But..." and then, "I'm not... That is, you can't... We can't."

Ingret reached up and pulled something out of the coil of her hair. A feather, soft and small. "I wouldn't bank on that. The old queen looked out for us."

Tharinn crossed the taproom and found that he could, after all, kiss her.

Sherwood Smith's literary accomplishments span the galaxy of imagination from Young Adult fantasy (her *Wren* and *Court Duel* series) to adult fantasy (most recently, her *Inda* series) to space opera (the *Exordium* series with Dave Trowbridge), science fiction (collaborations with the late Andre Norton) and media tie-in novels. Her latest books are *Coronets and Steel*, a marvelous Ruritanian adventure with magic, and *Treason's Shore*, which completes the *Inda* series.

In between writing and teaching, Sherwood participates in the SFWA Musketeers, enjoys watching The Three Stooges, and reads the letters of Jane Austen.

"The Art of Masks," she writes, is set in the world of *Inda* and is a sequel to *Crown Duel*.

THE ART OF MASKS

By Sherwood Smith

"'Masks are the artful semblance of lies.'" I flourished my rapier, gazing over the extended tip into the baroness's haughty face, as I quoted the old song. "''The truth is my weapon 'gainst all such disguise.'"

"Commoners are beneath notice." The baroness ripped off her mask. "And you are common." She tossed the mask away, then rested her beringed hand on the hilt of her sword.

"Common—" I whirled behind the elegant side table, "—is a term that people apply to what is ordinary." I gestured toward a crystal carafe and two goblets. "It is an epithet that nobles—" I flourished the carafe at her, "—apply to what is honest."

The baroness flung her head back and put her hand to the hilt of her rapier.

I poured wine. "You disagree?"

The baroness whipped her blade to guard as her henchminions stilled. "I do not converse with such as you."

"Silence can be art." I picked up the goblet in one hand, the rapier lightly-held in my other. "From you, I confess, it is a relief." I saluted with my blade.

The baroness paused. It was a dramatic pause, beautifully done as she flicked a fast glance from the goblet to my rapier, then back. "Silence," she drawled, "can also have a point."

And attacked.

High, low, feint, strike, disengage, thrust, smooth and fast, tight arcs that whistled in the air—and the wine did not spill.

Then, when I snapped the blade to pink her right arm—her two lackeys sprang to attack me in revenge—I drank from the goblet. It sloshed. Making me gulp. Though my eyes stung to a shimmery blur, my muscles knew where to twist, where to turn, and exactly when to strike. I risked another sip as my assailants changed places—*attack, block, thrust, feint*—I flung the goblet one way as I thrust once, whirled the blade, and thrust again.

The goblet clanged to the polished floor as all three bodies dropped with dramatic thuds.

The audience drummed their feet on the floor and rapped the bench backs, wild with enthusiasm.

The baroness defeated, my honor restored, everyone's problem resolved by my action, the 'dead' picked themselves up and joined me in a line as one by one the invisible ties to the story world snapped like the magical illusions the stage-mage banished in a shower of tiny sparks. As the stage hands swiftly carried off the few pieces of real furniture, we took our last bows, buffeted by a boisterous roar that was better than wine or song or kisses.

Mistress Tholog signaled for the curtain-door to roll out, diminishing the roar to a rumble.

"Splendid work, darlings." Camrad pulled off his wig with one hand and his gold-encrusted robe with the other. He still spoke in Emperor Mathias's rich tones as he leaned forward to kiss my cheek. "You surprised me with that goblet, Leste. I trust the Emperor's surprise was convincing?"

The others laughed as I made that mental leap: I was no longer Lasthavais Dei the Wanderer, who adventured across four kingdoms before she met and conquered an emperor's heart, I was just...me.

"Loved the goblet." Mirind said to me in her own voice, incongruous after the baroness's lofty hauteur. "You had me on the hop."

"I nearly tripped over my jaw when you poured that wine,"

said Bunop, who'd played First Bodyguard, as this play did not have music. Even his laugh sounded like song.

"I thought coming in low rather than high on my last thrust would keep your arm still." Danza, Second Bodyguard—as tall and broad as Bunop is short and slight—ducked his head, his grin shy as he dashed back his sweat-damp red hair. "I hope we do that again. Good bit."

Neither of them said, *You might have introduced it in rehearsal*, but I felt the question. I said, "We'd done that duel so many times, I'd wanted a little surprise to give a snap to the scene. I thought of it last night, and practiced with the goblet all morning."

The players laughed, alternating jokes with praise for one another. Danza repeated a couple of times, "It was the goblet that did it." And "Did you hear the benches drumming?"

I said, "The benches seemed to love us. But the galleries? I didn't hear any accolade from them."

"Oh, nobles." Bunop wrinkled his nose, his black eyes squinched like something stank.

"Who can predict, or please, the toffs? They were out there. That's good enough for the likes of *us*." Mirind turned out her hands expressively.

"Remember how presumptuous it might seem to some, our lowly foreign band daring a Colendi play before a Colendi audience, and in their oh-so-beautiful capital, yet. I'm just glad we did not get laughed off the boards." Camrad waved his curled wig to and fro, his extravagantly handsome features quirked with irony. "As Mirind says, they were here. They stayed all the way to the end. That means we're guaranteed to fill seats tomorrow. Let's wash off our paint and go celebrate!"

A touch on my wrist brought my attention to Viket, the new little prentice, her eyes round. "*She* wants to see you." And to Mirind, "You, too."

"Extra praise, no doubt!" Camrad's grin slashed white against his brown skin. "Join us when you're done."

"Where will I find you?"

"We'll send Viket for you." Danza gave the little prentice a friendly clap on the arm. "Want to come with us, Viket?"

"Yes!" She looked the way I had felt when I first joined four years before, thrilled to be included among the primary cast after the performance.

Mirind and I ran ahead of the others across the charming brick alleyway between the playhouse and the players' inn. So far, everything we'd heard about Alsais was true—even the alleyways were clean, walls plastered smooth and painted creamy white, neatly trimmed flowering vines on trellises and little half-moon balconies. The corridor between the upper story rooms smelled like beeswax candles and herbs.

Mistress Tholog's outer door stood open. We walked in, looking through to the inner chamber, where she sat at a fine table with the stylized lyre-frame legs one saw all over Colend, its polished surface covered with plays, a few very old.

"Leste, please wait in the outer room. You'll find a copy of *Leaf by Leaf* to read while I speak with Mirind."

Mirind's hands clenched once on the baroness's elegant velvet skirt, then she straightened up, walked inside, and softly shut the door. All I could hear was the murmur of voices, pitched for that small room.

I picked up the play, but it was one I'd read as a young girl. This version was the original Sartoran, which I'd had to practice. I opened it obediently, but I didn't see the words. Instead, I relived my performance, relishing the perfect execution of my surprise with the wine goblet at the end, which I knew was good. Even if the sophisticated Colendi nobles hadn't been generous with applause.

Mirind came out. "Will you tell the others that I'm going to bed, Leste?" She avoided my gaze and sped past me into the hall after my "Sure."

She couldn't have been in trouble; her performance had been excellent. Very confused, I crossed to the inner chamber. "Why did you summon me, Mistress Tholog? Weren't we great?"

Mistress Tholog gave me a short, courteous nod, then pressed her long, knobby hands together.

"The company," she said in her even voice, "was good. And

I am pleased that our risk, daring a Colendi play here in Colend, paid off. That will lend us tremendous prestige when we launch out on our next tour."

I didn't miss the faint emphasis she put on the first two words. "Mistress Tholog, you can't object to my little ruse with the wine. I wanted to give the scene a bit of surprise—but it worked! It gave Lasva such style!"

She said gently, "Your 'Lasva' was smug."

Protests, defense—argument—piled up in my head, but didn't make it past my tongue. When I was small, I'd been a blurter. One of the reasons why I left home to become a player, rather than pursuing it in my own country, was because people I knew expected me to be a blurter. Treated me like a blurter, even after I struggled to change.

But Mistress Tholog had been a player before my mother was born. Some whispered that the Mistress's background was Chwahir, as her name certainly was, and she had the pale skin and round face common among those war-like people. But no one held it against her, as she had no trace of accent in any of the four languages we ever heard her speak and her movements were so controlled, it was impossible to guess her cultural background from her gestures.

Her mouth thinned in an almost smile, making me hazard a guess she knew at least some of what was going on in my mind. "Leste, you are aware that we only dared to present this play because the Colendi are currently interested in the older, more robust plays, stories about great days gone by. We would never presume to present the more contemporary pieces, with their clever innuendo saying one thing that the slightest gesture, or the curl of a ribbon, can give the lie. Or at least another meaning."

When people tell you something you have already heard many times, that usually means you're hearing reasons for a decision you aren't going to like. I braced inwardly, wondering what I could have done wrong. Surely it couldn't be my performance. I hadn't dropped a word, much less any wine.

"Some say," Mistress Tholog observed in her precise voice, "that the young Colendi aristocrats are rather rough and even uncouth, compared to the years before the war. That is certainly true in my experience. In my day, they never swaggered around armed or spoke of duels, as they do now. Subtlety was prized and oblique meanings considered a sign of wit. When they were angry, the most you saw was an attitude of fan. The only cutting was done by tone, sometimes merely by where one stood in a room."

"When I was young," I said, again stating what we knew, but I was trying to show myself being cooperative, while trying to defend my performance. "We were taught that the Colendi aristocrats read muscle movements like we read books." *And that's what I do.*

She said in a smooth voice, not quite interrupting me, but almost, "They are raised that way, so even at their most uncouth, they are sharper observers than most. And so we come to your performance. Lasthavais the Wanderer *cannot* be smug. That last duel must be a last act of desperate courage or it is not heroic, a last stand for love. Your very skill with goblet and blade reduced your actions to a mere chastisement."

All my triumph vanished, leaving me cold inside my damp, sweaty clothes—my false semblance of Lasva Wanderer. "So the drumming on the benches by the regular folk, is that because they expect Lasva to be perfect?"

"The commonality expect Lasthavais to be above human concerns. A hero, to them, is always right. Lasva is a hero in a dozen kingdoms. But the nobles in the galleries expect to look past the trite poses of legend to a semblance of the real person. Who is numbered among the ancestors of at least half of them."

"Right." I resisted the impulse to shuffle, to rub my hands. "Do you want me to rehearse, or..."

"I have decided that Mirind will play Lasthavais, beginning tomorrow."

Her voice was still gentle, but it hurt worse than any mere blow from a sword.

"You know it was a near thing, which of you would be assigned Lasthavais, and you know you are a little young. You will take the baroness from now on. I think our play will be the stronger if you are not trying to suppress smugness, but give it strength. Mirind's baroness was desperate at the end, there, rendering her...not more heroic, for she made selfish choices up until the end and her duel was selfishly motivated. But one could almost sympathize with her to discover herself so very outmatched, offering a fresh perspective on them both. When we leave Colend, we might pursue this interpretation more. But not here, in the very city where once both lived, especially as none of us are Colendi. It seems...unnecessarily impertinent."

I sneaked in a deep breath so that my eyes wouldn't sting. Despite the sharpness of my hurt, I was aware that she was right. A smug baroness would make a very powerful antagonist for Lasva, and I knew the part well, for I'd learned all the parts of this play when I was small.

"Mirind will be having a dawn rehearsal with just me. We will all have our regular run-through at mid-morning. You may shut the door on your way out."

I paused in the hall, divided between returning to my room and changing, or just going out as I was, in my long, curling black Lasva wig, and my high boots, riding trousers, and the dashing tunic-jacket that people had worn back in those days, a fashion that had come back again, though without the layers of lace or the splendid sashes with their dancing fringes.

In other places, we'd often worn character to socialize. In fact, there were times when we'd done it a-purpose, as a way to cause talk and draw more audience for the next performance. But to wear Lasva's character in Alsais? Excuses ran through my mind—it was late, I didn't want to keep the others waiting while I washed off my face paint and changed, may's well just go—but really, I knew I wanted to enjoy this last excuse to stride about in Lasva's dashing clothes, to *be* Lasva, just pretend.

I'd always had a problem just being myself. Why, after all, had I chosen to be a player, except to see if I had enough talent to assume the guises of the great, since I did not have the courage it took to *be* great? My parents were courageous and great. I was just a clown.

So I ran down the stairs. Viket waited with one foot propped against the wall, a worn play-book angled toward the nearest glow globe on its graceful arch where the alley joined the walkway.

She cast an inquisitive look at me as she tucked the book into the carryall she always wore over her shoulder.

I said, "She wasn't happy with my performance."

Viket exclaimed, "But why? You were sooo *perfect*."

Perfect. Well, that was the problem, wasn't it? I thanked her, trying not to show how dismaying I found her unconscious corroboration of Mistress Tholog's words.

We did not go far down the brick walkway alongside the canal, just around a couple of the curves, past two of the flowery-railed arched bridges spanning the canals. Music and laughter floated on the balmy spring air, the golden light from windows enhancing the silvery light from the glow globes on lamp posts curved in the semblance of trees.

From the noise and crowds, it looked as if the other two playhouses had also finished their performances. I strode along behind Viket's quick pattering step, enjoying the swaggering ring of my boot heels on the patterned and smoothed brick, and the extravagant swing of my broad crimson sash.

If I half-shut my eyes, I could imagine the Colendi street the way Lasva must have seen it in her day. Had she ever walked beside this canal? How long had the playhouses been here, anyway? Had they changed over the centuries, like in the city of my birth?

Viket kept hopping and turning around on her toes. Everyone seemed to be out, wearing rich fabrics in extravagant colors and sweeping styles as they laughed, talked, flirted, watched one another, or shut away the world to an ever-changing backdrop for their duet. We walked past the low eaves and the golden-lit diamond-shaped windows of the taverns frequented by players and musicians, and on to a fine establishment with a circle of windows jutting out over a terrace, which was surrounded by a curve in one of the broadest canals. People in pretty lamp-lit gondolas floated back and forth, some laughing and singing, as those on the terrace looked out. Light poured from inside, and noisy chatter and laughter. I caught one or two startled looks and, once or twice, soft laughter behind fans. I nodded and smiled in the grand manner as I passed on by.

Across the way, musicians played for a small eatery set in a garden with tiny tables divided from each other by vine-trellises, where silhouetted couples bent toward one another. Perhaps it was somewhere here that Lasva met the emperor and fell in love at the first meeting of their eyes.

What if the handsome King Shontande, who everyone said looked like Mathias the Magnificent, came along? Except that Mathias the Magnificent had actually been Lasva's son and Lasva herself was closer to forty when she met the first Matthias, whereas I was twenty and I didn't want anything to do with romance right now. Or with kings. Unless it was on stage, where everyone knew what would happen next and the kings could be dashing, not working all day, pressured by the mountain of responsibilities that never end.

"Lasva!" Camrad dashed out, arms wide. "My beloved!"

Laughter greeted this greeting, followed by a voice, "You forgot your royal robes, O Mathias."

"So I did," Camrad exclaimed as he performed an elaborate bow, then drew me inside. "Permit me to presume."

Despite its fame as exclusive and expensive, the tavern was bright, crowded, and hot from too many people too close together. The blend of personal scents was like herbs and spices thrown by handfuls into a room.

I cast a quick glance around, half-dazzled by the brilliant light of faceted crystal glow globes. As usual, Camrad was the center of a crowd. He's so tall, and so handsome—with or without face paint—and he's got that deep, booming voice that is perfect for good or evil kings, or good and evil sorcerers.

I thanked him most royally as I pushed aside my rapier and sat down on a bit of bench next to Danza, who had squeezed up, ducking his head when I smiled his way. My curly black wig blocked my vision on the sides of my face and the lights spangled, winking off gems and the polished hilts of swords, as Danza offered me a share of his wine cup.

Swords, I thought, as the potent wine cup burned through my veins. None of the players carried swords. Except for me.

"Favor us with a bit of your wisdom, O Empress?" someone asked.

I couldn't see who'd spoken, but sniffed subtle Colendi scents close by. "Masks," I rolled out the words, "are the artful semblance of lies!"

"The empress is famed for her wisdom," someone called mockingly. "And her generosity, bestowing it without charge."

Was that supposed to be a joke? Quotations were the safest response. "I am known for saying what I mean." As I gave Lasva's line, I dashed back the lace at my wrists with a lofty air. "Wisdom comes with knowing when to mean more than one says."

Three more times it happened, someone showing how well they knew the play by calling out a line, to which I responded. People laughed every time.

With the laughter and the effect of the wine, my good mood had restored itself. I would finish out the evening as Lasva, and as for tomorrow, well, it's great fun playing a villain. I'd throw myself into the baroness, and smug? I'd show Mistress Tholog the very essence of smug!

These thoughts flitted through my mind as the exchanges went on around me, and I chimed in when I heard a cue. I gloried in the laughter until it broke over my words before I had finished them. On the next cue I concentrated, gazing past the splashes of light off gems and crystal and silk as I made out a female voice, in pure Colendi sing-song, crooning Lasva's lines just before I spoke.

In other words, I wasn't clever, I was obvious.

And they weren't laughing at the humor, but at *me*.

Camrad's eyes had narrowed into his wicked sorcerer expression. He broke in, extolling in rich, dramatic tones, "My very good people, need I remind you that we must respect the words of princes?"

That same mocking Colendi voice, with its fluid vowels and charming intonations, twisted Lasva's responsive line around.

"But we do not share them with players."

I felt the jab of that arrow in my companions. Danza leaned toward me to whisper, "Let's go elsewhere."

Camrad extended his hand; he was coming up with a suitable quote to make our departure.

But I was too angry on behalf of my fellow players. One of the baroness's lines flitted from brain to lips. I leaned around Camrad and spotted the Colendi female, my age, a heart-shaped face, slim form in celestial blue silk. I flourished my lace dismissively in her direction, very much in the baroness's style, and drawled with all the baroness's insolent haughtiness, "Your assumption of rank is only less preposterous than your claim to worth."

A tall, lounging fellow resplendent in a coat of rich green brocade said mockingly, "Mark the day, Falise. Your efforts appear to have inspired Empress Lasva to hide behind the words of her enemy."

Just the faintest check, emphasized by the oblivious background voices, now distinct; over them sang a voice on the other side of the tavern, rising and falling in a century-old lament. Danza ducked his head down further as Bunop leaned out, his wide dark gaze intent on that fellow in green.

The fellow in green ignored Bunop, Danza, and Camrad as if they didn't exist. He waited with a mock air of surprise for Falise, the young woman in blue, to make an answer.

Falise darted a firefly glance between the man in green and me. Everyone seemed to have paused—it felt like the room held its breath, though the lament rolled on, unheeding.

"Then let her follow," Falise said sharply.

The man in green shifted a lazy-seeming glance from me to Falise through heavy-lidded black eyes, as the others in their crowd exchanged clever smiles.

One of the women murmured; I only caught the end, "... very much their place."

Camrad bowed. "Whatever Lasva does, she does with grace. If you will step aside, we shall demonstrate how one departs with—"

So smoothly did Camrad bridge the moment, it almost worked, until Falise stepped out to confront me. "Does she fight with grace?"

"I can take a point." In an effort to break the tension with humor, I thrust my hilt forward with an overly dramatic gesture.

"And we can take our leave," Bunop responded, with a quick, graceful bow to the company. "Come, my dears—"

"But can she take a challenge?" The fellow in green utterly ignored Bunop.

Lady Falise was my height, the pearls edging her silk coat glistening, her dark hair braided up in a rope of costly pearls. Diamonds winked on her longest finger as she ripped her blade free.

"My dear Falise. These are *players*," drawled a young woman from their crowd, gems winking on her languid fingers lifting dismissively in our direction.

"Make space," the man in green said suavely, "so that Falise may play with the players."

Was he baiting her, or us? Camrad sighed, and Danza flushed. Bunop's fist tightened on his knee. My father insisted that sarcasm was the weapon of the weak, but there is nothing like self-righteous fury to condone anything, and so I drawled a line from *Jeje the Pirate Queen*, "Oh, the cowards hiding behind their coronets."

I meant it for that fellow in green, but Falise whipped out her blade—

—and attacked me.

My body reacted before my brain did, knowing its cue from so many rehearsals. I whirled, my sword whooshing out, and I met her blade with a loud, satisfying *clang-g-g!*

People jumped out of the way, some exclaiming, but I didn't see or hear them, I was too busy trying to react, desperately meeting her wild thrusts. It felt like trying to run through water, because I didn't know where she was going to strike next. In theater, you rehearse every stroke and also you endeavor to hit one another's blade in as dramatic a way as possible, and she was trying to hit *me!*

I'd been trained to defend myself, but it had been five years or so since I'd practiced those lessons, and I'd been doing theater fighting ever since. I'd desperately warded six or seven strokes when the crowd closed in, and a young man in brown silk exclaimed, "Put up! Put up! You want to kneel at Willow Gate?"

Falise lifted her point uncertainly as the fellow in brown stepped between Falise and me, closing her off from my view. Camrad gave us the private signal for *fast exit, you missed the cue.*

Bunop twisted and ducked, quick and sinuous, then took up a station on my left. Danza rose, a protective bulk at my right. I jammed my sword back into the baldric with hands that I discovered were shaking, and within a very short time we were out of there, the sound of mocking laughter floating after us.

It was a retreat, a defeat. Anger, humiliation, then a puzzled thought, what was it a defeat *for*? As I followed the others, the wig's black curls falling forward to hide a face I was afraid had suddenly become notorious, I mentally backtracked, trying to figure out why someone would jump out of a crowd and attack me, first verbally, then with a weapon.

We reached the quiet alley between the playhouse and the inn. No palace or city authorities had given chase. We were alone. Camrad sighed with relief.

I said, "I didn't start that. I don't even know what happened."

"I am aware," Camrad said, wiping his long hair back. "As are we all."

"She attacked you." Danza shook his head slowly at the unfairness. "No reason."

"Reason was, that strutting rooster in green." Bunop raised the back of his hand over his shoulder, in the direction of the tavern.

"He just wanted to see trouble," Danza muttered.

"Trouble between women," Bunop observed.

"Trouble just to have fun. That foolish female in blue seemed to be begging for attention," Camrad said. "Why not become a player?"

We laughed, though the comment was too pointed to be funny. Then Camrad turned to me. "Perhaps it's better not to go into company while still in character."

"At least not in Colend," Viket said, her eyes huge in the reflected light from the glow globe at the foot of the alley.

Camrad paused on the stair. "Are we agreed, we won't disturb Mistress Tholog, since there has been no further trouble?"

We laid our hands together in the players' pact. The rules in the company were strict: any fighting, any trouble with the authorities of a city, and we were out. No one wanted that, though Bunop's usually mobile, expressive mouth was tight; he had never hid his low opinion of real aristocrats, despite playing them on stage.

Our celebration was ruined. We all trooped upstairs to our rooms.

I carefully removed the Lasva wig and put it through the cleaning frame. Usually I enjoyed watching the magic snap and scintillate, leaving my things as clean as when first made, but my mood was somber. I took off the costume and put it through as well, then laid the things in the wardrobe; as I did so, I caught sight of myself in the long mirror on the wardrobe door.

I was startled by the sight of my face paint, smudged slightly from the long evening. The lining around my eyes, the cheek and lip rouge made me look older, different, so that my plain, straight light brown hair hanging in hanks around my shoulders looked like someone else's hair.

I washed myself up, and there was my ordinary face, to go with the dull hair. I stood there, staring into my eyes. I knew I should put on my nightdress and get into bed. The next day would be another full one, beginning with a rehearsal at mid-morning.

Yet...yet. I could not sleep. My mind was back at that fancy tavern, reliving the exchange, examining the laughter, the signs that I had missed, yet I still could not figure out why that Falise had attacked me. As for that scornful mirth after we left, as if we ran as cowards....

I prowled around my room once, then twice, and finally I

threw open my trunk and rummaged around for street clothes. I just had to go back and reclaim our honor. It wasn't for me. It was for the honor of players. *All* players, not just my friends.

I began to pull out my good cotton-silk gown, then I let it drop. It was horribly out of fashion for this kingdom, and it would be impossible to fight in. Also, if there was trouble, that might get reflected on the players. Much better to go as an anonymous person. After all, it wasn't I who had been insulted, but players, and so an anonymous traveler could just as well call out that snotty Lady Falise and teach her a lesson in a private duel.

So. What guise? All my early years I'd resented being a bean-pole, against having to play the boys' parts. At twenty, I could still don shirt, vest, breeches, tie my hair back like the boys do, and play the Hero's Friend. The walk, the gestures, were habit by now.

I was already wearing an invisible mask, if seen in a certain way, so why not don another? I buckled on my own sword, which was plain but of excellent quality. My father had seen to that before I left home. I threw my coin purse into the pocket of my tunic and hastened back along the canal, past slowly strolling couples and groups merry with laughter and chat. This time, no one paid the least attention to me. I reached the tavern, from which floated a tenor voice singing a ballad.

The man sounded fine, but he'd had little training. When he finished and a few of the guests tossed small coins onto a silver serving tray silently circulated by a small boy, I knew what was going on: a competition.

Only a few had thrown coins. The man bowed, his expression calm, but I picked up his chagrin in the way he turned his head as he walked out of the tavern. So everyone in the circle had to participate. I'd never seen that before, except among players— but this was Colend. In Colend, everything was competition, my father had said once, though they called it the life of art.

Holding the best table near the windows were those who'd baited us, Falise in company with two other ladies, and two lords, the one in brown silk and the lounging fellow in green. I had to get her alone if I didn't want a crowd, which would pretty much guarantee the authorities being called down on us.

So I headed toward a small table between them and the door, as an older woman took her turn in the competition. She offered a poem in Old Sartoran. The poem was funny if you understood Old Sartoran, the language of court, of high politics and ancient literature. The laughter sounded polite, not hilarious, and I wondered if people pretended to understand the poem because of the prestige Old Sartoran carries in courtly circles. It sounded to me like the laughter was forced, people laughing because others laughed. Whatever the truth, she got coins throw by everyone.

Including me. I dug out a small coin from my coin purse, because I had no intention of drawing attention to myself by being the only one not to throw one, but I noted before I tossed mine onto the tray that many of the coins were even smaller, down to copper-based tinklets. Ah. So there was another subtle signal.

As the servitor passed with the tray, I did a fast scan of the enemy. Falise faced the window, so all I could see was her profile. She laughed loudly, with the edges of her teeth showing, as forced a laugh as she'd uttered after the recent poem, but a different tone.

The next performer, an older man, began delivering, no, *unloading* a very long poem. He seemed to think that volume was better than expression, or maybe he was used to praise. He certainly had the manner of it. Under his chanting verses, Falise and her group murmured just loud enough for me to make our their courtly singsong.

The man only got a few coins; I'd decided to do what the majority did so I wouldn't draw attention. No one in Falise's group threw in a coin, so I also let the tray pass.

The man left, affront obvious in the line of his shoulders. Now the turns had reached Falise's group. I considered hissing when she performed, but no, that would draw attention.

When it was her turn, she also delivered a quick poem in Old Sartoran. Her eyes turned toward that lounging man in the green, whose poisonous drawl caused me to think of him as Lord Sarcasm. The rest of their group performed well, though in a courtly manner, and the man in green delivered a very funny poem that was obviously about current politics, as the listeners laughed at lines I didn't understand, as well as the funny lines that I did. His performance received a shower of silver coins. I'd been throwing tinklets. No one noticed.

I'd been so intent on watching each performer that I was caught by surprise when everyone turned my way. I wasn't invisible, just because I wasn't in costume.

"Well, fellow," Lord Sarcasm drawled—the word 'fellow' being neutral, but with that added lilt it meant 'one with questionable status.' "Do you need an invitation from the palace?"

Fellow. *Almost* not in costume.

I thought rapidly. I had to be good, but I didn't want to sound like a trained player. I gave them a short poem in modern Sartoran, so my lack of the purest Colendi accent wouldn't be obvious.

In not using my trained stage voice, I performed my poem the way I had when in my homeland.

When I saw the quick glances, the slight adjustings of posture that people give others whose status has just risen, I realized I sounded like a court-trained aristocrat. The evidence showed in the shower of coins on the tray.

So they had awarded my status at least as much as my performance.

Human beings are as silly as geese, my mother once said. *No, sillier.*

A song began, sung by a dark-haired woman who'd entered after I did. I'd scarce given her a glance, past noticing butterfly face-paint, making it clear she'd come from a masque ball.

My focus was on Falise and her noble friends. The woman's voice soared like molten silver in a sorrowful song that I recognized with a chill along my nerves: it was the original ballad that Lord Sarcasm's song was based on, only instead of lampooning one set of courtiers in favor of another, it lamented the cruelty of one human toward another.

The refrain arced up to a high sustained note, like the ringing of crystal. I knew that voice, and those dark eyes in their butterfly paint were familiar, too.

It was Bunop, in female dress, singing in counter-tenor. When the song was done, he curtseyed gracefully, then brought up a painted silk fan, wrist airy and arched as the fan gently fluttered to and fro in the mode of *duet or duel?* My amazement sharpened to indignation at his interference, but he did not look my way. His attention remained entirely on Lord Sarcasm, whose bony face had lifted, his coppery skin flushed a little, either from wine or from the perceived challenge.

Was Bunop going to interfere with me, or not? As the tray finished its round, Lord Sarcasm sauntered across the room to engage 'Lady' Bunop in conversation. Falise watched him go, her expression one of...relief.

As soon as he left them, Falise's two female friends came toward me. Falise was a step behind, followed by the fellow in brown, who had a pleasant face framed by pale hair ribbon-tied like mine.

"I have always loved that poem," the blonde in gold and crimson said to me.

"Is it popular at court where you come from?" The second one had brown eyes and curly brown hair the color of maple. Her courtly drawl was closer to a coo.

"Your delivery was quite elegant." Falise's manner was gracious, that of the expert bestowing a compliment.

Her friends snapped glances her way, and then back to me.

I bowed slightly in my chair, my hand coming up in the gesture of *manner no matter*.

"Where are you from?"

"What think you of our city?"

I raised my hand, as the next performer was beginning. He chose a complicated poem that would have been great, had his delivery not been wooden as he concentrated on all those internal rhymes, but the length gave me time to think. Now their group was down to four, as Bunop in his woman's guise continued to whisper to Lord Sarcasm—but the four had joined me. I was no closer to getting Falise alone for my challenge.

The length of the poem at least enabled me to ignore my new companions' questions as the tray went around, and the two females fumbled at their coin purses, both watching me. They were waiting to see what I offered! Surprised, I just sat, for I hadn't thought much of that delivery, and sure enough, they let the tray pass by as well.

The same thing happened after the woman whose turn was next. She'd probably had a glass too much wine, because she forgot a verse and tried to smile it away, but everyone knew that song too well. They smiled back, but she only got two coins, from her two escorts.

Bunop and Lord Sarcasm had vanished, the performers' circle thinning as the turns came around again. Time to get to my purpose.

The fellow in brown went first. He'd been quiet until now, patiently sitting at Falise's side, though she paid him scarce attention. He sang an old, old story-song, a simple one but well done, his light blue gaze resting on Falise, though her attention seemed divided between the females and me. The best part of his performance was the way he used his hands, dance-like with stylized gestures. I'd never seen that style before. It was very effective, and everyone else thought so, too—except for Falise. She threw down a coin, but her smile over her shoulder was perfunctory.

"I like what you did with your hands," I said as I threw down a silver.

The fellow blushed. "I learned it from an aunt, who—"

Falise cut him off. "We enjoy Nestan's outland styles. Refreshing." She smiled toward me, her manner proprietary.

Nestan thanked her quietly, his downturned gaze not quite masking his hurt, as the other two women exchanged a flutter of fingers in a private signal. They began a duet, one high, one harmonizing.

They, as had Nestan, got full trays. It was my turn. The time was late. Across the way, lights were being extinguished. If I was to make my challenge, it must be soon. I pitched my voice for courtly delivery, deliberately too quick, and...

"Masks are the artful semblance of lies..."

I sang it straight at Falise, who listened with her head tilted and eyes closed, as if listening to a performer. But when I ended, she opened her eyes and did not look at me, but at the women.

They pulled out silver coins as they complimented me in their pretty, sing-song voices, and Falise declared, "That is the way we should hear those words. Not sullied by presumptuous upstarts."

"Upstarts?" I asked, my heartbeat thumping.

Nestan gave the peace-making gesture called *so flows the river,* but Falise said, "Some outland players earlier. One had the presumption, no, the effrontery, to appear as my great-mother Lasthavais Dei in mask. I had to use my sword to drive them out."

"They were sooo fearsome," the blonde cooed.

The sidelong glances, sharp-cornered smiles, the tones that did not match soft words...I had it now. Snow chilled my nerves as I stared at Falise's friends, or enemies, rather, pretending to be friends.

The tray had made its round, the yawning boy returning to stand beside the impassive tavern keeper.

Some of the listeners got up to leave. The one in green sat alone.

It was now Falise's turn, and she leaned toward me. I could see in the lift of her eyes, her attitude, that she was about to ask for a request, and on impulse I rose and executed a flourishing bow. With a dozen steps I left Falise's honor back in that tavern in the graceful hands of the admirer she disdained and the enemies she propitiated.

Outside, the air was cool and smelled of coming rain.

A dozen more steps and I heard the swish of silk as Bunop joined me. He smiled, his stride lengthening as he kicked up the hem of his fine embroidered gown.

"You didn't," he said, glancing down at my rapier.

"No." I made a face, and so he wouldn't think I was a

coward, I said, "Those other women would have liked it too much." I frowned at him. "You?"

"No, no," he soothed, patting the air. "I gave our friend in green a surprise or two, I think, out in the privacy of the little courtyard. But no knife between his ribs."

"They're *mean*," I burst out. "As mean to each other as they were to us. Except for that fellow, Nestan. He seems to like that Falise. Can't imagine why."

"Love gilds the world," Bunop observed, kissing his fingers to a passing gondola, where a couple sat with arms entwined, faces together, and he leaned against the railing.

"She doesn't even seem to like him." I leaned next to him, enjoying the cool breeze rising from the canal.

"Oh, I suspect she does. Respect? Another matter. His rank is lower than hers, I learned from my drawling friend in green. Who attempted to impress me by telling me what fools they are, before he, ah, precipitously chose a swim in the canal."

Bunop mimed dumping someone over the railing, and I laughed.

Bunop finished, "Lady Falise is apparently desperate to be invited to court."

"She's not even a courtier?"

Bunop regarded me in the light of one of the arched glow globes. "'Not even,'" he repeated. "She's got rank and wealth, but you say she's 'not even' a courtier. You *are* a toff in disguise, aren't you?"

"I'm—"

He flicked the ruffles over his padded bosom. "I don't mean us right now, I mean you're not a player. You're a toff playing at being a player."

"I am just me," I exclaimed, stopping in the middle of the tiled path to face him. "I'm—" I was about to yell that I was serious about being a player, except isn't that the sort of thing that others are supposed to notice?

He stopped as well, his face paint not hiding the intensity of his expression. "If you get thrown out of the troupe, you can go back to another life. You wouldn't be ruined like the rest of us.

Or you would never have pulled that sword back in that tavern. Or you wouldn't have tried the trick with the goblet. Or," his voice gentled, "you would notice how much Danza follows your every move and word, the same way that young fellow Nestan follows Lady Falise."

Prickly heat burned all over me. "I didn't know that about Danza."

"Just my point."

"I mean, not because—because of rank, or any of that. It's because...because there's someone else. I think." My voice shook.

Bunop lifted a hand and brushed a strand of my hair from my face. "You don't have to say anything."

"But I think I do." I gulped. "Not about...*him*. Here I was, being so glad I didn't call Falise out to teach her we aren't cowards because I pitied her for not being aware of how those friends of hers must talk about her when she was not present. Well, surprise!"

Bunop kissed his fingers to me, then said gently, "Nobody thinks of you that way. You work hard. You don't slang others to make yourself look better, like that sorry fool Falise. But you do walk through the world with the comfort of privilege, and we can see it on the stage. You're comfortable, playing toffs. You take for granted things we work for."

"In other words, real words, I'm a snob." I felt sick inside as new ideas crashed over me like waves over a ship in a storm, and I started toward the inn, tears burning my eyes. "I thought you all liked me. Took me for who I am. I mean, who I said I am. I never lied. I just never said I come from Remalna or my real last name. 'Leste' is part of my name, I just changed it from Elestra."

Bunop didn't answer.

"Mistress Tholog said my performance tonight was smug." I grimaced down at the quiet waters of the canal as we crossed in front of the dark, silent theater. We'd almost reached the inn; just two windows were lit up on our floor. The rest were as dark as the theater and all the other entertainment houses along the canal. Soft laughter rose from an equally dark gondola floating by. "I'll be doing the baroness starting tomorrow."

As Bunop hiked up his skirts to mount the stairs to our inn, I put a hand across the stairs. "And you came to keep me from causing trouble, didn't you? Because I'm a smug toff pretending to be a player?"

"I went back to do just what I did," Bunop admitted. "But it didn't surprise me to see you there. With a sword at hand. So I waited, after I had my fun with my target. In case you might need backup." He yanked up his skirt, revealing a long knife strapped to his thigh. "As it happens, we didn't need steel, either of us, did we, to make our point?"

Despite everything I laughed—without sound, for we'd reached the hallway, which was dark, except for the faint gold of light under Mistress Tholog's outer door. "Masks," I whispered. "And lies. I'm sorry if mine caused any hurt."

"Everyone wears masks," Bunop whispered back, his fan shimmering as he flipped it open and mockingly covered half his face. "We spend our lives learning how to make them. But then some of us, sometimes, we learn how to take them off so we see real faces, and others see ours."

"That's not artful." I paused before my door. "That's...that's genuine. Sincerity. Candor."

"It's truth. It is after we experience the range of human emotion that we can make truth into art." He smiled, and flourished the fan. "And only then does art doff the mask and become truth."

Australian Sean McMullen is the author of fifteen science fiction and fantasy novels and over seventy stories, many of which have won awards and been translated into over a dozen languages. Sean gained the loyalty of a large readership with *Souls in the Great Machine,* in which a future Australia is ruled by a caste of psychopathic librarians and run by a human-powered computer. This was followed by the *Moonworlds* series, which featured a vampire who has been fourteen years old for seven centuries and is getting a bit depressed about it. His young adult novel, *Before the Storm,* was described by one reviewer as "the Terminator Meets the Bronte Sisters." For light amusement, he earned a PhD in medieval literature. When not writing histories of Australian SF and fantasy, he works in scientific computing and studies karate, foil and sabre.

He writes, "Being spirited away to Faerie by an enchanted lover is like an alien abduction: the transport is provided, and there is someone to get you past the security guards. Getting there by yourself, however, requires the magical version of Project Apollo." "Culverelle" provides the romantic background to his 2009 *F & SF* story "The Spiral Briar" and forms part of his novel, *Keeper of Boundarie.*

CULVERELLE

by Sean McMullen

Had Eleanor not been so fearful, she would have enjoyed the view from the slopes of the little hill. To the west was the lake, Derwentwater. The vista of the glassy-calm lake, its islands and the hills beyond, was laid out like a tapestry in the king's throne room brought to life. Turning north, she could see the village of Keswick and the Tower of Briars. She could also see the nunnery's ox cart trundling into the distance.

As instructed, she had come to this place at noon, and now she was waiting alone. She was dressed as a man, as the letter had specified. Her green ankle-length, unbelted tunic was even the height of fashion. It was trimmed with white fur, and puffed sleeves suggested broad shoulders. Her long red hair was hidden under a close-fitting cap.

A puff of smoke appeared on the east bank of the lake, followed by a deep boom. Moments later, a column of water erupted skywards out on the lake. *One of the new siege engines*, she told herself, hoping it was not a demon or dragon. The nunnery cart rounded a corner and vanished. Eleanor very nearly broke and ran after it, but the Tower of Briars caught her gaze again and reminded her why she was there. It was Sir Gerald's tower.

She had not seen Gerald for seven years. When his sister

Mayliene died, he had set out for the Tower of Briars to avenge her, and he had been there ever since. *She is so very long dead, yet she still robs me of my beloved,* Eleanor thought bitterly.

"Lady Eleanor."

The voice was like wind in dry autumn leaves. Eleanor turned. At the center of the road stood a figure wearing a helmet and chainmail hauberk. He seemed to radiate menace. The helmet's visor was down, and there were triangles inset with glass for eyes. The helmet reached to his lips, which were strangely delicate for someone of such threatening appearance. He wore black gloves, and a sword hung at his belt.

"The master armourer, Tordral, he, er, sent a letter," stammered Eleanor.

"I am Tordral."

He did not bow. That was bad. A man who did not bow was outside the rules that courtly folk lived by. She seriously considered running.

"You wrote that Sir Gerald has need of me," she said, moving on to the reason she had made the journey.

"He does, but he does not know it."

"You mean he does not know I am here?"

"*I* know that he needs you. That is enough."

Tordral advanced until he was within arm's reach of Eleanor. He smelled faintly of wood smoke, tar, resin, and sulphur. Although he cut a very impressive figure, he was not especially tall.

"A green tunic with silver lacework florals, no sword and no gauntlets," said Tordral. "You call this a man's clothing?"

"At court, it is quite the fashion."

Tordral circled her in silence, arms folded. Down at his lakeside workshops, the siege machine sent another boom echoing among the rolling hills.

"At court, they say you build magical machines," said Eleanor nervously, hoping to flatter him.

"I despise magic."

"And that kings take your weapons into battle."

"True."

"Armed only with a staff, you killed a knight who charged you on horseback."

"A trifling feat. Even you could do it."

"That you are at war with Faerie."

"True, oh so very true," he said, gesturing to the woodlands. "Now come along."

The trees towered like giant enemy warriors, and shadows hinted at enough fanged, clawed shapes to fill a bestiary. Nevertheless, most terrifying of all was Tordral.

"I—I cannot," Eleanor managed.

"Very well, return to London." Tordral turned upon his heel and set off for the lakeside.

"No, wait!"

Tordral stopped and turned back. "Wait for what?"

"I—I am just afraid."

"Afraid I might ravish you?"

That was indeed an issue, but Eleanor was too frightened to even discuss it.

"My lord, please, put yourself in my position," she cried, now at the edge of tears.

Tordral regarded her for a moment that seemed to suspend time. The interlude was broken by another echoing boom from the siege engine.

"I *am* in your position," replied Tordral.

The armourer's hand came up to the visor. With not a little theater, the metal mask was slowly rotated upwards...and Tordral ceased to be *he*.

No man could have a face like that, thought Eleanor as she stared, unaware that her mouth had dropped open. *In fact, very few women are so well blessed by fortune,* passed through her mind before being cut short by a dreadful qualm. The face was that of Gerald's dead sister.

"Mayliene!"

"Breathe a word of it, and you must learn to breathe through a slit throat."

"Are you a ghost?"

"No. Now come with me, and no more nonsense."

oOo

They entered the woodlands below Walla Crag. There was no path; Tordral just pushed her way through the bushes. Very soon, Eleanor realised she could never find her way back without Tordral to guide her. The glade where the armourer stopped was some type of ruin. A wide area of ancient paving stones had been recently cleared of weeds, moss, and the detritus of centuries.

"A thousand years ago, this was the dining hall of a Roman villa," said Tordral. "Here you will learn to fight for Sir Gerald."

Leaning against a ruined wall were a pair of shields and a half dozen swords. Beside them was a pile of roughweave clothing, such as an artisan might wear.

"I thought you—you died seven years ago," said Eleanor as they stopped.

"*Mayliene* died seven years ago. Tordral, the twisted one, was born then. Twisted by Faerie, twisted by mother church, twisted by family, and twisted by hate. What do you know of that story?"

Eleanor thought back fourteen years. The thought that she had never once visited the stricken Mayliene suddenly screamed within her mind. Were she not lost in the woodlands, she would have fled.

"An elf lord appeared before you in the walled garden of the Tower of Briars. You spurned his advances. You said you preferred books to courting. He was angered, he cursed you. His magic shortened your eyesight so—so that you could see nothing but a book held inches from your face."

"Now I want revenge, and after fourteen years I am powerful enough to take it," said Tordral, nodding. "What do *you* want, Eleanor of Derryton?"

"Gerald. I have waited fourteen years."

"Then help me fight."

"Help? Fight? But I am a woman and—" Realising that this line of reasoning was unlikely to get a sympathetic hearing, Eleanor fell silent.

"What am I?" asked Tordral, spreading her hands.

"A warrior?"

"A machine, ladyship. A war machine. Part of my body is before you, the rest is being built beside Derwentwater. When complete, I can either restore my brother's honour or make war on Faerie. Because I cannot do both, you too must become a machine. Now remove your robes and dress in artisan's garb."

Eleanor opened her mouth to protest, but Tordral had already turned away to stare into the surrounding woodland through the spectacles built into her visor. *Remove your robes.* The command was all at once shocking and thrilling.

"Why do you need me in particular?" asked Eleanor as she removed her fur-trimmed tunic. "A pageboy would make a better warrior."

"I need someone I can trust absolutely to fight for Gerald. You love him, even after fourteen years, so I can trust you."

"But surely—"

"If you refuse, then my brother's honour will run a very poor second to my war on all Faerie," said Tordral in a more deep and ominous tone. "Revenge means more to me than even Gerald. Faerie twisted me, so I chose the very name Tordral because I am twisted...yet I am in Gerald's debt. Before I twist Faerie as Faerie has twisted me, I would repay that debt."

For a moment, Eleanor stood naked. *This must be what it feels like to be seduced,* flitted through her mind as she glanced at Tordral's back. She picked up the roughweave tunic, smock and trews. They smelled of smoke and resin, but were otherwise clean.

"Are you done with dressing?" asked Tordral.

"Yes."

Tordral turned back to inspect Eleanor, arms folded. She nodded.

"Adequate, but next time bind your breasts as flat as you may with cloth, and rub dirt onto your fingers to make them seem less dainty. Now walk before me, back and forth."

Eleanor walked as elegantly as she would have before the king himself.

"You mince," said Tordral coldly. "You must swagger."

"Must I look so very like a man to fight as one?" protested

Eleanor, who was quite proud of her walk.

"You must have the *guise* of a man. The glamours of Faerie are powerful, but not without flaw. They can render an entire village asleep, yet cannot take hold upon a woman dressed as a man."

"So these rags are my armour against magic?"

"Yes, but you must still fight blade on blade."

Tordral handed Eleanor a sword with a fishtail pommel. It was heavy and awkward in her hands. The shield she was given was even heavier.

"Hold the shield's top level with your eyes," said Tordral. "Present the sword high, above your head."

Tordral had Eleanor make a number of strikes against a sapling padded with cloth. Her arms and wrists quickly began to ache.

"You are letting the shield droop!" snapped Tordral. "Were that tree an elf lord, your head would be free of your body by now."

"Its weight is beyond my strength."

"Hold it high, until your muscles burn."

"My muscles already burn."

"Then that is progress," said Tordral, drawing her sword. "Now face me, and remember that the shield alone stands between you and Death's scythe. Fancy that you are defending Gerald, who lies englamoured and helpless."

With a stab of alarm, Eleanor realised that she was now facing a live opponent. Abruptly the pain in her muscles vanished. Tordral twirled her sword as if it were feather-light. Eleanor staggered with every stroke that Tordral landed on her shield.

"Defend him!" shouted Tordral. "Defend him with your life."

Suddenly fear turned to anger, and Eleanor lashed out with her own sword. The blades met. Eleanor's sword was wrenched from her hand, and landed with a jangling clang on the ancient flagstones.

"Good, I am satisfied," said Tordral. "Now rest."

Eleanor shuffled to a wall, leaned against it, and slid down until she reached the flagstones.

"Why are you satisfied?" she panted, too fatigued to even sob. "I was pathetic."

"You did not turn and flee, neither did you burst into tears or cast yourself upon my mercy. You stood and fought, which shows spirit. Swordwork can be taught. Spirit cannot."

Tordral offered her a jar of ale. Eleanor greedily drank most of it straight down. For a time she sat in silence, recovering her breath. Tordral neither ate not drank. Eleanor gazed at her admiringly.

Like a man, she thought. *More than a man. As tireless as a watermill. A machine.*

"I once read a *roman courtoise,*" she said. "It was about a knight on a quest. To win his lady he had to pass seven tests—"

"Chrétien's *King Mark and the Blonde Iseult,*" said Tordral. "Love, trust, stand, learn, endure, forgive and fight. You have done the first three."

"So I must *learn* to fight, then *fight* the elf lord?"

"Yes."

"What must I endure?"

"Training. In just a month it is solstice, and you must work hard to be ready by then."

"And who must I *forgive?*"

"To tell that would be to spoil your journey, my lady. Now then, an end to rest."

"More swordwork?"

"No, legwork. You must learn to swagger."

oOo

This day, the first of June, 1449, thought Eleanor as she walked. *Fourteen years less three weeks since my Gerald was taken from me.*

In the ten days past, Tordral had trialled her with swords, spears, halberds and even axes. This had established that while Eleanor could now defend herself against an opponent, she could inflict no damage to speak of. On this afternoon she had been compelled to use a light hunting bow against a tree as wide as the shoulders of a man. At fifty paces she had been unable to hit it. Now the sun was low in the sky, and her arms and shoulders ached with fatigue, yet she was determined not to just shamble back to the nunnery and collapse onto a bed.

As they parted, Tordral had told her to introduce herself to Sir Gerald.

It took an extra half hour to reach a small wooden footbridge over the Derwent River. Here she found a knight sitting on a rock and polishing his sword. Sir Gerald looked up as she approached, but did not recognise her. Eleanor hardly recognised him, either. Although he was just two years beyond thirty, his face was gaunt, wild-eyed and haunted. His honey brown hair was fashionably long, but his face was unfashionably bearded. Veteran knights freshly returned from harrowing campaigns in the French wars looked no worse than did Gerald.

"Hail, goodfellow," he called as Eleanor approached.

"Hail, Sir Gerald," she called back, her voice deep and husky from ten days of calling battle cries with Tordral.

"If you know who I am, then you know I am not to be disturbed."

"This is Fay Bridge, where the boundary between worlds is thin," she replied. "On boundary days, such as solstice or equinox, one may walk between our world and Faerie at half-light. That is a boundary time, neither day nor night."

"You are most erudite for an artisan."

"I am a noble in disguise," she replied, truthfully enough.

"Are you another knight in the service of Tordral?"

"In a manner of speaking. I am El—Eldon."

"Then Faerie has wronged you, too, Sir Eldon?"

"All in Tordral's employ are enemies of Faerie. Faerie took my beloved from me."

"So you are at war with Faerie?"

"Not so. Just one elf lord is my enemy. I believe he is your enemy too."

Now Gerald stood up and bowed, then gestured to the rock where he had been sitting.

"By all the saints of heaven, welcome," he said. "This rock is called *Gerald's Watch* by the villagers. Sit guard with me, and tell your story."

Eleanor had not sat beside Gerald for fourteen years. She shivered with the intensity of the moment, yet dared not touch him.

"My beloved and I were to be married," she volunteered. "I was far away when the elf lord Darvendior came, so—so I could do nothing. He took my beloved. My story is simple, there is nothing more to it. I heard that Darvendior sometimes uses Fay Bridge to enter our world, so now I am here. It is too late for my beloved, but not for revenge."

Gerald sat staring at the ground for some moments, wringing his hands.

"Darvendior dishonoured my sister Mayliene," he said bitterly. "All the while I...I lay on the ground, englamoured and helpless. When she spurned him, he twisted her eyes. Our stupid parents feared her curse. They sent her to a nunnery, and there she pined for seven years. I had failed her, so now I devoted my life to her. Books, cloth, tools, lenses, whatever oddments she craved, I brought them. She learned the working of iron. Those of Faerie hate that metal, so she loved it."

"I heard she died," said Eleanor.

"Yes. I was fighting in France, a knight by then. I will not speak of her death, but suffice it to say that I swore revenge on the elf lord. I gave up my beloved, the wars, my prospects at court, everything, to return here and avenge my sister."

"So your beloved lives?"

"I am no longer beloved to Eleanor. I wrote a letter, setting her free to court some other knight and live out her years in happiness."

This was a supremely delicate moment. Eleanor had rehearsed her words for years, yet now her mind went blank.

"I have heard that Eleanor never married," was all that she could manage.

"Ah, then I hate Faerie all the more for it. Three lives, not two, twisted by Lord Darvendior's act of spite. But enough of the past. What part do you play in Tordral's plans?"

"I have a special talent. When all others lie asleep or helpless under glamours, I alone may walk free. I shall lie hidden near this bridge in the half-light of morning and evening. Should the elf lord enter our world this way, I shall be ready."

"He does not always come this way."

"Then I shall be patient. What of yourself? What are you doing for Tordral?"

"I have paid gold for him to build a weapon of earth, air, fire and water, the four great elements. It will be alive but have no spirit, a machine like a cathedral clock or a waterwheel. Scholars say that puts it beyond the reach of Faerie."

"Like myself."

For a rare moment Gerald smiled. "Why Sir Eldon, for all I know even *you* might be another machine built by Tordral."

"If Faerie may be brought low by machines, Sir Gerald, I would gladly become one."

"And what of Tordral himself? How does he seem to you?"

"He is cold and hard, yet I am sure few women who tread the soil of England would not melt into his arms. As a man... from the moment I met him, I abandoned good sense. I would follow him into the depths of hell and..."

Eleanor caught herself beginning to babble with admiration. *Govern yourself,* she thought desperately. *Take hold of your tongue before you tell Gerald that his disguised sister is a better man than he and that his disguised beloved...may love her.*

"Those of his company all say the same," said Gerald, unaware of the turmoil in Eleanor's mind. "So too do I."

Gerald stood up and stretched, then drew his sword and gave a few cuts and thrusts to loosen up.

"Time to ready ourselves," he said as he strung his bow. "The sun is low, and half-light is near."

"Sir Gerald, this is neither solstice or equinox, nor is it a feast day like Lammas. Why do you keep vigil, even though it is not a boundary eve or day?"

"I do it for myself, Sir Eldon. If I could not do something for my dead sister every day, life would be impossible."

Eleanor guarded the bridge with Gerald until the half-light was past, then they went their separate ways. Not far from the nunnery where she was staying, she took the fur-trimmed tunic of green and silver from her pack and put it over her roughweave clothing. Once more, she was a lady of high degree, dressed as a man. The abbess herself came to the gate when Eleanor pulled at the toll rope.

"For shame, my lady," the small, vivacious woman giggled. "Returning after dusk, and alone. Anyone might suspect that you'd had a liaison with a man."

The abbess was at least five years younger than Eleanor, and was one of six daughters born to a nobleman attempting to sire an heir. The nunnery was an isolated retreat where daughters of the nobility might disappear for a few months were there a need to give birth with discretion. The abbess ran the place with a very light and liberal hand.

"I did indeed spend the afternoon in a woodland glade with a man," Eleanor admitted.

"What was he like? What was he like?" gasped the abbess, clapping her hands with delight.

"Exhausting in the extreme."

"Oh wonderful, wonderful!"

Although genuinely exhausted, Eleanor lay a long time awake, indulging fancies of herself and Tordral confronting Faerie hosts and scattering them like a pair of foxes sent against chickens.

oOo

The next day, Tordral had a new weapon at the ruin. It was a small hunting crossbow.

"This is a goat's-foot crossbow, so named because of the shape of the bowstring lever," she explained. "You catch the string in the claws thus, draw it back so, and affix it to the release wheel." She held up a bolt with a barbed head. "This game bolt is for deer, but it is also suitable for elf lords."

Tordral handed the weapon to Eleanor and showed her how to hold it. Unlike the longbow, it required no great skill, strength or coordination to aim.

"Yonder tree is an elf lord," said Tordral. "Bring him down."

Eleanor aimed at the tree and squeezed the release lever beneath the stock. There was a sharp snap, like a dead twig being broken for kindling. She was stunned to see the bolt embed itself in the tree.

"I do believe I can use this," she cried, delighted.

"Perhaps," was Tordral's reply. "Now reload. By yourself."

Eleanor did not have the strength to draw back the bowstring using the goat's-foot lever.

"Here, I shall load for you," said Tordral in her whispery voice.

"What good will that do?" asked Eleanor, who had just plunged from the clouds of elation into the mire of despair. "You cannot be there to load for me when the time comes."

"No, but here and now we can determine if your aim is true."

Nine of Eleanor's next eleven bolts missed the tree.

"I am without hope! We should both admit it," she said despondently.

"Not at all, for one shot in four hit the elf tree, and the other shots were not wide by much. With a crossbow, you can shoot to effect."

"Only sometimes. I must shoot to effect every time."

"That can be managed."

"How? By having a dozen crossbows cocked and ready? There is no hope for me."

Tordral raised her visor, then gazed at Eleanor with beautiful but unfocussed blue eyes. Now she unlaced her helmet and took it off. Her hair was black, and above the level of her lips her skin was bone white. *So fair of face, she could easily have married a prince of the realm,* thought Eleanor. *So fair, yet more of a man than any alive.*

"No hope?" asked Tordral. "There was once no hope for *me,* Lady Eleanor. Put this on, see for yourself."

Viewed through the visor lenses of the helmet, the world was a blurred and confused place. Eleanor could not remove it soon enough.

"With the aid of learned texts and a spectacle maker, I enhanced what little vision was left to me by the elf lord," Tordral continued as she took the helmet back. "The same elf lord tore out my soul, leaving nothing but hate. I used that hate to stoke the forges that have made me into the machine of metal I am today."

"But you love your brother enough to help him."

"I cannot love, so I must use *your* love to help my brother. He will not see me voyage into Faerie and avenge every maid ever got with child by a handsome stranger with pointed ears and the eyes of a cat. To break the hold of hate and vengeance, Gerald must see the elf lord Darvendior brought low before his very eyes *You* must do that."

"Tordral, Lady Mayliene, in the eleven days past I have surely proved that I cannot even bring a lapdog low."

"Then become as I am."

"You had seven years to gain strength and skills."

"I am a machine, Lady Eleanor, a machine like a cathedral clock, a windmill or a waterwheel. My skin is iron, my eyes are glass, and my claws are steel. Now I am building a ship of air, earth, fire and water. It will take no strength to step aboard, but when I do, I shall become an even greater machine. I shall be strong, terrible and invincible. I shall slice through Faerie's glamours like a Saracen blade through silk."

In that moment, Eleanor's knees became as jelly, fever burned through her body, and a metallic taste came to her mouth, even though it was empty. Desire. Tordral was more powerful than any man, Tordral had no weaknesses, Tordral was wiser than any scholar, and Tordral alone could challenge an entire world and win. Before her was a hero greater than any knight in a *roman courtoise* or *chanson de geste*.

To offer myself to her would be to lose her forever, thought Eleanor. *I can give her give her nothing tender, not embraces or kisses, nor heartfelt words, nor soft caresses. Tordral desires only another machine. Be that machine.*

"There is one more weapon, if you have the courage to use it," Tordral was saying.

"Courage?" asked Eleanor absently.

Tordral handed her a metal tube bound to a wooden stock. It was about the length of a sword, and as heavy as the crossbow.

"What is it?" she asked.

"It is a machine of air, earth and fire."

"What does it do?"

"With this you can become a machine."

"But I have little strength."

"What are machines for, but to enhance your strength? Here, take the tube in your left hand. Now, put this pad of cloth between your breasts. Press the butt of the wooden stock against the pad, yes, like that. Now train it upon the elf tree."

Eleanor pointed the tube at the tree and groped for a release lever with her right hand. Finding none, she turned to Tordral.

"No lever," she said.

Tordral held up a length of string. One end was smouldering and trailing sweet-scented smoke into the air.

"Take this in your right hand, my lady. Now see this little pan at the top?"

"It holds some black powder."

"As it should. Point the tube at the elf tree, then touch the burning cord to the powder."

"Like this?"

The sound that followed was like a thunderclap brought to earth. Eleanor found herself lying on the flagstones, on her back. Her breastbone ached as if kicked by a horse, and her ears were ringing. Tordral stood over her with her arms folded, blueish smoke swirling all around, like a demon amid hellfire fumes. Tordral gestured to the elf tree. At least a half dozen scraps of iron were embedded in the bark.

"It is a type of gonne called a culverin. I am not sure who devised it. A very special and dangerous black powder renders it deadly. No strength is required to load it."

"To aim...it is like a crossbow," mumbled Eleanor, her ears ringing.

"Yes, and it can scatter a handful of iron scraps over an area half a yard across. All the magic of Faerie may not prevail against it."

Appalling though the weapon was, Eleanor had to admit that it was very hard to miss a target when using one.

"With a culverin, you get only one chance at a shot," warned Tordral. "Miss, and the loading of another charge takes as long as reloading a crossbow."

"May I try another shot?" asked Eleanor.

"As many as you desire."

My weapon, thought Eleanor. *This thing of earth, air and fire makes me a machine too. It is frightening, dangerous, inelegant, ugly and awkward, but it is mine. I am mistress of the culverin. I am worthy of Tordral.*

oOo

Four hours and fifty shots later, Eleanor and Tordral sat on the slopes of Falcon Crag, looking over the southern expanse of Derwentwater. On the flood plain to the south, a plume of smoke burst into existence, then a deep boom echoed among the hills. Out on the lake, a column of water erupted skywards.

"That giant culverin has all the form of my weapon, yet it has the might to destroy an entire ship," said Eleanor.

"It is called a bombard," said Tordral.

"All to kill a single elf lord?"

"The elf lord is yours. Keep your hands off my enemies and I promise to leave yours to you."

Tordral nudged Eleanor to reassure her that this was a joke. Contact. The faintest trace of affection. Eleanor fought the temptation to throw her arms around Tordral. *She would not understand,* Eleanor reminded herself. *Worse, perhaps she would.*

"I like my culverin," she said instead. "At first, it frightened me, but now I see its virtues."

"Very much like men," replied Tordral.

"What now?"

"More sword."

"Sword? But for nearly two weeks past you have taught me sword and I am but little improved."

"Yet improved you are. A culverin cannot be reloaded quickly, but a sword can be drawn in a heartbeat. If you but wound the elf with your only shot, best to have a sword ready."

"Full moon is tonight. I'll not be ready if the elf lord comes to our world."

"Tonight is for laying bait, not fighting. Solstice is fourteen days thereafter. Solstice is when you shall stand against the elf lord. I shall be sailing against all Faerie, a furnace of steam for my heart and a bombard to clear my path. "

"You make it sound so final," said Eleanor, shaking her head.

"As it shall be. Now, do you have a truename?"

"Truename? I am Lady Eleanor of Derryton, masquerading as Sir Eldon."

"No, you must have a truename, one whispered to you by your mother for protection against enchantments and glamours. Without a truename, some elf or sorcerer may name you, then use that name to bend you to their will."

"Mother is long dead."

"Perhaps I can be your mother. I have given birth to you as a warrior machine who carries a culverin and wears a sword. Incline to me."

Eleanor leaned across to Tordral, then shivered as cupped hands brushed her ear.

"You are *Culverelle*," she whispered.

Culverelle. Lady of the culverin. For a moment, Eleanor felt ready to burst with sheer pride. It was as if Tordral had walked within her mind and seen the name she most desired.

"There is more," said Tordral.

"Tell me."

"Glamours may be used to change one's shape, render folk asleep, draw out an enemy's strength, twist his senses, raise mist or even quench fire." She tapped a lens in the eye-slit of her helmet. "I have had my sight twisted, and Gerald once had his strength drawn out for the space of an hour."

"But I now have a truename."

"That makes you less vulnerable, not invincible. The elf lord could conjure a rainstorm to quench your match fuse before you can fire your culverin. Take these, and you may surprise him."

Tordral held out six small packets of reed paper.

"What are they? Amulets against spells?"

"No, just parcels of culverin powder mixed with shards of flint and suchlike. Watch."

Tordral took a packet and flung it against a nearby rock. It detonated with a sharp bang and a puff of smoke. Eleanor shrieked, then blushed.

"Flints struck together produce sparks, and sparks detonate culverin powder. These things are a fairground trick to amuse children, but they can also make fire when nothing else burns. Treat them gently, for they can go off by themselves."

Eleanor reluctantly accepted the remaining five packages. "You said you are laying a trap."

"Tonight is a boundary night, the last full moon before solstice. The elf lord will walk our world, and I shall give him much to think about. My trap is baited with my brother."

"Gerald?" gasped Eleanor, now showing concern more out of loyalty than love. "Might he be harmed?"

"Quite the opposite. Come now, we must cross blades for a time."

"One more word."

"Speak it."

"A sword or arrow will impale the heart, but the fragments of broken chain mail and iron scrap from my culverin will do little more than break the skin and cause annoyance. What has an elf lord to fear from me?"

"Iron, which those of Faerie shun. Iron, which quenches magic as surely as water quenches fire. With shards of iron in his skin, the elf can cast no glamours. After that, you must fight, sword against sword, mortal against mortal."

oOo

Eleanor had not intended to be abroad that night, but by pure chance she was still some distance from the nunnery and in her roughweave clothes when the entire world suddenly spun before her. She fell, but remained awake. Slowly, warily, she got back to her feet, then she walked on to Keswick. All was quiet in the village, where everyone was in a deep sleep. Eleanor walked the narrow streets, alone for being awake. A dog that she chanced upon could not be roused, even with a pail of water.

This is a glamour, and the elf lord is in our world.

Not far away was Gerald's tower, all shadows and highlights in the moonlight. Gerald would be there.

Gerald, Gerald, can you forgive me for loving your sister? Eleanor began walking in its direction. *We have both been waiting so very long. The heart still loves, but the arms long to embrace. I must learn to love you again.*

Here was a chance to seek out Gerald. Here was the opportunity to steal into his bedchamber, hold his sleeping body in her arms, caress his hair, press her lips against his.

Tordral was waiting by the open gate in the wall.

"A glamour is upon the village," Eleanor said as she approached.

"Indeed, but we have the guise of men and the substance of women. The glamour cannot touch us."

"Are you guarding Gerald from the elf?"

"Quite the contrary, for Darvendior has already been here. I watched from a distance as he entered the tower. He left not long before you arrived."

"You seem unconcerned."

"This night, he is here to observe. He has observed my brother, and now he has gone on to my workshops at the lakeside. He will understand nothing there, as it is all machines and iron. All of this is as planned. All except you. Here."

"I came to see Gerald. You said he would be bait."

"Yes."

"Is he safe?"

"Yes."

"I would see for myself."

"You would pay a price."

"I want no riddles!"

"Would you prefer lies?"

"Where is Gerald?" shouted Eleanor, making it clear that further wordplay was of no interest.

"Come with me."

They ascended the stairs within the tower together. Tordral pushed a door open, walked through, then stood aside and folded her arms. Eleanor took a step forward and stopped dead.

Moonlight streamed into the chamber, illuminating the naked abbess sprawled across the sleeping Gerald. The spring night was balmy and mild, and they were quite uncovered. Eleanor blinked, shook her head, then slapped her own cheek. Nothing changed.

"Fourteen years, I waited for him," she whispered through grinding teeth.

"I warned you of the price," said Tordral.

"*My* maidenhead is still mine, yet—yet..."

"Yet we two appear to be the only maidens in this room."

Eleanor glared at the couple on the bed, then advanced, drawing her sword. Tordral did not move. For a lingering moment, the point hovered above Gerald's throat.

"He has not been your beloved for fourteen years," said Tordral. "The abbess's little castle is no difficult siege. Doubtless it has been stormed and conquered many times."

"I waited for him!" shouted Eleanor. "Could *he* not wait for *me*?"

"He loved you enough to cast you free. Free to find a new beloved. Free to live a life in happiness."

"He knew I was unmarried, yet here he is in bed with that woman of indifferent morals!"

"What business is that of yours? Nearly a decade and a half have passed since he left you."

"But the sight of—of all this drives me to distraction. My reason takes flight, I—I want to slay them both."

"Then why not slay me, too?"

"What do you mean? *You* are not sharing that bed."

"True, but I did engineer this liaison."

For many, many heartbeats Eleanor stared at Tordral, teetering between hatred and incomprehension.

"To kill me, place the point of your sword just below my chin, then thrust it over the chain mail and into my throat. To get Gerald back, come away."

Eleanor glanced from Tordral to the lovers on the bed, and then to the door. Suddenly she raised the sword high, fought for control—then brought the flat of the blade down across the undeniably shapely buttocks of the abbess with all her strength. The woman remained asleep.

"That will really sting when she wakes," said Tordral.

"Do I look repentant?"

"Not really. Now can we go?"

"Go? Yes, with all my heart. This place reeks of the scents of lust."

They were in open fields and walking in bright moonlight before either of them spoke again. *Why?* Eleanor wondered. *Does she know I loved her? Was all this to quench allure?*

"Why?" she said aloud.

"It amuses the elf lord to bait Gerald. Now he thinks the abbess is special to him. The next boundary day is the solstice eve. He will make a special point of crossing Fay Bridge, englamouring Gerald, gloating over him, then seducing the abbess."

"Your story, repeated."

"Yes, but remember the rules of boundaries? Dravendior must return across the boundary place where he entered our world. If you set Fay Bridge a-fire, he cannot do that."

"Me? Fire the bridge?"

"Yes. With the bridge gone, Darvendior will be stranded. You must set the bridge burning and hold him back until it collapses. Will you do it?"

"Why should I help after you got my beloved into bed with that, that, butter dumpling?"

"To redeem yourself."

"Redeem *myself*? Why? What have I ever done to you?"

"Nothing, to me or for me, Lady Eleanor of Derryton. Never once did you visit in the seven years I rotted in a nunnery with crippled eyes. Not a single message of sympathy did I have from you until the night I slipped out of the nunnery, waded into the river as Mayliene, then waded out as Tordral."

Eleanor sank to the ground, then sat with her head in her hands. Tordral stood in silence with her arms folded.

"I could not bring myself to visit you," she said presently. "I...I hated you for—for taking Gerald away."

"I did not take him away."

"I know, I know...yet because he failed to defend you from the elf lord, he devoted his life to serving and avenging you. I lost him. I lost him to you, his own sister."

"None of that was my fault. I even asked him to return to you."

"I know, but—but nothing! There is no possible excuse. Can you forgive me?"

"I forgave you years ago. Do you forgive me for the abbess?"

In the distance, the glamour on Keswick and the tower suddenly collapsed, and there was a sharp scream as the abbess felt the slap of a sword across her naked buttocks. Tordral stood guard while Eleanor sat giggling hysterically.

oOo

A thin sliver of new moon hung in the sky as Eleanor crouched amid the trees, a little to the north of Fay Bridge. Gerald was at his vigil as half-light approached, standing between two flaming torches. A longbow was in his hand and an arrow was at the ready.

A tall, elegant figure with pale hair glided into existence at the center of the bridge. Gerald dropped his bow and toppled, and a wave of giddiness like the flapping of a huge wing brushed past Eleanor. Unlike Gerald, she recovered after a moment. She watched as the elf lord crouched beside Gerald. She could not hear the words spoken, but the enchanted traveler was laughing as he stood.

Doubtless boasting about what he is soon to do with the abbess, thought Eleanor.

She began to count as the elf lord walked away. Tordral had told her not to move until she had reached two thousand. That would let twilight run its course.

She reached ten.

What can an elf do in a count of two thousand?

She reached twenty.

Walk past the tower.

She reached thirty.

Reach the nunnery.

She reached forty.

Appear before the abbess and secure a night spent sampling the musky delights of...

"How may I spoil their evening, let me try my hand," growled Eleanor.

She stood up and strode toward the bridge, her culverin under her arm and a two large jars of seed oil in her hands. Gerald was lying with his eyes open. As she regarded him in the torchlight he blinked.

He is awake, so he will see the fight. May he be proud of me.

She lit her match fuse from a torch, then began splashing the oil over the bridge. She returned to the foot of the bridge, took Gerald under the arms, and began to drag him clear.

"Gerald, love, beneath the grime on my face I am your Eleanor. After fourteen long years I am back, to stand beside you and avenge Mayliene. Bid me good fortune within your thoughts."

With Gerald safely out of the way, Eleanor flung a burning torch onto the bridge. It blazed up brightly. She positioned herself to wait, match fuse smouldering.

"It is still twilight, my love, so the elf lord can flee back across the bridge to his own world. He will come at a run once he sees the glow of the fire."

Darvendior soon appeared amid the trees, a flickering, fleet-footed thing, lithe and pale. He slowed to a walk as he noticed Eleanor before the bridge, awake, alert, and armed. He was still too far away for a good shot.

"Stand aside, fellow," he called. "I have no quarrel with you."

"You shall not pass."

"You must have some skill with magic, to be awake and standing. Let me show you *real* magic."

He began to chant. Eleanor did not understand the language, but his words had the resonance of brass trumpets at the court of the king.

"Che si, feu li, as vray, tress fey!"

The glow from the fire behind her began to fade. *Glamours can control fire!* she now remembered. The flame of the remaining torch flickered, then popped out of existence. Holding up her match fuse, she saw the end no longer smouldered.

"Che si, feu li, as vray, tress fey!"

Over and over the elf lord was chanting as he slowly advanced on Eleanor. He was now shimmering and glowing with a light of his own, as if the brightness of the dying fire on the bridge were lighting up his body from within. Faerie could indeed stand against a culverin or bombard. There was no hope. Tordral's words of a fortnight earlier echoed through Eleanor's mind, almost smothered by the droning of the chant:

Take these and you may surprise him.

The fire behind her went out, leaving only the light of the approaching elf lord, as bright and handsome as an angel, as terrifying as entrance to hell. Eleanor fumbled in her pouch, and her fingers found one of the reed paper packets. Without another thought she slammed it down on the culverin, hoping that it was somewhere near the priming pan.

The packet exploded between her fingers. The powder in the priming pan ignited, then the blast of the culverin's shot echoed into a long shriek of pain and rage as scraps of iron tore into the elf lord's skin. He staggered about, frantically scratching at his wounds. Pain blazed from Eleanor's right hand as she dropped the culverin and dug about in her pouch with her left for another reed paper packet. She found two, drew them out, turned to the bridge in the twilight, then flung them at the boards. They flashed brightly, setting the oil-soaked timbers alight again. With her right hand streaming blood, she clumsily drew her sword with her left and turned to face the elf lord.

Gerald was up and standing between them, his sword drawn.

Iron quenches magic, and the elf now has iron in his body, thought Eleanor. *The glamour is broken.*

Blades clanged as Eleanor picked up the culverin. Although stripped of his powers, the elf lord was still a formidable opponent, but Gerald was a veteran of the wars in France. Cries of alarm sounded behind Eleanor. She pointed the unloaded culverin across the bridge. Several figures armed with swords and dressed in flowing cloaks materialised amid the flames. They began to chant.

"Che si, feu li, as vray—"

That was as far as they got. Eleanor thrust her culverin under her arm, tore her pouch of powder from her belt, and tossed it onto the bridge. It exploded amid the flames.

"Fall back or speak with my culverin!" Eleanor pointed the empty weapon at the elves again.

As the guardians from Faerie hesitated, their robes and hair began to burn. Shrieking with dismay, they turned and vanished back into their own world. Eleanor returned her attention to the fight in time to see Gerald's steel blade chop through the brass blade of the elf lord.

"Raise your hands, unless you want another blast of cold iron," said Eleanor, pointing the empty culverin at Darvendior and hoping for the best. He raised his hands.

oOo

They watched the bridge burn, saying little. Gerald knelt with his knee in the elf lord's back, and Eleanor kept the barrel of her culverin pressed against his head. To the southeast, a long, shadowy thing pouring spark-studded smoke into the night sky glided out across the lake. The *clank-clang hiss chuff* of its heartbeat echoed through the still air.

A machine's heart, thought Eleanor. *Tordral's heart.*

"Elf magic?" asked Gerald nervously.

"Not so," said Eleanor. "Tordral has become a machine more powerful than any enchanted creature. At morning's halflight, he will leave our world to do battle in Faerie."

"I don't understand."

"Nor do I. Let it rest there."

When Fay Bridge collapsed into the Derwent River, Gerald hauled the elf lord to his feet and gripped him very tightly by the hair.

"Pay heed, you abomination. Your path back to Faerie is gone, and while my children and my children's children rule these lands, it will *never* be rebuilt. You will stay in this world, and be mortal. You will grow old, ugly and wrinkled, and then you will die and rot. The satisfaction of knowing that you will suffer for decades is the *only* reason I am leaving you alive."

Pointing the elf lord in the general direction of Keswick, Gerald sent him on his way with a kick to the buttocks that lifted him from the ground and send him sprawling. As he hobbled away into the gloom, Eleanor and Gerald embraced.

"*Our* children, and *our* grandchildren," said Gerald over and over, then he began cutting cloth from his own surcoat to bandage her hand.

Eleanor was aware of exchanging endearments with Gerald, of embracing again and kissing, and of villagers appearing with torches and cheering them. On the lake was a long, dark shape, belching smoke and moving without need of sail or oar.

I thought I loved you, Tordral, but I was wrong, Eleanor thought wistfully. *I did not* want *you, I wanted to* be *you. Seven years I will give you, Gerald of Ashdayle. Seven years, and children to have grandchildren. After that, you owe me seven years of glorious freedom as the war machine Culverelle...and I shall take them.*

Sheila Finch is still not a native Californian, even though she has spent more years there than in England, where she was born. Her novel, *Infinity's Web*, received the Compton Crook award and her Young Adult book, *Tiger in the Sky*, won the 1999 San Diego Book award for best juvenile fiction. She's perhaps best known for a series of tales about the Guild of Xenolinguists (one of which, her novella, "Reading The Bones," won the Nebula Award in 1998).

When she's not writing or teaching, she likes to travel, practice Tai Chi, hike in the local mountains, or go 4-wheeling in the desert. She also cares for two rescued Greyhounds. Her website is: http://sff.net/people/sheila-finch, and her blog appears at http://lingster1.livejournal.com.

This story, she says, is one of several literary borrowings from the legends about Sir Francis Drake that first captured her imagination as a child.

FORTUNE'S STEPCHILD

by Sheila Finch

Will Sydney watched the crew of the *Golden Hind* slip away from the cooking fire on the beach, following the beckoning of the native girls. He was ignored. Fifteen years old already, third and youngest son of an earl—and thus without inheritance—he had attracted no female attention in England. Even here, farther north in the Pacific Ocean than either Englishman or Spaniard had ever ventured, it seemed the native women scorned his company. His mood, already glum, darkened.

One of the girls made a gesture to pile more meat on his plate, her fingers brushing against his. Embarrassed for her mistake, he pulled his plate away and did not look up. He had no appetite for food tonight.

He had signed on with Captain Drake as a passenger for this voyage into uncharted territory in the hope of gaining a little treasure, without which his chances of a favorable marriage upon his return to London were slim. And marriage to a rich woman, his father had lectured him, was all he could look forward to. So far, he had amassed a handful of Spanish coins when the captain raided papist settlements along the southern coast of this new land, and a sprinkling of cuts and bruises for his pains. Will imagined his older brothers laughing at his lack of success, but he was no swordsman. Neither, or so it seemed, was he going to be skillful with girls.

The moon had not yet risen. The scent of wood smoke and roasted meat lingered like a descant on the fresh sea air. There had been much drinking and merriment and the sailors' rough music of fife and drum at this last meal on shore; some of the men stumbled in their cups as they left. Will heard sweet female voices enticing them and the nobles, along like himself for treasure and adventure on the voyage, and he wondered what it would be like to be chosen. *If these rough men—drunken and unsteady—can do this dance of courtship,* he scolded himself, *why canst thou not likewise?* Surely he could manage a few steps? He was skillful with the lute; why could he not make his feet dance?

Shortly before he had taken ship with Francis Drake, his father had insisted Will dance the *volta* at the Christmas ball with a whey-faced maid whose feet he tripped over and whose name he could not remember. It was his first and so far only close experience with the female sex. Afterward, she upbraided him shrilly. He would have much preferred the life of a musician, but his father would not countenance such an idle pursuit, even for a third son.

Shaken out of his paralyzing shyness by the knowledge this might be his last chance, he looked up at the remaining girls. One, a slip of a thing with nut-brown skin and an easy smile, glanced at him. He hesitantly raised a hand in greeting.

"Lady—" he began, his voice squeaking with nervousness.

But she was looking at a man behind him and paid him no heed. Will sighed.

The captain and the parson, Mister Fletcher, remained by the fireside in the gathering dark. The chief of this village, resplendent in his tall hat of woven reeds, reclined by their side, unable to follow their talk but nodding companionably all the while.

"Abomination!" Parson Fletcher scowled at the disappearing crew.

"Nay." Captain Drake leaned forward to poke the embers so that bright sparks flew up. "Condemn them not, my friend.

Allow them some little pleasure, for tomorrow we sail and who knows when we shall sight land again?"

Another long sea voyage in perilous waters with little to show for it, Will thought. And he could hardly hope this time he would escape the horrors of the sea sickness that kept him in his hammock while the ship beat her way through stormy seas. This had not been a very wise decision, but a penniless third son had little choice but go adventuring with the Devon Sea Dogs whose exploits were the talk of London. Unfortunately for Will, though the captain had become fond of him, naming him "fortune's child," he parceled out the rewards according to participation in their securing. Will had to admit he was noticeably deficient in that enterprise. He was nervous in battle and far too slow. *Stepchild, mayhap!* he thought.

"These natives consider us as gods," the captain said to the parson. "I would not abuse their trust, nor would I have an Englishman give offence."

The chief nodded amicably, for all the world as though he understood Drake's words.

Will admired the captain. No one knew better than he how fierce Drake could be when battling Spaniards and sacking their treasure galleons in the Spanish Main. Truly, the captain had earned the name of pirate that the papists called him! But the captain had another side that Will had seen here. These natives had welcomed them when they beached the *Golden Hind* to mend the hull and scrape the barnacles that infested it after a long voyage; they brought venison and fruit to re-stock the ship's larders. The captain gave small gifts in return. Drake had taken care that neither noble passengers nor his crew took more than their fair share of the villagers' store of animal pelts or the shells whose insides were splashed with rainbows, the like of which never graced England's shores. *"They have little, but would give all if we had greed enough to take it,"* Drake had admonished them.

There was one girl, Will remembered now, about his own age, more intense than pretty, who had cast glances at him across the fire. Too late, it occurred to him that it was she whose fingers had brushed against his. She had vanished from the fireside.

He wiped the knife he had used to sup with on the sea grass, then put it in his belt and stepped away from the fire's glow. The captain and the parson were still deep in conversation. He heard only the soughing of wind in the pine branches, and the harsh cry of a bird whose shadow moved over the beach toward the white cliffs. A raven, he thought, watching it go.

He had no hope the rest of the voyage would be any more successful for himself than the first part. His second-oldest brother had given him his second-best sword for luck, but it had never so much as smelled blood on this voyage.

"Lad!"

He turned to see a fat noble, gaudy as a peacock in velvet and silk, a fine lace collar and a padded codpiece as if he walked the halls of the queen's palace in London instead of this beach half way around the globe. The man stepped out of the shadows, handsome blade at his hip.

"My lord?" Will acknowledged carefully. This popinjay was quick to take offence, and in spite of his appearance, Sir Thomas Oates was no mean swordsman. He took delight in goading the young men, none more so than Will Sydney. That he bore grudges and avenged himself on those who offended, Will had seen many examples.

Oates swept his cloak over one shoulder. Lurking behind him, Will saw two half-grown pages who served the noblemen aboard. "The chief's daughter waits on thy approval, lad!"

The pages hid their giggles behind closed fists. Will's ineptitude with both sword and maidens was apparently a source of much merriment to the crew and company of the *Golden Hind.*

He glanced away unhappily. "Goad me not, good my lord."

"Nay, lad!" Oates said gaily. "Surely thou wouldst not be seen as a girl, afraid of her own shadow when a comely wench beckons? Dost thou not know what to do with her?"

The pages doubled over with laughter. Will's cheeks burned.

"I shall repair to my bed and sleep, good my lord," he said, with as much dignity as he could muster. "Our captain has declared we sail on the morning's tide."

"Yet time enough for a night's enterprise for those that are man enough!" the fat man observed.

Oates minced away down the beach toward where the natives had built their reed and thatch dwellings. The pages turned to the thickets where the girls had disappeared. Obviously *they* knew what to do, Will thought sourly.

He kicked at pebbles as he walked, thinking glumly of the crowded cabin he shared. The captain had explained they could not return the way they had come, around the fearsome *Tierra del Fuego* with its fierce winds and menacing ice islands, for treacherous water and papist enemies awaited them. Drake had made many such bitter enemies on their hard journey past Spanish settlements on both coasts and around the southern cape of the continent. There was nothing to do but put themselves in God's hands, Drake had explained, and sail west into the setting sun.

No matter that he had declared his decision to seek sleep a moment ago, Will's mind was too troubled to let him rest. He decided to walk, trusting the night air would help his mood. It was a fair land, filled with clear streams and thickets of fir and pine where game and fowl waited to be taken. The Captain was right to name it Nova Albion, for it reminded them of England. Will had composed songs in praise of its wild beauty and set them to the lute while others worked at readying the *Hind* or practiced sword play on the beach. Seeking to comfort his troubled heart, he sang a measure from a new song. But the heaviness did not go away and he soon fell silent.

He walked on. He had not gone far when a sound of footsteps on the path startled him. He turned. The girl who had drawn his attention by the fire stood silently. *"The chief's daughter,"* Oates had called her, mocking Will, but in truth he thought she was not. Yet now he realized that she had served him goodly portions of venison and the tenderest vegetables. He had not taken account of this in the moment, but now it was clear. With a sudden rush of warmth, he remembered how she let her hand brush against his. Was it possible she liked him? He hardly dared entertain the thought!

She was taller than the other girls, and older too, though not so much older than himself. Her black hair was braided and adorned with small feathers. A necklace of the rainbow beads glowed against her dark skin. He felt a sudden stirring of desire; he was far from home and his heart was lonely. But he was immediately overcome with the awkwardness that always prevented him from acting. In truth, how would he make speech with one who had not his own tongue?

She came closer. He shook his head, dismayed at his own lack of courage. The popinjay was right, he thought; he was a maid himself, not a man.

"Go back, my lady," he stammered, knowing she could scarce understand him.

The girl said something. She had a gentle voice and he wished with all his heart he could know what her words meant, had he been able to hear them against the pounding of blood in his ears. There was no mockery in them, that much he knew, only—mayhap—an offer of friendship.

When he made no move, she took a small bright feather out of her hair and tucked it over his left ear. He trembled when her fingers brushed his skin. He opened his mouth to speak, but his throat felt full of dry pebbles and he could bring no words out. Marking his hesitation, she smiled.

Too shy and embarrassed by the sudden signs of his arousal, he pulled his wool cloak tight and hurried away, stepping over slick patches of dark kelp. Is this what his life should be from now on? He was angry with himself.

Off shore, the *Golden Hind* rode at anchor, sails furled, lanterns flickering at her stern and twinkling in the ports, their reflection shattering into diamonds on the dark water. The night breeze brought the sound of a lute and the voices of sailors preparing to sail on the morrow. The merriest times he had aboard were the evenings he played his lute with the ship's musicians, but he did not yearn to see them again soon.

The full moon rose over the low hills behind him. In a sober mood, he walked under white cliffs so like England's own, breathing the familiar salt scent of the sea. A shallow stream flowed across the sand where small boulders had tumbled down; he gazed moodily at the moon-silvered rills playing over his boots as he crossed. The world's beauty mocked him this night.

Someone came toward him from farther down the beach. Even shrugged deep in his cloak, Sir Thomas Oates was recognizable by the mincing manner of his gait. There was no chance of avoiding a second encounter with the unpleasant man.

"'I will away to bed!' the lad said," Oates mocked in a falsely shrill voice. "Yet here he comes, moping like a lovesick milkmaid in the moonlight."

Will said nothing to this.

"Bah!" the man said, as if Will were a bad taste on his tongue. "Some last business commanded me before we sail. None of your concern, boy!"

Will felt the small hairs on his neck rise in apprehension. He was puzzled that Oates would think to make any kind of explanation to him. But trouble was a pot that easily boiled over, his grandmother always said, and Will was in no mood to stir it.

"Out of my way!" Oates hurried by, limping as one overburdened might walk.

He looked like a peddler with a sack under his cloak, Will thought, astonished. Oates had come from the direction of the village, but that could surely not be. The captain had forbidden the village to them all, and the command included the company of gentlemen as well as sailors.

He continued his walk along the edge of the waves. In the shallows, fish moved like a tumble of silver coins, and somewhere high on the cliffs a wolf howled, its voice haunting the night. Clouds scudded across the moon, veiling and unveiling. Setting aside the thought of Oates, Will's mind returned to the journey home. What tales he would have to tell! He had seen things no Englishman had seen before. Yet how would his father be pleased by tales of other men's glory?

Suddenly, a thin cry reached him from the way he had come.

He stopped to listen.

Another. A woman's voice.

At first he thought, *A sailor and his maid?* The great

quantities of rough beer they drank this night might make even the gentlest man turn raging bear.

Again—and this time he recognized the cry for what it was: a plea for help. Alarmed, he raced back along the path.

Where the stream meandered into the sea, he found them thrashing about in sea-wrack just out of the water's reach, a man and a girl. The man's hands were tangled in the beads she wore about her neck. The girl struggled, but the man prevailed and the necklace came away in his fingers.

"Villain!" Will shouted, grabbing the man by the collar of his velvet cloak and tugging.

The man flailed; he was stronger than Will but his knees caught in his cloak, hindering him. He rolled on his back, dislodging a canvas sack from under his cloak, which now disgorged its contents on the sand. The man turned an angry face up to Will.

Thomas Oates!

Will was taken by surprise. His fingers slackened their grip. Oates cursed and scrambled up, drawing his sword. The blade flashed close to Will's face. Will was unarmed, his brother's second-best sword left aboard the *Hind*; he had expected to sup, not to fight. The girl slipped out of reach. Her eyes glittered in the shadows, and Will heard her quick shallow breath.

Will's voice came out as a squeak. "Wouldst fight an unarmed man?"

In answer, Oates lunged at him.

Will stepped aside, his feet slipping on the wet kelp, ducking under the blade which missed his cheek by a hair's breadth. Even had he been armed, or an accomplished swordsman, sword-play in the uncertain moonlight with a desperate man would have been a dangerous game. His sight blurred as sweat trickled down his brow. Through the haze, he was aware of the girl standing just behind Oates.

"Yield, boy!" Oates demanded. "Before I gut thee like a coney!"

Will dodged as Oates lunged at him again. He was more nimble than the fat noble, but it was only a matter of time before

Oates killed him, and then took the girl and whatever was in his sack, and this whole miserable voyage would have been for naught. And how long would it be before the captain or anybody noticed his absence on the morrow? Once at sea, there would be no turning the *Hind* back to seek his dead body.

The least of the nobles' pages on board would have known not to walk at night without carrying a sword! But he did have the knife he used to cut his meat at supper. Will's hand shook as he drew it. Crouching, circling Oates warily, just out of the man's reach, he held it ready to strike.

"What be this?" Oates taunted. "Wouldst prick me to death with a kitchen knife?"

Breathing hard, they circled each other, each just out of the other's range, though it seemed to Will it could not be long before the blade jumped the distance and took his life away. His heart pounded like a musician's drum.

Suddenly, Oates stretched out his arm and the blade sliced Will's wrist. The wound stung. He cradled the injured wrist in his other hand, the iron smell of blood rising to his nose. He was the most afraid he had ever been in his life—even counting the terrifying passage as they rounded *Tierra del Fuego*.

"Hah!" Oates took a step back and, without looking at the girl, seized her arm. "Get thee hence, *boy*! Let a *man* pass!"

Oates tugged at her, indicating by dumb-show she should pick up the contents that had spilled out of his sack. At that moment, the moon peered out from her cloudy veil and lit the girl's face. It was she who had favored Will at supper.

Now Will saw what the man had been carrying in his sack: a great quantity of the rainbow shells glowed in the moonlight. Will knew at once what Oates had in mind. The fine ladies of Good Queen Bess's court would covet such precious baubles as a necklace made from these bright shells! What could he do to stop Oates? He had not the skill to fight an accomplished swordsman—who would have to kill him, Will saw now, in order to hide his villainy from Captain Drake.

But there was one move he had observed from the older boys who passed the time on this long voyage at knife play with each other. Could he do it correctly? What other choice had he, save to run away like the coward Oates thought him? He slipped the knife from his injured right hand to his left, and extending his right hand open and empty before Oates's face as if he had dropped his weapon, he yelled at the top of his voice. Echoes bounced and tumbled from the white cliffs.

Startled, Oates hesitated, his eyes drawn to the empty hand. Quickly, Will stepped in on the man's unguarded side and thrust under the ribs, drawing blood. He saw the smile on the man's lips as he realized the momentum had caused him to lose his own footing. Will went down on his knees in the shallow water, just as the girl bent to the ground to pick something up.

Oates's sword flashed overhead. Will's ears filled with the roaring of the sea. The knife slipped from his blood-slick fingers into the little waves.

"We shall end it here, I think!" Oates snarled.

Will screwed up his eyes. Any moment the blade must enter his heart and take his life away.

It did not happen.

Instead, Oates cried out and dropped the sword. He fell, clutching his head, half sprawled across Will's legs. Then he was silent.

Confused, Will stared up at the girl. She said something in her own tongue, and smiled, a glint of small white teeth. Her hair fell forward, hiding her face, and he caught its perfume of wood smoke and pine forest. He wriggled free of the burden of Oates's heavy body. The fat man's mouth was slack and his breathing shallow, but he lived. The pumpkin-sized stone the girl had used to fell him lay beside him on the beach. Though it hurt, Will knew the wound he had taken was a mere scratch.

"I owe thee a great debt, Lady," he whispered, still giddy from the fight and its outcome.

In answer, she knelt beside him in the water. He stared into her liquid eyes, so full of starlight he thought he would drown in their magic.

"Bad man seeks to kill."

He gaped at her. Surely his ears had misheard? He opened

his mouth to speak, but she laid a finger on his lips.

His heart pounded like a drum. "I am dreaming, 'tis certain!"

"No dream."

He bolted upright and stared at her. "What art thou, Lady? Be thou a witch?"

She sat back on her heels and pushed long dark hair back from her face. "Thinkst thou it less easy to learn thy tongue than to speak the tongues of Raven and Wolf?"

"Witchcraft," he said, making an effort to scuttle away on his knees. He remembered a nursemaid, a country girl, who had hung herbs and feathers about his infant neck, weaving spells to keep him safe. His grandmother had sent her away. Then he remembered the feather this girl had placed behind his ear. To keep him safe from Oates's sword?

"A witch," he said again, warily this time. "But why then allow this knave to accost thee?"

"Raven's power be made of wind and water, sky and earth," she said. "No match for thy cold weapons!"

He wanted to argue this revelation—*Not a very useful power, then*—but she pushed him back to lie on the sand. She stroked his face and hair, and everywhere her fingers traced, his blood followed in a hot rush. Then she kissed him, and all thoughts faded in the pleasure that flooded his lonely heart.

"Will? Will Sydney! Where art thou, lad?"

Through the blood's pounding in his ears, he reluctantly became aware of voices. The girl moved away and he sat up. Fumbling with awkward fingers at the laces of his jerkin that had somehow come undone, he gazed at her. She giggled, but with him not at him, and his heart filled with tenderness.

A few paces away, Oates groaned. The sound of men's boots on the sand drew closer, and Will saw the flickering light of torches. Giving up on the laces, he scrambled to his feet.

"Will!" a voice yelled, nearer now.

The girl held out her hand to him.

"Lady," he whispered. "I must away!"

She grabbed his arm and tugged him toward the trees. "Stay," she urged.

"Nay! I must not," he protested.

But his heart asked, *Why not stay here with this maid who likes thee?* What was the alternative? Another long perilous voyage. More taunting from the other boys. And no welcome at home.

He glanced at Oates, now muttering and thrashing about as he regained consciousness. He kicked the man's sword out of reach. He would never be safe while Oates was alive. The knave would come after him seeking revenge as long as he lived. The knave's children would come seeking revenge on Will's children!

The captain and two of his men loomed up out of the dark.

"What be the meaning of this, lad?" Drake asked, gazing down at Oates.

"He tore this maid's beads from her neck, Captain," Will said.

"How so?" the captain demanded.

"He would have taken her against her wish." Will pulled the girl closer, and suddenly he was filled with the knowledge that he could be strong, and brave. "And he has been stealing from the natives!"

One of the men accompanying Drake picked up Oates's sword and handed it to his captain. The other lifted Oates's sack from the sand; opening it, he trickled the rest of its bright beads over his hand. He held the prize out for Drake's inspection.

"This knave has likely been concealing it till he could smuggle it aboard, Captain," one of Drake's men said.

"Taking a maid against her will be the greater sin," Drake said.

"I fought him off!" Will said proudly. He felt her stir under his arm. "Well, in truth, Captain, the maid helped."

Drake laughed. "Aye, no doubt she did! But now we must away. The glass lacks only a few hours 'til the morning tide." He gestured to his men to grab the reluctant Oates. "Secure this thief in irons in his cabin. It will benefit him to reflect on his evil, while I reflect on his punishment."

The men did as they were bidden. Will and Drake watched

them walk away, dragging the reluctant noble up the beach.

"Come, lad," Drake said kindly.

"Captain—" His voice came out too high. He cleared his throat and tried again. "Captain, I am no sailor, nor swordsman, and there is little for me to return to in England. I ask permission to stay."

Drake narrowed his eyes. "Sayest thou this of thy own free will?"

"Aye, captain. I do."

The girl, he was suddenly glad to find, remained silent. He knew not how he would explain her to his captain. Drake was a pious Christian who—Will was certain—would not take kindly to a witch whom Raven had taught to speak English. He hardly believed it himself.

"It be a fair land, my Nova Albion," Drake said thoughtfully, "But we may not come this way again for many a long year."

To return to the *Hind* would put him within Oates's reach, Will thought, Oates who would never give up his desire for revenge until the day he died.

"A man who stays here may not see England or Englishmen again, methinks."

"Aye, captain. I know this." He wanted to say more, words tumbling over themselves on the tip of his tongue, but he held them back.

Drake sighed. "The people of this land be well-disposed toward us. And thou art ever a child of fortune with a man's heart."

The captain looked down at Oates's sword that was still in his hand. "A fair enough blade," he said, and held it out to Will. "Go then with this maid, and raise up children to know the tales of Drake and the *Golden Hind*, and the Spaniards we fought on the Main!"

With that, he clapped Will on the shoulder and strode away down the beach.

Shouting with joy in spite of his resolve to act like a grown man, Will tucked his new sword into his belt. He seized the girl around the waist, lifted her off her feet, and kissed her.

"Thou art safe here," she said. "Raven will make it that, be the seekers many, yet their discoveries shall be as naught."

Already he knew to trust her words though he could not say how he understood them. He set her down again, took her hands in his and gazed into her dark eyes. "Glad though my heart be, I must ask. Why didst thou choose me?"

"Because thou art a singer," she said. "Together we shall sing new songs of our people."

"My name is Will," he said. "And I shall call thee Bess, to remember our good queen." *Until Raven teaches me to say thy proper name!* he thought.

Her eyes glittered with unshed tears. She spoke in her own tongue this time, and though he did not yet understand, he had no doubt that love if not magic would teach him every word.

After all, was he not Fortune's Child?

Judith Tarr did not want to be a knight when she was the same age as the protagonist of "The Woman Who Fell in Love With the Horned King," but she did want to be a dragonrider. Later, when she learned that dragonriders were based on the riders of the Spanish Riding School of Vienna and their dancing white horses, she knew what she really wanted to be when she grew up. Now she rides and trains and breeds Lipizzan horses on her farm near Tucson, Arizona, and writes novels about, among other things, horses and the Middle Ages—both real and imaginary. Her long list of books includes high fantasy, historical and prehistorical fantasy, mainstream historicals, and science fiction.

"The Woman Who Fell in Love With the Horned King" is set in the world of *The War of the Rose*, a fantasy trilogy written under the pseudonym Kathleen Bryan and published by Tor. It takes place after the end of *The Last Paladin*, and is the first of a series of stories about Lilias and the Horned King.

THE WOMAN WHO FELL IN LOVE WITH THE HORNED KING

by Judith Tarr

Baron Otric's children were both his greatest pride and his greatest frustration. Godwy, his heir, was a gentle soul whose only desire was to be a priest. He had no heart for battle and no gift at all for weaponry; when forced toward either, he knelt and folded his hands and gave himself up to prayer. In that, even his father had to admit, he was a great champion, and he could preach the birds out of the trees.

All the fight and fire had gone to the baron's daughter. She, having mastered such arts of a noble lady as she judged worth the effort, had set herself to master those of a noble lord as well. She meant, one way and the other, to become a knight.

She had no calling to be a Knight of the Rose or, heaven forbid, a Paladin. Her aim was more within the reach of a baron's child in the Westlands: to be a plain chevalier, and ride in jousts and fight in the occasional war, and defend her holding as a knight should.

Her mother abetted her without either shame or apology. Gudrun had been a shieldmaiden among her people in the north, and in the arts of war she was—even by the measure of southern chivalry—both able and deadly. Lilias was most well schooled, and she could stitch a tapestry and unhorse a knight with equal skill.

She should have been the son, people said, and her brother the daughter; then the world would have run as it ought. That was nonsense, in Lilias' mind. She did not need Godwy to tell her that the good God never made mistakes. They were each exactly as He had intended. And she was going to be a knight.

On the morning after her brother informed her father that he was entering the abbey at St. Dol, she escaped the uproar and went hunting for the pot. She had a line of snares through the rabbit runs, and she took her bow and her quiver of arrows. The wild geese were back in the lake, and her father had a great fondness for roast goose.

He would have calmed down by dinner, she hoped. "It's not as if he didn't expect it," she said to the wind that followed her down the track, even under the eaves of the ancient wood.

The wind played with the wayward curls of her hair. It was a spring wind, and light-minded. It danced through the new leaves and vanished in a dapple of sunlight.

She smiled. Her step was light, and so was her heart, now she had escaped the war. She breathed deep and spun full about and began to run.

oOo

Lilias knew every leaf and blade of that wood, and every clearing in it. Where the trees gave way to the reeds and sedges of the lake, there was a low hill, hardly more than a mound, and on its summit a ring of standing stones.

Wild magic lived there, both over and under hill. People in town and castle were terrified of it, but Lilias had never found anything to fear. It was strange, that was all, and little like human magic; it had its own laws and its own ways.

She had taken the long way round to the lake, and found nothing in her rabbit snares. By now it was midmorning; the air was growing warm. She had her eye on the lake, not only for the geese that flocked in it but for the cool of the water on her sweat-streaked skin.

Often she came over the mound, pausing to greet any of the wildfolk that might be dancing there. Today she happened to come from farther down the lake. She looked up as she went, at the loom of stones against the sky. It was empty of wildfolk; not even a sprite perched on a stone, grinning down at her.

Something fell down the hill: something brown, rolling in a tangle of slender legs and cloven hooves and velvet antlers. It tumbled to a halt at her feet, spraying grass and sand and stones.

She looked down at the body of a stag. At first she thought it was dead; then she saw the shallow flutter of breath in its flanks, and the arrow driven deep between the ribs.

That was a poor shot, to miss the heart and leave the beast so sorely wounded. The wound had bled copiously: blood clotted down the stag's side and belly, and stained the grass where it had fallen down the hill.

There was no sign of the hunter: no sound, no shape pausing on the hilltop. There was a great silence all around the hill, as if the earth had forgotten to breathe.

Lilias knelt. The wind blew again, and the waves lapped the shore. She had her knife in her hand for the mercy stroke; there was nothing else to be done, and a fine stag was even better meat than a string of geese.

As she took the head in the crook of her arm and raised the chin to slit the throat, the stag's eye opened. It was dark, clouded, and yet there was awareness in it. It fixed on her face.

She was a hunter. She could harden her heart against entreaty. But that eye froze her where she knelt. There was intelligence in it, more than any beast she had known, even the grey mare that she had won in a joust.

The knife dropped from her slack fingers. She lowered the stag's head to the ground; she ran her hand down its side to the arrow.

It was a hunting arrow, made of wood and fletched with grass-green feathers. It felt strangely warm under her hand, and it buzzed like a distant hive of bees.

She did not like things that tried to make her afraid. Her

brows knit; her jaw set. She called the magic that was in her, and the magic in the hill, too, since it was there and had no objection.

She drew the arrow from the stag's side and stanched the blood, such of it as was left in the dying body. She laid her hand over the wound.

Warmth poured out of her. The sun fed it, and the earth on which she knelt, and the stones on the hill above her. She belonged to all of them, and they to her.

The wound knit from its depths outward. As flesh mended and blood began slowly to restore itself, the stag's body melted and flowed.

She had erred; her magic had failed. Instead of healing the beast, she had wrought its dissolution. She reached in horror; then abruptly she stopped.

The stag was gone. A young man lay in its place, sprawled on the bloodied grass. There was a livid scar in his side. As she stared, it faded, turning from watered wine to the color of bone, white against the warm red-brown of his skin.

His body was the same ruddy brown as the stag's coat, and his hair was glossy black, thick and long and perfectly straight. He had long-fingered, elegant hands and narrow, well-formed feet; his eyes when she lifted the lids were human eyes, though very dark and deeply unconscious.

It *was* a man. He was solid and warm and breathing slowly. She resisted the urge to touch him again—and that was hard. He was as beautiful as any human thing could be.

The cast of his face was nothing she had seen before. It was all proud planes and keen angles, with a bladed curve of nose. It reminded her a little of a merchant she had seen once, a trader from the east, but that man's face had been smoothly rounded, and there was nothing soft or round about this.

She could be afraid, she thought. Or she could fashion a litter of alder saplings and willow withies, and cushion it with grass from the hill. She covered him as best she could with her leather coat—not that a man who ran as a stag was likely to care who saw him naked, but people in the castle would be horrified on her behalf. People were odd that way, in this world she had to live in.

oOo

It was a long way to the castle. The man on the litter never woke, though now and then, if the way was unusually rough, he would stir and mutter.

That reassured her, in its way. She was strong with riding and fighting and dancing, but she was wringing wet and near exhausted when at last she hauled him through the postern gate into the stable yard.

Two of the stablehands happened to be hanging about, taking their time with the morning stall-cleaning. They were delighted to drop their pitchforks and carry Lilias' stray up into the castle.

Apart from a grin or two and a muttered commentary on the luck of the find—that from Malec, who had an eye for a fine young man—they seemed not to notice how odd the foundling was. And maybe Lilias fostered that impression, and maybe she did not need to. There was magic loose in the world today, and not all of it was hers.

The room she had the stablehands carry him to was her brother's. Godwy was not in it; she could hear the rumble of war still going on in the baron's solar. She threw the windows wide to the sun and air, and called for fresh bedding and food and drink and, almost as an afterthought, something to cover him with.

Last of all, she summoned a bath in the small room that Godwy's squire would have lived in, if he had had one; and that was for herself. Baths were her vice, and she was frequently given to them.

When she was clean and combed and considerably more presentable, she found the stranger likewise and the servants discreetly gone. She was rather sorry to see him dressed in one of her brother's shirts; it diminished him somewhat, though he looked as strange and wild as ever.

He was awake, staring through the window at the sky. At the sound of her breath catching, he turned his head.

Dark, she thought, like deep water, and bright, like the flash of sunlight on its surface. His eyes were cold, measuring; then they warmed. She felt it in her whole body.

It was no worse than an arrow in the vitals. Lilias addressed him courteously. "You are welcome in Cor Benoic. My name is Lilias; my father is the baron here. Whatever you need, you have only to ask."

The lids lowered over those devastating eyes. "Carbonek," he said. It was a sigh. She could not tell if he was glad or dismayed.

"It was that once," she said, "long ago. Now it is Cor Benoic."

He sighed again, a long breath. Somehow her hand had found its way into his. She should recoil, but she lacked the will for it.

"Brenin," he said. "I would be—you may call—"

"Brenin," she said. He stopped struggling with the words and smiled.

Oh, he needed to stop doing that. And holding her hand. And looking at her. He needed to stop being there, except that if he did, she did not know what she would do.

Only idiots died of love. Or lust, which was more likely, all things considered.

She extricated her hand and mastered the rest of herself, and reached for the bowl of bread sopped in honeyed wine. "Here," she said. "Eat."

He ate, because no one ever disobeyed Lilias when she was in this mood. He drank the tisane of herbs that Cook had sent up, too, and then he slept, because part of that was a sleeping draught.

She had thought to try the waters in the hall, but the storm was still rumbling, with occasional blasts of lightning. Baron Osric was nothing if not stubborn, and Godwy was his living image. The last she heard, her father had threatened the dungeon, and Godwy had barricaded himself in the chapel.

No one took much notice of Lilias or her stray. It was quiet in Godwy's room, and there were books to read, not all of which were lives of saints; her brother did like a well-framed poem or a tale of old Paladins. He even had a book from the city, a compendium of tales from the great war that had changed the world.

Lilias had been too young to fight in that. Baron Osric had gone to do what he could, and come home whole, too, by the good God's mercy.

He had found little changed at home, whatever might have happened elsewhere. His demesne had always been somewhat strange. The wild magic was freer now, that was all, and more wildfolk flocked in the wood; and they no longer avoided the towns, though they still shied away from the churches and the abbeys.

The book fell open in her lap to an elaborately limned and painted image. In a shaft of sunlight in a woven wood stood a man with a crown of antlers like a stag. His feet were hooves; his eyes and ears were those of a deer.

The Horned King, the book said, *is one of the great Powers of the Otherworld, lord of wood and water, and master of the Hunt that sweeps the skies and captures wayward souls. His great rival is the Summer Queen; some say she is his consort, and others that she is his bitterest enemy. Who is to say that she may not be both?*

Lilias looked from the painted king to the living stranger. Sunlight fell across him, making Godwy's linen shirt seem even whiter against his skin, and catching blue lights in the long tail of his hair.

He did not look anything like the king in the book. His forehead was smooth: no buds of antlers.

He had worn those when he was a stag. That hardly meant he was a king, or a Power either. Or what would he be doing here, sleeping off the last of his wound, and not sitting on his throne in the Otherworld?

This was one of the Horned King's victims, maybe, enchanted and hunted and left for dead. There was nothing in the book about such creatures, though it told an old and long-familiar tale of the Wild Hunt and a captive soul and the lover who saved it from damnation.

Brenin was the stranger's name, that was all. It only happened to mean *king* in the old language.

He was awake again. "You aren't," she said. "You aren't—what—"

"I need a champion," he said.

Somewhere in his sleep, he had found his tongue. His speech was clear and barely accented.

She stared at him.

"I need a champion," he said again. "Someone to fight for me."

"I know what that is," she said. She did not mean to sound irritable. "Can't you fight for yourself?"

"It's not done," he said.

"You tried," she said. "Didn't you?"

He shook his head. "That was weakness and foolishness. I let myself be caught when I should not have been. The hunters never knew what they hunted, and I had no wits to tell them. All I had was hope, and a place where I had to be: Carbonek."

"Cor Benoic," she said.

"Yes," he said. "There were champions here in the old time. Blood of champions, so the sages say. I came to find one."

"That blood is long gone," Lilias said. "My grandfather won the castle in a joust. Its lord was dead, its last heir shut in a convent; she was too old in any case, and would bear no child, even if her vows had allowed it. Our line is respectable enough, and has magic enough, too. But it's not the old and holy blood, the blood of Paladins."

He heard her in silence. His face at rest was like still water. She could not read it at all. His eyes were as darkly brilliant as ever. "I came to find a champion," he said.

"You found me," she said, "but I'm not—"

"Yes," he said.

"I'm only a mortal woman," she said without bitterness. It was true, after all. "I can fight. I can dance and sing, and stitch a fine stitch. I want to be a knight, which may be mad, but there it is. I'm nothing to challenge a lord of Faerie."

"You can heal a wound," he said, "and unmake an

enchantment, and carry a stranger a good two leagues across wood and field to a place where he may be as safe as any creature is. That's great power, and great kindness, too."

"It's no more than anyone would do," she said.

"Anyone who is a champion," he said.

He was as stubborn as anyone in her family. That made her laugh, which baffled him, though he did not seem offended.

"Tell me why you need one," she said.

It was an apology of sorts. He struggled to sit up; she banked him with cushions and fed him bread and another tisane, this one without the herbs that fostered sleep. She shared that, to prove it was trustworthy, and because she had a feeling it would be a long while before she slept.

When the cup was empty and she had set it aside, he tilted his head toward the book and said, "That one you read of, that was my father."

She raised a brow. "*Was?*"

He nodded. His face was very still. "The war set us free, but its price was high. My father died in the last battle, defending the souls that rode with the Hunt. They were freed. So, in the end and beyond retrieving, was he."

His quiet voice made the words the more terrible. Lilias shivered. "I'm sorry," she said.

"It is what is," said the Horned King's son. "We are not a fecund people, and I was born late. I am young, and my following is few; I have magic enough, but without the eons of skill and craft that my rivals can boast. Still, the blood is mine, and among us that counts for much. I have the right to claim what was my father's, and the right to defend it."

"And to lose it?" she asked.

He bent his head. She could see, just then, how he would be if he wore the crown of antlers: both regal and gracious. "There is a challenge—of course. The Summer Queen claims the kingdom. She has the strength and the skill and the forces to hold it. But the old laws bind her. If my champion defeats hers, that ends our war. She has to accept me, and stand with me against any new rival."

"Ah," said Lilias. "I see. If your strongest rival loses the fight, no one else can hope to win it. All you need to do is find a champion for this one battle. But why a mortal? Why not a knight of Faerie?"

"Cold iron," he said, "and sanctity."

He shuddered even to speak the words. They were the greatest weapons against his kind, the strongest and the most terrible. Mortals had long known it, and so bound the wildfolk, driving them out of the world.

"Iron wounded my father," he said, "and a priest's prayer destroyed him. The Queen is no more proof against them than he was."

"But," said Lilias, "what is to prevent her from finding her own human knight? This world is full of them. All she needs to do is find the Midsummer Champion and steal him away. I'm surprised you haven't tried that yourself."

"She did," he said. "He is most impressive, for a mortal, and he dotes on her excessively—as he should. The Queen is famous for her beauty."

"Do you dote on her, too?" asked Lilias. Not that it should matter, or that she cared. She was curious, that was all.

"Not excessively," he answered.

That was well, and she should have been satisfied. But there was still the heart of the matter. "You'll need someone who can match him. There are a few; some will be at the jousts in Dinant, three days from now. I can take you there. You can—"

"I don't have three days," he said. "Tomorrow night is the dark of the moon. My champion must meet hers before then, or I lose it all."

"*Tomorrow?*" Lilias did not quite scream the word. "You haven't been in a great hurry, have you?"

"I have," he said, "been imprisoned. And enchanted. And, at the end, hunted. I'm supposed to be dead."

That quelled her, but only for a moment. "I know what you're asking. Truly, it is my dream to be a knight, and fight and win battles for my liege. But I'm young. I fight well for my age and size; I may be something to reckon with when I'm older. I'm no match for the Midsummer Champion."

"No?"

"No," she said with honest regret. "You can stay here. This world's not so bad, cold iron aside. It's easy enough to stay away from the prayers. I'm sure there's an order of mages that would take you, with such powers as you must have; or you can find something else to do. Maybe even be a knight. You can wear silver armor. And maybe find a spell against cold iron. There must be one. I can help you find it."

She was babbling. She stopped.

"I need a champion," he said.

He was persistent. So was she. "You need a knight of renown. Not the likes of me."

"You are more than you know," he said.

"Then you had better explain," said Lilias tartly, "because mysteries and evasions are a sore trial to my temper."

He laughed. He roared with it, laughing so hard the bed shook and the tears ran down his cheeks. He laughed until his voice was gone, and then he lay grinning at her, completely undaunted by the blackness of her scowl.

She had considered hitting him. It was not either fear or wisdom that restrained her, but plain practicality. He was not going to stop until he was done.

She waited him out. That was easy enough. What was hard was withstanding that wide white grin.

She did her best. She leveled her glare on him and kept it there.

When he spoke, it was hardly a surrender. "My champion may choose the weapons," he said, "and the means by which they are used."

Mysteries, she thought. *Evasions. Damn him.*

His eyes were bright. They challenged her to think; to see around corners. "Any weapons? Any at all?"

He nodded once.

"Will you give me your word on that?"

"I give you my oath," he said, "by the throne I hope to take, and the kingdom I was meant to rule."

It was not the great oath, the oath that bound the gods, but it was strong enough. She felt the earth shifting as he spoke.

The sky was full of wildfolk. They hung beyond the window, a transparent host of wings and scales and talons and wide bright eyes. "Very well," she said. "I will try. But there is a condition."

He waited, brows slightly lifted. He trusted her; his own gods knew why, because she did not.

"I must be back here in a night and a day," she said. "That's when Godwy is determined to enter the abbey, and he's going to do it, if he has to break out of the dungeon and crawl there on his knees. My family will need me then. Promise you'll get me back in time. No tricks, either. No hundred years in a night. One night of this earth, and one day. That's all I can give you."

"If that truly is what you wish," he said.

She eyed him warily. His face was open, his gaze limpid. She could see no deception in him.

He was royal blood of Faerie. There must be a trick somewhere. But he had sworn an oath, and she had made sure to frame the condition as exactly as she knew how.

"Done, then," she said. "We'll leave before sunset. There are things I'll need to take, and I'll need time to gather them."

He bowed to that. He was much stronger than he had been, but he was weak still. He was glad of the delay, she thought, and the rest it would give him.

She would get no rest until this was over. She squared her shoulders and firmed her chin and did what she had to do.

oOo

Lilias was ready well before sunset. She left a message for her mother, which told the simple truth: *I've gone to fight for the Horned King against the Summer Queen. I'll be back before Godwy goes to St. Dol.*

She saddled her first and so far only prize from a joust, the fine grey mare with the mane like a waterfall, and wrapped her sword carefully in swathings of silk. That was the only weapon she took. She wore no armor; she carried a water bottle and a bag with a loaf of bread and a wedge of cheese. She carried more with her when she went hunting than she did for this venture. But she was not intending to stay, once her task was done.

If, of course, she survived.

Brenin had borrowed Godwy's riding clothes and his brown palfrey. He was still a little pale around the edges, but the healing spell was nearly complete. He would do.

She saw no sense in waiting. For the second time that day, she left Cor Benoic and vanished into the wood.

oOo

The Summer Queen was waiting over hill and under stone. The place in which she stood was both a forest and a royal hall. Its floor was mown turf; its pillars were the trunks of trees rising straight and tall to a canopy of green branches. The sun of the Otherworld shone through them, dappling the floor with green and gold.

Wildfolk flocked among the pillars and danced in the branches. Some were no more solid than a drift of fog; others were as substantial as stone, squatting thick-legged on the edge of the grass. But only two stood within: the Queen and her champion.

He was no more or less than Lilias had expected, a tall man and broad, clad in armor of golden bronze and mounted on a massive destrier. The Queen was somewhat more surprising.

She looked like Brenin. She was tall and slender; her skin was ruddy brown and her hair blue-black beneath a crown of green leaves. She was dressed in green like a hunter in the wood, as if she had already laid claim to the Horned King's realm.

Lilias glanced at Brenin. Yes, it was the same face. His was blank; his eyes were burning. Hers wore no expression at all: no surprise, no dismay.

"My son," she said. Even her voice was like his, low for a woman's, with a deep music in it. "Welcome."

He said nothing. He rode ahead of Lilias, leading her to the center of the hall. The ground rose there in a low and flattened mound like a dais. His horse sprang up onto it, with Lilias' mare close behind.

A sigh ran through the wildfolk, a sound like a shiver, edged with excitement. Lilias was no master of unseelie courts, but she could reckon what happened here. The Queen welcomed the young king as if this had been her hall and not his. He claimed it in quite another and more visible way.

He dismounted with a flourish, tied up the gelding's rein and left him to graze. When his feet struck the turf, it yielded like a living thing, then steadied, and the whole of the hall seemed briefly to sway.

He smiled at the Queen, who it seemed was also his mother, and said sweetly, "I thank you for standing guard over my hall while I was away. Now I am back, you may go, with my gratitude and my goodwill."

That was breathtaking in its insolence, but the Queen seemed to find it delightful. She laughed and bowed, supple as a sapling in the wind. "I will go when I please to go. You may stay and dine with me if you wish, and pay me homage. I ask no tribute but your bended knee."

"From a lover to his beloved or a son to his mother," he said, "indeed. But a king to a queen? I think not."

"The king is gone," she said.

"Now he has come back."

"Has he?"

"You stand with a champion," he said. "I call the right of blood and heirship, and the right of choice. My champion chooses the weapons and their uses."

Lilias had not taken her eyes off the Queen since she came into the hall, though it was terribly tempting to watch Brenin speak. She did find that face fascinating.

At the moment, the Queen's was more so. She had not seemed surprised to see her son alive, and she must have expected him to speak as he did. But she seemed slightly puzzled by his choice of champion.

"Your champion?" she said. Her glance raked Lilias and dismissed her. "This may be a shieldmaiden's child, and more richly gifted with magic than some. But magic may not be brought into the circle. This must be body against body and skill against skill."

"Indeed," said Lilias. Her voice was not too wobbly, she did not think. "We are permitted three weapons, yes? I choose these: my horse, my sword, and my tongue."

"Your tongue?" said the Queen. "Remember. There is no magic here."

"No magic," Lilias agreed. "Only what mortal skills I possess, and what I bring of my own."

The Queen had to accede to that. "So be it," she said.

"So be it," said Lilias, to seal it.

The air rang like a great bell. That startled the Queen: her eyes widened. Had she not believed that Lilias could be a champion?

She was far from the first. Lilias smiled at her and bowed slightly, as one should to the queen of an outland nation.

To Brenin she bowed much more deeply, and her smile was deeper, too. Her heart was beating so hard she had to stop and simply breathe.

It was not fear. That was long gone. Nor was it battle madness, exactly. It was excitement, and a kind of giddy joy.

She sprang down onto the undying grass and handed Mora's rein to Brenin—her liege lord, she supposed, for this day at least. He did not object to being treated like a squire. With no thought at all, simply because the sun was so bright and his eyes were so full of light, she kissed him.

She spun away before they both drowned. The Queen's champion had ridden into the center of the hall. His armor gleamed no more brightly than his destrier's coat.

She faced him on foot, unarmored, dressed in plain leather as she liked to go hunting. Her sword was in her hands. She sank to one knee on the grass and laid it gently down, then unwrapped it.

She gave it the time it deserved. It was an old sword, and it came from so far away that it had forgotten where it was born. Its blade was thin and long and slightly curved, and the steel rippled like water. Its hilt was silver inlaid with ivory.

The air of the Otherworld keened as it ran over the blade.

She had laid spells of warding on it, and Brenin had bound them. It was still cold iron, and its presence here was a terrible thing.

So was the death of a king in this place where folk never grew old and seldom died. She lifted the sword from its bed of silk, and rose.

The knight in his armor loomed above her. His destrier was taller than she; its legs were thicker than her own.

She smiled. When she held out her hand, Brenin laid the reins in it. She was in the air even as she turned, swinging onto Mora's back.

She was still much smaller than the knight or the destrier. Her sword seemed as a light as a willow wand.

He drew his broadsword. It was nigh as long as she was tall, and weighed but little less. One blow could cleave her in two.

But first he had to catch her. Mora was a patient soul, but when she saw that monstrous blade gleaming above her, her ears pricked; her neck lifted; she sat down on her haunches. Her eagerness thrummed in Lilias' body.

"Yes," Lilias said to her. "Now we dance."

She was light and swift and brave as a mare bred for war can be. But that was a terrible great sword, and the destrier, though massive and heavy, was eerily agile as some of its kind could be.

Lilias had a plan, but it had one glaring flaw. The knight's sword was very much longer than her own, and his arm made it longer still. To touch him at all, she had to come in under the blade. She had to be supernaturally fast, to dart in, strike, and dart out again before he smote her down.

He made no move to come after her. Wise, that: his destrier had no such endurance as Mora had. The knight could stand and wait and only strike when Lilias came close.

She cantered a slow circle. The destrier wheeled with her. Mora tossed her head, champing the bit, but Lilias kept her to the same slow, almost motionless pace.

It was grueling for the destrier. Size, in a horse, is not always strength; and he was very large. But he was strong for what he was, and his rider would not have mercy on him simply because he strained and groaned.

Lilias rested the flat of her blade against her thigh, and slowed her breathing to match the rocking rhythm of the canter. She knew the moment when the broadsword began to rise.

Her breathing altered the merest fraction. Mora sprang like an arrow from the bow. Lilias' sword darted in, with nearly all her body following.

The knight twisted, lunged. Cold iron slid down the shining vambrace that warded his arm.

Lilias had gambled and won. His armor was wrought in the Otherworld. At the touch of mortal steel, it twisted and shriveled and melted away.

The sword, unlike the armor, was earthly bronze: it held to its substance. It was keen and deadly heavy.

Mora wheeled away from the blow. Lilias hung more than half out of the saddle.

For a long, breathless moment she hovered above the ground. Edged bronze sang past her cheek. With an effort that wrenched her shoulder and hip, she hauled herself back where she belonged.

There was no time to find her breath. The knight's armor had turned to smoke and fog and vanished, but he wore heavy padded leather beneath. She recognized his face without its helmet, vaguely: broad, ruddy, with close-cropped fair hair and furious blue eyes.

He clapped spurs to his destrier's sides. Mora cantered backward, a feat that barely rippled the surface of his wrath. He hurled all his weight and strength and every scrap of speed against her.

She might have outrun him if this had been a jousting ground or a battlefield. But this was a king's hall, and the circle was terribly, perilously small.

Lilias limbered the last of her weapons and struck.

She sang. Lilias had a strong clear voice, as strong as a boy's. She had honed it in the choir of Cor Benoic, and schooled it in her father's guardroom. It rang like a bell and cut like a blade.

The song was as scurrilous as any that came out of her

father's guardroom. It pricked; it stabbed; it mocked the Queen's champion mercilessly: his body and his person and his prowess, and all his line and lineage, too.

When she spun a verse on the subject of his mother and a sumpter mule, he broke. He lunged.

The destrier's shoulder sent the mare reeling. Lilias stabbed blindly, uselessly, as Mora stumbled and fell to her knees.

The broadsword swept over Lilias' head. She dropped and fell and rolled in the yielding grass.

Hooves flailed above her. Mora reared and spun, and squealed in rage, striking at the destrier.

Lilias scrambled out of reach. The sword was still in her hand, and that was a miracle.

Bronze bit earth where an instant before her hand had been. She staggered to her feet. The knight stood head and shoulders above her. His eyes had gone cold.

She saw death there, in this place where death had so little power. But the knight was as mortal as she; he had brought death with him, just as she had.

Jousts were not about killing, though sometimes men died. She had never fought in a war. She did not even know if she could kill a man.

One of them had to lose this battle. Lilias backed slowly away. Her sword was heavy in her hands, a dead weight.

Her eyes caught two figures standing beyond the circle's edge. They were so much alike, the Queen and the one who would be king, that it was difficult at first to tell which was which.

Lilias had no love for the Queen. For the other...

There was no sense or reason in it. With love, there never was.

The knight whirled his sword around his head and smote with all his force. She was gone—but barely. Her mind had emptied of thought. The sword in her hand meant nothing.

Some dim fragment of intelligence yet lingered. It was just enough to keep her moving. She had wagered everything on a bit of cleverness, and it had failed her. She had nothing left, not even her poor skill.

She moved to drop the sword, just as the knight struck again. Her fingers tightened around the hilt. The blade rose as if of its own accord. Her eye, wandering, saw the opening, the whole length of his body stretched before her, with the broadsword at the height of its swing.

Shimmering steel darted under those massive arms, angled, aimed, thrust.

Upward. Under the ribs and the breastbone. Up into the beating heart.

She almost died, too, in the shock of that pulse against her blade, as the broadsword swept downward. In the utmost instant, she threw herself back and away.

Fire seared her arm and side. The broadsword quivered upright in the grass, stained with the scarlet of blood.

The knight stood upright with Lilias' blade in his heart. As she stared, he went down like a mountain falling.

oOo

The earth shook. The air thrummed. The hosts of wildfolk roared and yowled and keened and, here and there, sang.

Lilias flushed. She knew that song all too well. The people of Faerie, it seemed, had taken a liking to it.

By the good God, did they know what it meant?

She looked up, still blushing, into Brenin's face. The Queen was nowhere that she could see. The knight's body was gone, and with it his destrier. There were only the two of them in the circle, and the grey mare grazing, one foot all too close to a trailing rein.

Lilias sprang to rescue the rein. When she turned back, Brenin was still there, and still himself, though she fancied she could see the shadow of antlers rising from his brow.

His people were waiting to swarm into the circle, to sweep him up and carry him off and celebrate his crowning. His will held them back, though it could only be for a while.

"Will you stay?" he said.

"Is it true what they say," she said, "of mortals who eat the fruits of Faerie? That they can never leave?"

"They can leave," he said, "eventually."

"But not soon? Not in a night in a day?"

His silence was as much answer as she needed. Her heart kept twisting and trying to break. "I have to go home," she said. "I promised."

"Then will you come back?"

"What would I do here?" she asked him.

"I still need a champion," he said.

"Even now?"

"Now and always," he said.

"And you want *me?*"

"Now," he said, "and always."

There was no sense in it, and no reason. If Lilias had been possessed of either, she would have turned her back and taken her mare and her sword and gone away, and never set eyes on him again.

Her hands were in his. That was becoming a habit. "When my brother is safe in the abbey," she said, "I'll come back."

"Do you promise?"

"By my heart," she said.

"I'll wait for you," said the Horned King.

It was clear to see now, the crown that he was born for. His eyes were still his own, and his face, so familiar and so blessedly strange. She kissed him again, longer this time, fixing it in memory.

When she must breathe or faint, she drew back. Already the gate was open between two pillars of the hall, looking out on mortal sky and mortal hill and the lake with its flock of geese.

His hand ran down her wounded arm, knitting flesh and stanching blood that she had not even noticed until it was gone. Where it had fallen in the grass, flowers grew, red as blood.

He plucked one, and then another. The first he kept; the second he kissed and laid in her hand. Its fragrance was dizzyingly sweet. "For remembrance," he said, "and to guide you home again."

Yes, she thought, with her hands in his and her eyes on his face. *Home.*

But first there was duty and a promise, and love, too, after all. She mounted her grey mare and rode away out of Faerie, back to the world in which she was born.

Madeleine E. Robins is a former fencer, a lifelong Anglophile, a New Yorker, a cake decorator and frequent dog-walker. She is also the author of eleven books (including Point of Honour, Petty Treason, and The Sleeping Partner), a production editor, and, not at all coincidentally, the mother of two daughters. A founding member of the online authors' collaborative BookViewCafe.com, more of her short fiction can be found there. She is currently working on finishing a fourth Sarah Tolerance novel (news about which can be found at sarahtolerance.com). Robins blogs occasionally at blog.bookviewcafe.com and more frequently at madrobins. livejournal.com.

About "A Wreath of Luck" she said, "When I think of daring and adventure, pirates come immediately to mind. But I know too much these days to throw myself into writing about romantic pirates (really: imperfect personal grooming, dishonor, scurvy—so not Errol Flynn), and so I found myself writing a romantic story about pirates. Who believes more in romance (and pirates?) than a bookish twelve-year-old girl like Amielle? She might be me at that age, seeing romance everywhere and hoping fiercely for a happy ending."

A WREATH OF LUCK

by Madeleine E. Robins

Amielle me Ortun had a genius for self-effacement rare in a child of twelve. Whether this was a good thing or bad is hard to say, but it is quite certain that without this gift she would not have been left behind on the *Plover* when the ship was captured. Her family fled at once to the lifeboat and, while the captain and crew were engaged in dying to protect their passengers, rowed heartily for the east and Meviel. By the time they realized that Amielle was not among them, the *Plover* was long gone from the horizon.

Amielle, a slight, spindly girl who preferred reading about adventure to undertaking it, heard the ado abovedecks and did what she generally did when there was a commotion: she hid. A few hours later, when the cries and footfall overhead had quieted, she slid from a cupboard in the Ladies' Cabin where she had been hidden and made her way up the stairs to find out what was what. The sun had set, but the moon had not yet risen; in the green twilight, Amielle realized with a shock that the persons in charge of the *Plover* were no longer the genial, brisk Captain ha Blifen and his well-spoken crew. These, without doubt, were pirates.

There were seven of them, a skeleton crew left by the captain of the *Drunken Daisy* to bring the ship to port on Isl'Alander;

the master, even to Amielle's unexperienced eyes, was a man remarkable for his beauty: tall, well-built, with light eyes, a square jaw, and long, waving dark hair. It was the hair that drew her eyes to the necklace he wore: a wreath of luckstones, each gem glimmering with the unmistakable spark of luck burning within. Amielle barely suppressed a cry of dismay when she recognized among them the beryl ring which had belonged to the *Plover's* captain and the opal luck which the *Plover's* mate had worn in his hatband. The effect was as shocking as seeing a wreath of human ears round the neck of an Egeni savage.

Seeing this, all thought of throwing herself on the pirates' mercy left Amielle's head. She slithered into the shadows while the master was giving directions to his crew, and waited to see what would happen next.

"'Til we meet the *Daisy* there's to be no raids; we haven't the numbers for it. Breggan, Lyd, you two take first watch." The master tossed his hair out of his eyes dramatically as he descended from the bridge.

Silly peacock, Amielle thought. *Fancies himself a figure of romance.*

Certainly, he was the only one of the pirates who might have been characterized in such a way. Of the six men listening, five were grizzled and ill-formed, with cast eyes, broken noses, missing teeth and puckered scars. The sixth man, a short, tidy fellow with spectacles, and his hair in a dark queue, looked more like an office clerk than a pirate. He certainly offered the master no competition.

All the pirates except the two left on watch went below, passing so close to the shadows where Amielle hid that she expected to be found and dragged into the moonlight. She crouched in the shadow of the rail, not breathing, until the last of them had passed, then waited while the two on deck disposed themselves, one at the helm, the other staring out over the silent, moonlit sea. After half an hour of this, Amielle slipped from her hiding place and, heart pounding, went below herself.

The door to the Ladies' Cabin stood open as it had been left, with piles of lace, silk, and linen garments strewn everywhere by the marauders searching for plunder. Along the passage, the door to the captain's cabin was closed; Amielle suspected that the master had taken that cabin himself. From the muttering that issued from the Men's Cabin she thought that must be where the crew had bestowed themselves. Amielle turned back to the Ladies' Cabin, stole in, and made for the cupboard. It was a small cupboard, and difficult to climb into, but Amielle had not yet achieved a woman's height or figure, and she managed it. Then, with her knees folded tight to her chest, she covered herself well with linens and left the cupboard door ajar for air.

Remarkably, albeit uncomfortably, she slept.

oOo

The sheets which covered her were moldy, and by the time the sun cast a stripe of light into the cupboard, Amielle was fighting the urge to sneeze. She was about to slide from her hiding place when she heard voices from the passageway and thought better of it.

"I'll get precious little sleep with you snoring in my ear, Breggan." It was a young voice. Amielle thought it must belong to the pirate who looked like a clerk.

"Don't make no mind to me, Lyd me boy. P'raps the captain'll let you take *his* cot." This seemed to be some sort of unsavory joke, for the second man laughed heartily.

"I don't think I'm the captain's meat," Lyd evenly. To Amielle's horror his voice came from within the Ladies' Cabin, not two feet from her head. "Your snores won't rattle the walls in here, I think."

Breggan made some indecipherable joke; Amielle heard him laugh heartily at his own wit as he went down the passage, then Lyd closed the door to the Ladies' Cabin. Amielle drew the quietest breath she could manage, realizing that nothing more than the cupboard door separated her from discovery. She pushed the sheet away from her face and peered through the slit of the door: the spectacled pirate, in an attitude of exhaustion, had untied the string from his queue. He shook out his lank, dark hair and scratched his head with an attitude of refreshment. His luck, a ruby in one ear, gleamed through the curtain of dark hair.

"Gods alive," the pirate muttered, and shrugged off his coat, rolling his shoulders. Amielle, whose muscles were stiff and sore with her unnatural position, watched enviously. The pirate turned to look out the port, peeled off his shirt, and began to unwind a strip of bandage which suggested that he had been injured in the taking of the *Plover*. With the bandage off, the pirate stretched, pivoted, and scratched as vigorously at her breasts as she had done, a moment before, at her scalp.

Amielle let out a gasp of astonishment.

The pirate girl seized her shirt to her chest with one hand and tore the cupboard door open with the other. "Out of there!" she cried, pushing aside the linens.

Amielle unfolded herself, slowly and painfully, from the small space, and slid out into the confines of the Ladies' Cabin.

"Gods alive," the pirate girl said again. "What will Nault say about you?"

Amielle was shaking her leg, which prickled almost unbearably with the return of circulation. "Is that the captain?" she asked.

"The master—until we reach Isl'Alander, anyway. I'd best take you right along to him."

"Wait." The middle-most of five children, Amielle me Ortun had negotiated the pitfalls of life in the Ortun nursery. She knew an advantage when she saw one. "You'd best put on a shirt first, hadn't you? Unless your captain already knows you're a woman." She put a sing-song lilt to her words.

Lyd pursed her lips and Amielle knew she had drawn blood. "It makes no difference," she said.

"Then why bind your breasts and dress like one of them?" Amielle shrugged. "If it makes no difference, then by all means let us go and—"

"All right! All right!" Lyd attempted to bind her breasts as she talked, but surprise and distraction had her making a bad job of it. "What do you want?"

Amielle had to consider. Her immediate objective was not to be turned over to the pirate master, for she doubted he'd see that she was treated kindly, and this Lyd, while a pirate, had not immediately offered to kill her, which she thought must be a hopeful sign.

"What do you want?" Lyd asked again.

"*Not* to be thrown over board," Amielle said firmly. "Here, I'll help you with that." She took the end of the bandage from Lyd's hand. "Really, all I want is to go on hiding until I can get away. No offense, but your captain doesn't seem the sort would let me do that." She pinned the bandage snug and tidy.

"Probably not," Lyd said dryly. "He doesn't care for females aboard ship. Thank you." She shrugged the shirt back on and buttoned her brown waistcoat over it. "But look, child. This ship's being taken to Isl'Alander, and even if you leave the ship there, where would you go? It's a port for privateers and pirates and—well, not for nice little girls like you."

"I'm good at hiding," Amielle told her. "I only gave myself away because—" she pointed at Lyd's chest. "And if I can get to this Isl'Alander, surely I can find a way home from there. If I'm not drownded for being a girl, that is."

"That's still most likely." Lyd sighed. "Look, child: I'm going to sleep. Perhaps I'll forget I saw you, perhaps not. If you're smart, you'll stay quiet."

Amielle, recognizing a good offer when one was made, nodded vigorously and, once again, climbed into the linen cupboard and closed the door.

oOo

For several days, it seemed that Lyd had all but forgotten about the stowaway in the Ladies' Cabin; it could have been forgetfulness that caused her to leave a trencher of stew and bread in the cabin from time to time. Amielle did not think so, but she was happy to eat the stew (which was tasty) and the bread (which was dry and weevily). Her chiefest problem, aside from unending anxiety about her fate, was boredom. Shut into the cupboard, it was all too easy to let her imagination run wide and consider her fate if she was discovered. Reciting romantic poetry to herself was very little distraction, and finally she gave in to that occupation which her governess had regarded as the worst sin a child could commit: eavesdropping. If she was not shut into the cupboard, she could hear almost any business not conducted at a whisper—and pirates, she soon realized, conduct little business at a whisper.

Amielle learned a number of things. The master's second-in-command was Gorle, whom the others called Fatty behind his back. It was Gorle more than the master, Nault, who managed things. Most of the men thought Nault too pretty to be captain, although they were willing to admit that he was a good pilot. Only Lyd seemed willing to stick up for the master when grousing started, as it did, like clockwork, when the grog ration was doled out. Lyd stubbornly insisted that the master was a clever fellow, smart even. And beside he'd been put in authority over them all, so there was no point fretting about it.

Amielle had heard that same tone of voice from the governess who had eloped with her riding teacher. She had heard the painfully nonchalant terms of praise from her older sisters when they fell in love but did not wish to be twitted about it. And because Amielle found Lyd rather admirable, she wished to understand what the pirate found admirable in the pirate master.

She asked Lyd. "That vulgar necklace was almost all I noticed about him. What kind of man wears the luck of dead—"

"You don't understand," Lyd said, more hotly than she might have done were it some other pirate under discussion. "Any man may choose to keep the luckstones of the folk he fights, and some do. Nault's just more *aboveboard* about it."

"Perhaps he needs to look fierce, since he's so beautiful," Amielle suggested.

"Well, yes, aye, that's it. The other men might not take him seriously if he did not appear ruthless."

"All that hair, and those blue eyes," the child went on. "But vicious, too, I reckon."

"Not always." Lyd muttered. "Sometimes he—"

"What?" Amielle urged. "Is he nice to *you*?"

Lyd shrugged. "When I was first aboard the *Daisy*, I lost my footing while I was up in the rigging, and I thought I was going to fall to the deck, but Nault caught me."

Amielle wondered: wouldn't any of the pirates have caught her? But Nault had, and when a man who looks like him saves your life, perhaps it was reasonable to fall in love with him. Amielle, at twelve, was certain there were aspects to the whole business she was not old enough to understand.

The next time Lyd came to "forget" a plate of food, Amielle asked another question.

"Should we not have reached Isl'Alander by now? We've been sailing for days since..." she trailed off. *Since you killed the crew and took the ship* sounded aggressive.

Lyd nodded, taking the opportunity to re-tie her queue. "We've been becalmed for two day—not a breath of wind on the sea. Gorle swears this ship is unlucky."

"Well, it wasn't until you lot captured us," Amielle said, a little sharply.

Lyd grinned. "I s'pose not. Other things been happening too, though. One of the grog casks leaked out almost the whole tuns' worth last night. Hold smells like a tavern, but there's naught to drink. And you may have noticed the bread—"

"It has bugs in it," Amielle said.

"Well, it always has some, but it's been worse the last couple of days. The men are talking about curses and jinxes. You stay in your cubby, little one. If they find you, they'll put it all to your account and I doubt they'll be kind."

In fact, Amielle had become bold enough to spend some part of the day curled out of sight behind one of the berths, reading her sisters' left-behind novels. When Nault had ordered a careful search of all cabins for items of worth, it was Lyd who volunteered to go through the Ladies' Cabin, and Amielle helped her fold the extravagant lace and silk left behind by her family. It would be sold to doxies on Isl'Alander, "and make a neat sum," Lyd told her.

"Don't you want to keep some for yourself?" Amielle asked.

Lyd snorted and gestured at her tidy brown coat and waistcoat. "What would I do with such stuff?" But she fingered the heavily-laced petticoats with appreciation. "Any road, Nault and the captain'd take my head if I kept anything back for myself."

Except for luckstones, Amielle thought, but did not say.

As they worked, Amielle learned a good deal about the pirate. Her true name was Lydanne me Kenn; her father had been a shipfitter, and she had run away to sea with her first love when she was only a few years older than Amielle herself. That first love had drowned within a three-month, and Lydanne had found herself on Isl'Alander and, in boys' garb, hired by the captain of the *Drunken Daisy*.

"Didn't you want to go home?" Amielle asked.

Lydanne shook her head. She was packing the folded dainties away in a chest for when they reached port. "Not by then. I love the sea. And the men are good enough fellows—"

"Unless you're on another ship," Amielle said. She still regretted Captain ha Blifen and the *Plover's* crew.

Lydanne did not disagree. "It's the way of things. But even if I could, I wouldn't go back to Meviel. Nothing for me there. This is my life; everything I love is here."

Amielle thought she was speaking of Nault.

After more than a week of no breeze, a wind picked up and the *Plover* began to make for Isl'Alander again. Amielle, hidden behind the berth in the Ladies' Cabin, knew at once that this was not a kindly freshening breeze but the making of a storm: the groans and creaks of the *Plover's* boards, the fearsome motion of the ship, and the increasing tension in the sailors' calls made that clear. Then rain began to beat down on the deck over her head, and the ship rocked and rose on great swells. Amielle, buffeted between the berth and wall of the Ladies' Cabin, climbed unsteadily into the linen cupboard, wrapped herself well against bruises, and sat to wait out the storm.

It was a bad time. The voices of the seamen on deck were lost in the wind, and she knew nothing of what was happening, except that the *Plover* sounded as if it was being wrenched apart. The tossing made Amielle sick, but she did not dare give way to her nausea lest someone hear her retching. The storm went on for hours; at some point, worn out by fear, Amielle fell asleep, uncertain if she would wake again.

She did wake, stiff and sore. The fearsome rocking of the ship had ceased, leaving a quiet that was eerie. She heard no voices, and for a moment Amielle entertained the idea that all the pirates had been swept overboard and that she would die aboard the *Plover*, for she had no illusion about her ability to pilot the ship herself. Then she heard footfall in the passage and almost laughed with relief. Likely it was Lydanne with food. But to be safe, she stayed where she was, arms wrapped around her legs and chin on her knees, with the sheets draped around her.

The door of the cupboard was wrenched open; a bony, one-eyed pirate was looking over his shoulder, calling to ask how many sheets were wanted for patching. He had reached, unlooking, into the cupboard, and grasped a sheet—and Amielle's wrist beneath it.

"Sweet Jophiros' knees!" The man dropped her wrist and Amielle attempted, impossibly, to squeeze herself further back in the cupboard. But the man pulled all the blankets and sheets down with a gesture, and Amielle after them. She found herself on the floor of the Ladies' Cabin staring up at the pirate, who was bawling to his mates to see what he had found.

Dragged onto the deck, blinking in the bright, clear sunlight, Amielle saw a shambles on the deck, and the pirates engaged in cleaning up. Nault stood at the helm, his dark hair blowing in the breeze and the necklace of luckstones glinting in the sunlight. Behind him, Lydanne, examining a torn sail, looked at Amielle with dismay.

"Found her in the front cabin, Nault. Been hidin' there since we took the ship, I reckon." The one-eyed pirate shoved Amielle forward.

Nault gestured to Lydanne to take the helm and swung down the stairs to examine his prisoner. "A *girl*." He might as well have said "a snake" or "a turd" for the distaste in his voice. He turned to look round at the rest of the crew. "Well, *this*—" he took Amielle's arm and shook her. "This explains all the foul luck we've had since taking the ship, hey, boys?"

The crew—saving only Lydanne at the helm—moved

toward Amielle, muttering their agreement with Nault. The kindest suggestion the girl heard was that she be turned over to the doxies of Madame Warmfist's on Isl'Alander: "They'll have a use for her!" The other men seemed to think that was too kind. "Brought the storm down on us," a fat, grizzled man said. "Took the wind clear away," another growled. And, worst of all, "Split open the grog barrel!"

"A woman on board's a jinx," Nault said. He tossed his head to get the hair out of his eyes. "Only question is how to deal with her. I say: over the side."

He took two steps toward the railing; Amielle attempted to resist, but the master was big, certainly bigger than a scrawny, twelve-year-old girl. She found herself pressed against the railing, bent backward so she could see the swift flow of the sea below her.

"Nault, stop! She's just a child!"

Amielle looked back to see Lydanne with her hand on the master's shoulder, restraining him. Nault had turned to regard her with a look that said he was not accustomed to being gainsaid.

"Step off, Lyd, or I'll have your ear," he said. And tossed his hair again.

"Master, give her to the brothel on Isl'Alander, if you like. But don't toss her overboard. A thing like that brings its own ill luck. You want to curse this ship?"

"Only curse on this ship is this brat, and over she goes. Take your hand off me or I swear—" Nault turned to face Lydanne; Amielle slid out from his grasp. "Now, damme, see what you've done?"

The master reeled around to grab Amielle, but Lydanne was still in his way. He swung at her; Lydanne was knocked sideways, her spectacles flying and her hair pulled from the tail in which she had tied it. As Nault turned to grab Amielle again, Lydanne staggered back and stood between them. This time Nault reached out to push Lydanne aside, then stopped. His hand, flat upon her chest, slowly shaped around the swelling there. His expression was all astonishment.

Lydanne, her glasses gone and her hair loose about her face, stared at the master, unwavering. She looked, to Amielle, like a warrior queen. The thought woke the romance in the girl's soul. *Now,* she thought. *Now he knows who she really is, without her spectacles and with hair down, now Nault will see she's pretty and love her and she'll save me and—*

But the master of the *Plover* only stood there, staring at the hand which cupped Lydanne's breast as if he had found a mouse in his boot. Lydanne stood still, watching the play of expressions on Nault's face.

Gorle, the fat seaman, broke the silence. "Gon to be a fight, then, Nault?" He sounded hopeful. The other pirates began a murmur of encouragement. "You and Lyd?"

Nault gave Lydanne's breast a hard squeeze—Amielle saw her wince of pain—and pushed her aside. "I don't fight *women.*"

There was a moment of silence in which the creaking of the ship and the whickering of the breeze in the sails overhead seemed unnaturally loud. Lydanne, on her feet again, straightened her coat and quickly braided her hair in its accustomed queue. One of the pirates muttered "Whuh?"

"Lyd's not one of us, Pico. Lyd's another thrice-damned *woman.*" Nault's voice oozed disgust. "There's two jinxes on this ship, and I say we be rid of both of them."

Amielle, still crouched in the lee of the rail, watched in dismay. This was not at all the way matters were supposed to proceed. Nault, in the face of Lydanne's bravery and beauty, was supposed to fall in love with her.

Don't you see how splendid she is? Amielle wanted to cry. But it seemed that none of them saw that, except her.

Gorle stepped forward and peered at Lydanne. "Zis true, Lyd? You a woman?"

An odd, small smile lit Lydanne's face. "I'm the same shipmate I've been for half a dozen years, doing my work and fighting beside you all when it was needful. What else matters? Boun—" she looked to the tall, one-eyed pirate. "Wasn't it me pulled you back onto the side when we were mending sails on the *Daisy* last year? And Pico, when you lost your blade taking this ship, hadn't I your back? Who saved your sorry ass then?

Breggen, you saved me more than once. D'you regret it now?"

The pirates looked at each other uncertainly.

"I'm no different from any of you. I love the sea—"

"*Love*." Nault spat. "Like a *woman* to talk of love. No wonder the winds died and the bread was weevilly—"

"But it's *you* brought the bad luck," Amielle burst in. She stood by the railing, her fist clenched, outraged. "You, with that vulgar necklace that tempts fortune with other men's luck! It's nothing to do with me—or Lydanne! Leave her alone, you bully."

It was a mistake. The pirates had all but forgotten her, and now she'd drawn their attention again.

Nault stepped along the rail and grabbed Amielle by the wrist, jerking her back toward the pirates. "Bully, am I? You're one piece of ill-luck I can rid myself of this minute. Over the side you go, brat. But first—" he reached for the ear where Amielle's own tiny luckstone dangled. She turned her head furiously, seeking to avoid his hand; the master roared his frustration and backhanded her. The world went gray and she sagged against the rail.

"NAULT!" Lydanne's voice was a roar in Amielle's ears. "Think shame to strike a child half your size. *Are* you a bully? If not, you'll fight *me*." She had her sword out, extended in a line toward Nault's throat. "Fight me, or prove yourself a coward."

Amielle fell backward when Nault dropped her. He drew his own sword with a sweep that almost deprived Boun, nearby, of his remaining eye, and dropped into a fencing crouch. The pirates stepped back hastily, giving Nault and Lydanne room for their business. Amielle, who had read of duels at sea but never seen a sword drawn in anger, found that it was not romantic or even exciting. She could taste her own fear as she watched Lydanne and Nault circle round each other on the broad, creaking boards of the deck. Nault did not love Lydanne: he meant to kill her. And if Lydanne loved Nault, well, she clearly had no intention of being killed herself.

Amielle folded herself back into the shadow of the railing and watched.

Nault lunged at Lydanne with a roar so loud it made

Amielle's heart jump, but Lydanne, unmoved, beat his point aside and riposted. Her blade sliced the fabric of Nault's sleeve; then there was a flurry of blows and parries, with the clash of steel and the thump of boots and the grunts and gasps of the two of them like music to a dance.

"Give over, Lyd," Nault gasped.

"Give over and die? Not likely."

"I've the luck." Nault flashed that beautiful, broad grin. The wreath of luckstones around his neck glinted in the sunlight, and Amielle was struck with inspiration.

"Unfair!" she cried. "Those stones give the master an advantage! Cry foul!"

"Whot?" Gorle looked around as if he could not remember who was speaking.

Amielle rose up from her hiding place in the lee of the rail and said again, "The master has an advantage; so many luckstones together when she's only the one. If the master doesn't fear being beaten by a *woman*, he should fight without the necklace."

"I fear nothing. Least of all Lyd, here." Nault reached with one hand to pull the wreath of luckstones over his head; his tawny skin glowed with sweat and his hair stirred in the breeze. With the necklace in one hand and his sword in the other, he was a very heroic figure. *And knows it,* Amielle thought.

Lydanne looked at the master with hopeless admiration, but she had not lowered the point of her sword.

Nault dropped the necklace on top of a barrel, well away from the crew, and turned back to face Lydanne. "Now we finish this," he said.

They fought. Amielle had no words for what she was seeing, other than that with each thrust and cut she was certain that one of them would die. They fought around the deck, causing the watching pirates to scatter more than once. Lydanne's blade caught Nault on the shoulder and cut him; a whistling downward slash missed her ear but took four inches of Lydanne's queue. But that was the last advantage Nault gained; Lydanne fought with grim purpose and economy, where Nault seemed to become angrier with each passing moment. Finally the master made a lunge for Lydanne's side that put him off balance; she parried the cut, then swept his foot out from under him with a kick, and the master was on his back with her point at his throat.

"Do you give?" Lydanne was panting so hard the words were hard to understand. She repeated them.

He nodded. Lydanne took up his sword and stepped back. She tossed his blade to Gorle as Nault got to his feet.

"Now, I suppose we must figure what's best to do with our stowaway," Lydanne said. Or began to. The words were cut off by Nault's hand across her mouth and a small, wicked-looking knife at her throat.

"Word to a woman isn't any word at all," he said. "First you, then the chit."

He pulled Lydanne backward with him toward the railing. The other pirates watched and did nothing. Any notions Amielle had cherished about honor among pirates were entirely gone now. Lydanne would die, and then she would die, and for what?

Amielle crawled unseen in the shadow of the rail until she found what she wanted: Nault's necklace, the pile of rings, earbobs, and pins strung together on a salt-stiffened thong. For the third time Amielle got to her feet and called attention to herself once more.

"Let her go, Nault." The girl held his necklace out over the railing with nothing but the green depths of the sea below. "Let her go, or I'll—" she shook her hand and the stones clicked and clinked together. Her voice was shaking, too.

Nault released Lydanne and launched himself, not at Amielle, but at the necklace itself, in a movement fluid with rage. Amielle stepped back, but not fast enough; Nault hit the rail with his hip, grabbing with both hands at the necklace, For a moment that seemed very long, he stretched out over the rail, his weight pulling on the thong. Lydanne reached out for Nault to pull him back, but it was too late; he fell forward over the rail, the wreath of stones in his hands, and disappeared into the sea. Only one stone—the emerald earbob by which Amielle had been holding the necklace—remained clutched in her hand.

oOo

There was no question that, with Nault gone, Gorle ha Deman was the most senior seaman on the ship. The pirates, including Lydanne, looked to him for what they should do next.

"Cap'n said head for Isl'Alander, zo I reckon that's what we do," Gorle said at last. Amielle sat binding Lydanne's wounds inexpertly, and Lydanne, wincing and drinking ale, had returned her spectacles to her nose and retied her newly-shortened hair. "Z' for you, Lyd, I dunno. Zif only you wan't a woman—" he sounded as if it had simply been a bad choice on her part. "I dunno what the Cap'n'll say about Nault. It's likely he'll blame you, though, and I'd not want to be in your shoes."

Lydanne nodded. "I had thought as much, myself. Gorle, if I take the skiff and bring the girl home, will you give me my share?"

The pirate considered. He was not a man, Amielle thought, much given to being in charge.

"I s'pose you earnt it, din't you? Even *with* being a woman. Go below and we'll count out what's yours. Oy, Breggen: provision the skiff and get her ready to launch. It'll be a week or more before you reach Meviel."

oOo

They left the *Plover* without ceremony or farewells. If Lydanne regretted leaving the ship, she did not say so. Instead, she settled into the skiff, took bearings with a magnet floated in a shell full of water, and began to row. For as long as it took for the skiff to lose sight of the *Plover*, Amielle said nothing. But finally she could stand it no longer.

"Lydanne?"

"Hmm."

"I am sorry about Nault."

The pirate woman rowed on. "I am too, girl."

"I didn't mean for him... I just didn't want him to kill you."

"I know. Thank you."

That didn't seem enough to Amielle. She thought for a few

minutes to the accompanying sound of the oars dipping slow and smooth.

At last, "I don't think he could have— I don't think he would have loved you."

Lydanne shook her head. "You're right there." One corner of her mouth quirked up. "But I could have loved him, see."

Amielle thought about that, but it made no sense to her. The pirate woman said nothing, but Amielle felt there was a good deal that could be said, as she often did when dealing with adults. She had an idea.

"Lydanne, would you like this? To remember—" Amielle offered the emerald earbob in the palm of her hand.

Lydanne stopped rowing and looked at the stone. "No, sweet. I'll remember well enough on my own. You keep it. Spoils of war." She fixed her gaze on the sea before them, the featureless horizon, and picked the oars up again.

Shannon Page was born on Halloween night and spent her early years on a commune in northern California's backwoods. A childhood without television gave her a great love of books and the worlds she found in them. She wrote her first book, an adventure story starring her cat, at the age of seven. Sadly, that work is currently out of print, but her short fiction has appeared in *Clarkesworld, Interzone,* and *Fantasy* (with Jay Lake), *Black Static*, Tor.com, and several independent press anthologies. Shannon is a longtime practitioner of Ashtanga yoga, has no tattoos, and lives in Portland, Oregon, with seventeen orchids and an awful lot of books. Visit her at www.shannonpage.net .

Jay Lake lives in Portland, Oregon, where he works on numerous writing and editing projects. Recent books include *Pinion* from Tor Books, *The Specific Gravity of Grief* from Fairwood Press, *The Baby Killers* from PS Publishing, and *The Sky That Wraps* from Subterranean Press. His short fiction appears regularly in literary and genre markets worldwide. Jay is winner of the John W. Campbell Award for Best New Writer, and a multiple nominee for the Hugo and World Fantasy Awards.

EMBERS

by Shannon Page and Jay Lake

Firenze, 1498

I peered around the rough-edged corner of the Palazzo Martelli, searching down the long, night-shadowed lane but seeing nothing save the muddy path to the river Arno below. The Ponte Vecchio glimmered in the distance, lit by a single torch at the near end. On my shoulder perched Fain; I hadn't trusted him to this task, so he murmured and cooed his dismay in my ear.

My nose caught the scent of lavender and the musk of men. Or rather, a certain man. Which made me curse quietly and draw back into the shadows.

Fain burbled at this.

"There is no humor here," I muttered. "For someone who claims not to use our magic, he's sore adept at getting to places before me."

The dove could not speak, not in the usually understood sense of the term; but as with many long-held familiars, our communication was subtle yet unmistakable. And at the moment, Fain was clearly disagreeing with me.

"All right," I whispered. "You call me wrong. But if Piero *does* cast, then why has he been working against us?"

Fain had no answer to that.

I waited until the bells sounded for Lauds, the last of the night's prayers. The man I sought did not reappear, and I dared not follow where he had gone. Only then did I slip through the first cold glimmers of dawn back to my small room in the rafters of the Palazzo Medici Riccardi.

oOo

As it is sometimes easier to hide amid a crowd than on the deserted streets of night, I spent the next afternoon in the markets and piazzas of the city of my heart. Despite the best efforts of the mad priest Savonarola, Firenze remained a vibrant metropolis, full of traders bringing commerce from every land. These far-eyed men tempted all with silks and spices and fine-worked leathers and, to a lesser degree, glittering gold and jewels. I permitted myself the luxury of admiring the pretties for an hour or two as I searched for the man Piero, though in truth I knew he lurked closer to the Arno.

Nestled in my bosom, hidden by the folds of cloth I had drawn around me to keep out the new-spring cold, Fain seemed to whisper, *Last night you avoided him; today you hunt him.* Or perhaps the dove merely slept, and those were my own thoughts.

At any rate, the point was well taken. I was of two minds about this entire business, to be sure.

Finally, as the late shadows pointed ever eastward, I made my way towards the river. I was forced to steel my sensitive nose against the assaults of the butchers who made their killings in the little shops lining the Ponte Vecchio. Why they perched here over the water was no mystery. Why folk downstream still drew from this river was the question.

Of course, ordinary folk did not know of the bad magic of drinking water tainted with the blood and offal of murdered beasts. They blamed night humors for their various ailments, or the curses of the vengeful departed. They weren't wrong in this, necessarily; those were certainly at work in the world as well. But the poisons in the Arno carried off more children and old women than any curse fomented by uneasy ghosts.

It was no truck of mine, I supposed. And there were fewer

people to die of starvation.

Gathering my suitably bleak thoughts, I approached the foul waters.

I stood on the packed clay of the bank a long while, staring into the moving path of the river, seeking to see anything of the bottom of it. Divination by water was a tricky art at best, and the winter rains had been formidable this past season. They were not finished yet, I was certain, though we were having a small respite these recent days. Merely mud, not deluge.

His presence spoke to me from across the river long before I raised my eyes to him. Rising over the odor of the waters with the improbability of our kind, musk met my nose and I knew, yet I would not give him the satisfaction of my gaze. Not until I was ready.

Finally, I looked up. Piero stood on the opposite bank amid a little forest of boats drawn up to shore, surrounding him like disciples ready to spread his message across the four corners of the world. He was too far across the rolling water for ordinary conversation. His black hair fell in curling waves to his shoulders, and it seemed as though I could see the light of his soul deep in his eyes, though even my powers were not so great. Especially not at this distance. In my bosom, Fain stirred, fluttering a soft wing against my breasts. I touched a hand to myself in order to gentle the bird as I spoke to the man across the water. My voice barely rose above a whisper.

"You know this shall not pass. You conceal yourself from me, yet we all know your game."

Piero smiled, catching every word, as I knew he would— just as I had caught his scent. "Lucrezia, your faith in me warms my mortal heart."

Your heart is not mortal, I thought. *And my faith is as nails driven through flesh.*

But that he would even stand and speak to me, even across the width of the Arno: this was progress, to be sure.

"You have been warned." I raised my voice as the wind rose to push it downstream. "Join with us, and we will make this right." Prayers and the focus of my power rode upon the words.

His smile grew, or perhaps that was just the glint of the westering sun on the water rendering odd shadows. "Sorceress, my path is clear."

The response he would have to give, of course. But I had my own path as well, and my task. Again, I summoned my truest voice. "Three nights hence we meet under the full moon, atop Fiesole. Join with us."

He took a step back. I had kept my words casual, but if I spoke the command for him to join with us a third time, he would be compelled to obey.

Piero reached for his pocket. The scent of his musk rose, blocking out the reek from the ancient bridge downstream. The aroma tangled the threads of my thoughts and caused my hand to slip within my robes, feeling for the softness of my own skin.

A nip from Fain returned me to my senses.

I opened my mouth to speak the thrice-uttered compelling words, but Piero was gone. "Join with us," I whispered anyway. The wind carried the spell off harmlessly, compelling the boats to nothing at all.

oOo

In a small forgotten room in the basement of Il Duomo, I met with the Lady. She had been my superior since the last turn of our order, and it amused her to meet here, in the cradle of the god of men. We sat amid bolsters of glittering silk and a great rack of gilded beams once intended for a festival altar, or perhaps a bishop's folly. The room smelled faintly of incense, wine, and sweat; surely, odors brought in the last time these play-pretties were folded away, before they had been banned.

"The city is restless tonight." She stroked the fur of her own familiar, a golden ferret she called Mani.

I waited for her to continue. The Lady did not speak idly, though often times her words journeyed a route opaque to my comprehension.

"The man of San Marco stirs the mists in complicated ways."

Savonarola.

Nodding, I let my mind trail back over the events of the past year. The mad priest's passion had attracted the attention of our kind, for its purity and its fury. After his burning of the vanities, however, we'd lost interest. Just another zealot, riding the wave of his time.

And miscalculating, ultimately. As they always did. So why did the man's activities concern us any more?

"He has touched on something that we might wish to see to," the Lady said, to my unasked question.

I continued to listen. Fain sat on my shoulder, casting a suspicious eye on Mani while holding his peace.

But the Lady stopped there, instead asking of my meeting with Piero.

"I do not know if he will come," I admitted. "I was unable to bind him."

She nodded, her face a mask of pale beauty and dark power. "Try harder. You have two more days."

oOo

Whether from fear or inattention or over-confidence, I had wasted far too much time. I did not even know where Piero spent his waking hours, much less where he made his bed.

Now I had to find him and bring him into our midst. No longer the luxury of avoidance for me, of ambivalence: the Lady had spoken her command. I complied.

It was easier thusly.

Or so I told myself.

A return to the river would be a waste of time. Like the Virgin Mary, he would not appear in the same place twice. So I turned to magic.

In a quiet alley intersection, witnessed by none but a nervous cat, I burned three sticks of rosemary and a twist of cinnamon bark under the blue cross of the sky above. I spoke the incantation into the scented smoke, then closed my eyes and followed my nose.

Lavender. Musk.

East.

Fain clucked like a tiny, agitated chicken. I steadied him as best I could with a trembling hand, then lifted him to his perch within my robes. "We go."

The bright sunlight of false spring shone as we walked, fast drying the mud of the streets. It was very nearly pleasant. Yes, something was certainly amiss.

Eastward we went, following the scent of the man. The scent that tugged at the very heart of me.

No: I would not harbor these thoughts. My path was clear.

oOo

I found him in a field of grass outside the city, halfway to the Palazzo Pitti. He had spread a dark green blanket upon which he sat, sipping from a tiny porcelain chalice that steamed like a cup of sin itself.

My heart thudded in my throat as I approached. His black curls glinted in the sun, bright from the natural oils and unguents that such as he would anoint himself with. A small spray of lace at his breast was mostly hidden by a blood-colored tunic. The eyeleted paleness was tickled by a few dark hairs peeking around the edges, the merest hint of a solid masculinity underneath. Fain kicked out with his claws, scratching the tender skin of my breast and sending droplets of warm blood to pool in my navel even as I walked.

Reaching within, I pressed my shift against the blood, praying that the stain would remain hidden under my robes as I approached the edge of the blanket.

"Come," he said. His eyes were dark dying suns as he lifted a silver pot over a second chalice. "May I?" Steam rose from the spout.

"Thank you." I folded my legs beneath me, sitting on the grass with what I hoped was an elegant motion. Fain murmured and settled, poking his beak out of the folds of my robe to gaze bird-mad at Piero, fooling no one.

He carefully poured out three teaspoons of a beverage darker than rock oil, then handed it to me.

I sipped. It was delicious: bitter, and hot, and full of fantastic magic. Coffee.

"You know this is forbidden!" The African beans would not come to this country for another hundred years or more.

"I do know that. Which is why I partake far from the city." He sipped the last from his own chalice, then poured another measure. "But you did not come here to debate mage law with me."

"No." I took another sip, rolling the beverage on my tongue before swallowing. It burned, but did not hurt.

"Come here." Piero patted the green blanket next to him. "It is not a binding; just a soft place away from the ants."

I watched his face: he spoke the truth. Besides, he would surely have already noted the aroma of my spilt blood, even from where I sat. I risked no further harm in coming closer to him.

Except for the lure of his sweet flesh, the thrilling of his musk-and-lavender breath, the black song of his eyes.

"No," I said, even as I moved onto the blanket beside him. "No."

Fain quivered against me, mewling and cooing. The breeze blew overhead, and the sun caressed my own dark hair, and the skin at my ankles. Far below us, the river Arno passed along its own path.

oOo

Back in my room, I cursed myself for such terrible weakness. Then I poured icy water from the basin onto the dried blood of my belly, not even permitting myself to gasp with the shock of it. I abluted my body thoroughly, until the porcelain vessel was red with my essence.

And still I could not sleep.

I would have liked to blame the noise from the street, for the crowds roiled and shouted below with the strength of madness and god-blinded passion and rebellion, but in truth, this was no different than so many recent nights. It would end badly for the priest, this much I knew. Whatever the Lady's game with him, I hoped she would bring it to bear soon. This tension would not hold for long before breaking.

Nor would my own.

Sighing, I rolled onto my side, gently so that Fain moved with me. The small comfort of his feathers and quick-beating heart did nothing for me.

I wanted Piero.

"No," I whispered to the darkness.

Yes, the darkness whispered back. *Yes.*

oOo

"Again you did not bind him."

"I am sorry, my Lady."

"In fact, it rather appears that *he* has bound *you*, in a manner of speaking."

That I could not argue with. I hung my head.

When I finally met her eye, I saw that she was smiling. And I recognized the look she wore.

Handing her a shade of a smile in return, I said, "I understand."

She nodded. "But hurry. We gather tomorrow at midnight."

oOo

I lay naked in the moonlight upon the softest bed in which I had ever rested my unworthy bones. Not *my* bed, to be sure; it belonged to a cadet daughter of the Medici family. She was on an extended holiday, taking the healthful waters in a convent outside of Trieste in an attempt to cure herself of an inconvenient swelling about the mid-section. Given enough time—oh, nine months, say—the problem would resolve itself, and she would return to Firenze.

By then, my work would be long done.

Fain perched on the footboard, curling his clawed feet around the ornately carved wood. He held his head so as to keep one eye on the open window and one on me. I settled even more comfortably among the silk-covered pillows and allowed myself a small sigh of pleasure. The feeling of the young Medici's linens against my skin made me question my very path in this life.

A gentle breeze sent me a breath of the night air and stirred the gauzy magenta fabric with which the girl had adorned the marges of her window. Queens' coronation gowns had been made with less fine stuff. But even this marvelous cloth could not keep out the smell of the street below: mud, horse shit, sour cooking oil...as well as lavender and musk.

Piero was at the window, and then he was in the room.

And then he was in the bed.

"I knew you would fall to me," he whispered as he covered my traitorous, willing body with desperate kisses. "I knew you would come here."

No matter that the note had been mine. I do possess some small magic, you know.

I writhed and turned beneath him, welcoming him to me, luxuriating in the feel of his leanness against my body. He had been in the fields recently; his skin smelled of grass, tasted of crushed sage and a hint of dust. I bit his arm, gently, savoring the lushness of him. Seeking to know him.

He growled and tumbled me over onto my belly, then clutched my thighs, moving his hands slowly and deliberately up to my rear. Cupping its roundness, he leaned in and returned my bite: first on the flesh, then dipping a quick tongue to my nether eye.

The mark of a sorcerer.

But then, I already knew that.

"Not so fast," I murmured even as the pleasure threatened to blind me. I allowed him one more sip at my pot of dark honey before I twisted around. In one swift motion, I turned him over and climbed up to top him, holding him down with strong hands.

Piero grinned up at me, even as he tried to hide the flash of shock in his eyes. He hadn't known me for such strength.

I leaned down and kissed him, filling his mouth with my own tongue. He tasted of me, of course, but beneath that he was fresh-baked bread and more of that cursed coffee. I could get used to kissing this man.

Pulling away, I reached down to untie his pants. "We are at

an imbalance," I said. "I am bare and you are clothed."

"We can fix that." He wriggled out of his trousers and linen drawers beneath, while his shirts fell away almost of their own accord. The dark hairs of his chest were even lusher than I had imagined. I buried my nose in them, then kissed his ruby nipples, one after the other.

I still sat astride him, holding his hips with my knees. His eagerness strained up to meet my sweetpocket, which I kept just out of reach, smiling down at him as though I were playing a game.

Finally, I lowered myself a fraction of a measure. "Join with me."

"Oh yes," he whispered.

And I lowered further. "Join with us." Then I took him into me, with the oldest binding magic of them all.

In the corner, Fain cooed and put his head under a wing.

oOo

The morning light found me alone in the tangled blankets and crushed pillows. I smiled as I allowed myself to remember our night, moment by moment, a slow, savoring retelling. After I'd bound him, he was my plaything for many hours, rough and tender both. And even though he had escaped with the dawn, I knew he would appear at midnight.

The Lady would be pleased.

With reluctance, I got out of the Medici daughter's bed and found my clothes and my familiar. Fain slipped into my robes, clucking at the love-bites and bruises on my satisfied flesh before he settled into place.

Then I left the room as it was. Maids would tell stories of witches and sorcerers haunting the night, and they would not be wrong.

I spent the day sleeping in my hidden chamber, conserving my strength for the ritual to come. So I missed the commotion in the Piazza della Signoria—the shouts of the crowd, the nailing together of the giant cross, the dragging of the chains. The sickening, mouth-watering smell of roasting flesh finally woke me.

Rushing down to the piazza, Fain fluttering about my head, I arrived in time to see Savonarola and two of his acolytes fall to the flames.

On the far side of the fire, Piero's gaze caught mine—a cruel and fiery echo of our first meeting across the Arno. He shook his head, gentle and sad, before he vanished. Such an audacious working....

oOo

"He *was* bound," I said.

"Yes." The Lady gazed at me, her face even paler under the moonlight. "I have to think on this."

"He cannot loose his magic in the world." I paced the small circle we had built with the stones of Fiesole, looking down on the valley of the Arno and the sleeping farms, each with their wary watchlight guttering to keep the likes of us at bay. The rest of the order would be here soon, and what would we tell them?

"I think he shall not," she answered, speaking slowly. "To pull himself from your call—he had to undo *all* his bindings. Not just the most recent one. And he was forced to unleash a great terror upon the entire city in order to do even that much."

I stared at her. The flames, the mad priest brought down, the vanities of piety burning brighter than even gilt and paste jewels. "Of course." Excitement and relief flooded through me. "So we *have* defeated him!"

The Lady chuckled. "Oh, no, Lucrezia—I am afraid we have done no such thing. Set him back a bit, perhaps; bought ourselves more time. But he will return."

At the bottom of the hill, I could see a small group of women beginning their climb. "What can we do?" I asked. "What happens next?"

"Be patient," she whispered. "Be vigilant. Wait and watch." Then she turned to greet the others.

oOo

I stood below the Medici girl's window. The bells of Lauds had rung not long past; dawn would invade the world soon.

It was dark within. The shutters were drawn. I could see no tender fabric, no welcoming bed. Fain slept unknowing against my aching breast.

One more glimpse. Just one more scent of lavender, and his sweet, sweet musk. That's all I ask.

The night air returned to me only mud and offal and the faraway reek of the Ponte Veccio butchers.

If this was defeat, I feared victory. I turned and walked slowly back to my room, my feet heavy on the rough cobblestones.

British writer **Tanith Lee** is the author of almost 100 books, over 270 short stories, as well as radio plays, television scripts, and poetry. Her work, which has been translated into over 17 languages, ranges across fantasy, science fiction, gothic, Young Adult and children's books, contemporary, historical and detective novels, and horror. In 2009, she was awarded the prestigious title of Grand Master of Horror. Her other major awards include the August Derleth Award for *Death's Master*, the second book in the *Flat Earth* series.

About "Question A Stone," Tanith writes, "My husband suggested this idea—not the first time he's done that! He also, having heard its description, named the inn. The two swordsmen and the swords themselves quickly made themselves known, including the backgrounds to the secret inner lives."

QUESTION A STONE

by Tanith Lee

About twelve miles from the city of Sincash Mahr, the inn called The Chameleon's Arms rose from the salty plain. Unlike the plain, or the massive mountains—so cruel and skeletal and tall—that themselves loomed about a hundred miles beyond the city, this inn was a paradise.

Once a palace, now a lodging-house of endless rooms and suites and courts, kitchens and libraries, gardens and cultivated forests, fountains, statues and secretive glades, it cost a fortune to stay there, even for one night.

But sometimes a single night is quite enough to turn a quartet of lives on their collective ear.

oOo

Amongst the weaponic admixtures of metals, those which use black iron, or red iron, are considered superior, whilst those which also employ the subtle and serpentine ore known as mercurix are both typical and unique. The natures of such blades possess quite distinctive characters. Arguably genders. Allegedly souls.

From *The Book of Swords XIV*

oOo

Talzen was tired, but hopeful. He had ridden for three days and much of the two nights between, before he came in sight of The Chameleon's Arms.

"There, Cinnabar," he said to his mare as they walked between the high gates. "Did you ever see a finer sight?" The horse, with unconscious wit, shook her head, her bronzy mane catching the many lights of the inn. Talzen laughed softly and stroked her neck. She was a princess among horses, strong as a lion and far more polite.

The gates, which were heavily gilded, were covered in myriad wrought-iron depictions of chameleons. The broad avenue that ran towards the front of the inn was columned on either side by fifty-foot flame-cypresses, each like a black plume, in the well-trimmed branches of which twinkled little chameleon amulets. Beneath the trees, spaced at intervals of twenty paces, stone chameleons held up lamps. There were plenty of live examples in the grounds as well, so Talzen had heard. This was an eccentric place, worth the hardship of finding. His last employment had been both dangerous and dull, an odd combination. But it had provided enough coins that Talzen could now wallow in chameleon comforts for a whole Sincashian tlok, approximately nine days. He was in fact only planning on a qath—four. His next bout of toil lay in the city.

After dark, as now, you could just make out Sincash's own lights in the distance, a muffled glow like a fallen rosy cloud.

The mountains on the far side were a different matter. He had been looking at them for quite a while as he rode. Others had named them the Bones of Fate. They looked it, carved now from the night and only sketched in white at their upper ridges with early snow. But the plain was still hot as a cauldron, and even once the sun was gone, the rough pushy breeze, strident from blowing for thousands of acres without any upright opposition, came in warm and tindery gusts, smelling of burnt grasses and scorched rock, russet dust, and the ghost of a sea long drained away into the south.

It would be good to lie in a bath for an hour, thought Talzen, with a Sincash flagon of plum qvass to hand. Then dress up and go down to a good dinner. And all the while knowing the horse was being groomed and burnished, and stuffed with royal roots and oats and sweet water.

Then, just as they came into the first courtyard, with a courteous servant gliding bowing towards him, Talzen experienced a premonition. He had had them before. This one was of the usual type. A heaviness in his gut, a sense of vague physical unease, as if at the onset of a fever; a sort of momentary flicker across his vision—as though the scene had trembled, like a backdrop in some theatre far to the west.

Talzen stood still and waited. The mare, accustomed to his ways, did as he did. Perhaps half a minute passed, or a handful of seconds. Certainly the bowing servant had only just reached him when Talzen felt the hunch lift away and fade into thin air.

He did not often have to suffer such things. Which was as well, since invariably the prediction was a true one, yet the character of the presage was *never* immediately revealed. Unhelpfully, it was always a simple warning, as if some spirit whispered aggravatingly in his ear, "No, I can't say *what* it is— but be *on guard*. Be wary. *Something* is about to occur."

To all appearances, Talzen was quite at ease as he spoke pleasantly to the servant, handed over Cinnabar with a list of instructions to a ready groom, tipped each man generously, and walked on into the entrance hall of the inn.

But Talzen barely saw the blue-washed walls and garnet-coloured pillars, nor the hundreds of chameleons painted or made from semi-precious materials, that covered almost every inch, including the mosaic on the floor.

Talzen's trained gaze went everywhere, unhurriedly and thoroughly, for the moment dismissing anything purely decorative.

However, ironically, when finally he spotted the Trouble of which he had just been warned, it did take a very decorative form.

The man was one of a company of five men, himself obviously their leader. Tall, straight and lean, with wide shoulders and the longest legs in the finest incised leather boots, he had hair blacker than any night and a pair of eyes the exact shade and quality of a tiger's. That he was the pivot of the foreboding was also undeniably clear. If not why.

All five strode across the foyer and off on the long walk that led a quarter of a mile to the main dining-room.

Even after they had vanished from sight, Talzen lingered by a pillar, pretending to study a small chameleon perched on a pedestal and seemingly made from a ruby, until it winked at him and turned grey as his cloak.

By the stars, thought Talzen, between amusement and alarm, *is that black-haired man the one I'm to be careful of? As if I wouldn't anyway. My God.*

With which his heart rapidly agreed, not to mention his loins, which were also determined to inform him that they, too, were now *very hungry.*

What a beautiful man. Handsome as a panther. Twice as dangerous, from the look of him. That sword—that's black iron and haematite—and mercurix, unless I've forgotten everything I ever knew. You don't put anything else into a scabbard of that sort, unless you're a total idiot. And he doesn't seem to be.

Inadvertently, Talzen found he had put his hand on the pommel of his own sword, which was itself of *red* iron and mercurix.

At this instinctive and lascivious pun, Talzen almost smiled. But he was taking no chances. Instead he followed the servant to his allotted room, and in fifteen minutes was lying naked up to his chin in water at first scalding, then as heady and relaxing as the flagon of plum qvass he drank.

Presently, irresistibly, Talzen's thoughts turned themselves again towards the black-haired stranger. They imagined him in other circumstances and rather less formally dressed. Almost sleepily, Talzen found his hand now strayed along the lean length of his own body to the *other* sword, which like a firm-fleshed, greedy waterlily was raising an inquisitive head above the lake of the bath.

Talzen reminded his thoughts of the warning. He told the

ardent flower to lie down again, and removed his hand from its temptation. Nor was he an idiot. He would not have survived this long at his trade of swordsman, if he had always indulged himself. And tonight he had better be sharp.

oOo

Andreis, black-haired and tiger-eyed, was not especially tired. He had, by that evening, already been lodging at The Chameleon's Arms for nearly two days. The work he and his men had carried out in the city of Sincash Mahr was accomplished. Remuneration had been prompt and extravagant.

The four men of Andreis's band had also decided to treat themselves at the inn, which he had gone along with, of course. They were never, except in a fight, his chosen companions.

At the inn, he had been able to spend some well-earned time by himself, nevertheless, leaving them to their normal hobbies of boozing, sex and gluttony. He spent hours in the libraries, poring over scrolls, books and manuscripts, or listening to recitals by the two-stringed cinorit and the sgy, the throat-flute. His men were due to leave after dinner tonight on another errand, travelling to the east. Andreis had therefore, with cheerful social deception, come to dine with them. He had also made private arrangements to couch, later on, with one of the inn's very appealing Honey Maidens.

Meanwhile, out in the spacious stables, his patrician stallion, Ruffian, who was the colour of black slate and with the most rare blue-grey eyes, would already, doubtless, be mating with The Chameleon's own chosen mare.

Andreis valued these oases in the desert of his labours. Valued them so much perhaps because aware he would, too, grow bored with an alternate overall oasis of rest and relaxation.

The entry hall, as ever, was full of people—arrivals, departers, servants, and several live chameleons, changing their colours with sorcerous abandon and occasionally sprinting across the hall to accompanying screams of fright or wonder.

Andreis additionally noted a young man in the foyer. Though travel-worn, he was a beauty of his kind, or so Andreis judged. A thick mane of hair, the shade of some light brown, polished wood, fell to his shoulders. Something about him, a sort of swagger apparent even as he stood quite still, studying a small chameleon on a plinth, suggested he too was in the sworded trade. There was a feral female quality attendant on his youthful masculinity, though nothing at all feminine.

Andreis turned into the corridor that led to the dining-room. His men were joking and jolly. He had trained them long ago to behave themselves in decent places. Only Bracer was sometimes a problem. Andreis decided he had better keep an eye on Bracer. And so Andreis forgot the young man in the foyer, and never even considered that the sword at the young man's side was, most likely, of the best, admixed, as was Andreis's own, from two or three blended smelts of Boar Iron Steel, climaxed by mercurix.

oOo

When Talzen had bathed and put on his best clothes, which were quite impressive, he too set off on the walk that led to the dining-room. He was entranced to find the corridors wandered circuitously between inner gardened courtyards roofed by crystal, and lit with painted lanterns, galleries of statues, armour and mechanical toys, and alluringly curving staircases guarded by marble chameleons, and each ascending—but to where?

His famishment had been stayed by the qvass, and in the end curiosity got the better of him. Already able to hear the faint welcoming rumble of the dining-room, he detoured and went up the very next stair. Its curve took him swiftly from the corridor, and next out on to a flat roof of the inn. Here was another garden, with exquisitely cut shrubs and small trees in urns of sandstone and alabaster, and a fountain playing from the translucent jaws of a chalcedony dragon. It was now quite a breathtaking night. The enormous stars of the plain were wheeling with unseen motion, like giant jaspers and diamonds, from the east to the west, and even the Smoky Way was quite visible, like a colourless rainbow of ice.

As he stared appreciatively upwards, Talzen became aware

of a different sound than that of plashing water and the wind-rushes of the leaves.

He had heard such noises enough times to know he disliked them.

"Honourable sir, let me go," entreated the girl. But the honourable sir failed to comply.

God above. Was there never to be peace anywhere?

Talzen did not, for a second, stir. He watched shadows and dim lights struggle in among the foliage, and heard now the clank of a metal jug falling to the tiles of the roof.

At this, Talzen went forward. He parted the branches and regarded a tall, well-built man, who was holding the servant girl by her arm and her hair. It was blue-black hair and a petal-soft arm, but that was not why Talzen spoke, and extremely loudly in fact.

"Excuse me, I regret the impairment to your hearing, old man. Let me help, as you're so deaf. She asked you to LET HER GO."

The man was glaring at him. He seemed oddly familiar—had Talzen already seen him tonight?

"Flounce off," said the man.

"No," said Talzen.

He moved forward between the trees and instantly the other drew his sword from its scabbard. It was a good blade, but made only of cobalt steel.

A buzzing and murmuring was audible. Some other people, until now up on the roof to watch stars or bill and coo, were clustering round to view what now went on. They had, of course, paid no heed at all to the girl's entreaty; it was a commonplace.

Talzen did not draw his sword. You did not draw a sword like Talzen's for such an impoverished little event, and thus were equipped in other ways. Talzen simply did this: slapped his right hand on the pommel to attract attention there, while shooting out his left foot to stamp down hard on the bastard's right foot; Talzen then clubbed him foursquare on the under-jaw as he leapt in the air. Down fell the unknown-known man and lay still as a bundle of bones.

Some of the watchers laughed, and a couple applauded. The poor little girl ran away. Talzen wished he might have calmed her, but she was gone.

He gave the amused audience one glance. Then he took himself back off down the stair and on towards his dinner. It was only as he entered the huge, ornate room, with its transparent ceiling and picture-painted walls, that he recollected his premonition. Trouble had been before him...it had even revealed its source. How could he have associated that oaf upstairs with such a source? Yet he should have done. For now Talzen recalled where he had seen the oaf before, and with whom. It was not hard to do, for there across the crowded room the *other* was, the panther with the tiger's eyes.

Ah, excrement on excrement.

oOo

"Forgive me that I must interrupt your meal," said Andreis, as he stopped beside the table. "But unfortunately you and I have something to discuss."

Talzen looked up at him in dreary self-annoyance. Which with a flick of expression sometimes bewildering to others, he changed to the lightest arrogance. "Pray sit. Have some wine. It's from Khavalisc. The 18th Year."

Andreis raised an eyebrow. "That won't be necessary. But I will sit." He sat.

Was ever such male grace surpassed?

Damnation, thought Talzen.

"Perhaps an apple then? They're at perfect ripeness."

"Forgive me again," said Andreis, who had too quite a wonderful voice, "but I dislike to share food or drink with anyone I shall presently kill."

Talzen's face settled. He looked at Andreis under his long lids and with grey immovable eyes. "Go on."

"I run a company. Our business depends on public perception of our shining skills. Where this fails, compensation is needed. Upstairs on the roof, it seems, and in front of quite a throng, you set on a man of mine. You knocked him out, which made a fool of him."

"No," said Talzen. "God did that."

Andreis did not smile. Nor lose his temper. He was cool as twilight on the frozen mountains. "You'll meet me tomorrow morning at an hour convenient to us both. The gardens here are licensed for dueling. What sword do you have?"

Talzen, whose face was now like pale bronze, stood up and let the other man see the sword, where it hung concealed in its revealing advertizement of sheath.

"That's good," said Andreis. "Red iron, yes?"

"And yours is black."

"Exactly. Well suited, then."

"Suppose I refuse," said Talzen.

"I shall have someone or other drag you down, and then kill you anyway. If you discredit members of my company, you lose me my livelihood. Commercially, I'm bound to eradicate the fault. No hard feelings. It's nothing personal."

Talzen sat down again. "I have things to do tomorrow morning. It had better be the seventh hour. Then I can get on afterwards."

"You shouldn't anticipate that," said Andreis.

"You are so sure of your talent."

"None more so."

"I, unfortunately, know nothing about you."

"My name is Andreis. From Ateni, and Khinai."

"And I am—"

"I know who you are. Some of your audience upstairs were thrilled to inform me. Talzen of Bucaresa Ruman. I regret I'd never heard of you 'til then."

"'Til seven, then. If it suits you."

"It will do," said Andreis. He stood up once more. "Don't be sulky," he added, with a freezing laugh that might not be feigned. "I won't keep you long tomorrow. It will scarcely hurt."

Talzen managed to give Andreis his most gorgeous and charming smile. "It won't hurt *me* at all," he said. "I can't promise the same for you, I'm afraid."

The dining-room all about had fallen deeply silent, as some

hundreds of ears were stretching, and eyes peering sidelong or over wine glasses, or into handy mirrors to get the view second-hand. Once Andreis had quit the hall, another swarm of conjectural conversations flurried up.

Looking now as sulky as he wished, Talzen drained his glass and, leaving another generous tip, left the table.

Although he swore by them continuously, he did not think he believed in any gods. Had he done so, he decided, he might have visited one of the tiny shrines and temples scattered about the grounds of The Chameleon's Arms. And there thrown a raw egg at the god of good luck.

oOo

Andreis climbed the longer stair to his private apartment. He had taken a suite, comprising a bedroom, two parlours and a large bathing chamber. Just as well, since now he wanted space to pace around, unseen.

He was very angry, but the anger of Andreis was generally cold.

Bracer was a numbskull, and he, Andreis, should have kept a tighter rein on him, for sure. But then the dolt had only gone off to visit the latrines; for God's sake, did he need a nursemaid for that? Besides, his rank conduct—also reported by the crowd from the roof—had caused Andreis to dismiss him temporally from his duties. The other three knew better than to grumble, and had ridden off on their own mission. Bracer by now, sore head and all, was on a waggon trailing back to Sincash.

Andreis ended his prowling and went to a window to gaze out on the night. It was a fine one, the sky an orchard of stars. He clearly observed the icy Smoky Way, to which twice women, and once a man, had compared Andreis himself—a cold and impossibly distant display, the heart of which might never be reached.

But Andreis was not inevitably cold. It was only a part of his armour, as, he suspected, that vivid charm and over-confidence of Talzen's might be.

How old was Talzen? Andreis believed some four or five

years his junior. *And I am not old.* It was a tragedy and a bitter crime to kill a man so young and...promising.

I would rather have taken him to bed than packed him off to paradise in the morning.

Which reminded him he must now cancel the Honey Maiden also.

Soon after, Andreis stripped, laved himself with water, and darkened the lamps before he kneeled to his own gods. He *did* credit other beings, supernatural and more complex, though they would have emerged as he had, and all men, from the vast potential of a faceless, formless, all-encompassing God.

"Forgive me tomorrow's sin. It is unavoidable."

A chameleon the colour of the night perched, glittering faintly, on the window's sill. Then, as if only to demonstrate that it could, it altered in one swift tidal blush, from silver-dark to scarlet, burned there an instant like a fresh ember, then slipped away along the wall.

oOo

A female sword is often likely to be outgoing and adventurous. She is most frequently found in the keeping of a strong and masculine man, and will very probably represent a number of his more secretive or aesthetic qualities, while additionally revealing some of those traits he himself has restrained. A male sword, conversely, may be flirtatious and inconsistent when not engaged in actual combat. He will often be found in company with a man whose female elements, while perhaps not overt, run parallel with his masculine side. This sword is canny and has something to him of the magician. However, under extreme stress he may be prone to break, if seldom physically then in some deeper and more insidious way. It is never wise to underestimate the personality of either the male or the female sword, nor the inner world where, partly, they always remain after mining, smelting, casting, smithing and seething.

From *The Book of Swords XXI*

oOo

This place is not like the inn. Not like the plain either, or the mountains. There are no cities, even distant ones.

Constantly the surface of the ground moves in slow, rippling waves. Decidedly it *is* ground. It is covered by a velvety lawn of moss or unusual grass, of a scintillant blackness. This resembles, maybe, the dense short fur of a cat. Yet it is constantly in a dancerish motion, not as grass—or fur—moves in a wind, but rather as the plangent and regular, muscular movements cross a tidal lake.

Strange tall plants rise from the lake-like earth. They are inky, or of a soft pewter shade. Transparent blue crystals hang from some, and quietly chime as they stir and swim forward, backward, with the rhythm of the ground-lake.

The surface is also fairly flat. Ghostly low hills seem to contain the area in a rim of deeper blue. Above, the sky—is it sky?—is hazy, milky. It holds light, mild, and very cool.

Now and then, only noticeable if a viewer can be very quick, veins of another substance, a sort of liquid copper, seem to glisten along the smooth curved edges of the rippling ground, or to spangle a moment in the crystal buds of the plants.

Sirrib is standing on one slope of a rounded hump, perhaps a rock, staring away over the landscape. She is visible only from the waist up. She has long white, streaming, gleaming hair, the white skin of a very young woman, and large coal-black eyes. Her lips are red. She is wrapped in a kind of stole or shawl of black and silvery fibres, which describe artistically her slender but definitely female shape.

Gradually you become aware that she keeps raising to her eyes a sort of spy-glass. She scans in all directions, and this way any other watcher in able to take in the full beauty of her form, as far as it is visible, and her face. She has a passionate face, frankly. Despite the priestess-like immaculacy of her features and bearing, her perfect mouth is nearly—dare one say—*greedy.* Greedy in a *lovely* way; who, that has themself any appetite, would not *desire* to be eaten by such a lovely, beautiful, ravenous rose? Imagine the perfume, and the holy pressure. But then, she is looking, not for *anyone*, but for someone. So much is evident.

Inadvertently or not, the watcher may then move about the contour of the rock. That way at last they must see plainly enough how Sirrib is herself growing up from the rock, since below her hipbones she seems embedded there. This does not impede her circling movement, but surely it must otherwise hold her in place. And she seems not to mind this imprisonment, if such even it is. In any case, the round rock also moves in constant ripples, and over them fleck tiny sequins of gilding, a serpentine highlight.

She lowers the viewing glass in both beautiful pale hands. A flock of slim, black and white birds flies over.

Sirrib shuts her eyes. She appears to sleep. And when she does this, all of her sinks slowly down into the slot in the rock. Only the platinum-blonde crown of her head is then to be noted.

Ripples of luminous tiger's-eye follow in the wake of the birds across the sky. And a mellow darkness, debatably nightfall, closes the vista.

oOo

His country is not like hers. It is all blood-ruby, brass and mahogany.

It is too, from horizon to horizon, a type of sea, certainly an enormous body of water, in which peculiar sub-aqueous creatures are in some form moving about, but in the slowest motion, like snakes indigenously active in treacle. Above, the sky may be a sunset, or a dawn. It is orange and crimson.

Flamuro himself is held in the hot, baked-to-a-cake solidness of the water, from just below his narrow hips. His torso is clad in a fabulous breastplate of brazen metal, incised with gold. His skin, where bare on face, neck, and muscular arms, is tawny as an eagle's wing. His hair is like a fire. His eyes are violet, almost purple in tone.

Flamuro too scans his world, from side to side, in all directions—if directions even exist here. He does not use a spy-glass. What he holds in his strong musician's hands is a set of pipes, each of which plays a weird and animal cry, sometimes like the fluting of a bird, or like the howl of a wolf, or the purring of a cat. He tries these sounds out, one by one, or sometimes in a chord, then waits a minute, as if listening to hear if any resonance is struck, away over the edges of the limitless and generally unmarkered sea. It seems also sometimes he thinks he *can* make out a reply. Then he tries that special sound again; aiming it in the exact direction as before. But in every instance, after each second attempt, he frowns slightly and gives up.

Once, once only—at least at this time—a pearly whiteness evolves and quivers through the nearly solid amber of the sea about him.

Flamuro is visible below the sea's surface only as a dark, possibly tapering pillar. A sort of merman? The pearly whiteness however, circles the dark extension of his physical presence below the lid of the sea. When this happens, he seems briefly pleased, looks down, lowers one hand into the surely-impassible syrup which, nevertheless, allows the hand to enter and—very slowly—to move. He tries to catch, or to caress, the glimmer of white, which, at his attention, flares abruptly to a lightning flash of sapphire. Then it goes out.

When this occurs, Flamuro curses. He has a voice, even if it is composed of similar sounds to those of his pipes. He seems angry, then sorry. A single starry tear that might be made of lava leaves one amaranthine eye. It drops in the sea and immediately vanishes, through being a perfect match.

The sky, if it is, is draining to mournful greyness, and suddenly Flamuro sinks straight down into the fixity of the water. Only the crown of his fiery head still shows.

Something with claws, and a lethal-looking tail, wends idly along through the sea.

A moon like yellow jade appears out of a hole in the perhaps-sky, and its light blanches everything to a blank, as darkness might have done but never does, here.

oOo

When mercurix is added into the composition of a pure sword, it will further inform the sword's nature. An occult empathy and random telepathy may then be experienced between a sword and its human keeper. But also, it has come to be thought, exclusively between certain swords. Some swords will accordingly seem to take against other weapons, though never those of inferior structure. Other blades may form between them bonds of friendship, or of the greater emotions. Several stories are recorded of such events, and of bizarre outcomes dependent on the effect. The curious sage, Solis of Zyre, when commenting on this alchemistry, claims that it is reckoned a phenomenon as unreadable as it is unpredictable. 'It has been said it would be far easier,' he tells us, 'to question a stone, for all the lesson we might gain from trying to fathom the metallurgic hearts of blades.'

From *The Book of Swords XXE*

oOo

An hour before the duel was due, Talzen woke, bathed, and otherwise prepared himself. After a light breakfast of rice and santh, he cleaned his teeth scrupulously and pared his nails. He felt miserable and had not slept well.

In the past, he had fought a number of duels. Of the ones which demanded a death, Talzen, self-evidently, had been the victor. But he disliked killing, which was either a curiosity or an obligation in a professional swordsman. On the other hand, he would, he had long ago decided, dislike *being* killed even more.

The notion of dispatching Andreis of Ateni and Khinai was dreadful. Perhaps it would be undo-able, anyway.

But Talzen had also the occasional handy attribute of a swordfighter: he found it next to impossible to believe he himself could die in that manner.

Across The Chameleon's Arms, Andreis as well had risen and made himself ready, with the addition of certain short private religious rites and physical and mental exercises. Andreis had, by this era of his life, killed sufficiently that he accepted it as a task. He attempted only to make the act as clean as each situation allowed.

He too, however, despite all his habituation and preparedness, felt depressed.

The notion of dispatching Talzen of Bucaresa Ruman seemed wasteful and unfair. Andreis did not, though, for a split second, imagine Talzen could kill *him*. This was less a swordsman's egoistic faith than the result of a prediction given him in his youth. He had been informed he would live into old age. And from various other things also then hinted at, and which had since taken place, he credited the prophecy...when he thought of it.

As both men descended to the inn grounds, the sun contrarily was just rising. Most of their fellow guests meanwhile were already up, drinking and eating hearty snacks before filing excitedly out to witness the fracas.

Upwards of five hundred people, estimated both Talzen and Andreis, were intent on providing an audience for the show. As the swordsmen walked out, by separate doors, on to the sandy paths among the glades, they were aware also of another crowd, this bundled up on the inn roofs, and looking down eagerly through telescopes.

The sky had been lavishly polished and broomed by the night wind, now fallen quiet. Birds trilled throughout the gardens. Many miles away, the mountains were barely to be seen, moltenly absorbed into the apricot east. Chameleons sat or clung on tree limbs, or the white arms of statues, but the chameleons, like the mountains, had copied carefully the colours of everything proximitous, and unlike the energized crowd, they went for the most part unseen.

The duelling ground was a wide open area, kept always mown and clear. It was surrounded by low flowering shrubs, which would obscure nothing of what went on. At the south end of the patch was a soapstone image of the Sincashian god of justice, who was represented as discouragingly eyeless, and besides lying down as if asleep. To the north stood an altar to all-gods, available to any worshipper, a kind gesture for anyone who might want to offer a quick one to some personal deity. Neither Talzen nor Andreis even glanced at these icons.

The sun of course was still low, and would get in both their eyes from time to time. Then again, it would not be directly overhead, scalding down and splashing on the blades at every twist and turn. Each man had fought in enough inconvenient spots and awkward lights, he scarcely bothered with the sun's angle.

One of the inn clerks ran up with a paper tablet for both to sign. This would safeguard the corpse's property for any heir. Andreis signed a signature of bold simplicity; Talzen a signature of flamboyant unreadableness.

At that, one of the inn's intercessory priests appeared and spoke a brief prayer to grant one or other protagonist reasonable judgement beyond death and/or alive following his successful kill.

Virtually everyone murmured the closing response, as politely did Andreis. Talzen only unnecessarily inspected his faultless nails.

The crowd withdrew to the margins of the open space. It had become the Field of the Duel. A deafening silence fell.

Even the birds, suddenly alarmed by something or perhaps having seen such matches before, disapproved and took off en masse like a shower of upward-tending, feathery hail.

With an obsidian rasp, both men drew from their scabbards their wonderful metallurgical weapons.

The sun, the day, time—the world—stood still.

Could anyone then look at anything save the naked blades? They were each like a searing flame or coal shot from the sun's core. One was black as death, one red as hell, and both visibly singing with mysterious inner rays, ambered on the black, lapis lazulied on the red. Who would doubt such swords could ever now be sheathed, until one at least had tasted the blood of a living heart?

Before that second, neither man had fully looked, today, at the other. Now, turning face-on, they must.

Talzen felt every bone in his body change to a liquid like red-hot qvass. It was not fear. *I am in love with him,* he thought, incredulous and horrified. *What can I do? I can't kill him—must*

I then let him kill me instead?

Andreis felt his heart flinch inside him. This was not fear either. He thought, *Can it be I want this man more than I want my reputation? Do I have to call off this bloody farce of duel, and make myself a laughing-stock worse than that dunderer Bracer?*

"Yes," he said, half aloud, cold as the southern continents.

"Yes," said Talzen, bleak as northern winters.

Any who heard the joint avowal took it for an oath of properly murderous intention. The audience itself went severally pale or dark or flushed with vicarious fear. It was a sacred if dire moment. Unmissable.

And what the audience had obviously relied on to happen next, next happened.

Both combatants were seen to raise their sword-arms, and leap together across the open turf.

Talzen thought: *No—what am I doing—*

Andreis thought: *I never meant to run at him—*

Each thought: *The blade has come alive in my grasp—*

Never ever before, through all their battles elsewhere, light or treacherous, threatening only or entirely merciless, had either man felt such vitality, such literal *life* in the sword he used. Now indeed, the blade used *him*. He had, for the first time—Andreis and Talzen equally—no control over any movement. It was the *sword* in each case which moved. Which *chose* to move. Nor could he let go of the fiery serpent, tusked iron and volcanic steel and quicksilver, that flared and lurched and *struck*—

They *struck* together, both blades, like clashing planets, they *struck* and veered away and roared with a soundless noise that was like an avalanche, or a great chunk of the sky that fell —and swung at each other and struck *again* and struck *again*—

Later the bystanders, some of them, declared they had been quite startled at this barbaric and ultra powerful mode of combat. They had expected the more playful finesse, the sallies and retorts and ripostes and tricks and nicks, which fine swordsmen generally utilized. But this, in its way, they must admit, was deeply engaging.

The air was sizzling and ringing, as if it were a glass bell being *struck* over and over from within, spinning and echoing, though never giving way.

Certain of the ladies and gentlemen fainted. Others felt drunk out of all proportion to any inebriant taken at breakfast.

On every tree or statue, had anyone noticed, the chameleons too were blazing like bits of the sun, ruby and jet, sapphire and topaz.

And the swords *struck*.

Now they *struck* like stars.

And then, in one cawing and coruscating wheel, blindingly they became a single *erupting thing*—which flew off on its own, sloughing the duelists so they staggered, and only a practiced athlete's balance saved them both from plummeting headlong.

There on the field of death, the sword of Talzen, *Flamuro*, and the sword of Andreis, *Sirrib*, plunged together into the ground. Which shook.

The irradiation and the swarms of sparks showering off, made complete accuracy of view difficult. Yet most or all present saw, and ever after swore they had, each sword, though still a metal blade, take on also the distinct likeness of a beautiful, partly-human but mostly spiritous creature. *She* was white and *he* was gold. That much seen, the rest was not in *any* doubt. Mouth to mouth, breast to breast, clawing and clinging, writhing and arching and calling like entities from some other far-off melodic yet blood-wringingly uncanny sphere, they were *coupling*. They were making the most willingly violent and gloriously will-less love. They were in congress. The sexual act. They were in paradise-on-earth.

How long coitus continued, very few persons were able to estimate. It seemed to last an hour at least...only the gods knew. But subsequent orgasm lasted, or so one scholar stated—if some years afterwards—for at least seven minutes by the shadow-track on a nearby sundial.

It was naturally, that climax, like a lightning strike. People believed they had been incinerated, and understandably shrieked. But no one was harmed. In fact, quantities later claimed assorted ailments had been cured, or a lost tooth grown back, such items.

As for the swords, they had seemed dissolved in the colossal light, and in the bellow of sound that *made* no sound. Then when the brilliance faded, there they lay side by side on the turf, not even dented, straight and still, lovely and unliving. Wonderfully fashioned inanimate objects of an ordinary and everyday world.

oOo

"Will I ever draw that—that *creature* again? How can I?"

"Neither of us knows. Maybe not. Or, maybe we can do nothing else. We'll nostalgically recall, won't we, Talzen, how their infamous lust brought us together here."

"In your luxurious bed. My God, Andreis, you must be rich as the King of Pazt, to rent a suite."

"And you only want me for my money."

"Oh, I *want* you. No, my turn for that."

"Be my guest. Like this?"

"Gods of fire... yes. Exactly—like—"

The day, begun in flame, but not blood, had gone on in flame.

They had picked themselves up, these two handsome men, from the place where they had, metaphorically at least, fallen on the field. They walked back, a couple of feet apart, courteously fending off the hysteric crowd, and each with his particular miscreant sword now firmly once more ensconced in its—*her*—*his*—sheath. No sooner up here in Andreis's opulent rooms than both unbuckled the swords and dropped them in a corner. Admittedly side by side. And then anyway other clothing unbuckled and undone, and scrambling on to the bed, or wherever first they came together—where *had* it been? Ah, yes, over there. Odds on, they were not the only couple to have been galvanized by the sorcerous dueted orgy seen in the gardens. Who cared? It had been of the best.

And no stigma now, no need to fight to a death. A miracle had occurred. Not the most stringently commercially-minded swordsman in the Six Hemispheres could argue with that. No one lost face. Only the impediments of garments and procrastination.

"I suppose you'll be off tomorrow," said Talzen, after a

further suitable interval of ecstatic exercise. "Off you will go. I'll never see you again. Just as well," he added. "I have no time—for this."

Andreis held him close enough for comfort. "I should have killed you, shouldn't I?"

"You have, my prince. You've stabbed and run me through more times than I can reckon. *And* killed me. Ah. The bliss of death."

"And likewise, you returned the compliment," said Andreis, adding with a mocking paternity, "my boy."

Days come and go. As do nights. Sleep makes demands and cannot be gainsaid. Even swords who, over vast distances both temporal and ethereal, telepathically meet and desire each other; even swords who manoeuvre their so-called 'keepers' into random action and related duels, in order blades can meet, mingle, meld and mate—even swords sleep sometimes, albeit, where feasible, side by side.

But when Talzen woke next midday, his lover, and his lover's sword, were gone. Talzen and his were alone.

They made their peace, as old friends usually must. By evening, sore but stoical, Talzen made on to Sincash Mahr. He noted as they went that his mare, Cinnabar, was relaxed and mysteriously smug, and was glad for her. He would try to be glad for Andreis, too, for Andreis's freedom—since Andreis would forget soon, of course. And Andreis himself all this while, thoughtful and slightly melancholy, his own weapon secure at his side, rode the sleek stallion Ruffian towards the east.

Nothing is forever. But then, forever, possibly, is also nothing.

oOo

The sage, Solis of Zyre, near the end of his treatise, however, adds that the questioning of a stone is, in actuality, not entirely foolish. He points out that any piece of stone, when closely studied by magnification, will render up certain truths. These may involve, through revealed strata, the ages of the earth, or even minerals, some valuable, or tiny fossils enfolded there.

Once, he claims to have found in a stone, the pristine mummified footprint of an ancient beast, now extinct. 'Stones,' he adds teasingly, 'are sometimes worth an inquisition.'

From: *The Book of Swords XZ*

oOo

From A letter by Andreis of Khinai
To Talzen of Bucaresa:

'And so I shall be journeying back across the plain in about a month. It would be a pleasure, and much more than this, to see you again, Talzen, at The Chameleon's Arms—I trust you'll permit me the honour of taking care of all finances during the visit?

'I admit I have some hopes you'll still be in the region. Having only recently learned my devil of a stallion, Ruffian, ignoring a pre-arranged tryst, instead possessed your charming and acquiescent mare, when last we all stayed at the inn. She'll be in foal. They always are. A nuisance for you, but I can promise the result will be a stunning horse. We might sell it, or rear it ourselves, what do you think?

'On the other hand, I *can't* promise you faithfulness, my boy. Nor you me, I believe. Maybe we can promise each other something. For the sake of the horses, not to mention the swords, which will be pining to renew their acquaintance. Not for ourselves, obviously, never that.

'While you wait for me, count all the chameleons. They say there are over three thousand. Tell me the total when we're together. It will help us pass all those long, tedious nights.

'Andreis, yours.'

Dave **Smeds** is one of today's most versatile writers; his repertoire includes science fiction, contemporary fantasy, horror, erotica, superhero, and more. His novels include *The Sorcery Within, Piper in the Night,* and *X-Men: Law of the Jungle,* and his short fiction has appeared in *Asimov's SF, F&SF,* and *Realms of Fantasy,* as well as many anthologies. *The New York Times Book Review* described his work as "stylistically innovative, symbolically daring examples of craftsmanship at the highest level." He particularly enjoys writing imaginary-world fantasy and often includes romantic elements and female viewpoint characters. Dave lives with his family in Northern California, where he has practiced goju-ryu karate-do for many years.

About "A Swain of Kneaded Moonlight," Dave writes, "the inspiration boils down to a simple observation that in situations where a male comes to the rescue of a damsel in distress, the damsel is usually playing a far more active role than the stereotype gives her credit for."

A SWAIN OF KNEADED MOONLIGHT

by Dave Smeds

Long ago, silver dripped from a crescent moon. The drops fell upon the land and became the glimmering brides. They were magical women. The great men of long ago won them as consorts—whether by force, seduction, or contract—and sired children upon them.

The brides lingered in the known realms until their children were grown. When their mortal flesh had aged and its grip upon them loosened, they slipped away. Now they are the stars that wander in the skies.

Or so they say.

I know there is some truth in the tales, because the moment I met Lissa, I saw the avatar marks. The color of her irises churned through shades from gold to burnt umber, as though smoke was pulsing in front of a setting sun. Her fingernails appeared to be mother-of-pearl. I admit those details fascinated me as they would anyone. But it wasn't our differences that mattered to me. It was how we were the same.

We were both eight. Both of us had lost our mothers to the cinder pox the year the Silk Coast traders brought it to our shores. And now we were both dwellers under the same roof.

That was a happy time.

Lissa was the ward of Firin, Lord of Osprey Harbor, who

had been her late father's friend. She slept in a bedroom she had known since age five. She was free to step out on her own balcony and wait for the fog to roll in and kiss her cheeks. She was able—with an escort—to explore the tidepools north of town or go out sailing on the bay.

I was Wyvva, the scribe's daughter. Of an afternoon, I would visit the chamber where my father composed the lord's bills of lading and copied ships' charts, and he would give me tea and candied lime and ask about my day. Of a morning, I would help Lissa learn the thousand runes of the North, the seven hundred glyphs of the East, and we would practice side by side with our quills and our iron-gall ink.

In the beginning, those lessons were my duty as a servant. They became a pleasure. All Lissa and I had lacked was a best friend, and now that lack was cured.

We played. We laughed. We became inseparable.

But eventually, the world around us turned to shit.

Now we were grown. My father's corpse had long since been heaved from the funeral bluff to join my mother's among the kelp and starfish. Lissa's foster father had gone into debt to his liege lord, the Duke of Mareswold, and been given little choice of what to surrender in payment. To me, Lissa was a sister of the heart. To others, she was a commodity.

Now our life was this tower room, with no view, and every breath heavy with inland heat. Now we were in the clutches of a maggot.

In a few minutes, we would meet a man who might, if luck continued to run sour, take her away to a worse place than this.

"How do I look?" she asked.

Her gown was dark as coffee. That and its cut took attention away from her curves. The wimple concealed her hair. Yet...

"Still worth throwing on a bed, I fear."

She turned green in the gills. I thought she might vomit on me. I stopped adjusting her sleeves and moved to the side. Unfortunately, that meant she glimpsed her reflection in the mirror.

She sighed.

We had tried to dim her beauty, but take a butterfly out of the sunlight and it is still a butterfly.

"I truly do not deserve this," she said.

"You truly do not," I replied.

A knock announced the arrival of our escort. Wood grated on metal brackets as the bar was lifted. A heavy key turned in the lock, and the door swung out into the sentry vestibule in the manner of a dungeon door.

The man in the vestibule was a guardsman named Obber. For all his muscles, he was a eunuch. The duke seldom trusted an intact male with the key to this chamber. I liked Obber. For all his leathers and the crook axe at his side, he was soft-spoken.

"His Grace summons you."

Had we been able to decline, we would have, but it was no good thrashing against the tide. We thrust our feet into our slippers and strode from our prison, faces smooth, postures stoic. Then it was down, down, down the steps of the spiral we had come to know too well these past many weeks, Obber clanking in our wake.

"Ah, here we are," I heard the Maggot say as Lissa crossed the threshold into the lord's parlor. "You can see every word I've told you is true."

I kept my eyes on the floor as I slipped into the maid's nook by the door, and Obber into the guard alcove. Once in place, I dared to level my gaze and take in the scene.

The Maggot was in his finest parlor wear, his shoulder cape embellished with gems large and small. He never dressed this way outdoors for fear some of his wealth might slip off and be lost in the mud. His guest was surprisingly shabby by comparison. The latter's ensemble was unadorned and, though made of expensive cloth, looked as though it would hold up on long campaigns spent in the saddle of a warhorse.

"His lordship Count Urley. The lady Lissa of Osprey Harbor." As usual, the Maggot was efficient in his introductions.

The count had perhaps once been handsome. Now his skin was tight against his bones, and creviced from weather, wear, and war. Perhaps when he had been seventeen, admirers might have called him slender. Now he was just gaunt. If he had anyone left who claimed to be admirers, they were remembering a man who no longer existed.

I could say one thing for him. His blood could still flow. He stared at Lissa as would a man half his age. Many who meet her find themselves disconcerted by the mutable quality of her eyes. Urley, however, gazed right back.

And licked his lips.

"Turn around. Let me see the other side," he commanded.

Lissa turned.

"Bend over a bit."

Lissa spun back around. Her spine had already been straight, as those things go. Now it straightened even more. Meanwhile I was trying not to choke on my own spit.

"No need for that," the Maggot told his guest. "Have no fear. I'm sure you'll find her mountable enough, should you make me a serious offer."

"I made an offer. Did it not sound serious?"

"It was inadequate by quite a margin," the duke informed him. "Or do you think an heir to be worth so little?"

"I'll pay more once she's proven herself."

"You can see the Brides' Marks for yourself. Has any woman bearing those signs ever failed to give her husband a son?"

"There's always a first time."

"In that unlikely event, you are free to demand a refund. But until I have payment in full in my treasury, you'll not so much as pluck a hair from her scalp."

They paused to exchange scowls, and Lissa saw her opening. "Your Grace? Do you need me any longer?"

The Maggot didn't bother glancing at her. He just waved his hand in dismissal.

Lissa retreated to the door before he could change his mind. I exited behind her, Obber dutifully ensuring that we headed back to the tower and not to the nearest way out of the castle.

Getting to the top level seemed to sap the last of the strength from Lissa's legs. I supported her by the elbow as we headed for the divan.

I had never seen her as listless and spent as this. But how could she not be, after the previous few minutes?

Obber's gentle comment caught up to us. "Do not fret, m'lady. His Grace won't let that scabby goat have you."

Lissa jumped. She had not realized our escort was still standing in the open doorway. Somehow even with his girth, he had the knack of disappearing from one's view.

Lissa tilted her head. "Will he not?"

"No. The goat's too cheap. Won't offer more than he already has."

I chuckled. How had we missed it? It was plain enough.

The worry lines in Lissa's forehead smoothed out. "Thank you for that, Obber."

"You are most welcome, m'lady." And with that, he closed the door. The key turned in the lock, the noise reverberating off the gaps between the tapestries.

oOo

By bedtime, it was clear Obber's assessment had been accurate. No summons had come, ordering Lissa to prepare to leave with the count. Lissa fell asleep at once, making up for the anxious wakefulness of the previous night. She was still asleep as I slipped out of my cubby into the main chamber the next morning.

I poured water from the ewer to the basin and washed my face. I tried to keep my mood high so as to greet my lady with it, but I knew too well the reprieve was temporary. There would soon be another suitor to take the count's place. He would surely be as old. Perhaps older—a greybeard desperate to make an heir while still capable of plowing the furrow. A younger nobleman could afford to select a wife from among the usual candidates, but not so with the ones who came, money in hand, to try to convince the Maggot to grant their petition. A woman who bore the Brides' Marks always conceived easily and always produced a firstborn son. That son bore the peculiar grace of his mother's heritage, and grew up robust, bright, able-bodied, and, if rumor was to be believed, unusually lucky in the face of chance. In short, he was progeny of the sort any lord or king wished to see as his heir. It didn't matter that subsequent children were more often than not female.

Lissa stirred. When I turned, I was surprised to find as radiant a smile on her face as I had seen from her since her foster father had confessed his inability to shelter her any longer.

"What is it?" I asked.

"My deliverer is on his way."

"Your—" I blinked. "How do you know?"

"I have dreamed it."

My insides bounced like sand fleas. This was what I had been fearing would happen. The ordeal had unhinged her mind.

"Um. When is he to arrive?"

"Soon." She brushed away the pillow-tangled hair from her face. Her cheeks were flushed, her lips plump, as if she had just been kissed.

"Wh-who is he?"

She closed her eyes, rolled on her side, and within moments was breathing deeply and regularly.

"Lissa?" I murmured.

She did not respond.

I decided it was best to leave her as she was. She slept soundly for another hour. Then, after a few minutes of tossing and turning, she sat up. Only then did she open her eyes.

She craned her head to gaze through one of the windows that ringed the chamber.

How those windows taunted us. Because summer was upon us, they were unshuttered, yet the ventilation gave us only minimal relief from the heat. The sills were set at half again the height of a man, so we had no view of anything but sky unless we shoved a chest against the wall and climbed upon it. Most of all, the openings gave the illusion that escape was within reach. But no. Even if we had possessed rope with which to rappel down the outer walls, it was a forlorn prospect. Lissa and I were both petite, but we were womanly enough that neither our bosoms nor our hindquarters would fit through such narrow apertures. They were pigeon's gates.

"Shall I ring for breakfast?" I asked, hand poised by the pull cord. I wasn't at all hungry, but at least the question might bring her home to port.

"Four days past full," she said. "That's good."

She was still staring upward. I sat on the bed next to her and was finally able to see what she was looking at. She was facing west. There through the window was a waning gibbous moon, a disc of silver within a rectangle of cerulean.

"Why is it good?" I asked.

She turned to me, as if just realizing I was there. "I don't know." She rubbed grit from her eyelashes. "Was I talking in my sleep?"

"I'm afraid so."

"What did I say?"

I told her.

"A deliverer. Wouldn't that be nice?" She mimed an executioner slitting her throat. Delivering her from this life.

She was her old self. Suddenly I was wistful for the Lissa I had so recently seen. The hopeful one.

"Breakfast?" I repeated.

"Bath first," she said.

"Before calisthenics?"

"No exercise today. I feel as though I spent all night hard at work. I want to do a lot of reading today. *The Tale of the Handsome Bladesman*, I think."

"Don't you know that one by heart?"

"It gets better every time. Don't you think?"

"I do," I admitted, and went to her cedar box to locate the book.

oOo

The day passed slowly, as every day of our imprisonment had. The maidservant who brought our supper let us know the Maggot had departed to visit the king's court. He would be gone four days.

"That's something to cheer," I said as we sat down to the meal.

"No, it's not," Lissa countered. "He'll use his time there to peddle my womb. There's no better place for that than court."

I patted her hand. "Then live in the present? Four days is four days."

She nodded, but without vitality. She ate only the soup and a few bites of bread.

oOo

Some time in the night, I woke with a start. Lissa and I were not alone. I was sure of it.

Heart pounding, I carefully, as surreptitiously as possible, parted the gauze curtain that isolated my sleeping alcove.

A man was standing by Lissa's bed. Moonlight glinted off the hilt of the sword at his belt.

I screamed.

Lissa thrashed and sat up, crying out.

I could not account for what I saw then. The intruder vanished. Not by ducking behind the bed. Not by running away. He had simply ceased to occupy the place he had been standing. The moonglow had been too bright and my eyes too well adjusted to the late hour to blame the effect on dimness.

The bar clanked to the stone floor outside. The key clicked sharply in the lock. Obber burst into the room, his axe in his raised hand. "M'lady? Are you well?"

"Yes," Lissa replied, with a calmness I knew was false but which would fool most who did not know her as well as I did. "It was just a dream."

The guard raised an eyebrow. Lighting a pair of chamber lamps, he made a quick inspection of the wardrobe, my maid's alcove, the privy nook, and the underside of Lissa's bed—the only places in our suite where anyone could be hiding.

He grunted. "Sorry to disturb. Good night."

As soon as he had secured the door behind him, I rushed to Lissa's side.

"Did you see him?" she asked. "The bladesman?"

"I—" Her question made me see what I had missed in the midst of my fright. The silhouette had been that of a lithe man wearing a hilted sword, the hat on his head embellished with a peacock feather.

As in the book.

"Was he handsome?" Lissa asked.

"I...I believe he was," I whispered.

"Then for all that you love me, don't scream next time."

She fell back on her pillow, eyes closing. It was then I realized she had not really been awake.

oOo

In the morning, she said nothing of the incident. I couldn't help but notice, though, that she moved around the chamber with a briskness she had not shown in weeks. Her brow was unfurrowed. She expressed interest in what clothes to put on for the day.

I hesitated to disturb this development with pesky questions, but at lunch I asked, "Your foremother, she had many powers?"

"So they say."

"Do you think it's possible you inherited more than you know?"

"You mean, more than the part that makes men want me as their broodmare? More than this?" She held out her hands, displaying the glistening nacre of her fingernails.

"Yes."

"I have no idea. I was so young when my mother died. She had no chance to tell me. Why do you ask?"

"I'll tell you tomorrow," I said.

oOo

That night, I waited until I was sure Lissa was asleep, then I pulled away the gauze curtain and sat on my bunk, watching. The hooting of an owl filtered in through the windows. The air wafting down took on a trace of coolness, though it was inadequate by my harbor-rat standards.

The moonglow began to shine directly into the chamber, and I thought to myself, a waning moon rises at night, so it is always in the sky during the hours before dawn, when dreams are richest.

Lissa's chest began rising and falling as dramatically as if she were engaged in heavy labor. Her mouth opened.

Her breath became visible. Grey mist. With each exhalation, the cloud grew at her bedside. Gradually, the cloud's shade deepened, and its shape grew more defined.

The cloud became the handsome bladesman. Tones of color inhabited his complexion. The metal of his accouterments began to gleam. He became as solid as any real man would be, lacking only motion to seem alive. And then he turned to me, lifting a finger to his lips for silence.

I nodded.

Lissa's breathing returned to normal. No more mist. Yet the bladesman remained. He caressed Lissa's check with the lightest of strokes before he quietly eased away from the bed and approached my alcove.

Gales of the north, he *was* handsome. Suddenly it occurred to me that my nightgown was clinging to my upper body like skin. I pulled the bedsheet higher.

"Who are you?" I asked.

"Do I need a name?" As I had, he kept his voice at low volume—quiet enough not to startle Lissa awake, and quiet enough that Obber would not hear us at all through the thick door and stone walls.

"Of course you do."

"As you wish. Do you have one to give me?"

I hesitated. The bladesman in the story was unnamed, save by description. That had been part of the character's allure. But I wasn't going to have a man in my bedchamber at night without knowing his name.

"Vannen," I said. It was the name my father had told me would have been used for my first brother, if my mother had lived long enough to bear a son.

"Vannen it is," he said.

"Why are you here, Vannen?"

"To rescue you." He drew his sword and thrust at the air.

My breath caught. He moved with such sureness I knew he could deliver a lethal blow to an opponent almost before a bout had begun.

"If you are ready, give a scream to draw the guard in, and I will dispose of him."

The thought made me hiccup. "No."

"Eh? I promise you it will be quick. Turn your gaze away, and I will be done before you turn it back."

"You cannot kill Obber," I said. "Kill the duke. Kill the chamberlain. Kill any of those spawn of privy piles that fetched us from Osprey Harbor. But not Obber. He has been kind to us."

Vannen swished his weapon right and left. He held it up to the moonglow. It shone. He had a right to admire it. It was a fine key to unlock our prison. Under other circumstances.

"It would trouble my lady greatly to think her liberty had been won at the cost of Obber's life," I said firmly. "Surely you were not made to bring her such pain."

He sighed. He thumbed the opening of his scabbard, poising the sword to slide it back in. "You vex me."

"I'm sorry."

"If I am to spill no blood tonight, what am I to do?"

I barely had to think about it. "Spill sweat instead," I said. "Show me your dance."

He cocked his head and gave me a smile. It was just like the smile in the story, the one that made the damsel give up her plan to remain a maiden all her days.

"As you wish," he declared.

He began the dance slowly, displaying the techniques in a way I could follow. Then he repeated them at speed. He thrust. He parried. He charged. He withdrew. I had seen fencing dances before, but not of this level.

Truly, Obber owed me his life.

After a quarter hour, the heel of Vannen's boot happened to bump against the corner of the wardrobe, a sharp thwack of hardened leather against oak. Lissa gave a soft cry and opened her eyes.

Vannen disappeared. A faint haze of mist lingered for an

instant, then that, too, was gone.

Lissa lifted her head from the pillow. "What's going on?"

I rushed to her side. "We need to make some plans," I said.

oOo

The next night, Lissa understandably could not fall asleep right away, but ultimately she managed it. Her breath turned silver. Our visitor manifested.

He was just a boy this time. Eleven, perhaps twelve years old. Mature enough to have some strength to him, but with none of the bulkiness of a man's physique. He had a long coil of rope draped over one shoulder.

I was sitting on the divan, the better to watch the magic. As soon as he was capable of movement, he joined me.

His smile was the same as it had been. He was still Vannen, even if he had no beard, no sword at his belt. In some ways, I found him more approachable. Not so intimidating. I put my hand on his knee as he sat down.

"I feel so much lighter this way," he said.

"Well, that is the idea," I replied. I gazed up at the row of windows.

He studied the openings as well, then measured out the width of his hips. "Yes. I think I will fit. Only one way to know."

We moved a trunk against the wall and he hopped onto it. He tied one end of the rope securely to a torch bracket and tossed the coil through a window.

Getting through the narrow aperture took him several minutes. Even if Lissa and I had been as skinny, neither of us could have managed it. Vannen had to twist and hold his body in position with the support of torso muscles alone. He had to grip the masonry with supple, strong fingers. He had to somehow keep from falling until he was all the way out and could at last seize the rope properly.

Finally he was suspended above the moat, ready to rappel down and swing to a courtyard or a lower window. Only his head remained visible. In the dimness, I made out the white of his smile.

I blew him a kiss.

I could only wait after that, until my yawns torqued my jaw and I had to lie down. At first light, I stirred. Vannen was back, worming his way into the tower as laboriously as he had exited. He was puffing and sweating. He almost fell as he got his last leg inside.

I helped him off the table.

"I couldn't get far enough," he reported. "I would have been seen. You would not believe how many sentries there are. What's the Maggot afraid of?"

"Thieves," I said. "He's always thinking about his riches."

"I see. Well, I'll have to try again tomorrow night. Maybe they won't be as vigilant."

oOo

The next night, he did not even get as far as the first time. Our plan had several weaknesses. Vannen could not be both a boy slender enough to make it out the window, and a mighty swordsman capable of surreptitiously killing guards all the way up to the top of the tower as he infiltrated the castle. And if he did make it to our door, what of Obber? Slip Obber a sleeping potion? Well, yes, if we had a sleeping potion. Lissa could dream that Vannen had such a thing in his pocket, but how would we get Obber to consume it?

And then the Maggot returned. Later that day, he summoned us. Our first thought was that Vannen had been seen, or perhaps the rope had been spotted dangling from the window. But no, our tormentor was in far too good a humor.

"My time at court was well spent. I have not one, but three wealthy lords prepared to make offers." He rubbed his palms together. "Now I get to play them off each other, until I get the best price possible."

Numb, we said nothing as we climbed back to our chamber. Once there, we silently sat down at our work table and picked up our bead-weaving, resorting to our old standby to keep us occupied with something other than desperation. The pastime was one of the few bits of Osprey Harbor culture we had been able to bring with us.

"Time is getting short," Lissa said.

"Yes," I mumbled.

"There is one thing we haven't tried. Please know I am serious about it."

"What is it?" By that point, any option was welcome, but her steely tone alarmed me.

"If I were already pregnant, the Maggot would have to stop offering rich oafs the chance to *get* me pregnant."

The bead in my hand slipped free and tumbled noisily off the table. "Wh—, wh—, what are you suggesting?"

"That Vannen lie with me, of course."

"Would that work?"

"If my foremother could become so much a part of this world as to breed with a human man, I don't see why Vannen's seed would not quicken once it's inside me."

"But what about the—you know. Do you think you could stay asleep while...while..."

"While the deed is being done?"

"Yes."

"I will have to find a way." She drummed her fingers on the table. "Tell me, do you think we could convince Obber to sneak us an entire jug of wine?"

oOo

By the time Lissa retired that evening, she was so drunk she needed my help just to make it from the divan to her bed. I helped her get undressed—no nightgown for her tonight—and covered her with a sheet.

Beneath the covering, she flopped her limbs apart so that she was lying spread-eagled. "There," she said, as if she had completed her part, and the goal was all but accomplished. She was snoring in less than a minute.

Hands shaking, I put out the lamps and tapers. I retreated to my cubby and pulled the drape closed. A real drape, not the gauze curtain that normally hung there. Something opaque. I lay back and stuffed cotton in my ears.

I didn't see how I was going to get through the night. I knew perfectly well I wasn't going to be able to sleep, no matter how it might help the cause of discretion.

The plugged ears only made my restlessness worse. I took the cotton out, hoping that if I were comfortable, maybe I would in fact fall asleep. But of course, I was wide awake when I began hearing rustles of movement from the middle of the room and knew that Vannen had materialized.

A soft whoosh told me the sheet had slid to the floor. I tried to banish the vision in my mind's eye of Lissa lying there as Vannen's shadow loomed across her.

The bed creaked as it coped with the addition of his weight. Subtle sounds of movement followed. Was he shifting her? Was he *priming* her? Was he already inside?

A garbled cry raised hair on the nape of my neck.

Suddenly it grew all too quiet.

After a few moments came the sound of a pillow being thrown at the wall. I heard Lissa muttering, and the sound of her pacing back and forth—I recognized the rhythm of her tread. Candlelight began to glow around the edges of the drape. Finally the partition was thrust aside. Lissa stood there in her nightgown, neck stiff, eyes bloodshot.

I didn't ask how far things had gone. Obviously not far enough.

"There's a tiny man inside my skull trying to bludgeon his way out," she whimpered.

"Shall I brew us some sailor-ashore tea?"

"Yes. And next time we get wine, don't bother serving me any. Just hit me over the head with the jug. It will save time."

oOo

The tea leaves were a little stale. Lissa's hangover was still plaguing her in the morning. She was petulant with me even when I was reading from *The Sailmaker's Wife*, one of her favorites. But as the day went on, stage by stage her mood shifted. She lingered in the bath. She stayed in front of the mirror after I had combed her hair, turning her body this way and that. Evaluating.

She dabbed scented oil behind each ear. I tied a ribbon around her neck, crafting the knot just so. After dinner, she chewed fresh mint leaves.

This time she needed no help getting into bed. In fact, she banished me to my cubby even before she retired.

I had promised myself I would fall asleep. I think I may have succeeded. But I snapped awake after midnight, suddenly sure that Vannen was in the tower.

Yes. I heard subtle indications of movement. But no creaking of a bed. In fact, no sound at all from the part of the room where the bed was.

I couldn't stand it. I lifted a corner of the drape and peeked out.

Vannen was sitting on the divan. He beckoned me with a gesture.

I joined him. "What are you doing?" I asked.

"Waiting. A little later in the night will be better. She's less likely to wake then."

"I see."

He was of course no longer the boy who had squeezed through the window, but he was not quite back to being the bladesman. He was less muscular, less impossibly handsome. Now he was appealing in a grounded way, an honest village man worth marrying and making a family with, not some charmer about to dash off to another adventure.

He smelled like mint.

"She dreams me well tonight. Last night her slumber was impaired."

"We thought the wine would help."

"No, she has to be alert enough to welcome me within her body. Otherwise the penetration is too startling."

I felt a blush coming on. I turned my face away.

"Are you all right?" he asked.

"Yes. I'm fine."

"If it would make you feel better, you might like to know I'm embarrassed by this as well."

I turned back. "You are?"

"I have yet to prove myself in bed. What man wants that? And if things continue to go poorly, I have not one but two women privy to my failure."

"For what it's worth, it's not my idea to be able to know so much. I'd be happy to let it be a secret between the two of you."

"I know."

I waved at the windows. "This would all be simple if she could just dream us far from here, where we were already safe. Beyond the duke's reach."

"If she had that sort of magic, she would not need my help. Are you weary of my company?"

My hand shot to my mouth. "I didn't mean it that way."

"Good. You don't want to make me feel unwanted. I don't think it would help."

"You should never feel unwanted. Until you appeared, the tide was over our heads."

He smiled at me. It was difficult not to blush again.

"What do you think he will be like?" Vannen asked when the pause grew long.

"Who?"

"My son."

"I couldn't say. How could I know?"

"Boys think like their mothers, even if they do it in a male way. You know Lissa. Therefore you know how her son will perceive the world."

I wasn't sure he was right, but I had to admit he had found a way to keep me talking.

He poured what little wine was left into a pair of goblets and we sipped as I spoke of this trait or that, whatever I judged to be the sort of thing the child might inherit.

The child. Somehow he already seemed to exist.

Eventually I had nothing more to say. I closed my eyes. I yawned.

He leaned over to whisper in my ear, "Thank you, Wyvva. I enjoyed this."

I felt myself being lifted in strong arms, to be deposited on my bunk. "Good luck," I murmured as he closed the drape.

He did not approach Lissa's bed while I was alert. It happened some time later, when my pillow had become a chariot to elsewhere, and I could not tell a human sigh from the flutter of a bat's wings.

oOo

At breakfast, Lissa looked incredible. "You're glowing," I said.

"I am not," Lissa replied.

"Are too."

She smiled like wharf pelican. "Maybe you're right."

"You know I'm right."

"Well, it is how I'm supposed to feel, isn't it?"

"Ideally," I admitted.

"I hope it's like this every time."

I almost choked on a piece of melon.

"You did realize we'll have to keep doing this every night until we're sure I'm pregnant?" she asked.

"Your foremother was a glimmering bride. Isn't once enough?"

"Maybe. But I have to be sure."

I carefully swallowed the piece of melon. Lissa stole a second piece from my bowl.

"You really slept through it all?" I asked.

"If I hadn't, 'it all' would not have been possible."

"True."

"It is odd, though, to know I have lain with a man, yet never spoken with him. Thank goodness for you. Tell me what he said last night."

I paused, spoon raised. "We didn't talk. I fell asleep before you did. I slept all night. It's better that way, don't you think?"

Lissa gazed at me so steadily, I lowered the spoon back to the bowl.

"Wyvva. I want to know what he said."

I hated that she knew so immediately whenever I lied. Conceding, I told her how Vannen had asked what traits his son-to-be might inherit, how he had gazed at Lissa so fondly. But

I did not tell her how long we had spoken, nor of how he had carried me to my bed, nor of his whisper in my ear.

That part was for me alone.

oOo

True to form, the Maggot could not help but play his prospects against one another as long as possible. Each time he received a better offer, he would summon us to his hall and cackle about it. Finally he intimated that he would probably accept the next one, and told Lissa to air out her best dress.

Meanwhile the nights went on, through the phases of the moon. Lissa's breath no longer had to be anointed by the orb's glow to make Vannen appear. He manifested as soon as she slipped into unconsciousness. He and I had more and more time each night to talk. I was always bleary-eyed in the morning from staying up late; I compensated with naps rather than have to retire when Lissa did.

Each night, he lay with her. We never resumed our conversations afterward; I did not want to sit there while he was fragrant with her scent. I stayed in my alcove.

Sleep seldom came quickly. From time to time, a soft masculine grunt would filter through the partition, or a drowsy feminine sigh. Inevitably, I sometimes could hear other sounds, ones more primal and rhythmic. Wet sounds.

Not once did I nudge the drape aside and peer out, but it hardly mattered. I could see Vannen so plainly in my mind's eye, his hair tousled, the sweat glistening on his shoulders, the muscles of his hindquarters tightening and relaxing. And then his whole body shuddering.

Lissa had always had more than I. But never before had I envied her.

oOo

Finally Lissa began throwing up in the morning. It confirmed what we'd been suspecting for some time.

She sent a note downstairs saying she was pregnant. Within

an hour the local birthwitch visited the tower and gave Lissa an examination. The Maggot barely waited until she was done before he burst into the room.

The birthwitch gave the sign of a swelling belly. The duke rounded at Lissa.

"Who did this?" he demanded.

"Count Urley," Lissa said. I nearly coughed out loud to hear her say it so calmly, unable to quench the awful image of that old man climbing into Lissa's bed, even knowing no such thing had ever happened.

The Maggot's mouth dangled open. "Count Ur—"

"He wouldn't meet your price," Lissa added. "But he met mine."

The duke's face purpled to such a degree I thought a blood vessel would pop. "He will not make a fool of me!" He whirled around and stalked from the room, slamming the door.

After Obber had reopened the door and let the birthwitch out, Lissa and I were finally free to burst into laughter. We muffled the noise as best we could in our sleeves.

It was worth dying now, if we had to.

oOo

That night, I keened my ears for the whisper of Vannen settling onto the divan. When I thought I heard it, I burst from my cubby.

"I have such news—"

The rest of the words lodged in my throat. Vannen was not there. The chamber was empty of anyone except Lissa, asleep in her bed, and me, teetering on the balls of my feet.

There was no reason to continue toward the divan. Chin down, I returned to my bunk.

At first, I told myself the night was young, and I had simply been impatient for him to arrive. But Lissa slumbered on, her exhalations never taking on their magical glow. No version of Vannen, be it bladesman or boy or lover, put in an appearance.

I stayed up until dawn, wondering what sort of good-bye I might have composed if I had known one was necessary. None seemed adequate.

oOo

As the next day wore on, we expected a summons. The need to punish us was surely burning a hole in the Maggot's bowels.

"If it happens, so be it," Lissa said aloud. She was exuding a sort of peace unlike any I had seen from her, even in the happiest portions of our girlhood.

More hours passed. It seemed the duke was reacting as we had thought he might. Inasmuch as we were his captives, he had plenty of time to concoct just the right revenge. At the moment, his anger was directed outward—at the supposed perpetrator of his ills. We had time for developments to fall in our favor.

Hopeful as we were, the form those developments took was a surprise. As evening deepened, a knock came on the door. A few moments later, Obber let himself in.

"Hurry," he said. "His Grace is off to demand satisfaction from Count Urley. He's all but emptied the castle of guards. If you come now, I know I can sneak you out."

"You'd do that?" I asked.

"I would." He waved his thick fingers in the direction of the door. "I have transportation arranged to get you down the road aways, but you have to be aboard within the hour. Take what you can carry. Nothing more."

We didn't need to hear it again. Lissa and I scurried about the chamber, gathering up necessities. We nearly collided as we both remembered the most important—the purse she'd hidden in a compartment of her cedar box. Wherever we went, gold would help smooth our way.

It felt wonderful to put on footwear meant for the outdoors.

Obber was true to his word. He knew the servants' corridors and the archers' crannies, which together became a route to an unwatched sally port. We were slipping into alleys in the mercantile district in less time than it took for the solitary sentry on the battlements to pace out a full circuit. All we glimpsed of him was the back side of his spiked helmet.

Finally we approached a large wagon. A pair of oxen were

already hitched to the yoke. The load was covered by a thick tarp.

Obber lifted the back end of the tarp. A rich aroma of beer escaped. On the wagonbed was half a load of kegs and barrels.

"Brewmaster is sending this all the way to Rowan Hollow. Load has to go in the cool of the night. His boy owes me a favor. He'll not say a word about carrying any passengers. From Rowan Hollow, you're on your own."

"We'll manage," Lissa assured him.

He grinned. "If I know the old goat, he'll put up quite a fight. His Grace will have to lay siege. Your trail will be cold before he gets the chance to go sniffing along it."

I kissed his cheek.

"We can never thank you enough," Lissa told him. "You are taking quite a risk."

"Worth it," Obber said firmly. "I lost my balls fighting in my master's Ten Valleys campaign. He never thanked me for it."

"How like him," Lissa said.

Obber gazed at Lissa's belly, as if able to see a bump there already. "I don't know how you managed it. I've never seen His Grace yank his own beard so hard."

He giggled. It was infectious.

Our eyelashes wet with tears, Lissa and I climbed into the gap between the barrels. Obber gave us one final nod and tied down the tarp over the top of the load, concealing us. His heavy bootsteps faded away.

Soon came the sound of someone climbing onto the driver's bench. A snap of the lash and we were on our way out of the alley and down the street.

The wheels, despite a recent greasing, groaned from the load as the oxen pulled us along, and the barrels, despite being well secured, rattled with each bump. The noise ensured our conversation would not be overhead.

"We can't go back to Osprey Harbor," I said. "They'd look for us there."

"Agreed. We'd only get Lord Firin in trouble. No, we have to leave Mareswold entirely. At night, if we can manage it."

"At night?"

"Assuming I can sleep on the road." She placed her hand upon mine. "Don't you agree it would be prudent to have a male escort?"

"I didn't consider that it was possible."

"You thought me done with him?"

I didn't answer. I was glad she couldn't see my expression in the darkness beneath the tarp.

"With him around, things seem to go well for us. I see no reason not to keep bringing him back as often as possible." She paused. "Do you have some objection to him accompanying us?"

"No," I answered at once. "Not at all."

"Then it's settled. All we need is a destination."

Strange as it may seem, we had never discussed this. Maybe we were afraid to contemplate the endpoint of our escape so completely, and be hurt all the more to be denied it. But now I believed we could make whatever distance we needed to go. With hope as tangible as that, the answer came to me at once.

"I know a place."

oOo

I awoke to the sound of owls tucking themselves in for the day in the upper recesses of the shack, amid the tangle of myrtlewood branches and thatch. I inhaled air perfumed with the scents of clover and elkbroom. For a moment, I was ten years old again, waking up on this very pallet during the one summer I had spent away from Osprey Harbor.

I rose and parted the curtain that ran down the center of the shack. Lissa, face already washed, already wearing her day dress, was combing her hair. She beamed at me.

"This is a beautiful place," she said.

"It is," I agreed. "Have you seen the ocean?"

"No. It's visible from here?"

"Just up the hill."

"You'll have to show me."

After we breakfasted on cold porridge and blackberries, we

climbed up. As soon as we reached the crest of the ridge, the wind thumped us like a family hound left alone all day and eager to show his love.

Off in the distance, blue water stretched to the horizon. We were too far from the shore to hear the waves crash, but we smelled the salt. The pores of our cheeks opened to drink in the moisture. We were inland exiles no more.

Not one human structure intruded upon our view. Not one sail. This stretch of coast was rocky, bereft not only of harbors, but of beaches upon which to pull a fishing boat ashore. It was not a place for lords to covet. Only shepherds saw its value. Of a winter, the winds here blew with fleece-thickening briskness.

We smiled as we took our fill of the scene. But in some ways, the view the other way soothed us just as much. For Lissa, it was the first chance for her to take in the full extent of our surroundings. For me, it was a sweet revisiting. Downslope lay the shack, where a small spring bubbled up, and outcroppings blunted the force of whatever breezes made it down from the ridgetop. A rolling terrain of pastureland stretched inland, the heather interrupted here and there by blackberry brambles, copses of myrtle or ash, and vernal ponds. By a small creek, its outlines hazy with distance, stood the farmhouse from which we had come on foot late the previous afternoon to arrive at the shack at dusk.

The time had come to retrace our steps. We picked our way down the slope and headed hand in hand across the fields toward the house.

oOo

We arrived just as my aunt Nebba was removing the day's batch of bread from the oven. We helped her finish churning the butter and sat down at the table with her and my uncle Foxmo. My cousin Mibb was out with the flocks, but his wife Taney sat with us when she was not keeping her toddlers out of mischief. The air grew addictively braced with the aroma of fresh loaves breaking open.

"Did you like the little place, m'lady?" Foxmo asked.

"Please call me just Lissa," she replied with cheer. "For now and for good. And yes, I liked it a great deal."

"Be good to have someone out there again full time." My uncle gazed out the window toward the coast. We let him savor whatever memory had bubbled up. I knew he had lived in the shack as a young man. It had been little more than a shepherd's cote back then. He had expanded it when Nebba had become his bride, crafting it into a bower that sheltered them through their newlywed days. But when Mibb was a year old and Nebba pregnant a second time, the old shepherd who had held tenancy of the land had passed away, and Foxmo and Nebba had occupied the main farmhouse, a better accommodation for a growing family. "It's not too isolated for you?"

"Isolation is what we want," Lissa said.

He nodded. "You'll have it. Even the king's tax collectors don't bother coming out this far. We pay our tithe at the village."

As I chewed on warm bread and butter, it seemed to me the most sustaining food I had ever eaten. We had reached a haven where the Maggot's trackers would never look. A bounty hunter clever enough to imagine Lissa and I had sought shelter with my mother's kinfolk would be unlikely to find anyone left alive back in Osprey Harbor to recall what village my mother had come from, and if he did, there was no one left alive in that village who knew to what far-flung corner of the realm Foxmo had drifted off to after he and my grandfather had quarrelled.

The whole way here, I could not vanquish the fear that we might be recaptured in the midst of our flight. Now I could. Now I had.

"We are in your debt," Lissa said.

"Pfff. Won't be long until I am in yours. I met your young man last night. Strapping fellow. Quite an archer. He'll have no trouble helping keep the flocks safe." My uncle pointed to a large pumpkin on the sideboard. The outline of a wolf had been painted on it. The hind half of an arrow jutted from the wolf's heart.

Lissa smiled. She had needed to hear Foxmo say it, for last night, we had suspected him to be a little unsure of us. It was all very well to speak of having a dream man in our service, one who could roam the fields at night, guarding against the predators that regularly swept down along the coast from the north, reducing the number of sheep the pastures would otherwise support. It was another thing to meet the man himself, shake his firm hand, and witness his skills.

"Did Vannen give his own word?" I asked. "Aloud?"

"As a matter of fact, he did." My uncle blinked. "Why wouldn't he?"

oOo

"What was that about? Vannen. Giving his word aloud?" Lissa asked as we stored crocks of olives and rounds of cheese in the root cellar in the hillside near the shack. My cousin Mibb was a full thirty paces away, making repairs to the hen coop so that of a morning, we could have eggs. It was the first time Lissa and I had been alone since we had returned.

I kept my face turned toward the shelves, pretending that wiping dust and cobwebs from the shelves was of greater import than the question. "It occurred to me Vannen might have other plans."

Lissa stayed so quiet I wondered if she had slipped out of the root cellar. I turned around. With the sunlight of the doorway haloing her, I could not read her expression.

"Did he *speak* of other plans?"

"No." I bowed my head. "I just got to wondering. What would some other man want, in his position? If he were just anyone, he might have any number of ambitions."

"He can't have other plans. I *need* him. *We* need him."

"I know. Of course I know. He is as you need him to be. But...is there more?"

She took both my hands in hers. "Wyvva. What troubles you? Tell me."

"Do you remember Frisk?"

"Your father's dog? How could I forget?"

"He was old when we came to Osprey Harbor. My father tried to leave him at a farm, where he would have fields to roam for the last fraction of his life. Frisk wouldn't have it. He wanted to be with my father. He cleaved to him out of love."

"Yes. He did."

"And do you remember that pup Kodder the Innkeeper had, the one we would see by the wharf?"

"Yes. Poor whelp."

"He stayed because he was tied up."

Lissa blanched. "Sister, if you think me evil, I could not bear it."

"When it comes to you, I only ever think of love," I said. "That's how it will be until I'm too old to chew a soup bone. I am like Frisk that way."

She hugged me. "I will do all I can to be worthy of that love."

oOo

Throughout the week that followed, Lissa and I were preoccupied with nesting. After our months of idling while confined in the tower, there was so much to do. We ended each day tired, and I slept all the way through most nights. Even when I did wake, I did not see Vannen. Mott was staying up after the rest of us retired in order to instruct him in the places where the flock should be, where wolves or grass panthers might turn up, and then Vannen would roam through the small hours of the night, taking the full measure of the territory that fell within Foxmo's tenancy.

But then came a night when the moon was at its fullest, and my restlessness would not cease. I rose, threw on the sheep-maid frock Aunt Nebba had given me, and slipped out of the shack.

Something whisked by my head, and I blurted an unladylike word.

It fluttered by again in front of me. A hawk moth. It continued on its way out across the fields, and as I tracked it, I saw many more of its kind, travelling in their swooping way, or poising like hummingbirds, or landing upon moorflowers to harvest nectar.

My breath caught at the beauty of it. I had forgotten the moths. Of a moonlit night in late summer or early fall, waves of them flowed over the heather like sea foam.

Over on the crest of the nearest knoll I made out Vannen's tall shape. He had one hand poised on an unstrung bow, the other hand holding up a sprig of elkbroom. A moth settled upon the sprig to feed. He bent his head to study the patterns of its wings.

I followed the path down from the shack and then up the gentle slope of the knoll, keeping alert for gopher holes and stones that might be hidden in the pasture's verdant mat.

Vannen watched me approach. With his face in shadow, I did not see how wide his grin was until I got close.

"You're in a happy mood."

"Your aunt left me one of her mutton pasties. And a cup of her cider. It was wonderful."

It was the emotion in his tone that made me realize, worldly as he might have been in other respects, he had never before eaten.

"She doesn't need to waste food on me," he added. "But I won't be the one to tell her so."

"Then neither will I."

He held out his bow to me. "Hold this, please."

After I had taken it from him, he ambled to the nearest clump of elkbroom, and headed back with a fresh sprig in his hand. A dirt clod crunched beneath his foot. Where he had stepped, the grass remained crumpled. He was solid. The things he did had an effect on the world. It did not seem possible that when Lissa woke, he would vanish.

I ran a finger along the bow. Fine yew, well crafted. As far as I knew, it materialized with him each night. If I took it with me to the shack, would it still be there in the morning?

"What are you, Vannen?" I finally dared ask. "Are you only her dream?"

His brows rose. He grew very still as he pondered.

"More than that, I think." He spoke softly so as not to disturb the especially handsome moth that had found his offering. "I suspect that I am not made, but taken from some other place and reshaped. But if I have another existence, I do not remember it while I am here."

"Doesn't that trouble you?"

"Do you mean to ask, am I content?"

"Yes."

He gestured at the silvered expanse of terrain, at the moths in flight. He drew breath until his chest broadened. "When I am here, I know I exist. I smell the heather. I hear the sheep bleat. I have a purpose and the skill to pursue it. So, the answer is yes. I am content. I would rather be alive than not. I am grateful for all that I have."

His voice mesmerized me. Its timber. The sincerity in its tone.

"I will tell Lissa you said so. She will be glad."

I toyed with the loose bowstring.

"There is one thing I want," he added.

I looked up. My mother's ghost watch over me, when I saw his eyes again it was all I could do not to untie my frock, place it on the ground as a blanket, and invite him to share it with me. "Yes?"

"I am lonely, of a night," he said. "I would have you join me more often. I would like to know you much better, Wyvva Scribe's Daughter."

I hiccupped. "I...I could only do that if Lissa has dreamed it."

He chuckled. "Silly girl. Of *course* she has dreamed it."

Suddenly I was having to wipe wetness from my eyes, and my heart began thundering in my chest.

Vannen removed his quiver of arrows from his back and rested it on the grass. With a nonchalant stride, he halved the distance between us.

I halved the rest. And kissed him.

Celebrated for her best-selling epics of European mediaeval history, most notably *We Speak No Treason*, **Rosemary Hawley Jarman** is also the author of the fantasy novel, *The Captain's Witch*. She has been dubbed "A Daughter of Mark Twain" by the Samuel Clemens Society for her services to literature. She lives in a cottage in Wales, UK.

About "Fire and Frost and Burning Rose" she says, "Ever since my first glimpse of fjord and glacier, the Norse legends have become emotionally significant. The magical sword I see as the archetype of mortal striving and desire. In this story I have departed from the Wagnerian tradition and it is a woman who, like the hero Siegfried, renders the broken weapon into a sacred force. The Ring has elements of the Sleeping Beauty, the longed-for princess, and the flames symbolise the ordeal to be passed through in search of fulfillment. Nothing changes, even today, so long as love is pure."

FIRE AND ICE AND BURNING ROSE

by Rosemary Hawley Jarman

(from a Norse Myth)

Throstan had lost an eye to the hard curved bite of a falcon, an agreed sacrifice, and now the falcon acted as his messenger. The eye had been gifted to the Maidlings as payment for the sanctuary which housed his treasure.

What his one eye saw was quite a spectacle. Sometimes it roused an amused pity or faint anxiety, but never did he feel that Merhild was at risk. Almost immobile, she stirred gently in her unguessed dreams. Throstan imagined her to be tranquil, at least untroubled by the workings of the world.

For her own safety had he bound his daughter in this sleep.

Throstan was one of several gods of the frozen realm shared with the white fox and the ermine and the somber snow bear, whose hide was his garment. The land was broad enough for them all. Parts of it were verdant, but here, breath frosted the air like a sparkling wine.

Sleeping, Merhild exhaled an irresistible perfume, like the golden lilies which had bloomed before the land was ice. It pervaded the air for leagues around. Young men were made mad by it, and, on finding its source, sickened and were lost. Merhild's beauty went beyond words, like flawless music. Her white lids lay soft over eyes of hummingbird blue. Her body, in its translucent single garment, was a dangerous innocence, crying out to be possessed.

Throstan gazed until the ice thawed a little under his boots. A young dawn touched Merhild's hair, a filamented gilt ripple from crown to ankles, almost like the broad boundary of lace which contained her.

This lace was a special commodity. Throstan had bargained for it, walking many leagues to find the Maidlings where they worked at patterning the skeins of past, present and to come, linking and looping the interstices of life itself. Faf, the falcon, was their overseer.

Throstan found them winding on to the giant bobbins thrice the height of a man; doubling and trebling and stretching and plaiting and knotting the delicate webs. They worked with star matter. It had fallen from the uttermost zone of sky.

Not all the Maidlings were fair. Wold was a thousand years old, at least. Grum was slightly younger. Flanik was hideous, leathery and squinting, but sly Sulva was lovely, and knew it. She licked her full lips as Throstan appeared.

The four continued to work with long clawed fingers (Sulva's were pretty), but their eyes fixed on Throstan and they whispered.

"He wants something," observed Grum.

"He's very handsome," breathed Sulva.

On went the pulling in and pushing through, the knotting and threading.

"We cannot stop, while the world turns," said Flanik.

"But he is a god," objected Sulva, smiling.

"Only a minor one," grumbled Wold.

They were insulting. He could have struck, scattered them, but it would be messy. He addressed them with gentility.

"Domina," he said to the eldest. Wold inclined her brow. Sulva drifted up through air to wind starshine on to the tall bobbins, flashing her thighs, fluttering back to earth. She winked at Throstan.

He made his request. Grum pricked out a pattern with a

sharp thorn.

There was quite a long consultation.

"Yes, it can be done, well done," said Wold at last. She beckoned toward the falcon. "The price is fixed. The price is high."

At this, Throstan nodded, then lifted his face. A feathered missile came down and blood spurted from Faf's strike. There was pain, silently endured, and Throstan gained respect.

"We have decided it shall be a circle, rather than a web," declared the eldest. She shook red drops from the glistening orb, and set it neatly into her lacework. Sulva drifted up to place a patch on the dripping eye socket, kissed off the hurt.

"Your daughter shall be inviolable," they promised firmly.

"The men are already coming," Throstan warned. The Maidlings shook with unseemly laughter.

"The more they *come*," said Sulva lewdly, "the fiercer our rampart shall be," and collapsed with mirth, pulling her pattern out of shape. Wold raised her hoary head and sniffed the air, heavy with Merhild's beauty, even at a distance.

"When will you finish?" Throstan had grown urgent. "They will fight over her. Hewing about them, blood will be spilled." (They looked up avidly; the Maidlings relished battles).

"By the time you see her again."

Returning home, weary, the truth met him pleasingly. There it was—a perfect ring, steely and tough as spiderwork, if spiders were of humankind. About the height of a tall man, deceptively delicate, lace patterned with snow crystals. Within, snug in a bed of blue fur, lay Merhild, dreaming.

oOo

The suitors were on their way, running on the ice, crazed, doomed, babbling love, helpless as slaves. Throughout it all, she lay, unknowing, emitting scents sweeter than nectar, in the frail fortress stronger than legions.

oOo

Gieshelm had been abandoned, so he was told, in the deep mossed foot of a venerable oak. Two thick roots cradled him. Occasionally, nuts rained down, and odd green beings brought him nourishment. So nurtured, he grew strong and tall and extremely pleasant to look upon, his skin the pale glossy tan of a maturing acorn. For many years he had thought his name was Acorn, but one deep midnight, a benign, greenly creeping thing had informed him that he was the product of incest between a great king and his sister. Better lie low on this knowledge, was the advice, and Gieshelm, not particularly interested, agreed.

Although solitary, he had never learned to be lonely. Forest beasts, hurt or sickly, migrated to him, dormice, robins, voles, hares, and he nursed and healed them with great patience and without question.

In the forest, Winter was yielding to Spring, warming like Gieshelm's blood through his steady heart and magnificent chest. This morning, he had foraged and breakfasted well and was reclining in his leafy home. Directly beneath him, the underground team had started work. Today they were noisier than ever. The earth quaked, and a few local squirrels bolted in fright.

He did not know the names of these subterraneans, and was unsure what they did, other than that it involved something metallic. Now the clanking and tapping and rattling and plinking was rising unnervingly near the surface, and crumbs of disturbed earth began to trickle around the tree roots. When something sharp and glinting rose very slowly up through the soil, he leaped to his feet.

A cavity appeared, followed by a small troll wearing moleskin leggings and an embarrassed expression. Shaking dirt from its head, it addressed Gieshelm politely.

"Greetings, esteemed overhead tenant. I am called Urn. I am here to apologise, and bring this gift in recompense." Bowing, he presented over his arm a short sword, which on close inspection appeared not quite so sharp, with a poorly finished hilt.

"Recompense for what?" inquired Gieshelm.

"Why, for terrestrial disturbance. Clanging, and such,"

replied Urn. "We are armourers. And some of us," he added mournfully, "are not as skilled as they think they are. I could," he said, "have brought you an ax. But this is more fit for purpose."

"Purpose?"

"Why, to harm folk. Legs and arms off, and so on."

Gieshelm frowned. "I never thought to harm anyone. Or anything." He remembered how, rambling in the forest, he had accidentally trodden on a skylark's nest hidden in long grass. He had been greatly upset.

The troll seemed intent on instilling blood hunger.

"You will when you scent her," he said firmly. "Should have brought an ax. You can hew a few limbs with an ax."

Gieshelm sighed patiently, holding out his hand for the sorry-looking sword. It would do to dig for truffles or fungi, or stir his cookpot.

"There'll be rivals, you know," Urn said stubbornly. "You're a fine-looking character. You could stand a chance. A glorious bride!"

Gieshelm shook his head, wondering whether years of life underground had addled Urn's brain.

"I thank you for the gift," he said. "I know of no bride. Nor do I yearn for one."

"You don't travel far, do you?" said the troll smugly. He rolled his eyes. "You should take a little walk some time soon. When the ice melts. When the wind blows from the West. Then you'll know what's what."

"I might," said Gieshelm.

"When the ice melts," repeated Urn. "The Spring wind's coming." He nodded, and turned, and tapped his nose cunningly, leaving a large smear of earth.

And Gieshelm thought: there *is* a little breeze, a funny, flowery little breeze. And it might be a good idea to take a trip, get away from the noisy trollcraft for a few days.

"Very well," he said. Urn was already wriggling his way down the collapsing shaft, face disappearing fast.

"Be lucky, prince!" he shouted, voice muffled by renewed clinking and clanging from below. "Sorry the sword's such a dud. A reject, if you must know...."

Gieshelm began his wanderings that afternoon. He wore a jerkin the colour of Spring, and the breeze made waves in his long chestnut hair. His legs were well-muscled but slender, his stride sure. The sun scattered gold on him through the tips of the trees.

His journeyings took him very near to the Maidlings' pitch. Faf flew out, stooped down to investigate this beautiful man, and flew back to where the bobbins whirled and the fingers flickered. And made his findings known, in detail.

Sulva had not made love for four hundred years. Now she remembered everything, and was overcome. Her bobbin was empty, her pattern faltered. She had forgotten how fast she could move.

"Flighty young harlot," said Grum, sliding to take over Sulva's abandoned pattern. "She's done this before."

"Oh, let her have a little fling," said Wold.

Faf settled on a blossoming branch, ready to fly.

oOo

Under the cold sun, the young men fought. They fought one another and they fought the Ring that surrounded Merhild's couch. On the misted horizons to north and east, fire seethed beneath the ice. Steaming white pillars, geysers of giant height, dashed upward. Their hissing eruption echoed steel on steel as those who craved the embraces of Merhild parried and thrust and killed and died. And with each fierce protracted battle, the scent of her allure seared their nostrils and spurred their blood.

The ice grew thin from the stumbling feet that rushed again and again with upraised swords in the urge to cleave the Ring. While within the sweetly fashioned garments (for none had thought to wear armour), their fleshly weapons burgeoned and burst forth, expelling the precious tribute of life itself.

Furiously the young men smote the fence of lace with their steel, and every strike made it more adamantine. And as the white geysers speared the air, so did the jets from the yearning loins lash the Ring of Merhild and, drying there, turn it hard as rock.

Smashed blades littered the ice and the fair young men groaned, dragging their mortal wounds away. Some, themselves broken, helped others through their deaths, and smiled a little as Merhild's perfume eased their dying.

Shielded between the spray of two leaping fire-fountains, Throstan watched. His eye observed the cruel beauty of the Maidlings' craft, now beginning to glitter—a wickedly angelic diadem under the rising moon.

Soft, Faf came through dusk to bounce on Throstan's gauntlet. Merhild slept on, in her ice-blue dream.

The wind blew, fragrant as her breath.

oOo

Throstan had never realised he would be lonely. He thought: she lies safe behind her seed-strengthened battlement, and I am bereft as if she were dead. He shifted his feet among the ravaged ice. Above, the moon blinked at the savage glow of the dragon-like bursts of flame.

It was time to fare forth again, seeking direction through mountainland. He marched south, and struck terrain familiar with a memory. The rising sun warmed his sightless right eye as he came down through foothills into the valley of the broad river Sereine, alive with fish and secret legend, and after a time stopped to rest in the grass. Here the path divided and in view came the figure of a fellow wanderer, a god who ruled over the southlands. An ancient, upon a stick. Throstan rose.

"Greetings, Nordin. How do you fare and whence?"

Nordin looked Throstan up and down and at his missing eye. "I see you've been with the Maidlings," he remarked. "I hope you had good value."

"How is your daughter?" inquired Throstan courteously. Nordin shrugged.

"Stubborn as ever. I have asked her to return home and be forgiven, but no. She appears to be enjoying herself."

Throstan forbore to comment. It was no secret that the maiden had lain with her own brother, now king of a distant quarter famed for its sky-wolves. He could see no scandal; it did not breed half-wits in spite of what folk said; it bred beauty.

Nordin stirred the air with his stick.

"I must be on my way. The journey home takes me longer these days."

"Strength be on your path, brother. One day we shall both feast in the hall of the great ones above."

Nordin nodded, amiably vague, and turned from the valley, disappearing from sight, although next instant Throstan saw his tiny figure reappear on a hilltop.

"The old dodderer has lost none of his powers," he muttered.

He walked on beside the sparkling river between banks laced with tiny white and yellow flowers, and through arched groves of willow and sacred ash. Deep pebbles twinkled in the clear-running current. He rounded a riverbend under the white cloak of a waterfall foaming into a pool, where it became a calm lake studded with lilies. He had entered a grotto sheltered in the high arms of a fjord, from which fell unceasing snowy cascades. And he was hearing laughter, high and ringing over the splashing fall. Trills and bells of sheer female happiness and foolery.

He saw them then. Two, flaxen, naked, slender, with small apple breasts and rumps scarcely covered by the long glitter of wet hair. He stood on the bank and watched as they splashed and ducked one another and wrestled and shrieked, and, breathless, embraced, their little hands like stars, groping and slapping, their mouths kissing, quick taunting kisses like the play of children.

Both had small heart-shaped faces and starlight eyes the color of young olives. They ran into the spray and played with the waterfall, then in the shallows stroked and washed one another, all the time laughing like music.

One plucked a lily leaf and set it between her teeth from where the other's quick mouth snatched it.

Now they stood with the ripples eddying round their thighs, and Throstan saw that their parts were nude of hair, the inner lips mimicking the buds of the water lily. Just as he realised there was something tantalizingly familiar about them, they looked over and saw him standing motionless. Their laughter ceased;

their eyes became attentive. Then from both came a smile that seemed to touch the water like a light. And a whisper, first one and then the other.

"A man!"

"A lovely one!"

They ran splashing toward him, raising great waves—calling him to join them, an unnecessary summons for while watching them, he had rid himself of all but his breechclout, which was swiftly snatched away by one or other of them, and ripped from his body almost with awkward results, his part being already excellently prepared for the welcome....

When they had sported together, warm flesh in the icy river, they rested, dozing on the bank. He had learned their names—Britt and Ola. She he knew by repute—old Nordin's wayward daughter.

A shadow fell over them. A third naked form. Beauty of body to break the heart. She stood ankle-deep in the river, gazing at him soberly.

He sat up and the two sleeping girls slid gently from his embrace. He saw long hair of gilt dewed with river diamonds and eyes blue as a tropical bird. He spoke a name.

"Merhild?"—Uncertainly.

"Oh," she answered. "Oh, Throstan. It was always her, was it not? She was my rival for your heart."

"Roshild," he said. And she nodded, came close, so that he could see the jewels in her hair were real, not water drops, and that round her naked waist was a cincture of rich red gold.

"You haven't forgotten me, then, my love?"

"Never, how could I? It was you who abandoned me. I knew where you had gone, but why?"

She smiled. "It was time. I had to take up my duty."

There was a pure gold lily tucked behind her ear. Real pearls peeped from the lips of her sex.

"Your duty," he repeated.

She moved away through the ripples, and he followed her. The others had woken and plunged after them. Roshild turned. She looked at the two with tender scorn. "I see you have met my cousin."

"Ola, or Britt?"

"My naughty cousin Ola, who bedded her brother and ran away. Britt is a distant relative on your side."

"I never knew that."

"You are a god. You should know everything," said Roshild mildly as she led them downstream. They halted where willows thickly curtained a bulge of rock in the cliff.

"Regard," she said.

She parted the fronds for Throstan to peer inside. A narrow chimney, deepening into precipitate darkness. There was the impression of immense space down below.

"Look well," she said.

Then he saw the gleam, secret, subtle, unmistakable, illuminated of itself, the deep, brooding hoard, the gold, the jewels, the price of a thousand kingdoms, quietly keeping its own counsel.

Roshild let the curtain repair itself, and the rock vanished.

"Ola," she said, and Ola splashed obediently to her command.

"Ola, why are you still here? Your old father asks for you."

"Oh no," the nymphs said it together. "We are here to guard the gold."

"A dragon guards it," said Throstan, frowning.

"The dragon's dead," said Britt. "Some idiot killed it. We are here instead."

"Little liars," said Roshild softly. "You are here to entice men. *I* am the custodian of the treasure. And you, my love," she suddenly turned on Throstan, "I hear you have sealed up our daughter. A falcon brought the news."

"That bird knows too much," said Throstan testily. He touched his blind eye. With the other he was looking at Roshild. Affectionately, but without desire. Their time together was over.

"You should let her find love."

Throstan frowned again, more savagely.

"Oh yes," cried the nymphs. "Love is lovely, love is fun!"

Roshild looked sternly at Ola.

"What did you do with *your* baby, cousin?"

Ola blushed, looking embarrassed. "The Acorns are caring for him." She shrugged and sat down in the river, where tiny fish swam in and out of her pink pubes, making her giggle.

"I have missed you," Throstan told Roshild.

"And I you, my beloved. But you do not need me. I am no longer frisky enough. Come, cousins."

And, startlingly sudden, Roshild dived, followed by the other two. They swam into the middle of the river. There was a last flash of gleaming buttock, then silence and a vanishing. Throstan stood alone.

Without warning, the falcon's claws struck his shoulder. He turned his head and Faf blinked rapidly at him several times. A clear unmistakable message.

There was something the god needed to see.

oOo

Sulva came at speed, her feet skimming the ground as she landed. Her flight was borne up by her voluminous garment rippled with stars. At first, Gieshelm thought he had strayed into the path of some great bird. He was struck dumb by her and found her beautiful, as the power of a dragon is beautiful, awesome, with her long snowy hair blowing like a lustrous banner, and her ice-white teeth revealed in an amorous smile. Her face was small and perfect, her lips red, her breasts bare, and her body was apparently only just contained by her clothing.

Gieshelm stood firm as she swooped and tumbled, finally coming to rest against him with clinging arms.

Nothing in his life had prepared him for this. At first, he was unsure what she desired of him, but only for a moment. He was confused by her passion, and also again aware of the strange fragrance which had increased throughout his journey, but before he could savour it, Sulva seized him by the hair.

"Come, my adored." Holding him by hair and waist, she bore him up effortlessly, and he found himself looking down on the tops of pine trees and the distant glacier. He thought he could smell the flowery breeze all about their flight, but Sulva wrapped her banner of hair over his nostrils and mouth, and he was thankful when they touched down breathlessly in a cave sparkling with rose crystals, on a bed of moss and bird feathers. There, she covered him with kisses, and he wondered: was this his bride, of which the troll had spoken?

He lay stunned and breathless. Now he could smell only food and drink and Sulva herself, her body like a clean sea, and the heady oils with which she anointed him from brow to toe. Her seduction of him was swift and total. She rewarded him with savoury herbal stews and strawberry wine. And having moisturized and fed him, she made love to him again, within the shimmer of rose crystal which, through the cave mouth, reflected the sunfall. At night, she lay with him in her arms and sang to him in a strange tongue like some demented bird. And he slept, until roused once again by her urgent demands.

oOo

On either side of the glacier, the geysers sprang like white lions at the air. Fire burned in their roots.

The wind shifted and the ice began to melt. The buds of the birch trees thickened.

Faf batted back and forth between all concerned. Mischievous Faf, messenger, talebearer.

Sulva cherished her young lover with devoted attention. His body was her solace and delight. She became importunate, but he responded with sweet obedience. The Spring wind awakened him where he lay drowning in her love.

"That scent comes more strongly now." He sat up, dazed. She smoothed his hair, frowning.

"Here, take some wine. It is made from honeysuckle. Smell that, not Merhild."

"Yes!" He rose from the couch, brushing the cup of wine away. "Merhild! I dreamed that name, a falcon spoke it to me. How long have I tarried here, lady?"

Silently Sulva cursed her tongue.

No, she thought. *I cannot let him become a sacrifice on that dreadful wall we made. I will not!*

Yet he was on his feet, throwing off the web of fine clothes she had woven for him, donning his forest jerkin, and taking up the sword, propped drearily in a corner.

Sulva stared at his fine body, his beautiful eyes. Even now, his purity shone, as if he had never known lust.

"I must find her," he said.

"Wait one more day, my darling. Drink. Sleep. Be still."

He sighed, and courteous as ever, did her bidding. She made him drowsy again, sliding over him, her white body draining him as a bee sucks a blossom. Then she watched him sleeping. Untouched by passion, his eyes were away where she could not follow.

She sat all night, sadly holding the tawdry tarnished sword in her lap. His breathing was hurried and as he dreamed he whispered: "Merhild, my glorious bride...."

"No," she answered. "Your inglorious death, my love."

He smiled in his sleep.

"Unless I help you," she breathed. Then: "My heart is breaking."

Even so, she began to caress the worthless sword as she had his body. The blade assumed a sheen, lustrous as fine gold. The tip became dynamic with a spectral heat. Gieshelm had awakened and was staring at what she had done.

"This may well pierce the Ring," she said softly.

"Will you guide me there, lady?"

"I shall lose you."

He answered quietly. Honestly. "You cannot lose what was never yours, lady. Forgive me."

She bowed her head.

It was nearly dawn. She held out her hand and took him from the cave into the sinking moonglow, and they flew together, borne on the winged flutter of hair and garments, and came down over the budding birches and pines to where the fragmented ice lay strewn with the crippled weapons and bodies of the dead. The ground streamed and pooled with blood.

Gieshelm was affected beyond speech at the tragedy. The Maidling looked without emotion.

And then she saw his eyes were filling with tears and, cursing herself, cried: "Yes! Now! *Bathe* your blade!" and seized the weapon, holding it up close under his eyes so that his tears fell on it and rolled from hilt to tip.

At that instant, she knew she had lost him forever.

The newly baptized sword changed. It gleamed, almost unbearably bright, reflecting moonlight giving way to sunrise. The point became a star and then a gorgeous rayed sun, morphing finally into a perfect rose, no ordinary gold this, but burning with its own energies, the gold of angels. Gieshelm raised it in an awed salute, and Sulva cried:

"That is the holy Rose that never withers. It will take you through the Ring. Go!"

The circle shimmered, implacable as iron.

A little apart, Throstan watched intently, the falcon on his glove.

"Go!" cried the Maidling again. *He cannot lose his life-force to the Ring. My own desire has quelled it for this moment.* She turned away, and moved to where Throstan stood.

Gieshelm went resolutely forward, and touched the flaming Rose to the circle. No quarter was asked of the pitiless Ring, none given. A sharp flare surged from the Rose, and the Ring, opening, shivered as in fear or ecstasy. Then suddenly it burst into sapphire flame, terrible, beautiful wildfires, racing in a perfect circle.

Gieshelm stepped calmly through. There was no pain, and when Merhild opened her eyes, it was like being bathed in bluest love. She rose up like a fountain, came in loveliness to meet his strong arms, his tender mouth.

"I dreamed you," she whispered. "I knew you'd come."

oOo

"What have you done, wretched Maidling?" Throstan's gruff voice.

Sulva smiled her most innocent smile. "Nothing but good, my lord. I fancy you have gained a most acceptable son."

"Is he worthy?" growled the god.

"Are not tears of compassion worth more than rivers of lust and blood? And look, see how happy they are. They are in bliss. And after all, he *is* a prince," and, slyly, "her cousin too. They are almost kin."

Throstan looked at her sharply, then thought: the tradition is good; our bloodline will be secure. His expression mellowed considerably: Sulva was very pretty—and frisky.

And she, who had no intention of waiting another four hundred years, said: "I swear, my lord, your countenance is more attractive than when you had both eyes. Would you care to visit my little home? I could make you extremely welcome."

"Why not?" replied the god.

Faf mantled his feathers in approval.

K.D. Wentworth was born in Tulsa, Oklahoma, and in a subsequent dizzying tour of the nation, managed to attend thirteen different schools by the time she graduated from high school in upstate New York. Returning to Oklahoma to attend the University of Tulsa, she earned a B.A. in Liberal Arts and has had the sense to stay put ever since, although she dodges the occasional tornado. She has sold more than eighty pieces of short fiction to such markets as *F&SF, Hitchcock's, Realms of Fantasy, Weird Tales, Witch Way to the Mall,* and *Return to the Twilight Zone.* Four of her stories have been Finalists for the Nebula Award for Short Fiction. Currently, she has seven novels in print, the most recent being *The Course of Empire* and *Crucible of Empire,* co-written with Eric Flint. She served two terms (2000, 2003) as Secretary of the Science Fiction and Fantasy Writers of America. She serves as Coordinating Judge for the Writers of the Future Contest and lives in Tulsa, Oklahoma, with her husband and a combined total of one hundred sixty pounds of dog (Akita + Siberian "Hussy") and is working on another new novel with Flint. Learn more about her at her website: http://www.kdwentworth.com.

CHE GARDEN OF SWORDS

by K. D. Wentworth

J n the white sweep of moonlight, Tana often thought the
Garden of Swords could almost have been located on any
of the great estates, filled as it was with roses and oleander and
night-blooming jasmine, the beds edged with aromatic herbs.
Almost. Except for the long double rows of graves.

Baron Emilio Iago de Cordova had not accrued his great
wealth and power by wasting even the most paltry of resources,
and defeated enemies were hardly to be considered that. Their
bravery and expertise had cost de Cordova dearly upon the
battlefield in his long-standing rebellion against the King, so
he'd ordered their corpses brought back and planted here, their
spirits magically imprisoned by the old horror of a sorcerer he
kept on staff.

When the mood struck him, he would stroll after dark
among his dead enemies and make them advise him on military
strategy. They paid him homage and trained his sons. Some said
he was even fond of his ghostly captives—in his own way.

The illegitimate daughter of a chambermaid, Tana had also
walked here since she was too young to understand why all these
tall, somber gentlemen wearing swords gazed at her so hungrily
in the starlight, but were never seen in the bright brashness of
day.

The first night she'd encountered them, she'd been left once again to her own devices while her young mother attended the Baroness. Tana had slipped out of bed and wandered into the starlit gardens, where each leaf and bloom glimmered silver under the full moon. The night was warm, for it was the depths of summer. Only four, she was restless and lonely. There were no other servants' children her age with whom to play, and her mother was far too busy with her duties to do more than see to Tana's most basic needs.

"Come here, little one," a tall man, who bore a buckler dressed with three gold stars, called as she turned into a long section flanked by rows of stately Italian cypress.

Startled, she stopped on the crushed gravel path, bare toes curled, and gazed up at him. Clad in red and black, he was lanky, with brown hair that tumbled over his shoulders. His eyes reflected the starlight and his voice had an odd echoing timbre. "Who are you?" she asked, remaining well out of reach.

"Sir Alik Gento." He made her a sweeping bow. "Born in far-off Shaldaria and lately attached to His Majesty King Bartolo Clodoveo's service."

"The King?" She had some idea from overheard conversations of who that was and in how much disregard the current monarch was held by the Baron. She twined one of her black curls around her finger. "He's a bad man."

"No, child, he is not," Sir Alik said gently. "He is a very good man, trying his best to preserve his kingdom against unwarranted attacks, but we should not quarrel on your first visit! Let me tell you instead of the Aentian Court, which lies many leagues to the east on the shore of the Caltanese Sea where the highborn wear clothing woven from gold and silver! Such men I have fought! Such wonders I have seen!"

"The poppet does not want to hear that nonsense," someone said behind her. She whirled. Another man loomed there in the moonlit dark, broader across the shoulders than Sir Alik and more muscular. His face was covered with a fine black beard. "Come sit on my knee instead and hear how I once escaped across the Darpathian Pass, pursued by snow tigers!"

Tana did not know what to say and only stared at the hulking stranger.

He grinned fiercely. "Sir Lorico Salka," he said, "at your service, sweet lady."

She gazed down the garden path and realized a great many men were watching her, each standing on a small plot of earth, some of which were grown over and grassy, others still bare as though recently dug. They were dressed in odd styles, some in fighting leathers, others in brightly colored shirts, strangely shaped helms, and fine boots, as though they had come from very far away where folk dressed differently.

"Who are all these people?" she whispered to Sir Alik.

"The Baron's enemies, child," Sir Alik said, "many of us recruited by His Majesty Bartolo Clodoveo from kingdoms as far away as Termania." He gestured. "Sit down, then Sir Lorico and I shall tell you stories."

She settled on the rock border and heard both men's tales that night. The two told of fighting and valor and honor, keeping one's word no matter what it cost, honoring women and protecting the weak. She went back to her bed very late.

After that, down through the years, Tana listened to the dark gentlemen's stories night after night when her mother thought her safely tucked into her small cot. Indeed, she would have slept in the gardens during the warm seasons but for fear her mother would discover what she had been up to and forbid her. As it was, she stayed up much of the night, listening to stories of far-off lands and dead heroes, magical doings and imprisoned princesses, and then napped the boring afternoons away.

The dark gentlemen planted in the Baron's garden were her playmates and her teachers. Their tales told of a world much bigger and more intriguing than the Baron de Cordova's estate. They made so much seem possible, even that she, a servant's bastard daughter, could matter, that somewhere, sometime, she might find a better life than serving the Baron as a lowly drudge.

She did not understand, though, that they were all dead until she was eight. "Why don't I ever see you in the day?" she asked Sir Lorico one night when his exciting tale of riding giant wolves through an evergreen forest was done. "It gets lonely."

"Because that's the way the magick works," he said. "Those of us out here in the garden are no longer of this world and the daylight is permanently denied us."

"I don't understand." She took his callused hand. As always, his flesh was so very cold, like the bite of snow in deepest winter or the chill caress of an icicle. She pressed it to her cheek, enjoying its exotic feel.

"Child," he said softly, "we died, every last one of us, defending King Bartolo Clodoveo from the Baron's unlawful attacks." His dark-brown eyes were somber as he gazed down at her.

"Died?" She dropped his hand, then clutched her own hand to her breast, feeling how, bone-deep, the chill lingered. How could that be? Dead people were buried and went to Heaven or Hell, then you never saw them again. Her mother had explained that to her when the Baron's elderly mother had "passed away," as they termed it, last spring.

"Yes, we are all quite dead," Sir Alik said from across the path. "Torborg, the sorcerer in the Baron's employ, bound us here by his vile magick for the Baron's pleasure."

"But dead people go away," she whispered, finally understanding why each of her dark gentlemen was associated with a mound of earth. They were *graves*.

"We will not," Sir Lorico said. "Indeed, though we wish it were otherwise, we cannot."

She thought and thought, the ideas chasing each other. So many stories she'd heard out here under the starlight, along with the gentlemen's confidences, sympathy, advice, and affection—all from dead men who should no longer be walking this world. She felt around inside her head for fear and found none. They were strange, but nevertheless all she had. "Then," she said finally, trying to work out how she felt about this startling revelation, "you won't go away. You will always be with me."

"That, my sweet brave child," Sir Lorico said, taking her hand again so that his arctic chill flashed up through her arm into her spine and whirling head, "is sadly true."

oOo

So the years passed. Though the dark gentlemen dimmed somewhat, becoming gradually more sad and wraithlike, that was, she supposed, only to be expected. They were still hers on the nights the Baron did not visit the garden, and she treasured each and every one of them.

One August day, when she was fifteen with scullery duties of her own in the kitchens, de Cordova's middle son, Manuel Olivarios, came upon her as she sat on a bench in the corner, polishing one of Cook's treasured copper pots.

"What's your name, wench?" he demanded. His clothes were very fine, green-dyed leathers and boots, a shirt of brocaded linen. His cheeks were ruddy with exercise, his mouth bad-tempered and sensual. He'd been away at school and she hadn't seen him for several years. He was so fine, he quite simply took her breath away.

She rose and curtsied as Mother, who had died two years before, had taught her, keeping her eyes focused on the tiled floor. "Tana, young Master." The steamy kitchen air was redolent with boiled cabbage and roasting lamb. On the vast stove, pots industriously bubbled.

"Tana!" Cook called, a note of panic in her voice. A rotund woman with ginger-colored hair threaded with silver, she gestured at the girl with one work-reddened hand. "Get over here and put that pot back where it belongs!"

Tana glanced over the young master's shoulder to meet Cook's worried gaze, her fingers tight upon the cool metal.

"Shut up, Cook," Manuel Olivarios said. "I have business with this morsel." He slapped his green gloves against his muscular thigh. "Are you a clean girl?"

Startled, she glanced up to meet blue eyes like flint. A spark simmered within his gaze, bright and dangerous. Her pulse thundered. "Yes, sir."

"Then come to my rooms tonight," he said and stalked off.

Trembling, Tana resumed polishing the copper pot. She bit her lip, fought the hot salt tears that wanted to slide down her cheeks.

Cook sighed and turned back to rolling out the pastry for the evening's meat pies. "No help for it, I'm afraid. You've attracted his attention with all that curly black hair. I did warn you to keep it tucked up under your cap or there would be trouble of this sort."

Tana knew something of what went on in bedrooms. The dark gentlemen had told her, often in detail that would have thoroughly shocked Cook. They missed such intimate physical connections, she knew. But in their tales, a woman and man freely chose one another. That mysterious quality called "love" drove their union. She had no choice here and certainly "love" had nothing to do with what Manuel Olivarios intended.

"I won't go," she murmured, scrubbing industriously. "I'll hide in the gardens instead."

"You will go to him if you know what's good for you," Cook said, scowling, "and then, my girl, you'll make him believe you desire nothing more out of life than to be his doxy for however long he wants you, or he'll beat you black and blue."

oOo

That night, as the quarter moon rose, Tana fled the great house into the exotic tangle of the gardens, heart pounding. She knew what Cook said was true. Surrendering to Manuel Olivarios was inevitable for one of her lowly station, and yet she could not bring herself to do it. She wanted what Sir Lorico and Sir Alik had been telling her about all these years. When she finally gave herself to a man, she wanted love.

At any rate, they were all there, her dark dead gentlemen, either standing or lounging on their graves, no older in death than they had been in the last moment of life. Moonlight danced silver along the length of their swords. Sir Alik held out his cold hand as she passed. "Child, you've been crying."

"No, I haven't," she said, willing her fingers not to reach up and wipe her wet cheeks. "I came for a story."

"Which you can have," he said, his dead eyes kind, "from any of us, so that cannot be what makes you so sad."

"I'm all right," she said, though her voice trembled.

"It is a man who makes her sad," a new voice said. "Count on it. That's always the way of it for young servant girls."

Tana turned. There, beyond the pink sweep of the blooming azaleas, she saw the mounded dirt of a raw new grave. A woman with long red hair perched upon it, polishing a deadly-looking rapier with a lacy handkerchief. She wore a frothy white shirt, midnight blue jerkin, leather trousers, and thigh-high gleaming black boots. Tana's mouth fell open. From time to time, the Baron's forces returned with a newly dead hero to inter here, but never before a woman.

"I am Calandria Padilla y Aznar," the woman said. Her eyes caught the quarter moon's light and gleamed as though lit from within. "Don't stare like a startled sheep, girl. One might almost think you've never conversed with a dead woman before."

"I—have not," Tana said, resisting the urge to curtsey. "Where did you come from?"

Calandria sat back, the rapier braced across her arm. She turned, revealing her profile. The woman's nose had been broken more than once, and then set badly. She had a strong face with bold cheekbones and might have once been even beautiful. The newcomer cocked her head. "You fancy yourself a wit?"

"I only meant—what battle?" Tana said, flustered. Usually the dead heroes loved to talk about themselves. This was a lonely place. Those of the great house, other than the Baron, avoided the haunted gardens. His sons came here for training, but only when their father commanded it.

"Oh, that," Calandria said. Her deep-brown eyes regarded Tana. "I fell protecting the King himself at the battle of Mardon Fields against your damnable Baron."

"The King?" Tana said, her hands fisted. "You've actually seen him?"

"Seen him?" Calandria laughed, but it was not a merry sound. "I dined at King Bartolo Clodoveo's table, played cards with his fussy little queen. I was a member of his personal guard these three years past."

"Then he must be very sad," Tana said, "that you are— gone—from him now."

"You mean dead," Calandria said. She raked her fingers back through her red fall of hair. "Always say what you mean, child. Dancing around truths, even monumentally ugly ones, never profits anyone."

"Dead," Tana said softly. She gazed down the long double rows of her dark gentlemen, all watching her in the moonlight.

"So how does the Baron do it," Calandria said, "imprison the dead here in this—" Her lips compressed. "—dreadful *place*, so that we have form but no freedom?"

The breeze rose, playing with the woman's long red hair."You don't know?" Tana said. Up and down the garden path, the dark gentlemen remained silent. Perhaps they knew. Perhaps not. She had never thought to ask.

"One moment, I was in screaming agony with a deep sword cut to my side, bleeding my life's blood into the thirsty black soil," the swordswoman said, "then I found myself here in the night, far away from the battlefield, surrounded by shrubs and posies, and unable to leave this damned heap of dirt!"

Tana thought of the little she actually knew as the night air soughed against her face, saturated with the scent of jasmine. "The Baron employs a sorcerer," she said. "His name is Torborg. They say—" She lowered her voice, for it was not wise to speak of the old wretch who was reported to have ears everywhere. "They say he has thunder in his hands, that he rides the lightning itself!"

Calandria's elegant red brows quirked upward. "Have you ever seen such goings-on?"

"Well, no," Tana said, "but I am just a scullery maid. No one performs wonders for the likes of me."

Calandria reached out and grazed Tana's tear-stained cheek with the tip of an icy finger. "A scullery maid in difficulty, I warrant."

Manuel Olivarios. It all came rushing back at her. She shivered, though the night air was warm as bath water. "I am summoned to the young master's bed this evening."

Calandria cocked her head. "And you do not wish to go?"

"Of course not!" Tana was shocked. "I am a good girl! I

have no intention of being—used—in that way, as my mother was!"

"Oh, there's nothing wrong with a nice bedding," the dead swordswoman said, "providing both are willing." A knowing smile crept across that bold, strong face.

"Well, I am not!" Tana's cheeks heated.

"Then—" Calandria balanced the rapier in her hand, sighting down along its wicked length. "—don't go."

If only it were that easy. "He is the Baron's son," the girl said while the stars shimmered overhead and the nightjar called in the darkness, "and I am only a lowly servant."

"You are whatever you make up your mind to be," Calandria said. "Do you think my mother, whoever she was, intended that I should grow up to take arms in the King's personal guard?"

Tana could not imagine any woman would.

"It does not matter how you begin your journey," Calandria said, tossing back her head. "What matters is that you decide what you want and then make that life come to be."

"I am but a servant," Tana said. "He is the Baron's son. I have no way to stop him from taking whatever liberties he wants."

"Only ninnies speak like that," Calandria said. She crossed her arms. "What you need, my girl, is a dagger."

"Scullery maids have no coin to buy weapons," Tana said.

"Well, I just happen to have one," Calandria said, "and pisspoor chance of ever needing to use it again, bound here to this wretched garden as I seem to be." She drew a gleaming blade from a sheath at her waist. Starlight glinted along its elegant length.

Tana stared at the former King's guard. The sorcery that imprisoned the dark ones here allowed them to manifest in the night, else they would not have been able to instruct and spar with the Baron's sons. But did the enchantment also permit their weapons to exist outside the gardens?

Calandria's icy fingers seized Tana's wrist, then pressed the double-edged blade into her startled grasp. Tana's own fingers closed around the elaborately-styled hilt with its sensual swirls.

It felt exquisitely cold, as though it had come from the depths of a snowbank in deepest winter.

"Hold it like this," Calandria said, shifting Tana's grip. The weapon was finely balanced, feeling almost like an extension of her arm.

"King Bartolo Clodoveo himself presented it to me," Calandria said, "the first time I bedded him." She smiled wickedly. "A blade in memory of a blade, you might say!"

Tana flushed.

"Now," Calandria said, "come at me with the dagger. See if you can slash my throat."

Tana's hand dropped to her side. "Lady, I couldn't!"

"Why?" The swordswoman's eyes glinted with reflected starlight. "Afraid you might *kill* me?"

Tana felt her face heat. That was of course ridiculous. The swordswoman was already quite dead.

"Or you can let this rutting brute drag you off to his bed and use you as if you were no more than a makeshift scabbard for his adolescent sword," Calandria said. "That is the fate of most comely serving girls in great houses. If you want to be one of his whiney little female sheep, it's certainly no concern of mine."

"No, I do not!" Tana raised the blade again and then leaped at Calandria.

The swordswoman laughed and easily caught her wrists. The chill of her fingers bit deep like the coldest winter's ice. "Not bad," she whispered, leaning close, her breath glacial on Tana's ear, "but be patient when you attack. Wait for an opening. He'll underestimate you, I promise." She shoved the girl back. "Now, try again and, this time, point the dagger at me, not the sky. You're not trying to skewer a blasted star."

Tana inhaled, focusing. She hefted the blade in her right hand, aiming the tip as instructed.

"Come on!" Calandria said, gesturing. "You're in the hallway, carrying a breakfast tray, and—" She yanked off Tana's cap, then anchored her cold, cold fingers in the girl's curly hair, jerking her off balance. Tana cried out as she stumbled, then swung upwards with the dagger. Calandria's blue jerkin parted before the blade. Starlight glinted within the wound as though the swordswoman's flesh sheltered galaxies within.

Calandria looked down at the blaze of light and laughed. "Well done, young miss! You show a bit of promise, after all!"

The light flared, then faded as the dead flesh magically mended itself.

Tana was breathing hard. She stared down at the dagger in her hand, then tried to pass it back to Calandria.

"Nay, keep it, child." A rueful smile tugged at her pale lips. She unbuckled the sheath and handed it over, too. "I doubt I'll ever have use for it again."

"The blade is so fine," Tana said, her fingers stroking the sensual curves of the hilt, "but I don't know if I can take it out of the gardens. It is magicked, of course."

"Unlike me, it cannot die," Calandria said. "Take it and then we will both see what happens."

Tana slipped the dagger into its sheath, then tucked it between her bodice and apron. No one would expect her to have such a weapon. Indeed, if her mother had possessed a dagger and the will to use it, Tana herself might never have been conceived.

She returned to the great house, but not to her own poor cot, which was where Manuel Olivarios would send servants to look for her when she did not present herself in his rooms. Instead, she went to Cook's quarters and asked the older woman meekly if she might sleep on the floor.

"You know he will beat you on the morrow," Cook said, braiding her frosted ginger hair for bed.

"But that is tomorrow, not tonight," Tana said.

Cook tossed her a worn shawl. "Sleep here, then, little cat, for all the good it will do you," she said. "Young masters always take what they want and it would require a mind far more cunning than yours, my girl, to make the world work otherwise."

Tana stretched out on the cold flagstones and wrapped herself in the shawl. The old wool smelled of boiled turnips, oddly comforting. Her fingers curled around the fine leather sheath embossed with gold, and traced the fanciful swirled pattern. Tonight, at least, it was real, but would it still be with her in the daylight?

oOo

Cook woke before dawn, grumbling. Tana rolled over, then found that she still held the dagger. Excitement fluttered through her as she quickly washed her face, hands, and arms, then followed Cook to the kitchens to help with the day's bread-making.

The morning passed as they kneaded the dough, pared carrots and potatoes, and sliced lamb for pies. Tana, as scullery maid, was tasked with scrubbing the pots and keeping the cooking surfaces clean. She was so busy, she lost herself in the morning's tasks and quite forgot after a while to dread the young master's revenge.

She was just brushing back a black curl that had escaped her cap when Manuel Olivarios appeared in the kitchens. "So there you are," he said, his face hard. "I thought perhaps you had thrown yourself off a cliff."

Heart thumping, Tana buried her wet hands in her apron and curtseyed.

He was dressed in maroon today, jerkin, boots, and belt, with even a jaunty maroon feather atop his hat. His linen was so white, she thought she had never seen anything so clean in her entire life. She wondered suddenly how his flesh would smell. The dark gentlemen out in the gardens were always nattering about the scent of their "beloved."

"Well?" He carried a riding whip in one hand and now tapped it against his thigh.

"There—are no cliffs in these parts, young Master," she said. Her fingers found the sheath hidden under her apron and caressed the dagger's hilt.

"No, indeed," he said, "or I would throw you off one myself!" His blue eyes glinted with anger.

She could draw the dagger and plunge it into his heart. He would not be expecting any sort of attack from her. She was only a maidservant, soft and defenseless, given to tears and pleadings. Her fingers tightened on the hilt.

Manuel Olivarios snatched off her cap so that curly black hair cascaded to the center of her back, then fingered a lock as though he had every right to make free with her person. "Why did you not come to me last night?"

"Because—I did not wish to." Her voice trembled and she had difficulty meeting those gleaming blue eyes. Nevertheless, she raised her chin.

"Why would you think even for a second this has anything to do with what *you* wish?" He slapped her.

Her head rocked back and she gasped, tasting blood from a gashed lip. The Baron's son seized her wrist and pulled her out of the vast homey kitchen, dragging her down the hallway behind him like an errant goat on a tether.

Her face stung and her heart pounded wildly. The dark gentlemen, with all their tales of courtly wooing and romance, had never prepared her for this. She glanced about, but her captor ranked above everyone but his immediate family. No one here would help her, even if they did come along.

She would have to help herself.

Twisting against his grip as they ascended the stairs that accessed the private family living quarters, she broke free and fumbled the knife from its sheath.

"Damnation, stop fighting—" Manuel Olivarios turned, hand raised to strike her again. His blue eyes widened.

She pressed the dagger's tip against his white throat. "Very well, young Master," she whispered. "I have stopped fighting. Is this better?"

"Where—d-did you get that?" He stood very still, then one of his hands crept furtively toward the dagger in his own belt.

"It was a gift." She nicked his flesh and a driblet of hot blood stained the pristine whiteness of his linen shirt. "I would not, if I were you," she said and snatched his dagger for herself, tucking it into her waistband.

"My father will kill you!" He tried to retreat from the blade, but she followed, backing him against the cool stone wall. Her heart raced. The stairs were deserted now, but soon someone would happen by. A body was never alone for long in a great house like this, staffed by so many servants.

"Not if I kill you first," she said, trying with all her might to be bold, brassy Calandria. Keeping the dagger at his throat, she leaned in and sniffed. Manuel Olivarios smelled of lemon-scented soap and oiled leathers. His shirt was redolent with sunlight and wind from being dried outside. How many women, she wondered, labored day and night to keep him so clean and sweet-smelling?

She inhaled, letting the scents dance through her head, and then grinned up into his pale, sweating face. With her free hand, she grazed the back of one knuckle against his cheek. "If you had invited me nicely into your bed, I might have come, but—" She shrugged. "As it is, I decline." With a sudden move, she scratched his cheek with the dagger's razor-sharp point, then dashed back down the steps.

"You are dead!" Manuel Olivarios called after her, one hand pressed to his bleeding face. "There is nowhere in this house that you can hide!"

But he was, of course, wrong.

oOo

Tana had grown up in the great sprawling house and, as a servant, had encountered many rooms of which even Baron de Cordova had no knowledge. She rucked a nest for herself in a pile of discarded burlap sacks in a disused storeroom to sleep the rest of the day away until it was full dark. Even if Manuel Olivarios did summon the courage to admit he had been bullied by a scullery maid, the Baron's men would not find her here.

But she thought perhaps he would not speak of what had happened between them. What a blow to his manhood that would be in everyone's eyes: held at knife-point by a mere servant, and a girl at that! She smiled to herself as she fell asleep, cradling the dagger to her breast.

She woke, hungry and disheveled, somewhere after midnight. The house was still, as though holding its breath, the only sound the occasional creaking of ancient timbers. She rose and crept down a back hallway to the kitchens. The scent of boiled mutton lingered, though the cooking fires had been banked, and everything washed and put away. She had a pang of conscience, for that was her job. Cook had been forced to find someone else or do it herself.

Foraging, she ate half of a leftover lamb pie she found under a cloth, and a slab of bread, then hurried out into the night before anyone came upon her. The sky was clear, midnight blue and fathomless, littered with faraway stars. The wind bore the scent of the sea half a league distant.

Tana went to the Garden of Swords and found all the dark gentlemen waiting. They seemed very thin this night for some reason, indistinct and attenuated.

"Ah, poppet, there you are!" cried Sir Lorico. "What manner of story will you have from me this evening?" His lean face was anxious.

She saw his loneliness, how terrible it was to be tied to a tiny plot of earth, waiting for someone to take notice of him night after night. "I'm sorry, Sir Lorico," she said. "I have no time for stories now. I must speak with Calandria."

"Ah, yes, the new one," Sir Lorico said, sinking back to sit on his long ago grassed-over grave. He bent his head, laced his fingers. "I could tell that she was going to be trouble."

Down at the end of the garden, Calandria's lean form was pacing restlessly, her hands pressed to her temples. Her jerkin hung open. Her collar was unlaced.

"What's wrong?" Tana asked.

"You mean, besides the fact that I'm dead and planted in this demon's garden like a blasted rosebush?" Calandria's fine dark eyes were haunted.

Tana did not know what to say. Her own problems, she saw now, were trivial in comparison.

"During the day, we are compelled by the spell that binds us here to sleep," Calandria said, "and when I sleep, I dream— of another world just beyond closed gates of diamond, a silver-green land where I could walk in sunlight again, feel wind upon my face, know love and freedom and adventure. Then I wake, and I am only here, chained in the dark forever."

"Torborg," Tana whispered.

"I suppose that is the wretch's name," Calandria said. "He does not visit us. No one does, save you and the damnable Baron himself, and he comes only to gloat."

Tana looked about the night-shadowed rows of jasmine, azaleas, and thorny roses. "Is he here now?"

Calandria raised her head and sniffed the night breeze. "No, but the boy is."

"Manuel Olivarios?" Tana drew the dagger and turned, seeking to see him first before he could come up behind and surprise her.

"Is he the one who troubles you?" Calandria smiled and Tana saw that one of her front teeth was chipped. She drew her rapier with a ringing hiss. "That awkward puppy?"

Tana heard footsteps crunching along the gravel pathway. She ducked behind the azalea hedge bordering Calandria's grave, gripping the dagger's hilt with both hands.

Manuel Olivarios walked stiffly down the path, stopping every few strides to talk in a low voice with the dark gentlemen. Tana could not make out what he said, or what they replied, beyond that several laughed.

"Sir Puppy!" Calandria called as the youth neared. "What brings you to my parlor this fine night?"

Manuel Olivarios stopped and gazed impudently at Calandria. "My father spoke of you," he said, one hand on his sword. "How you paraded about in male clothing and killed your shocked betters time after time. He was glad when the opportunity came to plant you out here among the roses, where you could do no more harm to his plans."

"What happened to your face?" She grinned. "Cut yourself shaving?" She lunged at him with her rapier. The Baron's son swore and leaped back. "Care to parry with me a while, Sir Puppy? You might learn something."

"I'm looking for a maid," he said, lingering beyond her reach. "One of the kitchen staff. Have you seen her?"

"And what would you do with this 'maid,' should you find her?" Calandria said.

He stiffened. "That is none of your concern!"

"You sound a bit tetchy, my lad," Calandria said. "Could it be that this `maid' marked your pretty face?"

"Have you seen her or not?" he demanded.

"A scullery maid, out here?" She snorted. "Do you think your father went to all the trouble of planting his enemies in this gruesome fashion so that we could keep track of his *maids*?"

Scowling, he thrust his hands into his pockets and sauntered out of the Garden of Swords, kicking at the gravel with every step.

"Well," Calandria said after he was out of earshot, "I guess you were paying attention to your lesson last night, scullery maid."

Tana rose, clutching the dagger to her breast. "Do not call me that," she said. "I do not yet know exactly what I will be now, but I am a servant in this house no longer."

Calandria cocked her head. "No, child, I think you are not. But—" she said, grinning crookedly, "you need more lessons in how best to employ that blade, and then you must find something else to wear besides those tiresome skirts."

oOo

Tana gave Calandria the dagger she had taken from Manuel Olivarios and then the two of them sparred up and down the soft crumbly earth of the grave until almost dawn. Tana took a number of painful shallow cuts, but twice scored upon the swordswoman so that the starlight trapped within her opponent's dead flesh blazed forth. The dark gentlemen, watching her progress from their own plots, shouted encouragement and advice.

Together she and Calandria worked on balance and timing, and above all, focus. Tana grew weary and sweat-soaked, but it was glorious, using her strength and mind to accomplish more than scrubbing stupid pots. At the last, Calandria taught Tana how to disarm an opponent in close fighting. "That, above all else, is the move most likely to save your life someday," the swordswoman said. They finally stopped as the eastern horizon grayed.

Calandria drew a hand back over her forehead and sighed. "What I would give for a few moments in the sun!"

Tana looked back at the dark gentlemen. They had already faded back into their graves. She turned, but Calandria was no longer there, compelled by the approaching day to retreat beneath the ground. She knelt and placed her palms on the cool loose dirt. It was wrong, she saw now, to plant these fallen heroes in the Baron's garden like a crop of potatoes. Whatever the nature of that other world Calandria glimpsed in her magicked dreams, the swordswoman should be free to go to it.

Tana thought about her dark gentlemen as she slipped back to the storage room to hide. They had seemed larger and more boisterous when she had been very young, but now had grown faded and indistinct, slump-shouldered wraiths of their former selves, talking of their lives with a hungry desperation, as though they were no longer real without an audience.

They should all be freed, but she had not the slightest idea of how to break the dark magick which imprisoned them here. Torborg, the Baron's sorcerer, knew what to do, and the Baron himself likely knew too. Neither would tell her even if she did dare ask.

But—what of the Baron's heirs? The oldest, Adriano Casimero, no doubt had been instructed in the nature of this dark resource, but he was out on the battlefield somewhere, leading the Baron's forces in yet another campaign against the rightful King. Torborg was said to be at his side, employing his terrible dark magicks.

Cipriano Gilberto, the youngest, was but a lad of eleven, still laboring at his daily lessons in sword and shield and dagger.

That left only Manuel Olivarios, the pampered middle son. Had his father trusted him with the secret of the gardens? And, if so, how could Tana make him reveal it?

She took this conundrum to bed with her as she curled up in the forgotten storeroom's burlap sacks, then dreamt endlessly of being trapped with Calandria and all the dark gentlemen beneath the Garden of Swords' deep dark soil.

oOo

She slept until dusk, then woke, ravenously hungry. She needed a good wash, clean clothes, and something to eat. The scent of roast pork filled the air, drifting up from the kitchens. Tucking up her black curls beneath her now-grimy cap, she lowered her eyes and skulked through the back corridors, edging into Cook's realm, hoping not to be noticed.

Cook glanced over her shoulder as she arranged parsnips on a platter. "Oh, it's you, is it? Come to steal a muffin or two?"

Tana's face warmed.

"I suppose you're hiding from *him*, still." Cook sniffed dismissively. "Much good that will do you! You'll see. The highborn always get their way, and I don't know why even for a second you should think otherwise, being who and what you are." She pursed her lips, then picked up a checkered cloth tied at the corners. "Here. Take this up to my room to eat and then tidy yourself. You smell like a field hand!"

The cloth bulged invitingly with bread and cheese and grapes. "Thank you, Cook," Tana said meekly.

"You cannot stay here unless you make peace with what has to be," Cook said, settling the platter into the hands of a serving boy. "Either go to him this night or take yourself off. It's one or the other, my girl."

Tana nodded, then scuttled up the back steps to Cook's quarters before she attracted any more attention. There she ate half of Cook's bounty, saving the rest for later, then gratefully washed.

Cook came up after the Baron's dinner had been served, the leftovers retrieved, and the kitchen made ready for the morrow. She sat heavily on her bed, staring down at her reddened hands. "Well?"

"I—shall go to him," Tana said. Her fingers traced the cold hard outline of the dagger tucked beneath her apron.

"That is for the best," Cook said. "You'll see. He'll soon grow tired of you, perhaps even after the first time. With that lot, it's all about the hunt. Once you submit, they move on to fresher game." Her pale blue eyes gazed at the wall, looking beyond the here and now.

With a pang, Tana realized Cook was talking about her own life. At some time in the past, she had been commanded against her will to someone's bed. *Not me,* she told herself. *I will* never *let myself be used like that! I want to see the wide world the dark gentlemen have been telling me about all my life! I want to matter!*

Cook made her ablutions, then crawled beneath her sheets. Tana waited until long after midnight, then slipped through the maze of corridors toward Baron's living quarters. Once she climbed the last set of stairs, she saw guards at each of the family's doors. Manuel Olivarios was expecting her.

Retreating, she went outside and regarded his rooms from the pathway below. This was the hottest month of the summer and all the windows stood open to catch the breeze coming off the sea half a league distant. Hiking up her skirts, she climbed the wall, slipping several times and scraping her knuckles on the ornamental flourishes before she achieved his balcony.

Inside, Manuel Olivarios lay naked, sprawled across his bed, sable hair tumbled across his face, hands fisted as though he dreamt of fighting. Drawing Calandria's dagger, she positioned the tip against his throat, stretched out beside his nude body, and watched the Baron's young heir breathe.

"Wha—?" He suddenly flailed awake.

She pressed the dagger harder so that blood, cherry-black in the dimness, trickled down his throat and soaked into the sheet. "Shhh, lover," she said softly. With her free hand, she smoothed the damp hair out of his eyes. "You said I was to come to you, so here I am."

"My father will kill you!" he gritted out.

"You said that before," she said, trying for Calandria's tone of cool irony. "I am quite terrified."

"Why—are you here?" He tried to ease away from the dagger but she held it firm. "If you wanted me dead, I would already be so."

"I want to know the secret of the garden," she said. "How does Torborg imprison the dead souls?"

"As if I would tell such a thing to a base creature like you!"

He seized her wrist and his fingers bit cruelly into her flesh.

With all her strength, she slashed with the knife, cutting his neck, though only shallowly. He cried out and his hand fell away. She pressed closer, her heart hammering. "What is the secret, lover?"

The door flew open, admitting the guard from the corridor. "My lord?"

Tana huddled against Manuel Olivarios, her free hand stroking his hair. "Send him away!" she whispered fiercely into his ear.

"G-go!" the young lord said. "And—say nothing of this."

The guard chuckled, and Tana knew that he could not see the dagger in the darkness. He thought the young master was merely bedding another in a long series of household servant girls. "Sorry, my lord." The door clicked shut.

"Now," she said, "tell me what I want to know!"

"What do you care about those old bones?" he said. "If you break the spell, they will be of use to no one, even themselves."

"They are people," she said, "or at least they were once. The Baron has trapped them so that they can never be at peace."

"They fought my father," he said uneasily, trying to squirm back. "He conquered them. It's only right they should serve him now."

"Do you know what they dream during the day when they 'sleep?'" she said. Her fingers were cramping with the stress of maintaining her grip. "They dream of a silver-green land under a bright sun where they may never enter! Think of yourself buried out there among the roses and worms, damned forever to attend some lording's spoiled sons, never to go on to the next world!"

"I don't believe you," he said. "They're just—" His hand slipped under his pillow and seized a dagger he had hidden there. With a flash, it pricked her throat. The two of them were at an impasse. She shivered. "What will you do now, tart?" he said huskily. "Shall we both die here in this bed?"

For an answer, she leaned in and kissed him hard on the lips, long and deep in the fashion spoken of so reverently by the dark gentlemen. His mouth opened in surprise and then he was kissing her back. It was—hot and sweet, unexpectedly pleasant. Blood pounded through her head, warmed her through and through. She forced herself to keep hold of the dagger at his throat.

His own dagger pressed harder as they kissed, but then gradually slipped. With a groan, he cast it away and closed his arms around her, pulling her suddenly pliant body against his warm chest. "So?" he said between kisses that made her head swirl.

His skin was soft, his mouth tasted of tomatoes and peppers from dinner. His fingers were skilled, stroking just where to draw the most response from her own unexpectedly sensitive skin as they slid beneath her bodice. This was what the dark gentlemen had meant, she thought dazedly, and Calandria too. *Nothing wrong with a good bedding,* the swordswoman had said.

But she could not forget what she had come for. "The secret," she whispered into Manuel Olivarios' mouth. "Torborg's secret?"

"I don't care!" he said, pulling her atop him. "If I am ever made the Baron, I shall have all those graves dug up and the bones burned so that I don't have the gloomy dead gibbering at me when I want to walk the gardens at night!"

She stared down at his face, dimly illuminated by starlight from the window. He was so very comely with those deep-set eyes and wide cheekbones, but shallow, spoiled, mean—and *vain*. "It will do no good to burn the bones," she said, caressing his ear with the tip of her dagger. He shivered as the blade skimmed over his skin. "They are magicked."

"I can break the magick," he said, then with a groan, sat up and buried his face in her half-covered breasts. "All the males in my line can. My father paid Torberg a great deal of money to give us control, so the gardens would exist beyond his death."

She pushed him away, then settled on her knees on the wide bed, just out of reach. Her lips felt swollen. Her skin still burned from his touch. "I don't believe you," she said. "If you could do such a thing, then you would not let Calandria Padilla y Aznar speak of you as she does."

"That harridan?" He eyed the dagger in her hand.

Tana let a small smile shape her lips as though she too had secrets to tell. "She says you are your mother's favorite, a weakling, a pampered little yappy lapdog, that you will never inherit, even if Adriano Casimero dies. Your father will pass the Barony down to young Cipriano instead, because you are utterly worthless!"

"The bitch!" He leaped off the bed and his naked body gleamed white in the night-shadowed chamber. "She hasn't been in that damned garden a week and already she's criticizing her betters!"

Tana turned the dagger in her hand so that she could watch the starlight trickle down the blade like quicksilver. "Calandria says she has no betters outside King Bartolo Clodoveo's court, especially not a bunch of jumped-up tradesmen like the de Cordovas."

"She is nothing!" Manuel Olivarios raked fingers back through his disordered black hair, quite beside himself. He seized a pair of leather trousers off the floor and put them on with savagely angry thrusts. "I will deal with her!" He burst out the door into the hallway, past the startled guard, who glanced inside the room at Tana.

"Lovers' quarrel," she said blithely, concealing the dagger in her bodice. She plucked a half-empty bottle of wine off his night stand and sauntered brazenly past the guard, down the corridors and into the starlit gardens.

Outside, the night air was thick with the last of the day's heat, though a breeze stirred the rose leaves and spread the scent of the night-blooming jasmine. Manuel Olivarios headed straight for the Garden of Swords, while Tana slipped along behind, keeping to the deepest shadows.

She could hear him muttering to himself and knew she had hit a nerve. It had not been difficult. Everyone in the great house knew that he was his mother's favorite and at sixteen, he was old enough to be off fighting at his brother's side if his father had thought him competent.

Just ahead, laughter filled the air, low and musical. Calandria. "Sir Puppy," the swordswoman called. "Have you come to dance with me again?"

Keeping low, Tana skirted the avenue of graves and approached from the other side. All the dark gentlemen were watching, their hands upon their swords.

"Bitch!" Manuel Olivarios spat. His hands were fisted and his naked chest was beautiful in the light from the quarter moon. "Whore!"

"My, aren't we in a state tonight?" Calandria grinned, revealing her chipped tooth. She trailed a finger down his breastbone. "Are we perhaps in need of a little workout? There are a few moves I can show you."

Tana saw Manuel Olivarios shiver. Well did she know the icy touch of that dead hand from their sparing sessions.

In answer, he only dropped to his knees and scrabbled in the mounded dirt.

Calandria settled on the grave and lounged back, one hand on her rapier. "You wish to sleep in my true embrace?" She laughed again. "How utterly charming."

"Silence, strumpet!" Manuel Olivarios kept digging.

Tana crept closer, peering through a gap in an azalea hedge. Torborg must have buried something with Calandria, indeed with all the dead heroes, to anchor the spell that bound them here.

For long moments the young master dug. His naked arms were plastered with damp soil, his face gritty. Then, finally, he found what he was looking for. He sat back, in his hand a tiny jade figurine, shiny with reflected starlight.

"This!" He bounded back onto his bare feet. "This binds your soul! I could crush it and then you would trouble me no more with your vile accusations!"

"Then do it, Sir Puppy," Calandria said. She stared at him evenly. "Set these tired bones free."

"And mine too!" cried Sir Lorico.

"And mine!" another voice joined in.

"Set us all free!" chorused from the double rows of graves.

Manuel Olivarios stared at the jade, then seemed to realize what he was doing and what his father would say, once it was done. With a curse, he shoved the tiny figurine back into the soil and covered it. He rose, brushed the damp earth from his breeches, and slumped, head down, back toward the great house and his de Cordova inheritance.

Tana waited until he was gone, then joined Calandria.

"You saw," the swordswoman said, nodding at the disturbed foot of her grave.

"Yes." Tana dug in the loosened earth, then held up a tiny jade owl to the starlight.

Calandria reached, then dropped her hands as though its touch would burn. "Destroy it, child, and set me free!"

"I cannot guarantee that you will find that silver-green land of sunlight," Tana said, a lump in her throat. "Here, you have at least a form of life."

"Here, I have servitude of the meanest sort and the binding of vile sorcery," Calandria said. She tossed her rapier at Tana's feet. "I do not care what lies beyond, as long as I can go from this terrible place!"

Tana nodded, laid the rapier aside, then searched until she found an herb bed bordered with ornamental rocks. Placing the jade owl on a rock, she picked up a stone and crushed the figure between the two.

The night *rang* as though it were a perfect crystalline bell. Tana felt the release flash through her bones, tasted it like white lightning on her tongue, could see nothing but a wondrous silver-green fire that filled her head.

When her vision finally cleared, the dark gentlemen were all straining at the boundaries of their plots, staring at her. "Now," said Sir Alik, "assist the rest of us to follow the lady!"

Tana labored through the night, digging and digging, releasing the heroes one after one, each of them trapped by a different jade figurine, wolf and horse, deer and eagle. When dawn neared, she had released them all, except for Sir Lorico.

"I shall miss you most, sir," she said as she dug for the last talisman. Her arms ached with weariness. Her fingernails were chipped and broken. A hot tear trickled down her face. "You have been with me almost my entire life."

"You do not need me, now, child," he said. His scarred face smiled sadly. "You should go out into the world and have adventures of your own, not sit here in the darkness night after night, listening to our worn-out tales."

"Yes, I shall have to go now," she said, her fingers closing at last around the cool jade hidden in his grave. She pulled the figurine up. It was a sleek little bear, perfectly carved by some unknown hand to hold the wicked magick that had imprisoned the fallen hero here for such a long time. She brushed the dirt off its miniature face, then traced the curves with her fingers. "When the Baron finds out, he will kill me for what I have done."

"You have a brave and true heart," Sir Lorico said. "Go to King Bartolo Clodoveo. Show him Calandria's rapier and tell him how you freed her. I warrant he will find a place for you."

Perhaps she would, Tana thought as she placed the jade bear on a rock, then brought down the stone with all her strength.

The night rang even louder than all the other times, as though breaking the last spell had freed the entire world. As she rose, brushing jade dust off her hands, intense green lightning cracked though there were no clouds, striking the ground again and again all around her. Her skin prickled as unearthly silver-green fire crawled over the land, lit up rose bushes and stone borders and benches, shimmered up her skirts and outlined her shaking hands. All around her, the gardens flared a brilliant silver-green down to the last leaf and thorn, almost too bright to look upon.

Heart racing, she turned her eyes to the stars. They blazed huge in the black sweep of the predawn sky, much larger than she had ever seen them, also silver-green, swirling, almost— dancing.

In the great house, a light appeared in an upper story window. Someone must have been woken by the lightning. The Garden of Swords stood silent now, just a sad row of graves emptied of their magickly imprisoned spirits. The green fire crackled, faded, then seeped away like water into thirsty earth. In the east, the horizon was now stained with the faintest tinge of vermilion. The sun was coming up.

More lights illuminated the windows. She heard voices, both male and female, as though servants and masters and mistresses were asking each other what had happened. Retrieving Calandria's gleaming rapier, she pulled off her maid's cap and let her black curls cascade down over her shoulders. The breeze freshened, bearing aromas both earthy and wild from the tide-struck ocean and its rocky coast. Though she had lived all her life just half a league away, she had never once seen the sea, only hearing tales of its restless beauty from the dark dead gentlemen.

Someone carrying a lamp left the house, headed for the gardens. The voices grew louder, more demanding. *Decide what you want,* Calandria said in her memory, *and then make that life come to be.*

So Tana tucked the rapier under her arm and set off to explore the shore of the vast briny sea.

Diana **L.** **Paxson** is the author of twenty-eight novels, including the *Westria* series and the recent *Sword of Avalon*, featuring history and magic. She has contributed to many anthologies including *Thieves' World* and *Sword and Sorceress*, and has served as a judge for the Pagan Fiction contest. After majoring in English with a French and Art minor at Mills College, she went on to earn a Master's degree in Comparative Literature with an emphasis on the Middle Ages from the University of California in Berkeley. In her last semester, she got the bright idea of throwing a tournament in her backyard, an idea which unexpectedly took root and turned into the Society for Creative Anachronism. She lives in Berkeley ("because there, we wouldn't be the weirdest parents at our kids' school") in a rambling house called Greyhaven with an arbitrarily variable number of people, cats, and non-corporeal entities in for a cup of tea. Read about her Westria books and more at http://www.westria. org/

BLUE VELVET

by Diana L. Paxson

Algiers at nightfall...scents of spices and excrement, voices raised in argument or song, warm air rising from sun-heated stone and a cooler breath from the sea. And drumming, always the drumming, throbbing in the blood and numbing the brain.

And my sense of direction, also, thought Claude, leaning on his sword-cane and staring around him. The ovoid cupola of the great El Djedid mosque rose above the rooftops; he was almost sure he had left the nearby market by the road that led back to his hotel, but he was abruptly certain he had never seen this alley before.

It was typical, he thought, of the misdirection that had frustrated him ever since he arrived. His business went well, but he had made no progress on the other quest on which his father's old friend had sent him. To find the missing girl, he must know where to begin. For a moment he wished himself back in Brazil, where he understood the language and the spirits of the country. The Arab drums stirred the blood, but their rhythms were strange.

Around a corner and along a wall whose stones might have been here since Algiers was a Roman town, he found himself in a street of basket-makers, that twisted like a drunken snake. Men taking in their wares glanced curiously at the infidel in his white linen suit, a low-crowned hat on his elegantly barbered blond hair. He could not hear the market any more. But this was still what they called *Al-Djazaïr Al Mahroussa*—"Well Kept Algiers." If he walked downhill he must come to the harbor, and that would bring him to the boulevard where the French had erected their civic buildings when they conquered Algeria thirty years before.

As he turned, Claude heard a cry and then the unmistakable kettle-mending clangor of steel on steel. It was a sound that any man of sense would flee, but after the first *frisson* of recognition, his feet carried him forward. Five men in white robes were mobbing another, whose blue *djellabia* flapped as he defended himself with a curved knife in one hand and in the other, a piece of board. At least, thank the good God, one could tell which were the attackers. Claude gripped the shaft of his swordstick; steel hissed as he drew the blade.

He had passed the point through the shoulder of the first man before they were aware of him. The fellow fell back with a shriek, and two of the others turned, wickedly curved blades gleaming in the last of the light. Claude settled *en garde*, point weaving gently, lips curling in a feral grin. The nearest man hesitated, then, with a glance at his fellow, charged.

With a speed beyond thought, Claude whipped his blade across the first man's face and dropped beneath his stabbing arm to impale the second with a neat stop-thrust. For a moment the bearded features writhed, far too close to his own. The knife, still obeying its owner's last instruction, sliced through the sleeve of Claude's coat. But there was no strength in the blow.

The man in blue had killed one of his assailants. The other, seeing three of his allies dead and himself outnumbered, grabbed the man Claude had blinded and scrambled after the one who had been pinked in the shoulder. Their prey came upright slowly, the fire of battle fading from his eyes.

"I thank you for your assistance." The native spoke with the careful diction of the mission schools, his voice unusually deep and smooth.

"It was my pleasure," Claude replied truthfully. It was not

the sentiment of a civilized man, but in the past few years he had learned to crave the release that came from pitting one's strength against another man.

"May I know the name of my rescuer?"

"I am the Baron DeLorme," Claude sketched a bow.

The other man salaamed. "You may call me Veludo." Claude raised an eyebrow at the Portuguese word. "When I traded in Brazil, they gave me that name because of my fondness for this blue velvet I wear." Veludo held out a fold of his robe, which was indeed made from velvet instead of the usual wool, noticed a long tear, and sighed.

"I also—" Claude grimaced at his hanging sleeve. Along the top of his arm, a thin line of red was beginning to show. "Did the scum wound you?"

"Only in my vanity," Veludo fingered the velvet again. He frowned as he noticed Claude's arm. "But it is you, *monsieur le baron*, who are wounded. You must come with me." He gestured gracefully. "We shall tend that cut and you may refresh yourself before you return to your hotel." He picked up the sheath to the swordstick and held it out with a smile. He was very dark, with the aquiline features of East Africa, but that was not unusual here. Algiers had been a center for the slave-trade for centuries.

Claude nodded. He had no desire to enter the Hotel Napoléon looking as if he had been in a street brawl. Besides, his cut was beginning to sting. He wiped his blade and slid it into the hollow stick. "Why were those men attacking you?"

Veludo shrugged. "I have business rivals. I was foolish to walk alone, but I thought that here, so close to my lodging, they would not dare."

The wrought-iron gate through which Veludo led the way opened into a courtyard filled with a sudden luxuriance of flowering shrubs, and a lemon tree in simultaneous fruit and flower. In the midst of the greenery, a fountain laid a blessed mist of moisture on the air. As they entered, a woman appeared from one of the inner doors, pulling a corner of her headcloth across her face before Claude could glimpse more than a flash of dark eyes and a scar. She took in the condition of the two men and snapped an order to someone in the house behind her before speaking to her master again.

Veludo turned to Claude. "Fadhma says that the baths will be made ready while she looks at your wound. By the time we have cleansed ourselves, there will be food—you will honor my table?"

Do I have a choice? Claude wondered, borne along on this tide of hospitality. But it sounded better than dining alone, or worse still, enduring the bourgeois inanities of the other guests in the hotel.

oOo

"What is your business?" Claude asked, sipping the mint tea the women brought in after the meal.

"I trade in fabrics—silks and velvets for great lords, and fine lace such as men give their wives."

"But Fadhma does not wear them...." The woman had been dressed in a sleeveless garment of the coarse brown wool they called *haik,* over the muslin shirt that was the common wear.

"Ah, but that is her choice," said Veludo, "her solidarity with the peasants who still resist your soldiers in the mountains."

And yet, thought Claude, if her gaze had been disapproving, her hands had been gentle as she bound up his wound.

"And she is not my wife, nor even my concubine," Veludo added with a smile. "She was fleeing the husband who gave her that scar, and I took her in. I do not even know her real name. She calls herself Fadhma after the holy woman of the Kabyles."

Claude nodded. He had heard stories of Lalla Fadhma n'Soumer, famous as a leader of the Kabyle resistance to the French conquest. Fadhma reminded him of women he had met in Paris who were always campaigning for some worthy cause. How many of them, he wondered now, bore invisible scars?

"What fortune brought you here to be my rescuer?" Veludo asked then.

Claude's business here was no secret, but he wondered suddenly if he might confide his other errand as well. "I belong to a Consortium of men who seek to invest in your country. I have spent some time at the emerald mines of Brazil."

"But we have no emeralds in Algérie!"

"True, but there is gold in the southeast, and rumors of diamonds. Most of my colleagues are men of substance—" he patted his flat belly, "in more ways than one, so they asked me to represent them. And hearing I was coming to this country, an old friend of my father begged my aid. His grand-daughter was abducted from the ship carrying her home from Italy. We believe she was brought to Africa, but an afternoon in the Casbah has taught me only how much I have to learn about this land…"

"That is more than the most of your countrymen understand," Veludo observed wryly.

"You asked how you could repay me," Claude said then. "Can you tell me where to begin?"

For a moment Veludo's dark gaze grew inward. Then he smiled. "I believe we may find news at the *Maison de la Rose*…."

oOo

Clearly, Veludo did not believe in wasting time, thought Claude as he pulled the hood of the cloak his host had given him over his head and followed the other man into the night. It was woven of a fine black wool, the edges stiff with gold thread. Beneath it, he wore a kaftan in saffron colored silk, the mate to his companion's blue.

"Your coat is ruined, *mon vieux*, and we must dress well," Veludo had said, offering the garments, "or they will turn us from the door."

Claude had heard of *Beit Ouarada*, the House of the Rose, but he had not expected to see it. The year in which he had watched consumption claim the life of a courtesan who had once been his mistress had soured him on the demi-monde. But the *Maison de la Rose* was supposed to be something out of the ordinary, even among houses of pleasure, a place where the French conquerors could shed the inhibitions of Europe and indulge their most fervid oriental phantasies. Whatever delights or perversions might be found in the hareem of a sultan could be provided here.

As they approached the gate, Claude could already smell the roses, wreathing the spikes atop the wall with scarlet blossoms and thorns, filling the warm air of the African night with their perfume. Light from the lanterns set atop the pillars glowed on the full crimson breeches and crossed bandoliers of the guards, whose ebony skins and smooth features showed that they had come from the Cote d'Ivoire.

Veludo said a few words to the guard, who seemed to know him, and beckoned to a small boy dressed in crimson and black striped trousers who had been trailing his fingers in the cool waters of the fountain.

"He will take us to Madame Ourada, and if fate favors us she will grant us a little of her time."

Claude had not realized that the lady who presided over the establishment was also called Rose. His heartbeat sped up a little. Whether or not this encounter was fruitful, it was bound to be interesting.

The boy led them through a series of gardens where the scents of jasmine and other night-blooming flowers mingled with the ubiquitous sweetness of the roses. Fountains plashed musically, and in gilded cages nightingales sang. But more vivid than the flowers were the women and boys who displayed themselves upon the scattered cushions, or strolled upon the paths, or danced to the plangent strum of the *oudh* and the delicate tapping of the drums. Gentlemen who had not yet made their selections moved among them, their crisp linen suits and knotted ties a stark contrast to the abandon of the others. It reminded him oddly of the Brazilian Carnivale.

Three girls swayed around him, veils concealing and revealing naked skin, one pale gold, one a warm brown and the third shining ebony. What was cultivated in these gardens was the beauty and grace of the unconfined human form. Claude's body moved easily within the loose robes Veludo had given him. How tempting it would be to cast off the bonds of duty and convention and join them.

The slender young man who was playing the *oudh* met his eyes with an amused, complicit smile. Claude felt his flesh stir in response. Was this why Europeans clung to their stiff clothing, so unsuited to equatorial lands? He had never been a lover of men, and he had always put his duty above his desires, but here, everything conspired to shake all certainties. He tried to distract himself by pricing the fabrics that covered those lissom forms, but he could still feel the touch of the musician's glowing dark eyes. It was said that the *Maison de la Rose* could satisfy all desires. Including, he thought in confusion, those you did not know you had.

Veludo was the center of a chattering group of girls who seemed to be showing off what they had done with his cloth. They blew kisses of farewell as their guide led the way past a screen of marble carved into a lacework of vines and flowers. Gratefully, Claude followed.

oOo

"You will take coffee with me?"

Ourada's voice, thought Claude, was like the syrupy Arab preparation itself, hot as the devil, exciting as a trumpet call, and sweet as love. To be in her presence was like standing near a fire. He met Veludo's amused gaze, flushed, and nodded. She was like Corquisa, he thought with a reminiscent throb of the flesh, or rather what the Brazilian courtesan might one day become. Honey-colored curves were alternately hidden and revealed by a loose garment of shot silk whose colors shifted from burgundy to flame. Midnight hair coiled across her shoulders, held by pins with rubies set in gold. The room was a worthy setting, with its silk hangings and intricately patterned Turkey carpets in deep red and black and gold. Hanging lamps in pierced brass cast sequins of light across the room.

She snapped her fingers, and the boy scampered off. Another gesture indicated the cushioned rosewood chairs.

"And what do you have for me, my dear?" asked the courtesan as they sat down.

"There is a bolt of black satin with roses of crimson velvet that I would like to offer you," said Veludo. "But that is not why we have come. We seek a girl—"

"Well, you have come to the right place, but for that, you surely did not need to speak with me...."

Claude felt his body responding again as Ourada laughed. A servant brought in a silver tray with three porcelain cups filled with a dark liquid and set it on a small table.

"This girl..." said Claude, taking his notecase from a pocket beneath his robes and sliding out the photograph of a young woman in a bell-skirted tartan gown leaning against a pillar. Despite the studied pose, she seemed to have alighted rather than settled there. The stiff line of the corset enclosed a torso just beginning to show a womanly curve, and there was still a hint of softness in the line of check and brow. Her hair had been parted in the middle and drawn back severely to fall in precise sausage curls from a dark bow. But it was the expression one noticed, the quirk at the corners of her mouth belying the mutinous line of the brows.

"A young lady of spirit, I perceive," said Madame Ourada.

"So I am told. She has red hair. The ship on which she had taken passage from Naples was found floating without passengers or crew. It is feared that they were taken by pirates. The girl, Adèle, was fifteen years old. It is understood that this is a forlorn hope," Claude went on, "but M. De Sartres asked me to search. He has received no request for ransom, and fears she was brought here to be sold."

Madame Ourada sipped a little coffee and set the cup down again.

"You Europeans pretend horror at the trade in slaves, yet it is not so long since your ship captains carried blacks in the thousands from Africa to the plantations of the Americas. Slaves are still sold in the Arab lands, but if you have visions of this maiden in the harem of some pasha, I can tell you that in these times there are few who would dare. It is the men of Europe who trade in white flesh now."

"Should I search in France, then?"

"I do not say that she has been taken to Europe," the lady replied. "Only that you must look for a European. The surintendant of the port of Algiers has a taste for young girls, but he is too powerful for anyone to accuse. I think you are the kind of *preux chevalier* who fights dragons and rescues maidens. A warning—if you go after him, you must be very careful."

"Drumont!" Claude straightened, staring. "But I have lunched with him! He is a member of the Consortium that—" He broke off, remembering the amused calculation in the man's porcine gaze. Drumont knew why Claude was here. Behind that bushy mustache, had he been laughing?

Madame Ourada raised one finely shaped eyebrow. "I have in this House an Italienne who was once his slave. She too has red hair. When she reached the age of eighteen, he sold her to me."

"She is called Celestina, yes?" Veludo inquired. "For her I have provided silk of the color of turquoise. This evening, is it possible that she is free?" He exchanged looks with Claude. "The gentleman will happily pay for her time."

"You, my friend, will provide me with that crimson flowered silk, not so? Because I also do not work for free." Ourada smiled.

"Madame, your beauty will adorn my cloth!" Veludo's teeth flashed white in the black beard.

I will pay for that, also, thought Claude. He took his cup and in a single swallow drank the dark bittersweet liquid down.

oOo

The boy led Claude to a small parlor. He could hear the sounds of lovemaking from the chambers they passed. Where every sight and sound was calculated to appeal to the senses, it was not easy to remember his duty. Even the thought of the girl he wished to rescue brought images of the child stripped of her armored clothing, with that bright hair flowing free, and with the thought came his own body's response. But if his flesh were as weak as that of any other man, he could hope at least to rule his will.

He rose from the settee as the door opened and a woman in a wrapper of aqua silk trimmed with blonde lace came in. She must be in her mid-twenties by now. Her hair had darkened to auburn, sparking with fiery glints in the lamplight. Her figure was buxom, though her waist was still trim.

"*Buona notte, Signorina,*" Claude stumbled on the Italian words.

"Oh, monsieur, I have been in this country for ten years," she gave a brittle laugh. "You may speak in French to me!"

Claude bowed. "Thank you for allowing me to speak with you."

"They say you wish to rescue another lost soul from that pig Drumont." The aquamarine eyes grew suddenly hard.

"Yes, if the maiden is there—"

"You will not save her from rape," Celestina answered bitterly. "But you may be in time to save her from despair. He still torments my dreams."

"What can you tell me about the household? Where would he be holding her?"

"You do not intend a frontal attack?" The brittle laugh came again. "That is well. Drumont is a power in Algiers, and he knows that he is not loved. The men of his house go armed, and in a heartbeat he could have a troop of Spahis at his gate. You must go in the back way, through the gardens." She leaned forward, describing the routes that were least used and the places one might hide. "Of course," she said at last, "all this might have changed. But in the days when the only thing that kept me in my wits was to plan escape, this was what I learned."

"Mademoiselle, you have my deepest gratitude. Is there anything I can do for you?"

"Can you save me from a life of sin, do you mean?" Surprisingly, her laugh was not so bitter as before. "To my family I am dead, but Madame allows us to save a little, and when I am too old to please a man I will have enough to support myself at some small place. I will tell them I am a widow, and truly, when I think of the women in my village, worn out before they are thirty with childbearing and drudgery, I wonder if perhaps I am the lucky one. Except for the memories." She shrugged. "We are all in bondage. Your maiden will never be able to make a good marriage now, but that is only another kind of servitude."

As Claude reached for his cloak Celestina laid a hand on his arm. "You are a good-looking man, so I should warn you. The pig also likes to play with men. I used to hear them cry out when he was finished with me." She gripped the muscle beneath his silk *djellibia*. "You are strong. I hope that will help you. I think that many men while they are in Europe are good only because of the rules around them, like a fat woman in a corset. When she takes it off, she has no shape. M. Drumont is like that—in Africa, he has no soul. Do not let him catch you, monsieur." She touched his face and a wave of lily-of-the-valley scent made his head swim. Then in a swirl of silk and lace she passed through the bead curtain and was gone.

oOo

Veludo had a key to the back gate of M. Drumont's mansion. Claude had seen him take it from a great iron ring holding keys of every shape and size. How many gates did those keys open, and how had he gotten them, and why? This was not the time to ask. In the twenty-four hours since their visit to the *Maison de la Rose*, Fadhma had been sent to speak with Drumont's servants, and learned that the master did indeed have a new toy, a *française* with red hair. She led the way now, a moving shadow among the trees. Once more, Claude wondered if he should have reported Adèle's abduction to the authorities, but if her shame were made public, her reputation would be forever soiled.

It was the still hour just before dawn. Among the pines planted around the house, a bird had begun to sing. The mansion of M. Drumont was built at the edge of the town, on a cliff overlooking the sea. Claude could hear the waves of the Mediterranean lapping at the shore. He hitched up the folds of the enveloping garment they had given him so that anyone who glimpsed him would think them two maidservants and pay no heed, where the sight of a man would have brought the guards.

How did the women here do any work, impeded by such garments? For that matter, how did the corseted women of his own country manage? *And what might they accomplish if they could move as freely as we do?* he wondered then. *Do we encourage such awkward costumes because we fear?*

As they neared the house, Fadhma paused and pointed. The back door was bolted from the inside, but Celestina had said that the window above the trellis was left open to catch the breeze from the sea. Claude checked the security of his toolbelt and the revolver, an old single-action Lefaucheux that Veludo had given him, and began to climb.

He tensed as the window creaked, then it slid free and he eased through. Here was the passage, with whitewashed walls and tiles around the doors. Heart beating heavily, he made his way down the hall and left at another hallway that ran toward the back of the house, counted one door, two, and there was the third, with a heavy bolt on the outside. With a prayer to the *Bon Dieu*, he drew back the bolt, let the door swing open, and stepped inside. He pulled the candle from his pocket and struck a match. There was a bed with a chamber pot beside it, but no other furniture in the room. As he eased forward, the coverlet stirred. Iron clinked as the girl sat up with a convulsive gasp.

"Who is it?"

Claude stuck the candle on the bedpost. The light flickered on a fine-boned face beneath a tangle of red hair, tender young breasts, and a mottling of bruises on the white skin. Celestina had warned him that they would have taken the girl's clothes. He tried to suppress his body's response to her pubescent beauty. *Celestina called me a knight errant*, he thought wryly, *and I do seem to make a practice of rescuing ladies, but I am still a man.*

As he unwound the headcloth, she clutched the coverlet to her breast. "You are not Zaira—but neither, I think, are you one of Drumont's *canaille....*"

"Claude DeLorme, at your service, Mademoiselle Adèle," he said very gently. "Your grandfather sent me to bring you home."

"You cannot..." She pulled back the covers. "They have fettered me." Her voice shook, but to his relief she had it under control.

Heavy links connected the shackle to a staple bolted into the frame of the bed, just long enough so that she could reach the chamber pot. There were abrasions around her wrists and on the other ankle as well. He lifted her foot so that the padlock was over the bed frame, set the edge of the chisel to the weld of the hasp and struck with the hammer. Both of them jumped at the ring of the blow in the small room.

"Oh, quiet, monsieur, or if you cannot be quiet, be swift! They will hear you and come!"

The tools jumped in his hands as he struck again and the candle flame flared. On the hasp, the line of bright metal grew.

"When the pirates attacked the boat, I thought that was the worst that could happen," she said presently. "But do you know how it is, monsieur, when you have been afraid for so long you have no strength to fear anymore?"

Claude gritted his teeth. He had known fear many times, but there had always been a way to channel it into action. Anger put strength into his blows.

"I was afraid again when the pirates sold me. I told myself it's not so different from being paraded with the other debutantes to be sold to lecherous old men, like some of the girls I knew at school. But at least they are not chained like dogs. When he is tormenting me, Drumont...talks. He tells me I'm a...pisspot. And other things... I lose more of myself every day. If they come, will you please shoot me with the pistol? What he does to my body does not matter. He is raping my soul."

Her eyes fixed and she gasped. He turned to see in the doorway a man with a black beard, a curved blade glittering in his hand. He said something in Arabic, and when Claude did not answer, laughed.

Claude dropped the tools and snatched up the revolver. The guard's grin twisted and he called out to someone behind him. Footsteps echoed in the hall.

"Run," the girl cried. "Kill them and break free!"

"I will not leave you here." He cocked the pistol.

"A strange lady, you!" said the man in accented French. "Give the gun. We too many. We take you down!"

"Not before my bullet finds your heart," Claude replied. "I am a noble of France, and there will be a terrible death for the man who harms me."

"You do not look like great lord. We say we killed thief—how could we know?"

"Help me and there will be a reward. Gold, land, whatever you desire."

"My master gives us gold...and women...." His avid gaze moved to Adèle. Claude gritted his teeth. Celestina had said that when M. Drumont tired of her, he had given her to be used by his men. "He has a long arm—"

"So does the Law. If you touch me, you will end on the gallows, and your master on Devil's Island!" Claude exclaimed. In the doorway, other faces appeared. "You dare not touch me."

"No need. Master comes."

"Good. I have a thing or two to say to him." He waited, revolver still poised, until the bravos stood aside and Drumont appeared, a brocaded dressing gown straining across his belly, his thinning hair on end. For a moment, the man simply stared. Then his face creased in a slow smile.

"Monsieur le Baron! I offered you my hospitality, but I did not anticipate that you would accept my invitation so soon. If you had given me some warning, I could have planned your entertainment. Now we shall have to improvise...."

Claude frowned. This was not quite the reaction he had expected.

"Listen, Drumont. This game is finished. If De Sartres had not asked for discretion, I would have you arrested now."

"I am sure he did." Drumont laughed. "He has a proud name, and the newspapers would descend on this story like vultures on a dead camel."

"Just so. You will free the girl and we will go."

"Free her? But no—I had something rather different in mind." He gestured to his men.

"Take one more step and I shoot you where you stand!"

"Shoot me and he shoots *her*." Over Drumont's shoulder, the long barrel of a carbine appeared, held by a man Claude could not see. "Besides, for you to shoot me would be murder, and gentlemen do not kill one another—"

"Except in duels." Claude remembered his first, with a

Brazilian gambler beneath a bloody moon. That killing had been forced upon him, but he would enjoy passing a blade through Drumont's belly.

"But to challenge me," the man said gently, "you must be free. I sent an invitation to your hotel. No one has seen you for two days. You will simply be one more European who wandered into the wrong part of the city and disappeared."

Fadhma and Veludo knew where he had gone. Would anyone believe them? That could not be allowed to matter now.

"Shoot him!" hissed Adèle. "It does not matter about me!"

"Put down your revolver and I will spare her life," said Drumont.

Claude's eyes narrowed, calculating trajectories. "Adèle..." he said softly. She had been at school in Naples; she must know at least as much Italian as he, and though Drumont might also have the language, his men would not. "*Quando dico, rotoli al pavimento...ora!*"

As the bed creaked, he fired. The carbine bullet sang by his ear, he cocked the revolver once more, and as Adèle hit the floor, shot twice at the link where the staple in the bedpost was connected to the taut chain. The fourth bullet extinguished the candle, but he had already marked everyone's position. While the others were still blinking, he grabbed Drumont, clapped the pistol to his temple, and swung him back toward the bed. Dawn must be nearing, for the window was a square of grey. The others were dim shapes in the gloom.

"Do not move or your master dies! Adèle, get up."

In the silence that followed he heard the rattle as she gathered up the loose end of the chain.

"You cannot escape," whispered Drumont.

"*She* can," said Claude. "All of you, step back until she is out of the room."

Drumont murmured something in Arabic and the men began to move.

"Adèle, go now! Follow the hallway to the stair and go out through the back garden. Give your word that you will not report this—"

Drumont snorted. "The bitch won't advertise her shame."

Glaring, she clasped the coverlet around her and crept past the grinning men. Claude waited, counting silently as he calculated the time it would take for her to get down the stairs. In the silence he heard the distant click of a closing door. Then he counted to a hundred again. That should give her time to reach the trees, and Fadhma would know how to take care of her.

"Now," he said to Drumont, "I will give you my word of honor to say nothing of what has passed here, and you will do the same, though I would rather see you hanged."

"And if I refuse? Will you murder me? If my men do not kill you, you will die on the gallows if you do."

Almost certainly, Claude thought grimly, for his only defense would be what Drumont had done to Adèle, and that he would never tell. "It might be worth it, but I will forgo the pleasure. Tell your men to return to their quarters. You and I will move, very carefully, to the gate, and there I will let you go."

Once more Drumont spoke, and again Claude wished he had learned Arabic before he came. He relaxed, just a little, as the men began to move, and in that moment the nearest whirled and knocked his elbow upward. As the gun went off, Drumont jerked away. Someone shoved Claude's left arm up behind his back while another grabbed his right wrist and twisted hard. The gun clattered across the floor.

"Monsieur le Baron," Drumont said viciously. "The game is finished indeed!"

oOo

Claude woke from a dream in which he was being paraded before customers in a bordello, to find himself in a room that might have belonged to the *Maison de la Rose*. His head was throbbing and his mouth tasted like the sewers of Algiers. Returning vision flinched from a tumult of color—Turkish carpets and brocaded curtains and a tapestry with a hunting scene. But the scent was different, a heavy musk mixed with sweat and other things.

Name of God, what was I drinking? he wondered. Then he tried to move. Agony flared from a dozen places—joints stressed past their limits and wrenched muscles, abrasions on his knuckles, an ache as if he had been kicked in the belly, a stinging across his back and a general soreness farther down. With the pain came clarity. He was lying face-down, splayed across a velvet bolster, shackles at wrists and ankles from which chains led to the posts of a bed.

Like Adèle... he thought, and with that knowledge full awareness returned.

He had got some of his injuries in the fight when Drumont's men took him. The taste in his mouth came from some drug that released sensation while it sapped volition. Once he was bound, everything that Adèle had suffered had been done to him in turn. That was where the other pains came from. He shuddered and closed his eyes once more.

"Welcome back." Drumont spoke behind him. "No, closing your eyes will not cause all this to go away—I know the signs when the drug begins to wane. I do not think you will need a second dose. You are helpless as a woman now...."

Claude winced as the other man traced the marks the whip had made on his back and then squeezed his buttock.

"You came to me as a woman, and as a woman I shall use you, until a new plaything comes along. And then...they have not lost the art of making a man into an eunuch in this land. You are old for it, and may not survive, but if you do, what a charming fate for a 'gentleman,' is it not so?"

"You cannot get away with this—" Claude muttered, more to shore up his courage than because he believed it to be true.

"I have been 'getting away with this', as you put it, for years," Drumont said reasonably. "This is Algiers, not Paris. Who is going to stop me? You aristocrats think you own the world, but where now is your privilege and power?" He sighed and poured wine into a glass. "You think you have suffered already, but you still see yourself as a lord of creation. It will be a delight to drag you down!"

He finished the glass, stood for a moment considering, and took up the whip. And then it began once more....

oOo

Even Drumont had to sleep some time.

Claude lay on the bed, still pinioned, breathing carefully in an attempt to manage the pain. They had left one lamp burning so that amid the luxuriance of his surroundings he could not forget that he had been stripped not only of his clothing but of all dignity. He had meant to try for a break when they let him up to deal with necessities, but he had no appetite for food, and scarcely enough control of his limbs to use the chamber pot. Resistance was out of the question.

He understood now the despair that had immobilized Adèle. He would lose everything, even his manhood, if Drumont had his way. Would he resist longer because he had no experience of submission, or would he succumb more quickly? Adèle had walked out of her prison. He did not think he could do so, even if his limbs were free. Had they treated him more harshly because they feared his strength? He had none now.

The house was quiet, but from somewhere beyond he could hear a faint susurrus of sound. It seemed to be growing louder, and that surprised him. He assumed it was one of the festivals that turned the city into a carnival. If this had been Brazil, he might have known, but he had not learned enough about the local version of Islam to guess what it might be. He supposed the celebration was heading toward the Kouba district, where an outlying village had been replaced by the estates of the conquerors.

He shifted position to the extent his restraints allowed and stilled, heart pounding, until the pain became bearable once more. There were three roads by which he might leave this place—escape, rescue, or death. He was too crippled for the first, and he could not hope for the second. Drumont had boasted that he was the authority here. Veludo knew where Claude had gone, but who would believe the word of a native cloth-merchant against that of the surintendent of the port of Algiers? Claude was young and healthy, and he had learned endurance in Brazil. Unless he could goad his captors into killing him, it might take a very long time to die.

The sound of the celebration was getting louder and, oddly

enough, it seemed to be coming from the gardens. Claude had no reason to think it had anything to do with him, but his heart beat more quickly. He suppressed an instinct to test his bonds. Better to save his strength until there was some reason.

Now he could hear music. The clarinet-like warble of a *zammarah* and the ecstatic shrilling of a *shabbabah* flute rose above the insistent patter of the drums. Somewhere below, a male voice shouted a question and was answered by a song that breathed mockery even though he could not understand the words. Through the open window, the scent of hemp smoke mingled with the perfume of jasmine. From the house, women's voices joined in the singing, and the male expostulations changed to laughter.

They were inside now. Through the floor, Claude heard the tumult grow. Drumont kept wine and rum and brandy. How long would it be before the revelers forgot their religion, and to their hemp-fueled intoxication added drunkenness? Claude forced himself to breathe slowly and deeply. He could not imagine what was happening, but a fierce joy tingled through his veins.

He tensed as his sensitized hearing identified Drumont's outraged protest above the babble below. There was a shot and a cry, lost in an immediate chorus of rage. A door slammed open. Claude heard the thudding footsteps of a heavy man and then the patter of many sandaled feet upon the wooden floor. He drew all of his forces inward, waiting, no longer aware of pain.

The door to his chamber crashed open and Drumont reeled through. He staggered to the other side of the bed, a revolver clutched in his fist, as a gaily dressed mob crowded in after him. Some had open bottles in their hands. This was no Moslem celebration, thought Claude, but a scene from a Brazilian Carnival.

Silks and gauzes in every hue floated around the smooth limbs of the revelers—and he knew them! He had seen those graceful bodies in the gardens of the *Maison de la Rose*. The young man who had smiled at him was grinning now, and there was Celestina, fixing Drumont with a basilisk gaze.

"Stop, you scum, or I'll shoot you!" he frothed. "I'll shoot *him!*" The bed heaved as he lunged forward.

The gun wavered as Drumont fought to find his balance. Claude put forth all the power that remained to him to wrench and roll, ripping one of the chains from its mooring and clamping his freed arm around Drumont's neck. The revolver went off with a deafening report. The bullet struck the lamp, spattering oil and flame across the tapestry. Claude knew only that he must hold on, hold until a dozen eager hands gripped Drumont's flailing limbs, and he could sink back, gasping, as his tormentor was pulled away.

Beyond them he glimpsed Veludo, still in his blue robe. In his hand glittered a small key. *Of course,* thought Claude as agony darkened his vision, or perhaps it was smoke as the hunters on the tapestry turned to flame. *He has all the keys....*

He barely noticed the tug as his shackles were opened. Soft hands rolled him onto one of the curtains. Drumont was still mouthing a gabble of threats and promises, but the roar of the crowd was louder still. He wondered if they would tear the man to pieces before his eyes.

"Arrest him," he formed the words, but he had screamed his throat raw.

"My friend, we cannot offer your kind of justice, only our own," whispered Veludo. "If such as these bring a French official to the gendarmerie, what will come to them?"

"Kill him!" cried Celestina, her face that of a Fury.

"No, bind him!" Veludo called. "There remain three shackles—they will do!"

As Claude was lifted from the bed, his rescuers thrust Drumont down in his place, on his back where white-rimmed eyes reflected the light of the growing flames.

"Come, my children," said Veludo. "Arrives the time to leave this abuser of women to the hell that he has earned." His eyes glowed, the eyes of a devil in blue velvet, thought Claude as more hands lifted his improvised litter and bore him away.

oOo

"I will not return to France," Adèle said steadily. Light

flickered across the native gown that hid the lines of her body as a breeze stirred the leaves of the lemon tree in Veludo's garden. Lying on a cushioned couch in the shade, Claude could almost forget the events of the past few days. Until he moved. He wondered if beneath the robe her bruises were beginning to heal. His own garment was similar, for as yet the constriction of European clothing was more than he could bear.

"I have written to my grandfather," she went on, "and asked that he send my dowry to the nuns at the convent of Our Lady so that I may live as a lay boarder there."

"That is no life for a young girl." Claude winced as he sat up to face her.

"In France would I find better, sold to some man who was paid to take damaged goods, and living in fear that society would find out what happened to me here? Though it might be worth it if I could tell them about that pig's end...."

Claude nodded. By the time the firefighters reached Drumont's mansion, the folk from the *Maison de la Rose* were long gone, and only empty bottles and scraps of finery in the garden bore witness that anyone had been there—those, and the half-melted shackles that still circled the surintendent's charred limbs. It would appear that Drumont's proclivities were known, and rumor speculated that one of his perverse entertainments had gone wrong. No one dared to probe further, for fear of where the trail might lead.

"Do not think I will be wearing out my knees in penance," Adèle said then. "Fadhma is teaching me Arabic. She has started a school for women in honor of Lalla Fadhma. I will use some of my dowry to help her there."

Claude considered her resolute features and nodded. It was a better future than he had been able to plan.

"And what will *you* do?"

"I too find no pleasure in the thought of returning to France," he said grimly. "But I have a debt to pay. M. Veludo wishes to extend his trade to West Africa, and needs someone to speak on his behalf to the authorities. When I am able to travel, I will go there."

"But won't that be dangerous?" she asked.

He raised one eyebrow. "What do either of us have to fear from the primitive, having survived the savagery of so-called civilized man?"

For a long moment Adèle held his gaze, and then, slowly, she smiled.

Samantha Henderson lived around the world before settling in Southern California with her family and an assortment of Corgis, cats, boggarts and rabbits, and occasionally a metric ton of mockingbirds. She also works as a church office coordinator, and writes poetry upon occasion. When not writing, she enjoys amateur theater and growing interesting molds in the back of her refrigerator. Her short fiction has been published in *Realms of Fantasy, Strange Horizons, Lone Star Stories, Goblin Fruit, and Chizine*. Her story, "The Red Bride" appears in *The Year's Best Science Fiction & Fantasy 2011*. Her Ravenloft novel, *Heaven's Bones*, was a Scribe Awards nominee and she is an active member of the Science Fiction Poetry Association. Visit her website at: www.samanthahenderson.com.

OUTLANDER

by Samantha Henderson

The whole disgraceful affair was my fault. I was the one who befriended that great beast of an Outlander, spawn of his border-clan House, and led him with such fatal consequences to my family's heart.

But Lukah Brehill seemed such harmless oaf, charming in a way rare among my fellows, and I thought it was a kindness to introduce him to proper society. He'd been sent by his House to pay his respects to Sireni and its Duke, and was housed among the rest of the young bucks of the Houses too far and unfortunate to live in the heart of the city spectacular. The Duke maintained the Gentlemen's Academy near his palaces, as much to keep track of the scions of the Great Houses as to provide a proper dwelling and education for his young nobles. Like other sons of the Great Houses, I kept rooms there as well as House Torelay, my family's compound.

Uncivilized as the border Houses are, no one of any intelligence underestimates the importance of such as House Brehill in defending the boundaries of Sireni lands. They raise sons trained on the battlefield rather than the dueling-ground, and have little time for the arts and graces that make city life so sweet. Lukah was a well-built man a head taller than myself, with a stance and a walk that spoke more of tracking the mountain-raiders in the forests east of the River Silpath than of dancing at court or arranging oneself beautifully in the Scholar's Gardens. His facial scars were earned after his first blooding—he'd killed one of a pack of raiders who had been terrorizing a crofter family—and they had been cut into his face by his own uncle. They were brute slices across each cheek, knotted and twisted as nature would have done, with no art to them.

No man of the Sireni nobility will show his face without scars, just as no woman will go unmasked. In the City, it's the fashion to seek a scarifier with a sense of the aesthetic, who will cut and shape and take into account the contours of the face, to flatter rather than disfigure. My father would have no less than the Duke's own scarifier when it came my turn. Lukah's scars, on the other hand, echoed our warlike past, when a man's scars were always earned and never things of fashion. I confess I felt a slight shame when I looked into my mirror and saw my own: double lines of raised pink tissue that curved under my cheekbones and flattered the angle of my jaw.

Our belligerent forbears founded Sireni to create a place of beauty and scholarship, where the finer arts might flourish. We are able to defend ourselves, for our Navy is unmatched, our border-allies stalwart, and our sons train in the arts of the blade, according to Sireni's charter. Surely we are right to seek a brighter, more glittering future, rather than dwell on our bloody past.

No one mocked Brehill's scion; there was no amusement to be had in such obvious discourtesy. But there was much sport, or so thought some of the Academy cadets, to be had in the clever digs and ripostes so easy to fling about the Outlander, who had no idea of the politics, alliances, and dalliances of Sireni's ruling families.

I might have joined in, but I liked this unspoiled youth and his good nature in the face of all sallies, something that spoke of clean air and honest work. Perhaps I was beginning to tire of the endless social dance of my fellows. So, when young Guisel of House Sacarsi tossed a towel at Lukah after a race about the Sparrow's Walk and bade him mop himself, for he was sweating like a farmer, I pointed out in the mild tones of an elder to a puling boy that *my* family were as good as farmers, and *his* House was not ashamed to provide manure from their swine for our orchards.

"Or do you fancy your apples and cheese, wine and good white bread are flown magically by little fairies from the Mountains of Plenty, Guisel?" I said, with the lightest of glances at his slightly-protruding belly. Guisel did like his food. He blushed faintly.

The Valmur twins, both masked in identical constructions of pale green feathers, had been present to witness the outcome of the race between the three of us and now giggled behind their fans. I wondered what Margi and Flor Valmur would do once one or the other was wed, for much of their aesthetic effect was due to the fact that the two of them dressed the same, masked the same, walked the same, gestured the same, and rarely spoke.

"Lukah knows I mean no insult, Kai," said the red-faced Guisel, turning to Lukah, who flicked him lightly on the thigh with the damp towel.

"I take none," he said in the broadest imaginable country twang. The three of us laughed all the way back to quarters while the Valmurs drifted home, accompanied by a formidable chaperone in a dull black mask that spoke only of barriers immovable.

"I know I'm a right oaf compared to you lot," Lukah confided to me in the baths later that day. "And I take none of the teasing ill. I confess this place is dazzling, with your gardens and palaces and ladies arrayed all o'er, like colorful birds with their feathers and silks."

I laughed. "Come visit my House tomorrow. We are not as dazzling as some, but we do shine somewhat."

Lukah *was* dazzled by my family—what Outlander wouldn't be? When my sister greeted him at my mother's side in the vestibule of our House, in the creamy robes of a maiden and the bird-of-waters mask she favored when we had company—he stood like a pole-axed ox before it fell. I was amused. I curse my blindness when I say it—*I was amused.*

He made a short, inelegant bow, and they nodded in return. I saw Lilliam's eyes through her mask glance at him, at me, and I shrugged in return. She must accept those I called my friends, graceless though they be.

At dinner, my mother was as gracious as a queen to a deserving subject, my father preoccupied but curious about the alliances between House Brehill and the other border clans.

Lilliam was more direct. "Is it true," she broke in, tilting the blue crystal-woven wings of her mask at him, "that Outlander women go unmasked?"

My mother's composure didn't break, but I saw my sister twitch when she kicked her.

"They mask in public, of course," Lukah replied, unperturbed. "But some of them, especially if they are married, will bare their faces before their own families."

I haven't seen Lillian's face since she was twelve years old.

"Interesting," she remarked in a voice that implied *most crude*, and my mother frowned—but whether at Lilliam's rudeness or Outlander impropriety, I didn't know.

At the fruit course my father withdraw, as it was his tiring-time, and my mother went with him, leaving Lilliam to pour our wine. She tore her bread apart restlessly, glancing at our guest from behind her mask.

Lukah had risen with me as my mother left the table, and sat again when I sat.

"A gracious lady, your mother," he remarked.

"A lady much occupied with the concerns of her House," broke in Lilliam, snappishly. "Although she plays the part of the idle hostess when called for."

There was an uncomfortable pause.

"My own mother busies herself about the library," Lukah said, finally. "I'm afraid she has no head for business, and leaves that to my sisters. The younger, at least. It was a great relief to her, I think, when Grisile reached her majority."

Lilliam's head snapped up and she regarded the Outlander intently. "Your House has a *library*?"

"Of course, my Lady," he said. "Surely all Houses of any

consequence do."

Did I not know his guileless nature, I would have suspected my barbarian friend of an internal chuckle at my family's expense. But I knew full well that in his naiveté, he was innocent.

Lilliam crushed a bead of bread between her elegant fingers. "We do not."

"Silly," I chuckled. "Of course we do."

Beneath the azure-lacquered rim of her mask, her lower lip curved down. "A History, the most banal of Cyclopedias, the Romance of the Cymbi, and a set of moral stories suitable for the children and wives of the nobility. Not what I call a proper library."

"My most-respected sister is, of course, an idiot," I said to Lukah. "With such resources as the Scholar's Guild commands, it's hardly necessary for a House to maintain such an investment in books and documents. It's best to gather all these resources together, to be available to all those who have an interest."

"What's filed and catalogued is what the Scholars consider significant," Lilliam snapped. "The rest molders in the archives, while the House Scions puzzle out questions of genealogy and laws of inheritance. Matters of science and the observances of natural history linger uncatalogued on the shelves."

"My mother could use one of your mind to assist her," observed Lukah. "The indexing of our House's archives is a formidable task, for we are plagued with many old documents."

"What kind of documents?" Lilliam bent to the task of further dissecting her bread. The presence of the unlettered barbarian must be disconcerting her. I both regretted causing her discomposure and delighted, in the sadistic way of elder brothers, in tweaking her for her superior ways.

"My grandfather traveled beyond the Great Waste, past Kudershar, and sought ancient books and scrolls from the merchants that traveled there," he told her. "And my granddam was not pleased at the quantity of stuff he brought back. There was a collection of the poetry of el-Kasmiel, I recollect, and a great pile of old records having to do with the household of the Kudershari Khan. One of them, at least, was many years dead."

Lilliam ceased making doughy pills and placed her hands on the table before her. Her nails were painted to match her mask. "And histories? The Kudershari were a great people for record-keeping, I am told. And for accounts of the lands beyond them, bordering the Gauthel Sea."

Lukah's fingers touched the rough cloth over his heart. I must get him to a proper tailor, I thought.

"I regret I do not know. It's the provenance of the women of the House, I'm afraid. My mother once found something in the shambles that might have been a history, if such interests you. A tiny thing, bound in violet leather."

He motioned, sketching something that could fit in the palm of his hand. "As far as I could see, it was an account of the villages along the Gauthel Mountains—just a page to each, with drawings in green and gold. My mother told me it detailed the primary goods produced by each croft: a merchant's tool, made small for travel. I regret my Kudershar was not good enough to read much. But it was a beautiful thing, that. Each town became, in telling of it, a child's tale."

Suddenly Lilliam rose and curtseyed to Lukah, a scrap of a bob just shy of polite. I was glad he didn't know enough to realize he'd just been insulted. She swept out of the room without saying goodnight.

"You mustn't mind my sister," I said, pouring us both another measure of wine and putting my boots up on the nearest chair. "She's a sharpish harridan at times, with none of my good temper."

"Oh, I don't mind," said my unsophisticated friend, likewise putting his feet up and swallowing his good red wine down to the dregs in one motion.

oOo

I stayed that night in my old rooms while Lukah returned to his Academy quarters, accompanied by a servant and unaccountably steady after an enormous quantity of wine. I slept in and, seeking a late breakfast in the morning room, walked into an argument between my father and Lilliam about the Torelay orchards.

My House owns rich lands past the south fork of the Lithia, where we grow the black pears that are really dusky purple, with firm flesh fading from violet beneath the skin to pale white at the center. They're good to eat, mild and juicy and sweet, but better for wine: the rich, fruity pear-wine drunk by House and commoner alike at the fall harvest celebrations. The bud blight struck our orchards three years ago, and we haven't had a good crop since.

My father turned to me and I saw Lilliam's fist clench against the creamy fabric of her dress. I stifled a smile. Somewhere in the dusty reaches of the Scholar's archives, she had found an account of what she took to be the blight and the methods of its treatment. My father was a man of action, not scholarship, and was too impatient to listen when Lilliam set out her plans of attack: burning the blighted trees, then bringing in saplings crossed with native pears resistant to the disease. She said the Torelay black pears, famed through Sireni and beyond, had become inbred over the generations and were weak in the face of diseases a bastard tree would throw off. Such advice rubbed my father wrong—he saw the Torelay trees as the height of breeding, and to speak against their purity denigrated the work of his ancestors—or rather, the dedicated orchard masters who worked under them.

"It's time she was married," he told me, raising a hand to cut her off. "It's time she turned her interests to service inside her husband's House, keeping his accounts and household matters in hand. Such is the use of scholarship, not interfering with the affairs of men."

Although I love my sister, I had to agree—our family business was the public face of the House, as were the men with their scars. Behind the façades of mask and home was the place of women.

"Kai," said Lilliam, when my father had left. "You are surely not as stupid as you look. You know will we lose everything— lands, status and House—if the blight continues. Will you talk to Father?"

"It's no use, love," I said. "He's adamant, and for all I know, he has the right of it. Our stock had held strong for hundreds of years, since the founding of the City. The Torelay trees will outlast the blight, you'll see."

Her day-mask quivered. "Of all the plagues of humanity, the pride of Men is the worst," she huffed. "Are you inviting that great hulk of an Outlander to supper again?"

"I will if I want to," I retorted. "You're to be nicer to him this time."

"I was perfectly polite."

"No, you weren't, miss. I'm heir of this House, and my friends will come if I like."

"Oh, I don't mind," she said with a flip of her day-mask as she left the room, leaving me alone to my smoked fish.

Lukah did come again, and again, much to my sister's annoyance. My parents became fond of him for the same reasons I had—his simplicity and good humor—and he often stayed at our House. Lilliam was left to tend us of an evening. Patiently, Lukah answered her questions about his House and the borderlands, although she was sullen to the point of rudeness.

oOo

I don't know how, exactly, Lukah came to earn the enmity of Sanmano Boradkor, the Duke's eldest son and Prince of the City. He still could be remarkably oafish at times, and was clumsy in the pouring and drinking of wine, and I knew that such irritated the Prince. Still, it didn't explain the increasingly dark looks and snappish tone Sanmano took on the occasions he encountered Lukah.

My friend, of course, was childishly blind to the problem.

The affair came to its dreadful conclusion, a sequence of events I will rue to my death, the day Lukah passed the Prince in a close corridor of the Gentleman's quarters. Lukah nodded respectfully enough and with adequate grace—I had managed to teach him something, at least, but in the narrow hallway he managed to elbow Sanmano in the ribs, so that the Duke's son halted, gasping.

I wasn't watching closely, but I still cannot understand how it happened. It was close quarters indeed, and Lukah was tall, but not freakishly so. It was almost as if he'd done it on purpose, which, of course, my simple friend would never have.

"Your pardon, your Grace!" called Lukah, jovially enough. "I will never get used to the fine and narrow masonry of this place."

For some reason, he'd put on the broad accent of a countryman, and it must've irritated the Prince further.

"Watch yourself, you clumsy fool, or get back to the pigsty you came from," he growled, still grasping his side and struggling to stay at his full height. Lukah must've elbowed him harder than it seemed.

The Prince's companions and I looked askance at each other. A dreadful silence filled the hall. Lukah stared at the Prince, not even reddening at the insult. I moved to grasp Lukah's arm and hurry him away.

"I did apologize, your Grace," he said, shaking me off, never looking away from Sanmano. "And I don't appreciate my mother's and my sisters' House being called a pigsty." His accent was, if possible, broader than ever.

The Prince straightened his perfectly straight clothing and brushed an invisible speck of dust from his embroidered sleeve.

"From what I hear, the women of House Brehill are no less piggish than yourself," he sneered. "Tell me, do your women scar themselves like men on the mud fields of the Silpath, as you did?"

Someone gasped—it might have been me. Silence deepened and enveloped us all like black smoke does the candlelight.

Lukah took one giant stride forward—by all the Gods, I wish I had had the foresight to fling myself in his path—and struck the Prince of the City full across the face.

There was a moment when everything seemed suspended, then Sanmano fell heavily on one knee. Two of the Prince's companions seized Lukah by the arms and dragged him back. I took his shoulder and did the same. He didn't resist—we couldn't have moved him if he had.

A trickle of blood snaked from Sanmano's nostril as his third man—Jago of House Coreilli, if I recall correctly—helped him to his feet.

"I call the blood duel," said the Prince in a voice like iron, a voice too calm for any kind of comfort. "Since the hovel your House calls home lies beyond all civilized ken, I shall send the challenge to House Torelay."

I found my voice. "Very well, your Grace." The three of us managed to move Lukah, like a heavy but unresisting tree, down the corridor.

"I hope, Kai," continued the Prince, as he took Jago's proffered handkerchief and mopped the blood from his face, "I hope that you have learned the foolishness of taking a barbarian into the bosom of your family."

I said nothing. I was not to learn that lesson then, but later.

oOo

I led Lukah through the streets in silence as we made our way home. He was quiet until we reached House Torelay's gates.

"Kai," he said, "sending the challenge to Torelay—does that bode ill for your family? I would not return the Duke's ill-will for your hospitality."

I saw nothing on his face beyond his scars and simple honesty. The hypocrite.

I sighed. "No, not for an affair of honor such as this. It's merely that he must send the challenge to your House or, failing that, a House with which you are allied. Since you've eaten at Torelay's table, and since you are my friend..."

He took my hand. "I hope you will always stand my friend, Kai."

I returned his clasp. "Assuredly, I will."

Knowing now what I didn't then, I say again—the damnable hypocrite.

"Why did you do it, Lukah?" I said, as the majordomo hurried to unlatch the heavy gate. "And why did you hit him so hard?"

He shrugged and laughed. "I didn't think I did."

Lilliam met us, wearing the dusky plum-colored mask she often used when she planned to visit the Scholar's Library. Her street cloak told me she'd already been there.

"The idiot," she said, her eyes shining, when I told her the news. "The absolute idiot." She turned to Lukah. "You *are* an idiot, you know that?"

"Lilliam!" I growled at her as I hadn't since we were young, before I was scarred and she was masked.

She tossed her head and swept away down the hall. I turned to Lukah, ready to apologize.

He was watching my sister's back as she walked away, and he was smiling.

oOo

The challenge was delivered that evening. I wrote the reply and Lukah signed it. The fight would take place an hour after dawn, at the fencing grounds beside the Academy. There was to be no private meeting by the riverbank in this matter, and no time for cooler heads to negotiate a way to satisfy everyone's honor without bloodshed. Lukah took a light meal and went to bed early, with a cheerful attitude, slapping me on the back on the way to his rooms. I stayed up later than I liked, gnawing a knuckle and thinking how I might get my friend out of Sireni.

The problem was this: Lukah knew how to fight well enough, but the weapon of the blood duel is the small sword. I'd seen Lukah work with rapier and epeé, and he was skilled enough to hold his own in short matches supervised by the Academy fencing masters.

But Sanmano was an expert in the small sword, with no weakness in technique that I had ever seen. He was shorter than Lukah and his reach was not as long, but he was lithe, and the indolent poise he favored when at his ease belied the speed of a panther. His anger, hot that day, would have cooled into a deadly calm by morning, and he was not likely to make a mistake. He might very well kill Lukah, and there was no way I could think of to prevent it.

Lukah and I rose early, and he breakfasted on a capon wing

and hot water. I couldn't eat. We arrived at the Academy just as dawn broke. Lukah stretched and practiced footwork in the inner sandpits as we waited. I sat and watched him, and couldn't speak.

He had dressed in the rough fabric of his House, with only a silver pin with the wolf's-head of Brehill at his left shoulder as decoration. As the bells outside chimed the half hour, he sat beside me.

"Cheer up, Kai," he told me. "I'm not that easy to kill. And if I don't live past this day, know that my own foolishness was at fault, and you were nothing but a friend to me, and made my time in Sireni a delight."

"It's time to go," was all I could say.

Before he rose, he touched the wolf's-head lightly. "If I am killed, give this to your sister. I will have failed indeed if I do not irritate her in some way, at the last."

oOo

Even from the bowels of the Academy, I could hear the rumble of the crowd. I can't remember the last time a blood duel—a fight all but guaranteed to end in the death of one of the combatants—had been fought. No scion of any House would miss it if he could ride, walk, or be carried to the fencing grounds.

I blinked as we passed from the darkness in the corridor to the bright morning light. The crowd silenced for an instant. Lukah's face was solemn now, although he had been cheerful a moment before. With an almost theatrical gesture, he frowned and adjusted the strap of his glove before moving to the corner where the challenged was to stand.

Immediately, those assembled began to whisper to each other. The Ladies of Sireni were not worried that an interest in bloodshed should be thought unfeminine, for they were gathered five deep in the risers behind the bravos of the Academy. The Valmur twins were there, dressed in lavender this day. The women's masks glittered in the pink light of dawn, studded with crystals the color of the sky, opal, forest, blood and sea—smooth against their faces, horned like devils, or enhanced with wings that rose on either side of their faces. Most wore gowns better suited for the ballroom than a duel, silks and linens finely embroidered and dyed to match their masks. They bent their heads together and twittered like birds. Lilliam stood with them, in a cream gown and the bird-of-waters mask she had worn the first time Lukah came to dinner. She stood as still as a post, watching us. Her fists were clenched at her sides, and it seemed to me her eyes burned though her mask.

It saddened me to think she might wish for Lukah's death.

I took my place beside Lukah, who studiously ignored the fuss. A ripple of sound heralded the arrival of the Duke and his entourage, who took their place in the judgment stand where they could see every figure of the fight. I was glad to see my parents in the crowd behind the Duke—the affair could hardly interest them, save for Lukah's slight association with our House through me. It was gracious of them to show themselves in his support. I saw also that Guisel Sacarsi chose to stand behind Lukah's side of the ring, and I flashed him a grateful look.

I couldn't help but feel sorry for Timon Boradkor, Duke of Sireni. He was in a terrible position, for although he had the power to forbid such a fight, the fact that his own son was a principle would make him—or Sanmano—look a coward if he did so. His face was white and drawn, his scars pink against his pale skin, for all he stood tall and maintained an air of indifference.

I would bet my inheritance that he had stayed up late the night before, thinking how he might cancel the fight with no loss of honor.

Another murmur, and the glittering mass of spectators separated to admit Sanmano Boradkor and his second, Jago Coreilli. Sanmano strode to the challenger's corner, looking confident and fit. Jago whispered in his ear and Sanmano smiled humorlessly.

At the Duke's gesture, the rapiers were brought forward. A fluttering gasp rose from the ladies at the sight of the deadly steel. Jago and I bowed, each to each, and examined the selection. All were fine weapons—I chose what seemed the heaviest, thinking it was most like the weapons Lukah was used to. After testing the balance, I carried it to Lukah for his approval. He hefted it and nodded. Out of the corner of my eye, I saw Sanmano tracing a complicated figure in the air with much skill and little effort.

Usually the seconds are armed as well, and it is our task not to join the fight but to hold our weapons beneath those of the duelists to strike away any blow out of bounds, and to halt the fight when protocol is breached. But in a blood duel there could be no foul, no enforced mercy. Our job was only to witness. I have never felt so helpless in my life.

A signal from the Duke, and the match was on.

oOo

The *Code Duello* specifies what footwork may be used during a duel, with the consequences of violations clearly set forth. There is no such restriction in the blood duel, save that the combatants are forbidden to leave the ring. Sanmano, trained for years under the watchful tutelage of both his father's sword-masters and the Academy trainers, instinctively fell into regulation footwork, while Lukah, trained on the battlefield and in desperate scrabbles with border raiders, had a style less graceful but more efficient. I hoped the sheer audacity of Lukah's technique would so disconcert Sanmano that the Outlander would have an advantage. Indeed, he did drive the Prince to the edge of the ring more than once with merciless blows from the base of the blade, wielded as if it were a saber. Soon Sanmano's skill and swiftness began to tell on my friend—again and again his rapier twisted past Lukah's guard and came dangerously close to his throat. As one, the watching crowd held their breath to watch the deadly dance, or sighed as a length of lethal metal almost went home.

Once Lukah didn't twist away in time and Sanmano's blade opened a cut on his cheek. Lukah didn't flinch—though I did—and the wound wasn't obvious until thick blood ran and a dull red drop fell on the sand. There was a collective gasp, and somewhere in the crowd a woman screamed.

"Hold!" called the Duke, as he must at first blood, and the

combatants sprang away from each other. I mopped Lukah's cheek. A fine sheen of sweat was on his face, but his breath was steady.

"He takes first blood," I said, low and urgent. "You can stop this now, without shame. Only apologize."

He took the cloth I held to his face from me and pressed harder.

"Please, Lukah. Don't waste yourself over one silly incident. If you apologize now, he must accept, and you can go home again to Brehill and forget Sireni."

He smiled at me then, kindly. "I can never forget Sireni."

He thrust the bloodied linen back at me. "And such little faith in my skill from my second! You wound me, Kai, deeper than that over-coddled dog's-meat could."

I saw he was laughing at me. I looked past his shoulder and caught Lilliam's eye. Her lips tightened.

"Resume," called the Duke, when it was clear that Lukah would not make amends. There was finality in his voice. Save that one or the other showed mercy, the match could end only one way. I resolved to make myself watch, whatever the outcome.

It seemed that Lukah had benefitted from the respite: for a while, Sanmano's blade could not come near him. But presently his response time slowed, and he began to give ground, one step at a time. Behind the lightning flash of steel, Sanmano smiled.

And then—Lukah's sword swung wide, as if his arm had tired. The Prince saw his opportunity and thrust, with all his strength behind it, straight at Lukah's exposed torso.

If I hadn't seen it, I would have thought it impossible to bring a rapier across the body from that angle and with that speed. But Lukah did it, catching the Prince's blade with his cross-guard and twisting it. A lesser player than Sanmano would have been knocked over, but he maintained his balance, hopping out of the way and keeping his grip on his weapon.

With Sanmano clear, Lukah bent to grasp something from his boot. I cried out with the crowd when I saw it—a long knife with a thin blade, that could be hidden in a boot sheath. He crouched, holding the knife in his left hand with equal skill as the sword in his right.

Sanmano backed away, his eyes widening.

"Hold!" shouted the Duke, the force of his voice causing the startled and indignant murmurs of the onlookers to fade away. "Lukah of House Brehill, you are in violation of the *Code Duello*, and dishonored in the City's sight."

"You are mistaken, your Grace," called Lukah, never taking his eyes off his opponent, holding both weapons at the ready. "The *Code Duello* of your own City Charter states that blood duel may include a short blade for the weaker hand, no more than the length of his forearm, if the challenged combatant desires it. I am the challenged, and I do so desire it."

There was a shocked silence, and my irreverent friend grinned.

"Nonsense!" bellowed the Duke.

"Nay, it is not," said Lukah. "Ask your own Scholars."

A white-swathed figure hurried to the Duke's side, gesticulating. The Duke bent to him, his face growing as pink as his scars.

"I never heard of such," I heard him growl.

"It is part of an earlier charter, but never struck from the record," said Lukah. "Is your Grace is not familiar with it?"

A second Scholar joined the first, and the Duke's face grew redder and redder.

"It seems that it is so," he called out, finally. "But Sanmano must have a *main-gauche* as well."

"Of course," said Lukah, in a tone of surprise. "I wonder that the Prince was not so armed already."

Jago Coreilli took an offered weapon, bringing it to Sanmano. It would have been better for the Prince, in retrospect, to refuse the second blade and chance the fight with only his small sword. The dagger, thin and light though it appeared, unbalanced a man trained to fight one-handed. He took the blade for pride's sake, and it was his undoing.

The Duke signaled again, and Lukah leapt at Sanmano like a tiger. I couldn't help but feel sorry for Sanmano. He fended off the long blade and the short as well he might, but could not bring the *main-gauche*, the left-handed weapon, to bear. It dangled uselessly in his fingers.

With a sweep of his foot, Lukah brought the Prince heavily to the ground and pinned his sword hand to the sand with the cross-guard across his wrist. He swung the sharp blade of his knife under Sanmano's chin and held it there, the point pricking the soft flesh of the neck. Sanmano's eyes bulged, wide and helpless.

"Hold your hand!" The Duke's voice was ragged.

Lukah did not take his eyes off his opponent, but he smiled. "And forsake my honor? It's a strange thing you ask, Master of Sireni."

The Duke opened his mouth and closed it again. Whatever he might do afterwards to the heir of Brehill, there were witnesses in the hundreds here. The weight of Sireni history and Sireni honor lay on his head.

"I will accept one thing in exchange for the Prince's life," said Lukah, in a voice that rang over the audience. "The hand of Lilliam of House Torelay in marriage."

In the shocked silence came the twittering of birds. No, it was the women where they ranged in masked rows, my sister among them, turning to each other and whispering, hands covering masks covering mouths, jabbering like sparrows.

It hit me like a blade in the gut, cold spreading through my limbs. This brute, this Outlander, this barbarian, with a man's life at the tip of his blade, this *creature* desired my sister?

Someone broke the silence with a strangled cry of *"What?!"*

It was me.

The Duke considered the scene before him, tension pulling his scars high over his cheeks. Sweat glistened on the bulging muscles of Lukah's bared right arm, but the sharp blade beneath the Prince's chin didn't move. All sorts of calculations were going on behind the expressionless façade of the Duke's scarred face; he held the threads of history in his capable fingers. As Master of the highest House of Sireni, he could not force any marriage, but he could forbid the banns.

Even in my anger, I understood his hesitation—I had been

trained in the Duke's halls. The Heir to his House could be killed with impunity before him. A woman of a Sireni House in the ruling family of Brehill, barbarians though they be, could be a powerful tool, and would strengthen the defense of the border. Torelay was well-regarded, but not so highly placed or intermarried with House Boradkor that giving my sister into the hands of a brute like Lukah would be seen an insult.

And yet, to give in to such a demand, to save the life of his son, who was, as his scars attested, supposed to be a warrior, would be seen as a weakness. It might be best to let the heir spill his blood on the marble stairs.

I certainly thought so.

And then my sister, who had stood like a statue through the fight, the reversal, the incredible insult, moved, flowed like water from the throng of her masked companions and bowed her head to the Duke.

"I will consent, your Grace," she said. "With your permission."

I strode across the ring, little caring how close I came to the grinning oaf and his victim pinned beneath him. I took the dais steps two at a time and stood before the Duke, my shocked parents beside him, my sister masked and demure at his side, looking at the ground between us.

"Your Grace," I managed through clenched teeth. "You cannot permit this travesty."

He flicked a glance at me, and I knew he dismissed my rage as inconsequential to his decision.

Still, the Duke played his game close. "I will not buy my son's life with a maiden's honor," he said.

Lilliam didn't look up as she spoke. "My honor will not be besmirched by a House marriage. And if it were, it is nothing to the life of Sireni's heir."

It was a brilliant move. In an instant she had indebted House Boradkor, bound them to us with bands of iron. And yet....

"Lilliam," I began.

"Be quiet, boy," said my father.

I would have defied him and the Duke, at what cost I

shudder to think of now, but Lilliam flashed me a glance that pierced right through me. I had not known her eyes were so blue, so bright, so cold.

She turned them back to the ground.

"There are conditions," she said in a voice as sweet as honey-wine.

The Duke smiled coldly. "There always are."

I couldn't see if she smiled in return.

"The Torelay orchards," she said. "House Boradkor holds them in surety. They are to be released fully, with no debt or interest owing, into the possession of my family."

Beside me, my father tensed. I hadn't known that he had mortgaged our lands and livelihood to the Duke's House. But with harvest so minimal for three years—of course they might be.

There was a lot, I realized, I didn't know.

The Duke pursed his lips. "Under your family's ownership, the blight has decimated the orchards. Are all to be denied the harvest libations for your House's pride?"

She tilted her mask so the iridescent surface caught the sun and looked him straight in the face.

"Will all respect, your Grace," she said. "That is Torelay's business."

The side of his mouth and the corresponding scars quirked up. "You said conditions," he said.

"My father is to be Master of Games this coming year."

The Duke glanced at my father, who stood up straighter under his scrutiny. Beside him, my mother whispered something beneath her breath. The Master of the annual Games which followed the harvest season wielded great power in Sireni society. The position a jewel greatly desired and jockeyed for among the Houses. The Games Master determined which House hosted which game, and who could sit where along the paths of the races, and who took precedence in the ceremonies that were as important and challenging as the feats of athletic skill. A good Games Master could make the fortune—monetary and social— of his House.

"You don't ask much, do you?" The Duke's tone was wry.

"Perhaps I do," Lilliam replied. "But your son's life is surely worth sacrifice on both our parts."

"But...but..." I sputtered.

Lilliam flicked her eyes my direction and bent to the Duke, whispering. He turned a blue glare on me.

"And you, boy," he said, "you are forbidden to challenge the barbarian, do you understand me?"

I shut my mouth and turned away from Sireni's Master as he called to Lukah to release the Prince. Out of the corner of my eye, I saw him rise and offer a hand to Sanmano, who tentatively took it. Lukah pulled his opponent to his feet unceremoniously and slapped him on the back with great good humor.

Oaf.

oOo

My sister bears her burden well. This day, I am on my way to visit, to bring the blessings of House Torelay to her and the child she carries. Along the road, my escort and myself passed the lands where Torelay's orchards stand, and the laborers told me that the blight is passing. On the edge of each carefully geometric line of trees was a pear tree of a different sort. Bees hummed merrily in their blossoms, traveling freely between them and the pure black Torelay pears. A heavy smell, tinged with the flavor of wine, drifted across the dusty path.

Ah well. I think I shall not mention such to my father.

I kept quiet, too, about what Lukah told me after the wedding, an affair of ceremony and lace that left me in no good mood, for all I had to pretend to the guests that I was happy. Since the daughter of a Sireni House was wedding a noble ally, the Duke declared that the wedding journey of my sister and late friend would embark from the Ducal docks, a tradition from our beginnings as a sea-people. The bridal party, all in costume like a pack of carnival monkeys, trooped down to the ships to bid them farewell.

I bent to kiss Lilliam, the trim of her elaborate wedding mask scratching my cheek. The silver wolf's-head of House

Brehill was pinned to her shoulder.

"Say the word, sister," I whispered, "and I will get you off this ship and to safety, and hang the consequences."

"Don't be a fool, Kai," she said fondly.

There was nothing else to do. Lukah, my once friend, my present brother-in-law, stood beside her, and I had to shake his hand or risk more scandal.

When Lukah grasped my hand, he pulled me to him and bent to my ear.

"I'll tell you a secret, Kai," he whispered. I tried to wrest myself free, but his grip was too strong. "The Prince was quite right. About the Outlander women refusing the mask for the scars of battle. It doesn't happen often, mind, but it does happen. My own sister Grisile was blooded on the field when I was a child, after she killed her first Westerner. I don't see her much; she rides the borders most of the year. I think your sister will like her."

He released me and I sprang back, speechless. With a grin, he stepped up to the deck, beside my poor sister in her scarlet robes.

oOo

Remembering that day, seeing the pear trees, I wonder about another thing that I didn't think much of at the time. The memory lies like a tiny, flawed jewel in a forgotten corner of an unused room.

When Lukah defied the Duke and cited an obscure version of the *Code Duello*, a thing it seemed no one in Sireni was aware of but him, I saw his eyes flick, so briefly, towards the crowd, towards the women assembled like bright birds.

Towards my sister.

And I remember she seemed to give an infinitesimal nod. The horse snorts beneath me and stirs dust from the hot road, and I glance at the orchards where the burned stumps of the trees once blight-struck are visible between the fresh green growth of the new stock.

That day on the dock, as the boat pulled away, and they

stood side by side...

...beneath her great mask of scarlet and gold, and beneath his brute scars...

No. It's impossible.

But I did have the slightest impression—

—they were both—

—laughing at me.

ABOUT THE EDITOR

Deborah J. Ross has been writing science fiction and fantasy professionally since 1982. Under her former name, Deborah Wheeler, she published two science fiction novels, *Jaydium* and *Northlight*, both from DAW, and short stories in *Asimov's, Fantasy & Science Fiction, Sisters of the Night, Star Wars: Tales From Jabba's Palace, Realms of Fantasy, Sword & Sorceress,* and other anthologies. After working closely with the late Marion Zimmer Bradley, she has continued the Darkover series: *The Fall of Neskaya, Zandru's Forge, A Flame in Hali, The Alton Gift* and *Hastur Lord*, and an original epic fantasy trilogy, *The Seven-Petaled Shield*, forthcoming from DAW. She's a past Secretary of Science Fiction Fantasy Writers of America and is a member of www.bookviewcafe.com.

Deborah lives in a redwood forest with her husband, fellow writer Dave Trowbridge. A veteran of almost thirty years of Chinese martial arts practice, she now studies yoga, piano, and Hebrew. She invites you to visit her blog at http://deborahjross. blogspot.com/ and to chat with her at http://deborahjross. livejournal.com/

ABOUT THE ARTIST

Artist **Mitchell Davidson Bentley** spent the last 20 years moving physically from place to place and artistically from traditional oils to cyber compositions. Trained in the traditional medium of oil by his mother, and inspired by his grandfather's love of science fiction, Bentley began his career as a full-time science fiction artist in 1989 from his home base in Tulsa. While actively involved in the science fiction art world, Bentley also moved from Tulsa to Austin to Central Pennsylvania where his search for knowledge earned him bachelor's and master's degrees from Penn State University. Over the same period of time, Bentley shifted from the more traditional oil painting to airbrushed acrylics, and since 2004 has been working exclusively in electronic media.

As art director of Atomic Fly Studios, Bentley produces cover art, marketing materials and Web sites while he continues to produce quality 2D artwork marketed through the AFS Web site and at science fiction conventions across the United States.

Bentley has lectured at universities, worked in film, edited publications and served as Artist Guest of Honor at more than a dozen science fiction conventions. He has also earned 35 awards, is a lifetime member of the Association of Science Fiction and Fantasy Artists, and is serving as President. Visit his website at

Books Published by Sky Warrior Books

Purchase them through online resellers and better independent bookstores everywhere. Visit us at www.skywarriorbooks.com for news and upcoming books and promotions.

Alma Alexander

2012: Midnight at Spanish Gardens (E-book, Trade Paperback)

S. A. Bolich

Firedancer (E-book, Trade Paperback)

M. H. Bonham

Prophecy of Swords (E-book)

Runestone of Teiwas (E-book)

Serpent Singer and Other Stories (E-book)

Carol Hightshoe (Editor)

Zombiefied: An Anthology of All Things Zombie (E-book)

Gary Jonas

Modern Sorcery (E-book, Trade Paperback)

One-Way Ticket to Midnight (E-book)

Quick Shots (E-book)

Michael J. Parry

The Spiral Tattoo (E-book)

Phyllis Irene Radford (Editor)

Healing Waves: A Charity Anthology for Japan (E-book)

Deborah J. Ross (Editor)

The Feathered Edge (E-book, Trade Paperback)

Laura J. Underwood

Ard Magister (Book One of Ard Magister) (E-book)

Dragon's Tongue (Book One of the Demon-Bound) (E-book)

The Hounds of Ardagh (E-book)